Foxes pass daintily by

Estelle Holloway

Estelle Holloway.

By the same author

"Elinor with the Pleading Eyes"

"Hounds, Hares and Foxes of Larkhill"
The Story of the Royal Artillery Hunt

"Portraits of the Tedworth Fox"
The Story of the Tedworth Hunt

"Not to Astonish Others"
The Story of the Avon Vale Hunt

All books obtainable from
Mrs Estelle Holloway, Oriel House,
Bolland's Hill, Seend, Melksham, Wiltshire SN12 6NQ

Copyright © Estelle Holloway

ISBN 0 9512104 3 2

A CIP catalogue record for this book is obtainable from the British Library.

Printed and Typeset by West Somerset Free Press, 5 Long Street, Williton, Taunton, Somerset TA4 4QN.

Published by the author

The moral right of the author has been asserted.

Obtainable from the author or all good bookshops.

Foxes pass daintily by

Some words of appreciation by Rory Knight Bruce, MFH,
Correspondent to *The Times* and *Telegraph*.

Occasionally one happens on a book whose redolence and narrative is like encountering a new room in a loved and familiar house. Estelle Holloway's *Foxes pass daintily by* is such a work.

With its credible heroine who passes from juvenile city mistress to accomplished rural heroine, there hovers about the book the natural magic of gossamer. Foxhunting, racing, the 'hothouse' (which seems to be the current word of fashion) of family life in the Big House, all may be found within its pages.

Yet throughout there are vignettes of moral purpose and manners, nuances of behaviour and observations of taste, which recall a more innocent age and are, in themselves, a delightful reminder of the joys of horses and the countryside.

Anyone who has met Estelle Holloway cannot fail to be struck by her infectious elegance, warmth and kindness. This is apparent in her writing, which leaves the reader with a warm glow as to the better side of humanity.

Foxes pass daintily by calls out to be read by an open fire with a small glass of whisky on the arm of a well loved chair.

CHAPTER 1

On this mid-November evening Henry Pritchard, chairman of TorrTechTron, decided to walk from his office at Canary Wharf because he knew his end was near, and he told his chauffeur to wait with the limousine by the entrance to the astonishing, monumental Underground station on the new Jubilee Line.

Canary Wharf on the regenerated Isle of Dogs! Where once herons waded the grimy marshes behind West India docks on the River Thames. Now the whole balance of East London was being shifted to this vast High-Tech development area for a digital hardware age, and TorrTechTron had prospered with the age. The synergizing technologies and optoelectrics company was founded by Henry, and TTT had become phenomenally successful, making him a very rich man indeed.

However, tonight the future was bleak and a less dominant man than Henry Pritchard might have felt depressed. Suicidal almost. But being a classical scholar from one of England's most famous public schools, it had made him philosophical regarding tragedy. For the moment, there were pressing problems and the most urgent was how to look after Fleur, his executive-secretary and mistress of ten years.

Standing in the circle of Westferry Circus, he looked for the last time at the vast square tower of Canary Wharf pierced by a thousand lighted windows. They appeared like stars suspended in damp mist, while behind the tower's massive stubby 'wings', river fog swathed halogen street lights which beamed from lamp standards resembling meat-hooks. Further in the background across the river the ghostly white tent of the Millennium Dome shimmered like a giant mushroom rising from the ground, its thirteen one-hundred metre masts stretching skywards above curled canvas lips. He walked on towards the Jubilee Line Extension never ceasing to marvel at the economic regeneration of this exceptional place, and feeling proud to have been part of the private sector development. Richard, the chauffeur, opened the rear door of the limousine for Henry and they drove up river through Limehouse and Wapping to St. Katharine's Dock where Fleur rented one of the new up-market flats.

A successful career woman in her own right, Henry knew that she, having never married, depended on him for love, sex and companionship, and until tonight this had been understood. Although in the long term he was confident for her future, he decided his immediate course was to persuade her to leave him. Start afresh. Go right away. He elected to walk the last fifty yards across a cobbled parterre and the limousine drew up by the rope-and-post guard-fence to the off-river Thames dock. Henry, or Harry to his friends with bowed head, passed a late night restaurant specialising in crab, lobster and other sea-faring delicacies for yachtsmen and well-heeled landlubbers alike. Something made him turn his head. Then he saw Fleur, alone, sitting at a plain deal table by herself and the only customer. No matter that the décor was expensive, the young woman sat alone and a tall, wide mahogany door in the background seemed to detach her from everyday life. The yellow walls and red curtains suggested gaiety, but the restaurant looked as bleak as a dentist's waiting-room. Fleur had become a 'caféist', a 'single', and until now Henry had never realised the price Fleur had paid for her loyalty and love.

She looked up and, recognising him through the plate-glass, rushed outside. She was wearing no coat and he put his arm around her as protection from the rain, so that she snuggled close to his thick overcoat. In the darkness he kissed her. It seemed appropriate.

Even after a short half-hour Henry knew the interview was not following the plan he had devised on her behalf.

"Get out of here!" Fleur seemed appalled. "Go. Get out of my flat!" Her red hair was wet with sweat and glistening due to the shock of his sudden announcement. He moved towards her, hands outstretched in an attempt at consolation. "Fleur, you're not concentrating or considering the new arrangements I've made for you."

"I heard you. I heard you. I'm to be promoted out of the way. Kicked upstairs!" Her eyes blazed. "How many times have I seen you do this to disposable employees!" Those eyes, glittering with tears, appeared to him like opals.

"It's not what you imagine. Try to grasp the advantages." He was irritated by her lack of comprehension.

"You said that I'm to be posted out of London to your new factory being opened in Watford, on promotion, as marketing executive. Suddenly — out of the blue. Just like that. With no warning, and after working with you for nearly ten years."

"It's been a shock to me too," he agreed. "Try to understand."

"Then why promote me? I don't want to leave you. Why send me away for no reason when I don't wish to go?"

"Listen," he pleaded. "You must believe me, that it's for the best." He sat down on the pale cream damask sofa not believing in the moment, and uncharacteristically for such a dominant, fifty-year-old man, he knew he had lost control over the situation. Through November night-mist, a Thames river-boat siren sounded mournful, to match their mood. The window of the first floor flat looked down towards dark, iridescent water in an enclosed dock, coloured black, viridian, with hinting silver flashes. Ships, some Port of London grey, the rest private yachts, together with repainted barges, rose and fell with the tide, their masts black against floodlit facades of the buildings opposite.

"I've never seen you like this before," he commented haughtily, attempting to puff out his chest in the usual paternal manner. "Surely you have more sense than to cry. Tears are for typists! And you have succeeded where so many have failed. Don't spoil yourself now."

Answering him bleakly, "You made me what I am. Sophisticated, hard working, efficient. And in love with you!"

There was silence. Later he commented "I thought I saw a rational woman. Poised. Calm. Beautiful."

"Certainly you gave me confidence."

"You have a sound business sense in the world of electronics. A natural."

"I have always been willing and eager. Eager to learn. I remember you interviewing me."

"You seemed too young when I saw you. I didn't want to take you on."

"That certainly wasn't *my* impression."

"I took the risk, to give you a chance."

"You . . . . . you," she burst out. "The chairman. Smiling. Sitting behind your powerful desk. Always that smile of yours. The perfect mask."

"Let's get this into perspective. You begged me to give you the job and teach you."

"Agreed. And I was very susceptible . . . . . plastic."

"How d'you mean?"

"Plastic. Soft. Like wax, you moulded me."

"A little girl asking for it. Learn not to run after people unless you need their influence."

"That's cruel."

"But true. You were willing enough to sleep with me."

"I worshipped you, besides I had just lost my mother. But you taught me never to cry. Have feelings. There was no room for emotion, you said. And now?" She paused, uncertain.

"What are you now?"

"I've no idea!" He saw her struggle to fight back unwelcome tears which belittled her in his eyes. They had never spoken so openly before and he was surprised she dared be so candid, as candour to him was equivalent to insolence. She had worked hard ever since he could remember for all her years at TTT because there was little time for anything else except for those few hours when he visited her or took her out. When he thought back over the years, working hard was so ingrained in her psyche that he couldn't imagine her doing anything else. He got up to pace the room. A tall man, habitually he looked on lesser mortals from a height, now he struggled unable to appreciate her distress. "Surely emotions are for teenagers," he muttered then , more kindly, "Seems our lives are divided into periods,"

"Periods?" Fleur said puzzled.

"A series of short periods. One period following another, like months in a year." Thankful she did not interrupt he continued "For the best of reasons it seems our period is over and I must look ahead for you."

"For me. For me. You never discussed what I wanted. Never thought I had feelings. Nerves. Wishes of my own. Never gave me a choice." He pitied her seeing she held a pain-stabbing head in her hands. "This is *my* flat. I've struggled to find the money to rent it and now you force me to leave it behind and go miles away. I love docklands. I love the river. I'm an EastEnder, born and bred." There was pride in her voice, later she went on "I suppose Colin knows?"

"Naturally. He's my chief executive."

"You arranged this with Colin before telling me? Chopped me up between you as though I'm a commodity. A take-over!"

"Childish!" He could not comprehend the new turn of events.

"You arranged this with Colin. And Elizabeth?"

"What's that suppose to mean?" She was silent so he went on "Elizabeth being Colin's wife wanted to know. She's fond of you." He stood there, his head bowed in humility as the thread of the conversation seemed lost between them and there was little point in continuing. He idly rattled loose coins in his pocket. *"There will never be another Fleur!"* Anxious to distract her and to offer the honeyed-spoon he went on "Let me pour you a drink. It'll soothe you."

Then she, taking a glass from him, "What have you put in?"

"Whiskey. What else. Strong".

"Phew!" she choked, shaking her head.

"Understand my dear, we are offering you promotion because you deserve it. Don't you trust me?"

"I've always had faith in you."

"Isn't that the same thing?"

"You always appeared to know your own business, so I never queried your motives."

"I took it you were alright."

"I'm not blaming you but it simply isn't enough. No, not nearly enough."

"You should say what you mean."

"Do you? when do you ever *say* anything?" she countered.

He trod up and down. Step by step, his thoughts struggling for expression, as though pulled out of secret archives. "I took it we were always very happy. I was never so happy and will never be so again!"

"You didn't ask me if I were happy."

8

"I thought we agreed to take it as it comes."

"You agreed! To me it was half-good because I hoped for the future. I've waited patiently for years. I love you and have never ceased to. I imagined . . . . ." she laughed wryly. "Yes, can you believe this? I was so *naive*. I imagined that since you had a wife, but you lived apart . . . . . well nearly . . . . . or so you said, that we might one day be together for always and have a family of our own. Just how naive can one get!"

He felt sorry for her knowing she was not a scheming woman and she was genuine, although living alone she was inclined to daydream "I'd have liked that. But it is not to be."

The conversation petered out being inconclusive, with neither side prepared to negotiate.

"I shall miss you. Unbelievably," she sighed.

"Things might have been different. It's not in our stars."

"Why bring that into it?" Harry never took an important step or decision at TorrTechTron without consulting his horoscope.

"I must go now." Was there more he wanted to say? Could he say anything else? But he decided not, even though his mental turbulence almost overpowered him so that for one brief moment he considered confiding in her, then he became more composed and added rather stiffly "Please think about what we are offering you, it is in your best interest. Telephone Colin Goldring when you have reached a decision." He opened the sitting-room door to cross the passage and turn towards the staircase.

"Colin! Colin Goldring. I'm to telephone *him* how I decide?" she screamed. "You rat!"

"That's enough. He's entitled."

"I might have known you'd sidestep. You haven't the courage to face me yourself." He winced under her attack. "Now you've told me what a Mr Samuel Whiskers you are, I shall leave the firm because I am not going to Watford!"

"You go too far!" He walked down the first two steps.

"Too far. Not far enough." She picked up a Chinese vase from a niche above the stairway. Sensing her movement he turned, amazed, as she threw it at him. The vase caught him across the face grazing the bridge of his nose. He swayed for a moment, then with an effort descended the stairs. Reaching the hall he steadied himself. He did not look back.

'He'll never forgive me for this,' Fleur thought. 'I cannot return to the Company now. Even if I wanted to.'

She found herself shaking from fear, grief and shock. Brilliant jazz-lit arcs, minute at first, then increasing in size and amplitude obscured her vision. Migraine and whiskey all mixed up made her sick and, head down the loo, waves of vomiting crashed against pent-up emotion.

Later, when feeling some relief, she dragged herself to her white bathroom and leant over the basin. Pressing down a mixer-tap, the air trapped in cold water under low pressure, similar to a Jacuzzi bath, made a refreshing sound to resemble natural mineral water. It had always fascinated her, reminding her of holidays in France with Harry. The cool water bathed her face, then realisation dawned that lately there had been no dinners, no private dances together, and also that they had not been on holiday since the summer. Harry was such a secret man that she had learned not to ask indiscreet questions.

She sat back on her heels, the thoughts damming her pain. "I think I guessed this was coming," she said to herself, "but I just couldn't believe what I saw and was too scared to do anything about it, Harry — it's not like you — to dump me in this way." She pushed her face under the water in a sad attempt to drown rage, then re-emerged with her coarse wet ringlets making her look like a seahorse-maiden.

Drying her face, the pupils of her eyes focused through the supernova of now quiescent migraine to see a pallid, oval reflection in the mirror. "Perhaps I'm just a beautiful face and that's all." But she knew at meetings and conferences for electronics manufacturers, other men envied Harry her intelligence and discreet charm. There was nothing loud or common about Fleur, ten years of Harry's society had assured that.

Walking into the bedroom she lay on her bed in the dark. It was a white, designer-generated room furnished to modern minimalist style. The dim light from the doorway appeared to outline the image of her late mother as she materialised from the floor. She had been a small woman, with a tiny compressed mouth and a sallow face lined with guilt. A single mother living in a London County Council tower-block, she worked in a car factory making motor components, and scraped up every penny to send Fleur to a south London convent school, where the nuns' dedication and her eagerness to learn gave her a scholarship to business college. Mother was determined Fleur should have a bright future. She then died leaving many debts.

Fleur as a child had been slightly repelled by her thinness and often wondered who her father was. Perhaps he was handsome, because as a child she knew she was exceptionally good-looking. Mother had a Puritan strictness, although the parched surface of her body hid a love which warmed and comforted the child, without her faintly understanding it.

Lying in the dark Fleur remembered 'fifties tower blocks in Limehouse with concrete staircases, built to re-house slums. Her middle-class convent school became hopelessly confused with rack-rent landlords, graffiti, emerging drugs and latch-key kids.

Every day she had made a tedious journey by Underground from Limehouse to school at Wimbledon, passing through an invisible curtain of houses with gardens and swimming-pools, green open spaces, parks and tennis courts. At school she had friends, but she couldn't ask them home for tea or accept invitations to tennis parties, swimming or a barbecue. Other girls liked her but thought her odd. Only the nuns understood. Returning in the train she wondered what life was like in leafy suburbs with quiet houses in pretty gardens. Did they feel different? Think strangely, these persons with deckchairs and swinging-sofas-under-canopies. Only TV aerials were the same.

To walk home from Stepney station she would put her school hat in a satchel and cover her school coat with an old mackintosh to hide from cat-calling, roller skating, skate-boarding, motor-bike kids with chips-in-newspaper smoking round street corners. The last bit of the way made her run through paper-blowing waste as she feared louts with square faces. In Limehouse she was different. She had no friends.

After two years' work at business college, the nineteen-year-old found herself sitting in Harry's office, and later he told her he had found it fascinating to find someone as strait-laced as herself. She remembered he was half-smiling at her intensity during the interview as though he recognised her as special.

Three months after her mother's death, Fleur found comfort in Harry's bed. He was the perfect sinecure for an over-intense, lonely girl. "You gave me a great deal, but I will not take your promotion and the move to Watford," she said to the empty room, its echoes mocking her. She was aware of a restlessness. Financially an independent woman, although with little saved, she was emotionally dependant on Harry and she felt as though caught up once more in that invisible curtain. On one side was Jacuzzi water, a white minimalist flat and the broken pieces of a Chinese vase, and on the other, a square face leering at her. She had quarrelled with the chairman of TorrTechTron and physically attacked him and she knew how ruthless he could be. Revengeful. Unforgiving. Now she must unthink ten years of TTT. Her flat was up too close so she must stand back. It was impossible to stay and Fleur knew she must go away, anywhere for a few weeks just to think.

Turning on the light, she packed a suitcase. Shoes, sweaters, hair brushes were tumbled in in confusion and she slammed the suitcase shut. Changing into a plain dress, she threw a favourite long cloak over her shoulders. Then paused. On a shelf stood an absinthe glass they had bought in Paris during their first holiday together.

"Why does it have a spoon full of holes?"

"To place in a sugar-cube."

"Why?"

"The wormwood in absinthe is bitter. Bitter as rue."

"I see . . . . ."

" . . . . . the water dripping through the holes turns the liquor a cloudy yellow. 'L'Heure Verte' they call it in Parisian cafes. The Green Hour. The Happy Hour."

"Absinthe. It sends you mad so they say."

"Who can tell? It gives the mind novel experiences. Changes shapes and sizes. Reverses day to night."

Fleur crammed the glass into her handbag because she felt it held both past and future. Then determined to sew up the tears in her heart she walked out into a ten o'clock city.

Goodnight today. Welcome tomorrow.

Harry stumbled to the front door of Fleur's flat. He saw Richard, his chauffeur for twenty-three years, hurry across the cobblestones to assist him, with his nose twitching like a rabbit. Being not merely a servant but his master's best friend, Harry suspected that long service with the family told him that things were going awry. He was aware that the chauffeur thought his wife, Lady Lydia Pritchard, a harridan, and kept out of her way.

River mist had condensed to rain. Richard placed a Shetland rug over Harry's knees, as he hated car heaters and thought they blew in noxious gases.

'Isn't it extraordinary,' thought Harry, 'I've always looked after my health, and now!'

Priorswood House was twenty minutes drive through darkened streets and shuttered shops, and he amused himself to see Richard's eyes searching for the reflection of his employer's face in the driving mirror. The bruise on his forehead was turning red to black, and he saw Richard scrutinising it intently before looking away. Relentlessly the chauffeur's eyes returned again, and yet again, in the obvious search for a clue to the evening fracas.

They arrived at the house where Lydia had not waited dinner for them because only rarely did she bother to say goodnight.

"The study, sir. Will you be sitting in the study?"

"I think that's best."

"Shall I fetch you some supper? On a tray. Everyone's gone home."

"Stop blathering about, Richard. You can get me a drink."

Richard looked dubious. "What about a nice cup of tea."

"Whiskey." But Richard stood his ground. "Better for you tea."

"Does it matter?"

"Matters to me, Mr Pritchard."

"Make it a small one then. You can do me some grog." Harry heard him mutter. "It will be a very small one!" Compromise being reached, with honour satisfied, he went to the butler's pantry to fix hot water and demerara sugar. Harry knew he would add a little ginger to the hot drink before bringing it in on a silver tray.

"Satisfied are you here, Richard? On the whole."

"Always been satisfied. Very satisfied. You've been very fair."

"It's been a long time."

"Twenty-three years this Christmas."

"Christmas? Christmas so soon! Perhaps I'd better make it twenty-five years you've been with us. Better for your pension."

"Very generous of you." And picking up his meaning. "But it's not time yet."

"I think it's a good idea. Twenty-five. We shall see, though."

Richard made up the fire, putting on logs and coal as he guessed Harry would not go to bed yet.

"You consider me fair then?"

"Very fair. Fair. And just."

"But devious?"

"Not for me to say, sir".

"You must say what you think, Richard."

"Yes sir. I'd say you were devious. But just. Difficult sometimes to see what you're driving at."

"And you're not alone in that!"

He wondered whether to confide in him, as he trusted him as well as any man he'd known. Besides he knew Richard to be very partial to Fleur, treating her more like a daughter of the family. Without him the affair would never have been workable. However, thinking better of it: "You'd better go off home now."

"Nothing you'd like?" He seemed unwilling to leave Harry alone. "Anything more I can do."

"Nothing. Leave me now. I'd rather be by myself."

The house was silent as though bereaved, only Harry and the fire kept vigil. Lydia seldom bothered him unless she wanted money to indulge her passion for racing. Occasionally they visited Ascot or Newmarket together, when a faint warmth recalled their early marriage. Recently Lady Lydia had commenced breeding racehorses herself on a small Essex farm he had bought for her. With her battered felt hat, the monocle in a weak left eye, and a rolling limp, she was a figure of amusement and respect on the racecourse to both trainers and jockeys.

'And very successful she is too," he reflected. 'Should be profitable, especially with her Irish connections, and give her a great interest. Besides she'll be extremely well off and provided for.' He knew that Lydia was aware of Fleur's existence and was too confident a woman to regard the girl as a threat.

Fleur! And he felt his face. Raising the tumbler to his mouth, he saw the firelight fracture, then recombine into a torus of light to transform the pale orange liquid, and in the bright lumin he perceived her rage as a heartbeat. This surprised him, so that his thoughts being in phase with the lucid beam, he mellowed towards the girl's outrage. He was a fair man and did not hold it against her.

Harry did not love people. He enjoyed them, sought their company and shared his time with them, but he had never loved. He appreciated his family's care and was very grateful. But he could not love. He had much to offer wife, children and assorted liaisons. Status, money, culture and travel, also interests and even excitement, together with classical good taste. But no charity which is love. All the chairman had to offer was money, the ubiquitous panacea of the Western World.

Harry had no pity. No pity and certainly no regrets, because he had no pity towards his person. He saw himself like an olive which falls from its branch in due season, falls with a blessing to the earth, and a thanksgiving to the tree which gave it life.

Fleur stepped out of her block of flats, formerly a docklands warehouse, but now restored and refurbished. This vast emporium was once used to store imported spices, rare wood, ostrich plumes and African ivory. Other stone buildings surrounding the dock were new, they only appeared old. Since working with Harry at Canary Wharf she had looked upriver towards Limehouse for comfort. Missing her mother, Limehouse was home in spite of difficulties, and some years previously she had looked with pleasure and amazement at the development of the old London Docks further still up river to become shops, offices and flats, and she was able to rent one of the apartments. Now she was leaving it and everything it meant to her. When nor-easters blew, strong and chill from the North Sea she would stand on the footbridge at the mouth of the dock watching salt water tidal waves racing up river. The storm in her hair. Memories came of Surrey and West India docks; Rotherhithe, Millwall, with its gas stench, Blackwall and Woolwich. She knew them all on the banks of this devious, serpentine Thames. Now she must give the agents her notice to quit.

She turned to face the restaurant where Harry had found her that evening. In a world of London commerce people had hundreds of acquaintances but few friends and Fleur felt disloyal if she went out with other men, or accepted a date.

'What have I become,' she thought. She had money of her own and a luxurious home. But with too much absorbing work and an elderly lover she was still the odd-girl out. Young couples were overpowered by Harry's money and his authority. Older friends disapproved of the age-gap. Half-consciously she recognised that Harry had been her protector and he was a shield against imagined square faces, who haunted her dreams.

She pressed on. The water in the dock resembled a velvet-black mirror reflecting in ghostly ripples the white masts and blue, furled rigging of sailing yachts. Her high heels clicked as she crossed steel plates which sprang up and down on the walkway which bridged a trickling stream and a few minutes later the Tower of London, that grim fortress of English history, behind its battery of floodlights appeared on her left. Right-handed the statue of a Roman centurion bonded to the remains of his Roman wall, pointed to the Underground. Five minutes later Tower Hill tube station stood ready to swallow her up.

"Victoria Station. A single," Fleur could think of nowhere else to go.

At the main line station none of the destinations of night trains appealed to her. 'An hotel for the night is the sensible thing,' she thought, but thrown back on herself, restlessness drove her on, and she felt she had to move. The Victoria coach station came to mind with dim recollections of the annual week's holiday taken by Mother and herself at Weston-super-Mare, and Fleur crossed the road wearily, her cloak an ill-protection against driving rain. The air smelt acrid due to diesel fume.

Past associations often evoke present difficulties. To Fleur, the new Victoria coach terminus was a revelation compared with the old, age-torn, dirty, run-down station of her youth. She was puzzled, being unaware of its refit. Once the grubby arch was a magic doorway to sand, sun, bathing, ice-cream and the tired smile on Mother's thin lips as she rested in her deckchair. Here for one week only Fleur played ball with other children, swam and built sandcastles. She was one of a carefree holiday gang. She had friends and was no longer the odd-girl out.

And now ? As she walked under the vast roof, she wondered how many acres of grey-flecked tiles, edged with darker squares covered the dear, grubby cobbles. Night coaches were leaving for Southampton, Edinburgh or Cheltenham, but nothing for Weston-super-Mare, and Fleur traversed the complete area of platforms before sitting down on a brightly painted bench next to an 'Automat'. Her headache had returned to compound her worries. For a brief moment she considered telephoning Elizabeth Goldring, to ask if she might stay with her for the night, but decided her friend was too close to Harry.

The old waiting-room and stall where you bought tea had disappeared. Disconcerting glass doors separated people from the fume of buses, while metal columns were painted grey-green, with thin orange circles, informing passengers of their coach numbers. Listlessly — Fleur watched a young man wearing a long, black coat, who carried a HARRODS FOOD HALL bag, and was eating a pasty as he strolled by. 'It's ridiculous,' she decided, 'to sit and watch coaches. But if I don't go now, I never will. Pulled back by indolence and the least resistance of familiar things.'

READING — SWINDON — CHIPPENHAM — BROXFORD . . . . . 'Broxford? Where on earth is Broxford? Never heard of it and I don't suppose many other people have either!' she thought, and without waiting to see the coach's final destination 'It's going west so I'll buy a ticket. At least it will pass the night.'

Condensed mist oozed in rubbery drops down the coach windows, and the reflection of her deep brown-green eyes looked streaked with glycerine tears. She dozed and dreamed in her seat as the coach drove westwards along the M4. Had she been stupid? Her feelings towards Harry were softening, because she recollected that he said he was getting old. Strange. Something he had never conceded before. And the memory of his words shocked her. But why send her away with no explanation, only promises of promotion, a company car, pension and private health care, this was the puzzle. She began to feel like his divorced wife, who has thrown her alimony back in Harry's face.

The night passed by. She felt the miles lengthen as though she were flying, gravitating faster and faster. When they stopped she awakened with a breathless choke, while the bus halted for unending periods at Reading and Swindon. Workers on shift embarked, then dispersed once more to their night stations. Dreaming again, she saw herself walking along a dark, narrow road crossed by a highway teeming with lorries and screaming cars. She cried out because she was a hundred miles from home and unable to return.

"How can I ever walk back?" she asked tormented. And Harry's voice answered her "Never. It is endless night!"

CHAPTER 2

Early morning Broxford was cold and grey, although to walk away from the nightmare coach was a relief. Here fresher air spoke of sanity being far from city or urban life. Fleur found Kosy Kaf with its linoleum floor and paper tablecloths, and coffee revived her so that after half an hour she nibbled a rockcake, as she had not eaten since lunchtime yesterday. Looking around she was comforted by the softer speech and dated country clothes of the other early risers. However, the country cafe highlighted another difficulty when she began to realise she had exchanged one emptiness for another. Even the quietus was eerie. What was there for her in this unknown village? Had she been right to come? Since childhood there was only one sheet-anchor, one paradigm in her life, that she could depend on. *Work.* This was the paradox. Her only real rest, refreshment or relief, lay in effort.

Work for a high-flying executive might prove no problem in the future but not in Broxford sitting in Kosy Kaf an hundred miles from home.

I must get work, washing up or sweeping to give me a few days to organise myself. Fleur asked the fat waitress for a local newspaper, to scan the SITUATIONS VACANT. Milk-roundsmen were wanted, and an HGV Workshop fitter, together with Site Sub-Contractors and Tractor Drivers. 'I don't know how to drive a tractor or work an unknown machine,' she said to the rock cake. Then an advertisement ringed by a coffee cup stain caught her attention:

'GIRL FRIDAY urgently needed. Household, horses, dogs, desperate for help. Please come and look after us. Tel: Bowden's Grove.'

The advertisement intrigued her, and she puzzled what it would be like to live with a country family, and pictures of Wimbledon swinging-sofas, leafy gardens and barbecues swam into her tired mind. Do they think strangely? she said to the rock cake crumbs, these people from my teenage years? She pressed Button A in the telephone box when a tired voice of subtle flavour answered. In response to her query a woman said: "Brilliant. Can you come at once? With so many horses in the yard the house is chaos. Take the bus and ask for Bowden's Grove. All the drivers know us. We'll have breakfast ready as you must be starving."

The bus wound its way up steep hillsides and along twisting narrow lanes bordered by dry stone walls, as here, some aeons ago, southern England had smashed into the northern isle to create Britain and raise these jagged hills. Pheasants whirred from wall to trees, sensing beaters and keepers about.

"Bowden's Grove," said the driver as the bus passed a high brick wall leaning outwards, its cracked, recessed panels green with lichen and moss. She dragged her stuffed suitcase through the wrought-iron gates tied back with binder-twine, her long red hair twisted down one side of the damp black cloak. Fleur normally drew wolf-whistles from persons in trousers. That morning she saw the driver shrug as it was not his business.

To Fleur's right a small Regency lodge guarded the rusty gates. Dislodged coping stones had shifted roof from wall, so that when she stepped across the grass to look through a glassless window the only inhabitants were some white rabbits in a box and an ancient mower. To the right and past the lodge three acres of formal gardens stretched into an orchard, while beyond a wooden fence, horses were grazing. A sturdy attempt at order said that gardening was an important aspect of someone's life at Bowden's Grove. She heard clumps of bamboo rattling behind herbaceous borders, while roses steeped in horse manure looked bravely towards winter.

The left side of the drive disturbed her, nerve sharpened as she was. Rows of marching black-brown trees captured veils of November mist in haunted silence, and she walked with her shoulders turned towards the friendly garden, the weight of the suitcase straining her wrist.

Then she saw the house, eighteenth-century ashlar, with its sixteen-pane sash windows and Portland stone columns flanking a maple door, beneath a delicate fanlight. No matter that the roof was in want of repair, or the steps uneven, and the bargeboards had seen no paint since the reign of George the Sixth. Fleur had looked at the pictures in *Country Life* often enough to know that this was the real thing, and that the minor landed gentry were alive and well, albeit very quiet about themselves. No developer had touched the cream Bath stone decoration and no-one had 'improved' the hand-wrought iron of a minuscule rose garden designed to resemble a bouquet. A large hand-written notice nailed to the gate said:

'We are in the kitchen. Side-door please.'

"You've buggered it up, Harry!"

He winced, but did not contradict anyone as chic and formidable as Elizabeth Goldring.

"You should have said!"

"I couldn't."

"Told her . . . . . explained." Elizabeth had the thinnest legs in London being very tall and weighing a fashionable nothing.

"She's gone!"

"So you rang and told me."

"But where?"

"That we will see."

"You appear confident."

"Darling. People don't just disappear. Fleur's perfectly competent to

18

look after herself." Elizabeth walked over to a mirror, and her reflection showed a plain woman of indeterminate age, with a long nose and thin raspberry-tinted lips. The tiny hat she wore would have looked ridiculous on anybody else, but on Mrs Goldring it balanced her high, spikey heels. She turned, smoothing the severe Italian-tailored suit.

"Harry — I've often wondered. Does Lydia know about Fleur?"

"Yes."

"And? What does she think about her?"

"Amusement. I think she's pleased that Fleur keeps me amused."

"She's changed, you know, fading almost."

"Changed? Who? Fleur?"

"A spinster before her time."

"What's that supposed to mean? Fading?"

" . . . . . a spinster before her time. You work it out. With a woman you'd snarl anything up. Even Lydia!"

He sat slumped in his chair. "Drink your coffee, it's getting cold." She didn't say that for Fleur, sex went with the job and that the girl was strangely innocent and naive. "Something happened. Last summer. At the CIEE."

"Where? When?"

"In Switzerland. Wake up Harry. Take note. Colin took me to Lucerne for the holiday and Fleur went with you as secretary to the Conference."

"Nothing's changed. Nothing happened," he growled.

"If you say so. We're all prisoners . . . . . every one of us. Born in a gaol from the moment we open our eyes. Just once in a lifetime the jailor forgets and leaves the door open. Perhaps it's her only change."

"Pah! So she runs away. Deserts."

"For once, she can choose to choose. Just the once." Elizabeth drew on black kid gloves. "I must go."

"Wait. I need you and Colin to vet this. It's a Codicil to my Will. I want you both to see if it's workable."

She took the sheet of paper from him, glancing at its contents. "When do they want you in?"

"Tomorrow."

"So soon." Elizabeth winced and put the document in her handbag. Being a few years older than he was, she treated him like a kid brother. "Goodbye then, my dear," and she took his face in both her hands kissing him on both cheeks. "Look after yourself. You're an old Poppet really. Except that you're the only one who doesn't seem to know it."

Mrs Mara Bowden-Hesketh wore jodhpurs and no shoes. Her blue sweatshirt decorated with animals' heads said: 'Raining Cats and Dogs.' She looked tired, and her tousled curls were turning iron-grey. Fleur thought she had once been pretty.

"Brilliant!" although there was a hint of disapproval in her tone. "Come in. Sorry about the pack of dogs," she said as two lurchers and a Jack Russell descended on Fleur. "I'll take your cloak. It's *soaked!* Poor you!" She regarded the designer wool dress with a query, and there was an unspoken comment that Fleur's Italian shoes were really too marvellous for the country.

The back hall was painted a light terracotta with great bunches of hydrangea, roses and herbs drying on racks. She led her into the untidiest kitchen she had ever seen, whose centre-point was an ancient AGA. The dog pack bounded onto a battered chintz sofa, while buff walls were plastered with calendars, bills and aides-memoire, in lieu of book-keeping.

"This is my daughter Bridie. She's deaf but understands everything." Bridie gave Fleur a disinterested smile from beneath a fringe of mousey straight hair. She guessed that Bridie was a little younger than herself.

"Have you come to do the washing-up? Poor you!"

'That's the second time in three minutes I've been called 'Poor You',' thought Fleur. Bridie's voice had the metallic rasp of the deaf. She pointed to a chair with a broken back by the refectory table and went on reading *Hounds*.

"Make yourself at home," said Mara and Fleur guessed that it implied she should fit herself to them, as she was the 'cuckoo in the nest'.

"Are you looking after the sausages, Father?" she went on. "This is my father, Colonel Bowden. Sometimes he helps with the cooking, if we can get him out of the garden!" Fleur felt the overworked fluster of Mara's life.

"Charmed, my dear. I hope you stay with us a long time," and he gave her hand a kind pat making Fleur warm to old-fashioned charm.

"They never do stay long," Bridie rasped. "You have to like punishment to survive here."

Fleur wished she would have her eyebrows plucked, as they were too heavy for a girl of her age. To Colonel Bowden she asked "Is that why the house is called Bowden's Grove. After you?"

"It's been in the family forever, James II so they say." And leading her to the fireplace. "Those are my father's initials. I bought my elder brother's half-share in the 'fifties."

"She isn't interested in stone carving. She wants her breakfast."

"Who's 'she' Bridie? The cat's mother? This is Fleur." She looked from mother to daughter and saw strained exasperation on Mara's face.

"Yuk!" from Bridie. "Mind if we call you Flurry."

"Metamorphoses," retorted Fleur, feeling needled.

"Don't take it to heart. We're quite friendly really." Bridie pushed away four dirty cups, a milk bottle, some saddle-soap and a tin of mustard to make way for Fleur's plate.

"Maybe we're an endangered species!" agreed Mara looking at Fleur quizzically as though poking fun at her. "A clash of cultures!" Making Fleur think of the cuckoo again.

"Sausage, mushroom, bacon, egg m'dear. Always give the troops a good breakfast, even in the heat. I was with the Sudanese Force y'know, for four marvellous years."

"We know. We know . . . . . stationed forty-five miles from the Abyssinian border."

"Have some respect, Bridie. He's eighty-two."

"Grandfather's so boring!" Then to Fleur. "Can you ride?"

"No."

"She's only just got here," her mother cut in, and turning to Fleur, "with eighteen horses in the yard, the house is completely neglected."

"Are they all yours?"

"And where would we get the money to buy eighteen hunters and young-stock racehorses," snapped Bridie.

"We do have four of our own and the mare and foal."

"They are client's horses, with more to come over the holidays. That's how we scrape a meagre living."

"I thought there was money in racing," sighed Fleur.

"There might be if anybody had time to do the books. You'll learn next season, if you're still with us." Bridie's big hands were inherited from her mother, the nails cut off square like a man's.

"My daughter's a wonderful rider," put in Colonel Bowden, placing a fond hand on her shoulder. "Mara's raced in Singapore. Won point-to-points in Hertfordshire and hunted with the Charleville Blazers in Ireland. That was before her husband died. Good chap, Hesketh, one of my best officers."

Fleur ate her breakfast feeling she had dropped out of the sky and through a black hole into another civilisation. She had nothing in common with these people. They seemed kind enough and she suspected that Bridie was simply pecking, like the English always will, should they meet someone who doesn't walk the way they do. A type of self-centred isolation.

'Fleur? or am I Flurry?' she thought with feeling, breath and warmth slightly returning in spite of a blazing headache and dull depression. She wrapped her hands round the coffee cup without a handle, and saw Mara's gaze speculating on faint white circles, where rings had been hastily torn from Fleur's lightly sun-tanned fingers.

"I had to leave. We quarrelled," and in the silence "I can't explain."

"Nobody comes here unless they have to!"

"It isn't as if . . . . . "

"That's enough!"

"May I give you some more coffee, m'dear? Would you like a cigarette?" from Colonel Bowden.

"Only father has any manners. We didn't expect you to say anything."

The family exploded into racing talk. Fleur noted how dirty the curtains looked while the sink was piled with greasy plates and saucepans. 'Why don't I just go? Just go! Where?' Then something of a tenacious spirit grabbed her. "I will be Flurry!" she murmured, although no-one heard.

"Why white rabbits in a box?" she said defiantly. They stopped talking. "In the lodge. I saw them."

"That was the last girl," grated Bridie. "A kinda hippie effort we had called Belinda. Thought the country was weaving Angora sweaters in sunlit gardens. She returned to a pad in Pimlico yesterday. Said a boyfriend would collect the rabbits."

"If they don't leave this evening," Mara said to Flurry, "take the Land Rover and bring them up to the stables. They can go in an empty loosebox for the night." Flurry thought 'No-one ever says please in this house. An order is an order.'

"Does anyone else live at Bowden's Grove?"

"Only Sean who manages the stables. He comes from Ireland, county Cork and he's been with us a few months."

"Sometimes I think he knows more about it than we do," interposed Colonel Bowden.

"You'll never see him," snapped Bridie on the defensive. "Because he's always in stables."

"Fleur may like to ride!" Her mother was quiet, positive. Bridie regarded Fleur's face and hair with jealousy.

"Oh! glamour!" and stalked out of the room.

"It's her being so deaf!" Mara sighed. "We make allowances, I expect she'll go and play with her motorbike. I'll show you your room."

The house was originally medieval with a new facade built during eighteenth century prosperity. They moved to the older part of the building, where a King Post from the ground floor to roof truss supported an oak staircase dark with age and beeswax. Mounting the steps, Mara's tall form, by nature agile, showed a slight sway of her hips, as she placed each foot firmly on successive steps. Across the landing, black timber panels enclosing plaster, bordered an upstairs passageway.

"You're in the West Room. Careful of the boards, they're a bit uneven. Have you lived in the country before?"

"Always London."

"You'll find us very dated and twenty years behind the times. We like it that way. I'd better lend you some jeans. We go to Broxford at least once a week and there's a good Nearly New Shop, as well as Oxfam and Save the Children. They always have something, so you needn't spend very much." She looked doubtful, then continuing, "I don't know how long you plan to stay with us, and as you gather, we cannot afford London wages. Let's see how things go."

Flurry knew that Harry gave generously to Oxfam and with a shock she realised she was expected to wear clothes gifted by others. Flurry saw Mara looking at her puzzled face with amusement and she thought she understood that Mara, born to a house-in-the-country, ponies, boarding-school and probably married young to live as an army wife, was hardened to postings in Germany, Northern Ireland, the USA or the Far East. You took things as they came and had to part with an only daughter, leaving her at school in England, as a fact of army life. Even the agony of widowhood must be borne bravely. Flurry conceded that as a straight-forward, honest woman of integrity, struggling to keep Bowden's Grove together, she wouldn't take to a City-flower who might not like hard work!

The West Room had exotic pink roses on green wallpaper. A massive clothes press, large enough to have hidden Charles the Second for weeks, was held shut by a tightly rolled newspaper. She unpacked, placing the absinthe glass on the chimney-piece shelf, with the spoon balanced across the rim. Then she collapsed on the king-size bed, with its quilt and feather-bed smelling of naphthalene. In the distance was the vroom-vroom sound of Bridie's motorbike driving round and round the orchard.

Fleur believed she'd made a bad start, maybe because her emotional state over Harry's loss showed plainly on her face and they didn't want to employ trouble! 'I needn't stay,' she thought, but the beautiful, old-fashioned, threadbare room with its three hundred years of family chatter comforted her, cocooned her in a woollen shawl, and she shuddered at the thought of exchanging it for a five-star hotel bedroom without Harry.

Sleeping and dreaming, she felt transported back to London and pictured herself standing with Harry looking at TorrTechTron offices on Canary Wharf from across the river. It was a sunny day. They stood on the Greenwich side with Wren's Royal Naval College glowing cream, rose and slate-blue in warm light.

He took her hand as they walked towards that strange little brick

23

'bee-hive' on the waterfront, which was the entrance to the Greenwich Foot Tunnel to the Isle of Dogs. As a child she and Mother had occasionally walked through it. Its narrow tube whiteness terrified her. St. Katharine's Dock looked way, way over in a hazy north-west. She wore a black dress.

The 'beehive' drew them nearer and swallowed them up as they descended steep, coiling steps beneath the mud of the Thames. An abyss. To an underworld where strange rectangles of brilliant white tiles transcribed a circle which closed to a pulsating, constricting white tube growing smaller and smaller. Horrified she walked, but did not move, being no more than a reverberating black 'shriek'. A black question-mark on white tiles. She was nothing. Nowhere. Running with high heels clattering on those white tiles.

Sweating and frightened with her face buried in the hot feather quilt, she awakened to the clatter of horses' hooves on the cobble-stones outside her window. Thankful that someone might be near, she threw open the sash window, and looked straight into the face of a young man with a wide grin, a shock of unruly hair, and the straps of his racing skull dangling unfastened. He rode one tall horse and was leading two others.

"Good day to you!" And he rode on towards the yard. She thought he sat his horse as though he were part of it, with his long flexible back lightly following every movement. He was a Centaur with his great black mare and presumably that must be Sean.

She sat on the side of her bed pondering and shaking away her nightmare. She felt she must not think of London, as she had achieved a friendly room, a roof over her head and there were other people living in the house. But she flushed with embarrassment remembering Mara's quizzical look, as thought she were laughing at her. Beneath the muddle and confusion she suspected that Mara was one tough lady who didn't take kindly to weaklings. It stiffened her determination. She was a Londoner, a Cockney, born within the sound of the Bow Bells, tiled Greenwich Foot Tunnels, tower blocks, graffiti and all, so pulling on a shirt and jeans she resolved to show them what she could do. Make them laugh on the other side of their faces!

Shutting the door and blowing a kiss to her lovely room, Fleur went downstairs. As everyone had left by three pm, the new Flurry dusted down the kitchen walls as became her metamorphosed self, and swept the off-white ceiling between black oak beams. Even the strings of onions were given a shake-up. At three-thirty, grease and carbon from the AGA were calling for an armistice with the Brillo pads. Windows polished with kitchen paper shone a quarter of an hour later.

When the hall clock struck four, cupboards were disgorging their contents. A row of cardboard boxes was steadily filling. They bore labels such as: 'Rubbish', Half-eaten jam or pickle', 'Broken cutlery', 'Mouse-traps minus their springs', 'Stable equipment, eg saddle-soap, horseshoes, etc. Not kitchen', 'What do we do with these?'

Cats and dogs fled in anguish when the chintz sofa-covers disappeared into the washing-machine and Flurry made a fervent prayer that the respective worn covers might emerge more or less unscathed.

Standing in the centre of the stone floor Flurry could see a grey shade of her mother. Small, tight-lipped, she adjudicated the spring-cleaning. Her daughter visualised the endless concrete steps she had once scrubbed, leading to their council flat in Limehouse, and the cheap oilcloth polished each day without fail in the kitchenette.

A furore of floor scrubbing exploded at four-thirty. Spiders, beetles and lizards abandoned house. So that at four-fifty when Bridie entered the kitchen from the stables, she removed her Wellies, and for the first time in her life, placed them on the spread newspaper provided.

"Knickers," she said.

"I've had a good apprenticeship," snapped Fleur, now Flurry.

Five o'clock precisely brought Sean in for tea, when Flurry was scrubbing under the refectory table. He gave an approving glance at her backside and went out again.

She did not meet him until an hour later, when it was dark. Remembering the rabbits, she left the house to find a car. Flurry had never driven a Land Rover, and she hated the thought of asking help from anyone. 'Perhaps I'll have a word with Colonel Bowden tomorrow,' she decided. 'He is at least civil.'

Driving Mara's small Traveller was easy, if fussy, bearing no resemblance to the sports car Harry had given her. The sky was solid black in the west, the faint white gleam of a young moon giving outline only to the larch covert, impenetrable now in early night. Avoiding larch boughs invading the drive she imagined what might be clawing and grasping at the lights of the little car, so that she looked towards Colonel Bowden's friendly garden preferring the familiar rather than the strange side. The known being more comfortable than the unknown.

It took her some time to focus the car-lights, push open the lodge door, and carry the rabbit-box to the back seat. Constructed of rough wood, with a chicken-wire top, splinters caught her fingers. "Lucky old Belinda," she protested. "Oh! to be in Pimlico!"

Returning to Bowden's Grove, she hesitated to drive into the stableyard not knowing the rules, and lugged box and rabbits over the cobbles past the kitchen windows. The family were consuming tea and crumpets round the table and there appeared to be no place laid for her, while soundless lips gossiped unknown news.

The yard built in the form of a hollow square comprised a tackroom and twelve loose-boxes. Lit by the hard beam of a security light, an archway surmounted by a clock tower led towards the back lane. Clock hands, long since stopped, pointed to eleven o'clock, while a slated steeple held aloft a sharp-nosed fox, galloping over serrated metal grass.

In the order of the neat stableyard, horses rested or munched quietly, and an orange lamp showed rugs airing in the tackroom, Flurry sat on the box to wait, while interested rabbits nibbled her borrowed trousers.

In her imagination, the rectangle of the kitchen window melded with the doorway to her London flat. On the cream-carpeted staircase, the sheen of Chinese ceramic from smashed pieces of the bird-vase held minute drops of Harry's blood. Tonight she heard the back door slam and a sharp whistle.

"Hi, there! Isn't that the prettiest face in the whole country, we have here. And her sitting on a box with no tea!" With that Sean gave her a pint mug with a buttered crumpet balanced on top. She said nothing, not being oriented for compliments.

"From London, are you?"

"Yes. Last night. I arrived this morning. On the coach." He said nothing, giving her space. "I brought the rabbits in the Traveller, because I'd never driven a Land Rover."

"We'll sort you out in the morning. Drink your tea," he remonstrated, sitting on the box. Sean wore an ancient hunter-green sweater with linen elbows and patches, liberally sprinkled with bran, till he resembled a snowstorm.

"Do you take sugar? In your tea?" The brew was hot and very strong.

"No. No thank you. Makes you fat."

"Is that right now? You're not being fat?"

"Important in London. It doesn't seem to matter now."

"You never lived in the country?"

"How do you know?"

"So they tell me."

Too weary to argue, she agreed. "I suppose so."

"They cared where you worked. You being fat."

"You have to look smart. To project your image . . . . . the firm's image. Project just the right message."

"Then it must be right." He looked amused. "What will we be calling you now you're with us?"

"I am called . . . . . " she paused uncertain. "Flurry!"

"That's a good Irish name to be sure. You're here to ride the horses for us."

"I can't ride." She saw he looked disappointed. "It's just a job, housework, washing-up, to give me time to think. I don't know how I got here. Or who I am."

"And you're needing a friend and a warm bed for a while."

She felt confused as though language had taken on a new dimension. "Look, I'd better go indoors. They'll want breeches washed for tomorrow." She wondered why her poise as a competent business associate had evaporated in a livery stableyard.

"Let's have those rabbits." He picked up the box, slipped the bolt on a stable door with his elbow, switched on a single bulb and went inside. The loosebox was high ceilinged, large and airy, the window on the far side being equipped with bars and armoured glass to dissuade intruders. A drinking-fountain above its porcelain bowl was built into one corner, a metal hayrack having been bolted into the adjacent angle. He fetched a bale of wheat straw, broke the pink binder twine, spreading the contents on the brick floor which sloped towards a channel constructed across the door, to drain water or urine. Releasing the chicken-wire lid, Sean picked up each rabbit, stroked it for a moment or two to soothe the animal, before freeing it in the straw.

"One buck. Two does. Rabbit pie for the New Year."

"I don't like rabbit pie."

"You'll be liking Mara's. The best this side of Youghal," he pronounced it 'yawl'.

"Wherever's that?"

"County Cork. My grandmother comes from the Blackwater River, it enters the sea at Youghal." His lean muscular body looked scrawny, and nobody would call Sean handsome as his face was too pale. His eyes were light blue of the true Celtic colour, in conjunction with dark blonde hair.

"Have you been to London, Sean?"

"Hardly at all. Only Ascot for the horse sales to sell our Irish horses. Or Tattersalls."

"I didn't know."

"USA, Paris. Poland sometimes, Germany, Saudi."

Considering him she concluded: 'You're no stable boy.' "We go . . . . or did go to Paris," she added aloud.

"That's a grand place now, for a holiday. With the racing." She waited feeling an unasked question.

"Perhaps I'd better go in," then stepped away, uncertain, the stableyard being kinder than her room.

"And in the morning you'll be getting up on old Jenny for me."

"Jenny?"

"Mara's grey pony, quiet as a lamb is Jenny."

27

"No!"

"And what will you be doing after Christmas when we're working ourselves to the bone riding out two or three horses a day?"

"I shan't be here."

"And you letting us down, like we're not your friends."

"Are you?"

He scratched his back up and down the door, refusing to contradict or prolong the argument. Sean was not a man to be drawn and he made her feel she was losing the initiative.

"Goodnight Sean. Thank you for the tea."

Some days later Flurry tackled the staircase. She knew how to polish because Mother's father had been a cabinet-maker in Hackney. 'Not too much wax. And hot cloths. Always warm your cloths.'

In the main bedroom above, Mara waited until she heard Flurry finish polishing and walk downstairs, then sitting on the unmade four-poster bed she picked up the telephone to talk to her cousin Annie of Broxford Court. Weak sun filtered through the sash-window illuminating a rococo mirror over the serpentine dressing-table, while Bertie, her beloved Jack Russell terrier slept, dreaming of rats, on the bedside rug.

"Annie darling, how are *you* . . . . . we're fine, fine. How's the knee? Too misery-making that it's swollen again . . . . . the doctor says what? . . . . . that you're too fat? Aren't we all . . . . . and you must reduce three stone? I don't believe it! We have the most brilliant new girl, but what she was doing in Broxford at six o'clock in the morning, heaven only knows. She's not the type . . . . . London in point of fact . . . . . difficult to place her. Not like anyone we know. Sometimes she can be a bit tiresome, don't you know, because she cleans and cleans, so unlike good old untidy us! Everything has to have a place! And polish." She took a gulp of coffee from her walnut side-table, littered with bills, unanswered letters and bank statements in the red. A photograph of her late husband Alex Hesketh, taken in army uniform, gazed at her kindly from its silver frame. Bertie grunted in his sleep, when an extra large dream-rat popped out of its hole. "Annie! you don't say . . . . . I don't believe it! Surely not. Divorcing Robert, after all these years! I know you've had troubles . . . . . haven't we all and don't trust him! As well as you know who! But don't do it . . . . . really. You'll be lonely . . . . . don't I know. I'm still forlorn, grieving after Alec died, I still miss him, nights are the worst . . . . . I know . . . . . I know . . . . . Robert's hardly darling Alec. But divorce!" Her fingers kneaded the duvet on an unmade bed. "Annie I shouldn't really . . . . . think again . . . . . he had his girl-friends before and you've turned a blind eye . . . . . but you say it's different with this wretched girl. What's her name? Julie Baker? And the car he's given her is from Somerset . . . . . that's miles away. How killing! Makes one think of Exmoor . . . ." Mara could hardly believe her ears!

"I do sympathise! It's because of this child she's having . . . . . you're sure it is his. Tests and so on . . . . . DNA and things. But please be *careful*. You'll have to compensate him I suppose, because he hasn't any money of his own and there'll have to be a settlement.

"Does he know you're thinking of divorce? . . . . . not directly. But you think he guesses by your silence. By you're *not* saying anything. Be careful! You know how unpredictable Robert is!"

She put down the phone. The news shocked her as Annie was more than a first cousin, being friend, confidante and buffer against hard times. She threw herself into the warm duvet seeking erotic comfort against soft, hugging pillows, as she had never recovered from Alec's death due to a heart attack in Ottawa. He was seconded on army duty, and one day they had enjoyed skating on the Rideau canal, corporate golf, or summer riding and fishing. While the next - widowhood.

It was his voice. His caresses. His hands about her body, and their laughing companionship that she missed. Now Annie and Robert were breaking up.

And she wept for them.

Bertie woke up shivering, one front paw raised, as terriers do when emotions fly around. He jumped up onto the bed pushing a fox-like head into his mistress's hands, as Bertie understood everything and was concerned by every nuance.

CHAPTER 3

Monday at Bowden's Grove was a rest day. After morning stables, the farrier arrived to attend to any shoeing needed, but after eleven o'clock they were free.

Flurry walked to the stableyard with its clocktower and running fox weather-vane, where Jenny, Mara's elderly pony, stood tacked up and ready, because Sean had been pestering her for days to ride out. She wanted to go but was worried about her ignorance of horse matters.

She needn't have troubled herself, although at first she was non-plussed, and then utterly fascinated by Sean's instructions as to how to approach a horse before getting on from a mounting block.

"It's balance now. Everything depends on balance. Sitting a horse and using your body as a counterweight. Remember you're riding one of God's creatures, and not like a monkey on a bicycle."

Mounting his black mare Hecuba, "You say you've never ridden before?" he queried opening the gate under the arch for Flurry.

"Well, hardly. Actually every spring we went to this conference for electronics manufacturers at a grand hotel in Surrey. Some of the other girls, secretaries, business associates and a few wives hired horses and rode round the park. It was great. The horses were very tame. Then Harry, that's Mr Pritchard, my boss, disapproved. He did not encourage it, so I never rode again." She did not explain further and Sean thought it wise not to press her. The girl refrained from saying that Lydia with her racing meant that she and horses must be kept well apart. In special compartments.

The pathway led across fifty acre Home Paddock. In the garden on their right, Grandfather was digging up his begonias ready to store during cold weather, while left-handed Bridie rode round and round the paddock on her motorbike. She refused to look at them and with a show of jealous anger she roared over the bumps, scattering grass and clods in her wake. Only the all-weather gallops were spared. Flurry could feel her misery from afar. "You should be kinder to Bridie," she told him.

"And if I am now, isn't it the poor girl who'll be getting it the wrong way?"

They passed through the paddock gate to walk along the road towards Broxford. The day was fine, albeit cold, and Sean was wearing a well-worn tweed coat, with a long skirt. The excellent hang from his shoulders accentuated the lithe form of his supple back. Passing a local farmer's wife in her car, he swept off his cap with a flowing gesture and deep bow, which depicted natural manners, but without show or self-conscious pride.

After half a mile they turned left, to travel a lane leading to the village. Flurry was enjoying herself. At the hotel riding stables nobody had ever mentioned things like controlled relaxation! Or inviting the horse's back muscles to move freely. But then, hotel nags bore no resemblance to the high-class hunter or 'chaser that Sean was likely to ride. Jenny was old, but Sean said she was a good Welsh Mountain grey pony, nicely put together and well-schooled with a light mouth, and Flurry had increasing confidence in her.

"Make her walk out now with even strides and a good rhythm. Squeeze gently with your lower leg muscles." And Flurry knew that she could learn more from Sean in half an hour than in a year on any old cob. Learning meant a lot to Flurry. It was fabulous and she was enjoying every second.

Further down the lane, beech trees linked branches overhead to form an eerie green tunnel. The trunks were supported by a network of bleached roots, like bones, while in turn the tunnel gave way to a covert fringing the steep culvert bordering a vicious left-hand bend. Just before the hairpin, Sean picked his way right-handed down a tiny path laced with beech roots and scrambling ivy.

"Hold Jenny's head up. It's steep." Below them the Byebrooke spluttered, foamed or dashed over rocks. Clear water, now green, then black, sometimes appeared sparkling or a dead plush.

"Morning Bert," called Sean to a little old man walking with his gun and a brace of hare on one shoulder. The water between them was an unnerving green, the pale colour of baby lettuce.

"'Ow be on then, Sean . . . . ." Bert Rawle was a Somersetshire man and had never lost his Somerset vernacular.

"Well. And yourself?"

"Fair, fair to middlin', thank 'ee," Bert replied, sucking at a small brier pipe.

"Here is Flurry. Come to help Mara."

"Aye. She needs that." Flurry thought Bert looked like Andy Capp, the cartoon in Mother's newspaper.

"Tell Mara, I be bringing the trout 'saternoon."

"Brownies? End of season?"

"Aye," and bursting with importance the smallholder continued "You'll have 'eard the 'happence?"

"What?"

"Car. One o' they big Merc jobs went right over the 'airpin." Bert took his pipe from his mouth pointing it upward. Sean and Flurry both looked up. The steep bank high above was engineered to a stable slope, when the cutting was constructed by Road Works out of the farther bank.

"That'll be second time car's bin over. Reckon Council'll 'ave to do sommat 'bout they 'airpins. Light or summat."

"Somebody should get themselves killed . . . . ." conceded Sean uneasily.

"Was anyone hurt?"

"Not s'far as I 'eard. But they got to do summat. Lights or else."

On Tuesday, the meet of foxhounds was at the Rocks, and six horses were being loaded into the big horsebox. On hunting days, Sean and Bridie took it in turns to ride to hounds and today it was Bridie's turn to wear her black coat with hunt buttons, which cheered her up no end. She loaded her grey gelding, Surtees, and was looking forward to a good run. Meanwhile, Sean loaded his own black mare, Hecuba, together with four horses which belonged to clients. Each horse had a leather head-collar and wore a travelling rug with its owner's initials.

Sean put on his well-worn 'ratcatcher' coat, before tying a stirrup-leather across his shoulder and chest, to signify he was leading a second horse. He then climbed into the driver's seat and drove the HTV Ford Cargo lorry out of the yard. He wanted to put up his three clients early, and arrange with the strong lady-rider, who was a front-runner, where to meet her with the second horse.

Mara did not go to the meet, but announced that she was driving to Broxford to shop. Christmas presents are cheaper if you buy early.

"Flurry darling, check the mare and foal in Lawson's Meadow. I shan't return till tea-time."

The ponderous front door of Bowden's Grove opened from the hall after some persuasion. Below the front door's elegant eighteenth century fanlight, two steps down revealed twin marble columns which guarded each side of the entrance. Mara shoo-ed away stable cats sitting on the granite treads.

"Don't let them in. Tabby's in kitten and she'll make cat's cradle of my bed."

Flurry helped her carry assorted bags to the car. There was a saddle for re-stuffing, plant trays, two black hunting jackets destined for a belated dry-clean, and a hat that a friend needed for someone's wedding.

As she lifted the bulky trays into the boot, grey mist swathed sleeping larch trees in Six Acre Covert which lay across the drive. Beyond the fence, the larches, planted in rows, looked like seaweed-decorated masts of sunken sailing ships. Flurry knew she must walk through Six Acre Covert to reach the mare and foal and this made her shiver with apprehension. Near her on the semi-circular lawn in front of the house, November leaves choked the bird bath, while the stone nymph of the lily pool looked chilly.

After a splutter or two the little car deigned to start, Mara wound down the window. "Father's seeing his solicitor, an old friend of years and years, and they're having lunch, so he'll be gone for hours. There's plenty of lamb for your lunch and give the chickens some water, I forgot. See the house has a rest! Please! don't do any more cleaning, or people will talk! Bye-ee!"

Flurry stood on the drive watching the green Traveller make its bronchitic way down the drive towards the lodge. She felt bereft, the loneliness culpable, as though she were to blame in some strange way. She stuffed cold hands into trouser pockets knowing that Bowden's Grove, when you are by yourself, could be misunderstood.

Turning indoors she walked towards the medieval part of the house. Boards expanding in the damp, then drying near chimney-stacks made footfalls. The windbraces strengthening the roof above the long gallery and over the labyrinth of the Smoker, kitchen, pantry, bootroom and scullery had their own strange shriek, as though dead voices were gathered in harmony. She had never been alone, by herself, in a large house in the country. She felt frightened. There was no-one to cling on to and she longed for Harry's strong reassuring presence, and her love for him. 'Why don't I go back to London' she thought. But she couldn't see her way clear. 'I came here to think and no constructive thoughts come.'

Unable to idle Flurry decided to wash all the Wellington boots, as nothing is nastier than putting on cold, damp boots. She knew small animal fleas from squirrel, fox and badger inhabit the cloth lining making your legs itch. With venom she sprayed the legs of the boots with anti-flea aerosol, then carried them to a wash-house sink. Bertie, the Jack Russell terrier, slunk under wine-racks, fearing the worst. A lead-covered sink was wide and shallow, being equipped with a wooden-slat draining board. Hot water, by a miracle of plumbing, was delivered to the sink. Cold water you pumped. Lumps of mud, leaves and horse droppings were washed down the ceramic pipe to find their way into some mysterious sump, as nobody knew where drains at Bowden's Grove led. Perhaps there were none.

The odour of bromine rose from the veterinary flea spray and dozens of pale pink geraniums stored by Mara on the shelf behind the sink, sneezed. Draining the row of boots on grey flagstones, she carried them towards the AGA, fixing them upside down on plate racks above the stove. A Victorian contraption, she wondered how many plates could be warmed? How many people lived at Bowden's Grove during the days of yearly babies, a governess and 'tweenies? She sat down on an oak Windsor chair with its sack cushion. Tweddles the cat gazing up with his one eye, jumped on her lap. She wiped her own eyes with her sleeve, where tears were falling too rapidly, her confidence lost, with no belief in herself. She wondered if she had ever been happy? She had worked? Yes. Achieved her ambitions? Yes. Done better than expected, but happiness is such an ephemeral thing, that maybe her love for Harry had been only an illusion.

She stroked Tweddles, and Bertie, thinking danger of a good bath over and commiseration called for, came out from under wine-racks. She caressed both cat and dog drawing comfort from warm fur, and like riding Jenny the grey Welsh Mountain pony, a slight feeling of euphoria spun through her body. Flurry had never kept an animal before because neither council tenement nor luxury flat allowed pets.

She got up with the cat under her arm and went to the 'fridge to take out a piece of Cheddar cheese. Purring and soft whining commenced, as both animals loved cheese. Bertie wagged his tail, pushing her leg with one paw, while Tweddles waved one front paw in the air, claws extended to grab the slivers offered. The old house closed round the warm AGA.

"You are a couple of the most lovely animals!"

Later on Flurry was able to eat a little of the lamb and bread Mara had left for her. Food was good at Bowden's Grove. Two pairs of eyes watched every movement. The air relaxed.

About mid-day a pair of smaller boots felt dry and putting on a stray pair of anyone's socks, she went out of the back door, walked round the house, across the drive and through a wicket-gate into Six Acre Covert.

The day was beige streaked to indigo. Somewhere there were animals at large in the covert and footfalls were scarcely heard on nerveless grass, sodden with November and rotted larch needles. Autumn was dead with winter not yet arrived. Six Acre Copse, next to the covert, was leased to the Forestry Commission and the agency had planted quick growing larch to protect groups of ash, oak and beech hardwoods. The path was wide enough for a timber-carriage to pass along, or tractors to strip lower branches and clear undergrowth. A fallow deer, startled, galloped by, its tiny slots hitting the pathway to echo and re-echo amongst the stands like a whispering gallery. She clutched her second-hand Barbour with its torn sleeve round her thin chest. The milieu was too silent. Too lonely, although the copse was noisy with the subtleties of animal life. She hoped she had left behind fears of attack after moving from Limehouse to St. Katharine's Dock, but when under stress the residue kept repeating itself like pickled onions after a pub lunch.

A half mile walk brought her to the edge of Six Acre, when the path ran beside a barbed-wire fence protecting ploughland planted with winter barley. The U-shaped field was enclosed by trees. She struggled to lift the metal gate, pinching her fingers in a loaded spring-catch, then slamming it shut she made her way across a set-aside headland.

Weed, grass and mud deadened the footfall of a horse walking behind her until a man's voice said: "Are you lost?"

"No. Are you?" She thought 'Why does walking in hard quiet make anger surface? Like hard lumps of whey. Hard acid lumps.'

He was gazing at her obliquely. A big middle-aged man on a tall horse, she felt belittled by him.

"You're out of order, walking through here." He tapped a boot with his stick. He wore brown boots with a zip, the kind worn by polo players. She felt him looking at her red hair. Insolently. As though she were a tart.

"With that hair you remind me of someone I know."

She hurried on and he came upsides of her, his weight back to make his horse walk with a slow pace to match her speed. "You know you *are* lost!"

"Don't be silly. I'm checking the horses."

"So you're a horsewoman are you?" And his cold query, nearly insulting, infuriated her. "I wouldn't presume!" she snapped.

"A gal like you shouldn't be walking along a lonely path." And she winced at his familiarity, but warned, Flurry made no reply. A powerful man, he had the arched back and deep seat of a strong rider, albeit hard on horses.

"Where are you going?"

"To Lawson's Meadow to check the mare and foal."

"Mara's got another foal has she?" His face appeared amused but the hooded eyes remained expressionless. "You've not been with horses long?"

"Not at all. I don't know anything about them."

"Thought you said you were Mara's new girl?"

"I didn't say anything. I said nothing at all."

"Couldn't believe you rode." There was something about him that made her think he was a Londoner. A townsman. He was too brash for the country and his tweed coat too loud a check, as Flurry was beginning to recognise the somewhat dated 'uniform' that country people wear.

"You're trespassing, walking through here."

"Don't you ever give up?"

"Should I? This is my land." He sounded smug and looked around with a proprietorial eye, so she was perplexed.

"I thought this land belonged to Grandfather and Mara."

"Is that what they told you. They never give anything away do they. They rent it from me. You *are* Mara's new girl, I thought so."

"I work in the house. Cleaning. Boots. Chickens. Dogs. Anything that comes to hand. Mara's gone shopping and I'm to see to the foal.

Satisfied? And may I continue with what I was asked to do without an inquisition. Good day."

"I'm Robert Davies." He pulled at his tweed cap on grey hair in tight natural curls, as if unsure whether he might raise it in acknowledgement, or treat her as an underperson. "You're the re-Christened Flurry. Thought you might be. I knew you were."

"Then why ask?"

"We'd never met." His eyes scanned her systematically as though assessing every point. Proportion. Muscle. Length of bone. Shape of head. Teeth. Feet. Neck. Size of eye . . . . .

"Satisfied?"

"Nothing as charming as you ever comes to Broxford." He patted her shoulder, so that she snapped away. "Knew who you were. Women talk to women."

"I'm surprised you listen to gossip. Grooms' gossip!"

"It's my dear wife, they all gossip to each other don't y'know." Then changing tack. "I breed racehorses, National Hunt mainly though I do a bit on the flat. Everyone knows Robert Davies. I have four yearlings coming along, they'll make your eyelashes flutter. Mara's a fool, she never goes for the best, or uses fashionable sires for her stock, it's always what she can get on tick, or other people's problem horses. She'll never make it."

"Money isn't everything. I'm beginning to understand that."

"It is in horses."

"Mara's a friend, and . . . . ."

"She's everyone's friend and they all take advantage, like her ass of a father she'll never learn. She works her fingers to the bone, and for what? For nothing. She's a good horsewoman, and good with young stock, but she'll get no-where." He looked around with a self-satisfied smile, acquisitively, although with no interest in the height of the winter barley crop, or the well-being of cattle grazing along the strip wood. Suddenly he continued "A gal like you doesn't want to hang around too long. A waste of time. You want to get on with your life." Flurry coloured feeling as though he guessed her secrets and had an affinity with her.

Walking across these lonely fields she was glad of his company, and he both attracted and repelled her. Nothing these days ever seemed straight forward.

They had reached the end of the plough. Beyond a further fence November larches whiskered with dead lichen and spent needles, awaited their passing. Flurry struggled with the gate.

"Allow me" and springing the bolt with his whip the metal gate swung open. Stands of eight foot high laurel bordered the track through

Lawson's Covert on the way to Lawson's Meadow, and the way grew narrow, wet leaves forming an arch overhead. Flurry hurried. Alarmed now. His horse walked steadily behind her however fast she trotted. Laurels gave way to a wide circular copse and here natural hazel with ancient blackened nuts still clinging to sharpened sticks sprouted from amongst fallen beech, soft and rotting. Sudden depressions like graves edged with giant stones made the pathway twist and turn. With relief she saw Robert take a different route right-handed, the big chestnut jumping fallen trunks where stones did not impede the take-off. A tall man, he had to lean forward on his horse's mane to avoid overhanging branches.

The path returned to orderly Forestry Commission copse. In the centre stood a small roundhouse with a pointed roof.

"Hangman's Castle," he volunteered. "Did you know? They say it was a Blind House once, where sheep stealers awaited the gibbet."

She shivered with apprehension. "They didn't say. Is the door locked?"

"Just tools and things." He continued to walk by her slowly. "Stubborn, that's what they are. I don't know why I put up with them on my land. But it's my wife. She won't hear a word against them. Says blood is thicker than water." The trackway opened out to a wide grass covered drove, they went on side by side in silence.

"And that Sean. Don't trust him. They never ought to have taken him on. I did warn them. He's nothing but trouble."

"Sean's super. I'm not listening." Flurry was surprised at her vehement defence of the young man.

"His grandmother's a witch."

"That's silly."

"Not in County Cork it isn't." He smiled. "You may not believe me, but it's true. Little dot of a woman. Dresses in black and wears a feathered hat. I believe she makes flies out of that hat to catch trout in the Blackwater. You can see her . . . . . the gardens sweep down to the river, where she drives her chair down to the bank and fishes. Not much else she can do, except fish and sell horses. They say she was the greatest horsewoman in all Ireland. And can those women ride! I pride myself that not many can beat me, but she'd go where no human could jump. Wills her horse over. 'Throw your heart over and your horse will follow,' she'd say. Then she broke her back. Taught her grandson all he knows."

"Was there an accident?"

"They say she followed hounds down the side of a quarry. She used to sit right back, and taught her horses to slide down on their quarters, just a trick, but one day the horse came down. Broke his neck and her back. That's the story. she's a witch with a horse, I know because we've bought horses through her. Young stock. Have the greatest respect for her judgment, nothing they don't know about horses. However don't trust them, they never *say anything,* and don't trust that Sean. I've told Mara time and time again to get rid of him but she'll never listen. Good day. Your mare and foal's over there, through the gate, next time you come bring the Land Rover by the road. Or has it broken down again!" And he cantered off down the side of Lawson's Meadow.

She felt puzzled about this man. Sophisticated, educated, a womaniser, he was obviously a deft hand with his method of flattery and hinting, to confuse his target. Presumably he was well-known in the district, being a landowner and certainly no stranger or vagrant, so why should she feel disturbed? It was not just his condescension in a lonely field. She was experiencing definite fear.

The mare trotted over to be patted and crunch a Polo mint from Flurry's hand. "Who's a good girl then?" she asked the horse, and the animal's friendliness brought some colour back into her wan cheeks. The foal attempted to suckle its mother, but she was more interested in the Polos. The baby was wearing a tiny New Zealand rug, with tapes in lieu of a surcingle, so that the ends were tied in a neat bow on its back. By the time Flurry had picked over the straw in the field-shelter and put it to rights, also checked the water-trough, it was getting late. She decided to walk home by the road, which was longer but safer, luckily Bert Rawle came along in his rusty little truck.

"'Ow be on then, Flurry? Them's gone to market?" Flurry was pleased to see his kindly, cheerful face, with the pipe firmly stuck in his mouth. "I felt lonely . . . . . walking across the fields."

"What you'm used to I 'spose. Friend o'mine went up to London. Got on that there Underground. Went round and roun' 'ee did. Couldn't of got awf!" They rattled on with Bert singing snatches of hymns.

"Sean says you sing in the church choir."

"An' play the organ. Weddings mostly."

"Better than funerals. November makes me sad and those larches!" She shivered. The van turned right-handed by the ruined lodge and up the drive towards Bowden's Grove.

"'Minds me. A chap . . . . . new chap he were, came to play for a funeral. Now hymns, yes, or a nice wedding. but what's the 'volontry' for a funeral. So 'ee looks in the music cupboard, an' what does 'ee find?

'Sheep May Safely Graze.' 'I'll play that', 'ee says, so that's what he plays. 'Well,' says the vicar afterwards. 'That were nice. Us enjoyed that . . . . . very 'propriate. *Because we've just buried the butcher'*!"

Flurry entered the house by the back door, which was never locked, as they'd lost the key and hurried up to the comfort of her homely bedroom.

Meantime in the local market town, Grandfather stumbled up the steps of Messrs Payne, Jude and Ellis's office. Henry Payne, the solicitor, was a long-standing friend of the family and Grandfather was ushered into a large, booklined room overlooking a rose garden.

"Uncle my dear, and how are you?" said a very stout lady, kissing him. Colonel Bowden's sight was failing, thus he could only guess at beloved Annie's luxurious grey cloak and her velour hat, trimmed with tail-feathers. They sat together holding hands, as Uncle and niece had always been very close, she being the daughter of his elder brother Julian and the first-born in the family of the next generation.

"Dear, dear, a sad day indeed!" intoned the solicitor. "But I believe you're wise, Mrs. Bowden-Davies. With divorce in the offing, you never know how much a husband can claim . . . . . may I say . . . . . from a rich wife."

Grandfather could only feel, not see, the diamond bracelet on Annie's plump arm, because he was blind on his left side.

"Now you are setting up this Trust, well in advance, that does alter things." There was no need to tell Henry Payne that Bowden's Grove was the original family home. However, when Julian, Annie's father, as a successful merchant banker married the rich heiress to Broxford Court, Miss Gertrude de Courcey, who was an orphan with no father or mother, he sold his half-share of Bowden's Grove to Grandfather. However, lack of money and poor management during the time Colonel Bowden was in the army, meant that Bowden Grove's land was re-sold, leaving the house with only five acres of the fifty acre Home Paddock. This had long been a worry with so many horses in the yard. However, Annie was always generous to her uncle and cousins. Now Grandfather felt uncertain. Changes could be imminent.

" . . . . . and" went on the solicitor, "should you die before your husband Robert Davies, because you are childless, he receives only the interest on invested capital. Your entire estate is held in Trust . . . . . from the date of your signature . . . . . " The solicitor read out four long pages of legal procedure.

"To take effect immediately," said Annie.

"Robert is not aware of the Trust? And how it will affect him?"

"No," agreed Annie. "He has no idea. I don't leave documents lying about, like my husband does." Grandfather sighed remembering Robert's misalliances.

The solicitor tapped the tips of his fingers together. "I am very uneasy, because I can see terrible problems arising. Wouldn't it be wise to discuss the prospect of divorce with your husband, rather than springing it on him suddenly. The consequences could have their dangers."

"On New Year's Eve my old hunt, the Charleville Blazers, is visiting us. I want nothing to mar their pleasure."

"Even at your husband's expense?"

"They mean a great deal to me. More, far more than you can ever know."

"Amen to that," said Grandfather, squeezing Annie's hand in understanding.

"Mrs Bowden-Davies. Are you afraid of your husband?"

Annie thought for some time. "Yes, I am."

"Can he be violent?"

"He can be. That is why we must say nothing. And then tell him . . . . tell him to leave my house . . . . . in your presence."

Payne went to the door to call his chief clerk, together with a secretary, to witness the signature of Mrs Annie Bowden-Davies. She appeared undeterred by unforeseen danger.

Leaving her bedroom, Flurry walked down the steep twisting back stairs. The carpet was torn, so you had to be careful with the electric bulb fused, and no light. The stair smelt of onion, cats and damp. Crossing the dining-room she entered the 'Smoker', a family gossip-room, so named because gentlemen retired to the Smoker to smoke their cigars. The room had blue velvet chairs and two sofas grouped around a large chimney-piece. Mara's dried flowers were arranged on a low table, while Persian rugs brought from the Middle East by Grandfather set off brocade curtains, perhaps new in the 'sixties. Flurry loved this room because it was her ideal of warmth, friendliness and elegance. Coming from a long line of skilled cabinet-makers she had natural good taste. Flurry looked around. The room was larger than the whole of Mother's flat; and more colourful than her stylish, minimalistic, white apartment.

Memory bounced back and forth from Mother's oilcloth on the kitchen table where they ate, to the pale sofa of St. Katharine's Dock flat under it's swan-necked, flexible, halogen, standard lamp. There was nothing in-between. Only space. A blank. Had she been born into a typical family there would have been a melding, linking childhood to being an adult, with holidays in the country, children's parties, Barbie dolls and a My-Little-Pony with a choice of green or pink silk mane. Catapulted from Limehouse to Wimbledon each day under Mother's watchful eye, she had accepted the corseted-cossetted existence of Harry's patronage without ever growing-up. Work was her only free-expression.

Now at Bowden's Grove she was living backwards in time, and was experiencing those in-between years so cruelly sliced out of her life. For the moment she felt uncertain as to the significance of these thoughts, which had been brought to the foreground by meeting Robert in the woods.

She stood by the window on the wide elm board floor, she had polished so energetically during the past week or so. A cobbled pathway led to the stableyard built with cream stucco walls, its clocktower and sculptured roofline appearing unnecessarily elegant when attached to this small house in the country. The eighteenth century builder must have thought a great deal more of his horses than home comfort. She could hear the arrival of the big horsebox to herald Sean and Bridie's return from hunting.

She knew Bridie disliked her and was bitterly jealous, this made Flurry feel both sad and mad at her. Grandfather was always charming, but a bit ga-ga, while Mara was the enigma. She no longer laughed at her work, although doubtless felt that 'new-brooms-sweep-clean' and would not commit herself for or against! Flurry knew she must *earn* respect, but a challenge excited her. She must succeed. At the same time Sean appeared sublimely indifferent, except that she caught him gazing at her when she half-turned away from him. 'I'd better go down and do some work', she sighed, and went to look for them, finding Bridie in the tackroom. Two lurchers and a sort of sheepdog bounced out, to lean against her legs like big dogs will, given a chance. Only Bertie was a house-dog and lived indoors.

"Have a good day?" she asked Bridie.

"Aye?" Bridie's straight hair was plastered down on her slightly elongated head as she took off her velvet cap.

"A good day?" more loudly.

"Fair. Nothing much doing till the two o'clock fox. Then a run. Scent's catchy though. Too dry. We need rain." There were saddles, bridles and headcollars to clean. "Get yourself a sponge," she went on. "Wring it out almost dry and use the glycerine saddle soap, it's the block there. On the dish. Try stirrup leathers first, they're easier. I'll take the bridles to pieces."

Sean came in and tapped Bridie on the shoulder. The tension relaxed from her body as she leaned towards him, but he turned away saying "I'll be feeding and doing the lorries." Sitting down he pulled off his spurs and brown hunting boots, while turning to Flurry. "And you want to be careful. Bridie will kill you if you get the tack mixed up. Keep each horse's tack by itself, and don't be forgetting yourself. Is there a cup of tea?"

"Who's boss around here, Bridie?"

"HE is," and she obediently filled, then plugged in the electric kettle.

41

"You shouldn't let him push you about. Refuse to be a doormat."
'Maybe,' she thought, 'that's what I was for Harry. A doormat!'

The tackroom was quiet and industrious. Soap-filled nails on chapped hands polished away sweat, grease, mud and scratches. In the shadow of a whitewashed wall, dimly lit by the half-door, Sean's black hunting coat and grey velvet cap, made by Patey's of London, hung indistinctly above a row of saddle racks, some metal, others wood. A dark chest, immense in size, stood, its lid open, leaning against plaster cracks. Inside, leg bandages, tail bandages, sheets, over-reach boots and a dozen alternatives at whose use Flurry could only guess, were packed with towels, together with a ginger cat, purring, and some pheasant's tail feathers. A board, lit by light from the barred window festooned with cobweb, had hundreds of rosettes pinned upon it, recalling victory in blue, red, green, yellow, pink-purple and gold from every hunter-trial, horseshow, point-to-point or team-chase in the country. Some were clean, some dusty and curled. Another board laid down the rations for each horse, together with a further chalk-written roster for daily exercise or hunting. The organisation required was a surprise to Flurry, who as a working executive herself, was beginning to understand the intricacies of running a livery yard and it intrigued her. Through an archway in a second room, gold and brown stripes of Newmarket or navy blue rugs, were drying on racks pulled up by cords into the roof above the anthracite warmth from the cockle stove. Padded rugs were stored by themselves in case of fire.

After half an hour Sean returned and Bridie made them tea, when Flurry remarked, "This afternoon I talked to the most unpleasant man I have ever met!"

"Where?"

"Six Acre and Lawson's. His land so he said."

"Robert Davies, and it's *not* his land."

"A big man. A big man on a tall horse. Wears sort of polo boots."

"You're learning. The boots."

"Why shouldn't I notice his boots?"

"Is that right now. And you wouldn't notice the horse a week ago!" He held out a bridle to Bridie. She got up placing the dirty bridle to hang on a type of multiple meathook suspended from the ceiling. With deft fingers she undid the noseband and cheek-pieces, taking reins from bridle. His request gave ease to her afflictions. A response to her silence.

"Can't he do that for himself?"

"She likes it. Cleaning tack."

She knew Bridie was besotted with Sean, brushing her body against him, smelling him, in spite of his obvious repulsion.

From Bridie, "What did he say? Robert?"

"Walking with me across Six Acre, he said he did not know who I was, and that I was trespassing. And then decided he knew me after all. He was insulting, but has *charm*. Ingratiating."

"Robert has charm alright and likes to spread his largesse about."

"Annie's," snorted Sean." He had no money of his own."

"I think he was trying to give me good advice. Or make me think he was. I got the feeling he was warning me. Trying to be friendly and make me listen to him. He's certainly plausible."

Sean lost his indolence. He threw the paper away walking up and down, as though fighting with himself. Flurry wondered what link there could be between Sean and Robert, or even Sean and Robert's wife.

Bridie, watching him, echoed, "He's a creep."

"Seems to dislike us at Bowden's Grove," from Flurry.

"Envious." Sean and Flurry looked at each other. Signalling. Not to say too much in Flurry's presence, making her feel an outsider again.

"Jealous," Bridie said at last. "Annie owns the Court."

"I see, and it's not his land. I *thought* he didn't look country!" Flurry laughed. "I've noted how you all lean on gates, to look at the crops and cattle and things!"

"She's learning!"

"Strange . . . . . how he almost seemed like a Londoner . . . . . like me!"

They went on working when Bridie said suddenly, "Annie breeds a few foals for the flat."

"Robert said he did."

"Did what?"

"Bred horses."

"Doesn't know what he's talking about. It's Annie."

"What's she like?"

"Too good for him. She helps Mummy out sometimes when she's skint, because clients don't pay their bills."

"Which is usual," yawned Sean.

"Annie may be good about money, but she can be hoity-toity. You can't cross her."

"As if you'd know!" he snapped, mastering her thoughts, so that she scowled, and a cold finger of antipathy pointed between them, making Flurry query Sean's involvement with the Bowden Family. There was much going on beneath the surface that puzzled her. The kettle boiled once more and mugs were filled up. Flurry found cleaning tack hard on the hands, as the grease on stirrup leathers was filling her nails, while the evening grew darker, only the pool of warmth from the stove keeping out the chill.

"What horse was Robert riding," Sean said to improve the silence.

"Big. Chestnut, I think," and Flurry creased her forehead in concentration.

"Tiger Bay. Two white socks fore, and two white stockings hind."

"What do you mean?"

"White hair on the legs. Socks means up to the fetlock. Stockings as far as the knee" Bridie explained.

"You should look, and you'll be telling a horse miles away," from Sean.

Bridie chipped in, "Two are never the same . . . . . perhaps only one in a million. Like fingerprints."

"I didn't realise."

"If it were easy now, they'd be wanting to put a 'ringer' in a race, to help with the betting."

"Too many people in the know," agreed Bridie, picking up a broom to begin sweeping. "Turn the rugs on the racks, Flurry!"

"Please!" Flurry sensed her stick her tongue out at her when her back was turned. Ignoring the childish outburst, Sean took a newspaper from his pocket and, leaning against the half-door, read the racing results by the amber light from the stove. Mara's car could be heard coming up the drive, and Bridie ran indoors.

"You should be kinder to her. She hurts."

"So you keep telling me!" and Flurry was surprised when he went on "I have a niece, she's six. In Cork City streets you cannot hold her hand because it's too small. Too soft. So it's reins for little Marie, red reins with tinkling bells on. We get along fine, her looking into shop windows and feeding ducks in the park. You keep her in front of you, the bells ring and it's fine."

Flurry felt suitably reprimanded and he held the door open for her to proceed him into the nervy night. Cobbles twisted their feet. The skyline of the roof still netted night clouds, and as they walked towards the side door, they could see the uncertained window of the Smoker. Mara had a drink in her hand and was talking to Grandfather. Bridie stood by the door resting one side of her foot, as though uncertain whether she was hearing correctly.

In the silence of talking mouths, Sean said, "Let them alone."

"What is happening?" He shrugged. "You can guess!"

"If you say so!" He appeared to agree without committing himself.

"Do you know?"

"Would I say if I did!"

CHAPTER 4

Vr-oom. Vr-oom. Vr-oom. Flurry woke to the sound of Bridie's motor-bike being revved up in the yard. It was then driven to the paddock where it commenced its dreary circuits on the winter grass. It was only six o'clock in the morning and still dark, so that the lights flashed and faded as the motorbike circled. Flurry, unable to sleep, went down to the kitchen, where she found Sean, propped up against the AGA, studying racing form as usual. Without looking up he told her, "Mara said to clear the small box, and get the bags on the truck."

"Stablehands get more pay than domestics," snapped Flurry.

"Is it your cards you'll be wanting this morning."

"Oh! Shut up! Can't Bridie do it, rather than make all that noise?"

"And you saying we should be kinder to the girl."

"What's the matter with her now?" He refused to be drawn, and Flurry considered saying that why couldn't he help. Then thought better of it. "I might as well be in South America from understanding you lot," she muttered. Then, like a miasma, a film of her questioning thoughts blocked any further back-chat because she had to be careful. Bowden's Grove might be her only chance to reclaim lost teenage years, and she couldn't afford to throw it away until she had learnt how this strange, foreign world worked. She must succeed.

At breakfast Mara observed: "A Nervous Mum wants something to ride as it's a Saturday. I told her she can have Jenny, but only for two hours." It was Sean's turn to hunt and Bridie objected. "We've a load up as it is. I can't cope with Nervous Mum as well."

"Then Flurry can drive the small Bedford taking Jenny. The mare knows her," Flurry protested in spite of herself.

"You'll be alright." Mara seemed confident. "It's only a four-and-a-half ton truck."

"I've never driven a horsebox."

"Just like a car, except first and second are crawler gears . . . . . "

". . . . . more like a tractor . . . . . :

". . . . . the turbo doesn't come in until later."

"Charming. What happens if I get stuck?" But nobody seemed interested.

At first she thought she would never get used to the diabolical steering and unaccustomed width of the lorry. Then confidence grew, and daring to engage top gear she arrived at an open grassy space one mile from the County and District foxhound meet. Flurry parked near Bridie who walked across to her.

"Check Jenny's bridle and see her chain's done up two-and-three-a-side, or we'll have your Mum taking off. And tighten the girths before she gets on. Then check twice afterwards, 'cos Jenny blows herself out, and Mum hasn't the nous to do it for herself."

Flurry was pleased to see Bert amble towards her.

"Mornin'. Lazy old wind. Goes right through you, rather'n blow round."

Flurry shivered. "Please Bert. Lead Jenny down for me. She jumps a bit, and I'm not used to the sloping ramp." Together they settled Nervous Mum, who trotted off to meet hounds. "I thought Jenny was such a quiet pony."

"Not when they see hounds they bain't. 'Sides your Missus makes pony restive. Know 'ers nervous-like."

The two leant on the fence catching excitement in the air, where nature was like a heartbeat, and hunting the expression of its soul. Her first time. First experience of hunting, and she didn't know what to expect. Flurry shivered in the damp, bitter wind. Anxious. Waiting. Bert took his pipe of out his mouth, carefully packed it with tobacco and lit it using three matches. After a while he said, "Would Sean give I a lend of his lorry, t'take calves to market?"

"I'm sure he will. I'll tell him tonight." Reminding her of him, she hoped to see Sean mounted being entranced by his horsemanship albeit ambivalent towards him as a person.

Faintly on the aether of the parish, the huntsman blew his horn to take hounds to the first draw urging the pack in front of him to find a fox. Below the watchers, forty acres of cold pasture sloped gently down to a stone wall, while beyond it a meadow of coarse grass rose to a dark covert of maple, oak and beech, stripped and winter bare. Far distant hills were grey-silver.

Meantime, the fox hearing hounds, crept downhill leaving the covert blank. Streaming across the valley floor, the pack, resembling a flight of swallows was uncertain. Behind them the field followed slowly, led by their field Master and Flurry was fascinated to see hounds work. Horses were restive, expectant, and she felt excited, half wishing she might ride too. Suddenly there was a whistle and a blood-curdling 'Yoi'. The huntsman took hounds to the holloa, when they quickened, to swing left-handed along the far end of the covert, but were still unsure of the line. Then opening with a sudden burst of joy they pushed their fox across two fields and up the hill out of view, where hound-music reverberated through the trees.

Girths were tightened, and the field galloped parallel to the covert, Flurry saw Sean riding his black mare Hecuba, wearing his old-fashioned, long-skirted black coat, now nearly grey. He was accompanied by a large lady riding side-saddle and in a dove-grey habit. She was mounted on a weight-carrying pale horse, and Flurry, with a pang of jealousy, which caught her unawares, wondered who she was. Behind them rode Robert Davies, with his hunched, thrusting shoulders, resplendent in top hat, red coat and mahogany tops. 'That must be Tiger Bay,' Flurry thought. 'A chestnut, with two white socks fore, and two white stockings hind.' It appeared from a distance that Robert was trying to pass Sean, but Hecuba was too fast for him, and with a vicious yank on Tiger Bay's double bridle, Robert dropped behind.

"Us'll drive toper 'ill, see 'un come round" and Bert made for his rusty pick-up truck. Flurry wondered if she should leave the horsebox unattended. "Don't you fret. Big Jim's on duty. Nobody won't get past Big Jim. Jim's wigerlanty." She was not quite sure what a wigerlanty was supposed to do.

In the open back of the pick-up sat a black dog with long legs and fiendish teeth, together with a rope, spades, a storm-lantern, cattle-drench, a blue calf-net and Bert's dinner. Flurry did not like the look of the dog.

"Patter's alright. Patter's a good, honest dog."

They rattled along through country lanes at breakneck speed, and had the truck not been open-topped, fumes from the broken exhaust might have asphyxiated them both. As it was, Flurry's throat felt sore.

They climbed a steep hill to an open sandy terrace and Bert parked to the left of a thick forest. Below them the country stretched to an infinity of small hills and fields like patchwork. Directly below in ten-acre Locksmith Wood, floating like an island in the damp air, the huntsman was tooting his horn to say he was still in covert, while faintly on the stiff wind his voice could be heard encouraging his hounds. Flurry listened intently, captivated by the mystery of huntsman in communion with nature.

"Eleu in there my lads! Eleu. Eu in, little bitches. Loo in!"

On the terrace a knot of hunt supporters stood by the five-bar metal gate. "Morning' Bert," they said. "Morning Flurry!"

"So you're Flurry, pleased to meet you," said a farmer's wife with a smile that turned up at the corners. She was a comfortable-looking body with brown hair, knitted cap and glasses. "Hear you've revolutionised Bowden's Grove!"

"Hi there!" and the local haulier joined the group, holding out his hand. A handsome man, he felt sure of himself.

Flurry dragged herself away from watching the hunt. 'They all seem to know me. They're country, where everyone knows everyone else, unless you retire to one of those suburb-style complexes, then you only know other 'townies. And she thought of the old saying, you're a 'foreigner' for twenty-five years, then a 'newcomer'. After that it's only time before they'll *speak* to you.'

47

"Bill's taken on hounds to Locksmith's for the first check," said the haulier. "But they can't prove the line." Far below, the field could be seen holding-up on the near side of the woodland. Flurry watched, breathless, keenly, nerves on edge, hoping to see the fox. Bert brought the black dog up to the group on a piece of rope.

"You want to be careful of that dog," joked the haulier, winking at Flurry. "Never mess with a Patterdale. Have your hand off."

"Patter's a good dog."

"I mean it! When a Patterdale grips. He grips. Have your hand off!"

"Daft bugger!" interrupted a person dressed in a cap, waistcoat and trousers, Flurry was unable to decide whether the apparition was man or woman.

"Take no notice, dear," laughed the farmer's wife. "Only their way."

"It's true y'know. Up in the Fells and Lakes the Patterdale terrier runs with the pack. That's why he has long legs. When they mark to ground in he goes and despatches the fox. A terrible grip has the Patterdale."

"That's Dales 'unting," objected the HeShe. "Not Wiltshire."

"Didn't I say Dales."

Flurry watched as the banter went from one to another. 'How easy these people are with themselves. As though they grew out of green grass, flying leaves and rushing cloud packs,' which made her think of her own position in this close country community. Then she felt Patter's damp nose sniff her hand and she looked down into the deep shining eyes of a faithful, friendly dog.

"Good boy, Patters."

"There's no such thing as a bad dog," observed the farmer's wife. "It all depends on how they're trained. Trained with kindness."

"Not like people," agreed the haulier. "Some men are born evil."

The old Major standing near them contemplated the waiting horsemen, some conspicuous in red coats. "I agree there don't y'know." The Major who sported a moustache above which grew a bulbous nose, had been silent until now. "I believe in evil. Knew a chap once out in Panama when I was posted there. Seemed all right. An engineer. Decent enough chap on the surface. Then he got into debt, the usual thing. Gee-gees and women, so he goes to a moneylender. To cut a long story short, he shoots the moneylender and, worse than that, reloads and shoots the brains out of the wife and three-year-old child. That's evil."

"Did they get him?"

"Never. Disappeared. Just disappeared."

"But what makes them evil," said the farmer's wife. "Children aren't born bad."

"Some are." The Major blew out his moustache. "Small minded. Socially inadequate perhaps. Gets into trouble. Harbours a grudge which can only be redeemed by murder. They're born evil. It's the response of the stupid."

"You can have clever murderers," Flurry hardly knew why she was joining in.

"Wily perhaps. Clever maybe, but unimaginative. Some men live in a fantasy world, which no medicine and no psychiatrist can get through to." Flurry had the feeling that the Major was trying to say more but was unable to, and her thoughts tied in with 'speak' again. What did the word mean? Like a hundred little innuendoes, nods and winks.

In Locksmith Wood three couple of hounds broke from covert, to feather. They moved quickly, noses glued to the ground, sterns waving frantically. Then Primrose gave tongue, followed by Polish, Pointer and Dagger, when the whole pack took up the cry. The huntsman blew away from covert, with quick pulsating notes.

"There goes the bugger," said HeShe. "Yoi!"

A big, light-coloured fox with a white tag piloted the pack up the hill towards the supporters, gaining at every yard. Charlie leapt up on to the wall in front of the watchers, and turned as though to say to hounds 'Come on you lot! You are slow!' Sir Charles then made his way nonchalantly, to escape into the forest.

Meantime, the huntsman, knowing his country well, galloped up a grassy lane flanked each side by stone walls. His second whipper-in followed him, while his first whip cantered diagonally across the meadow to take up point duty. The field followed the huntsman at a respectful distance.

Suddenly, cutting across the meadow to make a chord with the arc of the lane, the dove-grey lady riding side-saddle accompanied by Sean approached the five-bar metal gate. Bert dashed forward to open it for them, but the gate was securely chained and padlocked. The huntsman grinned as he flashed by. The lady collected her seventeen-hand heavy horse to approach the gate slowly, and getting close, his hocks well under him, she jumped the gate which was raised some way off the ground, making it a formidable fence.

"Well taken, Mrs. Annie," shouted the haulier, and to Flurry "Get a fence like that wrong and it could be curtains. Broken backs for horse and rider."

"So that's Annie. I might have known!" Flurry murmured, heartily relieved and watching Sean intently. His black mare stood well back to fly the obstacle like the good steeplechaser she was, and he raised his grey velvet cap, bringing his arm forward and then back in a bow, which was characteristic of him, although his eyes were fixed on Flurry, with her red hair shining against black trees, and one thin hand clutching the collar of her Barbour to keep out the cold. Feeling his gaze she dropped

49

her eyes.

"'Tis true that Sean's Gran taught 'em both to ride," Bert assured the company confidentially.

"I didn't know that Annie's Irish?" She was surprised.

"She is on 'er mother's side."

"Is Sean's Gran the Black Witch?"

"So they say, Missie," laughed the haulier. "But most of it's gossip 'bout Annie and Sean," to make Flurry look up quickly, mouth open silently. "Annie was Master of our County and District, that's why she rides up front."

Collecting herself, "Why did she give up?"

"Robert was jealous — so they say. Because the country wouldn't have him as Master, although he put in for it several times. Hunt Committee don't trust Davies and didn't think he knew what he was doing. They tried him as field Master for one season and he made a pig's ear of it. A lot of mistakes."

"Proper muck up," agreed Bert.

". . . . . as well as upsetting the farmers. Robert and the Hunt chairman had a dreadful row, so Annie felt she had to give up her mastership, as not to take sides."

"Is it true," Flurry asked, "that they don't speak to you till you've lived here twenty-five years?" The haulier raised an eyebrow and Flurry felt herself watched. Queried. As if there were something to know. "What about Bert? Is he a foreigner too?"

"He's honorary, 'cos he's born and bred Somerset," laughed the farmer's wife. "Honorary Wiltshire."

She pondered yet again the meaning of the word 'speak' guessing it meant secrets in this High Peak of country living. While they were talking, the field Master brought up a large body of horsemen and Robert Davies was struggling in the front rank, spurring and whipping his horse to keep up.

"Better'n not let the Colonel see 'im do that. Get sent 'ome."

"Doesn't Robert ever ride with his wife?" Flurry asked.

"No stomach for her and Sean's kinda riding. He's inadequate. Not their sort. Just grudging, and only imagines he can ride."

"Quite so. Quite so," agreed the Major. "It's in the breeding. Genes tell." Once more Flurry thought he was going to say more but thought better of it.

Presently a holloa was heard on the other side of the forest. "Do you always make that dreadful screech, if you see a fox?" Flurry asked the haulier.

"Not if you know what's good for you, you don't. Lifts hounds' heads and makes the huntsman mad, if it's the wrong fox. You have to be sure. Very sure."

"D'you know the one 'bout the sausage factory," chipped in Bert. "In goes pig and out comes pork, bacon, sausages, trotters, bristles and bonemeal. Only one thing left . . . . . it be the squeak! An' they gives the squeak to Violet, 'ere! That's why 'er 'orrible 'olloa." Flurry was entranced to find that the HeShe's name was Violet! They returned to the pick-up.

"I'm surprised a nice gal like you gets up with the likes of Bert Rawle. You want to watch him."

"An' you want to watch that 'aulier. Puts tenpence-a-mile on the bill for 'is cattle truck, if you don't watch out!"

"Take no notice, my dear," smiled the farmer's wife. "Good friends are like happy families, always have to get at each other. But they'd do anything to help one another!" She patted her shoulder. "And don't you worry — we'll always put you right!" Flurry wondered if this had something to do with 'speaking' to her and was grateful.

"True. True," agreed the Major.

The haulier had to have the last word. "And watch that tinker's truck. Drive round a corner too fast and the wheels fall off."

"Daft buggers," snorted Violet. they drove off and the pick-up rattled downhill with Bert singing *"Oh! God our Help in Ages Past!"*

Flurry found Nervous Mum, untacked Jenny, putting on a blue sweatsheet and loaded her into the small box. She was glad of Bert's help as she found raising the ramp too heavy for town-muscles. On the way home, and struggling with the low crawler-gears before getting up speed, she felt gratified to think that Mara trusted her to deal with both horse and box. Horseboxes, even old ones, are expensive, and accidentaly turning it over was a thought too terrible to contemplate. She realised that tied up and trapped on her side in a confined space, Jenny must be terrified, and would thrash about in blind panic, breaking her legs that could never be mended. Dear Jenny! She must be very, very careful.

When Flurry drove into the stableyard Mara was waiting for her.

"Annie wants us both to go to tea."

"When?"

"Now. Today. You take Jenny, untack her and wash her off, and I'll feed in half an hour."

"She's, Annie I mean, is still out hunting."

"She's having a short day. She often does."

Flurry did not say that she hardly felt up to meeting the glamorous Annie, nor the distasteful Robert, as she had a cold coming on, besides going out to tea had a certain ring about it. Going out to tea! You didn't do such an old-fashioned thing in business circles. It made her think of school again, when other girls went to tea with friends, while she went back to Mother, who had done her best, but Flurry knew she would never be whole until she had sewn up the tears in her life. So 'going out to tea' had a certain storybook quality, and what did you wear?

"I've nothing to wear for tea!"

"Trousers are OK," and Mara led Jenny away.

"Won't Bridie want me for tack?" she shouted after her retreating back.

"Sean will help.'

Running after her, "He hates cleaning tack."

Sean can do three times the amount of work than all of us put together. "He only looks indolent. It's a pose, and keeps us up to scratch." Mara did not say how Annie had guessed that Sean might be smitten with Flurry, and could not wait to meet the wonder girl. Sean was not easily caught.

"Royal Command," grumbled Flurry. "Why don't I stand up for myself more."

In the dying afternoon light, Mara drove her Traveller to the lodge gates and turned left. They skirted the garden, turning left-handed again to skirt the paddock and down the small lane towards the hairpin. She switched on the car lights as they approached the beechwood tunnel, and Flurry shivered.

"I rode down here with Sean. Isn't this where the Merc went over the edge?"

Mara changed to second gear to negotiate a very steep hill, dropping down in front of them. "There is a large disused quarry on our left. This was once the approach road that horse-drawn drays used, to extract the stone."

"Is it still used?"

"No stone has been quarried here for a hundred years. Too expensive. Tomorrow you can go on exercise with Bridie and she'll take you along the ridge path, it's a brilliant ride and then down what we call the Z-Path."

Gaining the bottom of the hill they turned left at the fork, so that Flurry realised they had completed a half-circle. Passing through a pair of elaborate wrought-iron gates, Mara stopped the car in a tree-lined avenue leading to Broxford Court.

"Look up, and you can see the quarry."

It towered above them. In the foreground, like unconquered ramparts, two terraces had eaten into the precipitous hillside. Diagonally across the two terraces linking top to bottom was a wide oblique trackway, known locally as the Z-Path. The countryside is unique, formed when millions of years ago, granite rocks were thrust up by the sliding forces which compressed the south of England into the Midlands and North. The crumpling and piling forms a broad swathe of North Wiltshire.

To the west and most dramatic of all was a peak of primordial rock. Blasting had not demolished it. But rain and weather had sharpened the peak to a chisel-like point, while at its base four cushions of rock formed the topmost shoulder ridge. Cold, white beams of a sun already set, outlined the peak in an icy frame.

"Round here they call it *The Finger of God*. They say a woman was brutally murdered, but the murderer was caught on the Z-Path, and killed himself." Flurry wondered at the intense stiff finger, with its four knuckles of the clenched hand of God. Like the apocalypse, the peak gazed down on Broxford Court, looking pale and haunted in the fading evening. Such a panorama in black and white called forth deepest emotions of pain and primordial lust, so that Flurry closed her eyes, unable to witness her exposure to its presence. The very lack of colour was an irrelevance.

Continuing their journey they approached the eighteenth century house. In bizarre contrast light shone from every sash-window to bathe the façade in a pale orange glow. An ambitious giant portico of Corinthian columns surmounted by a pediment was lit from below by lamps held in the paws of two lions rampant. Steps led to the front door. Annie gave permanent orders that whenever a guest was expected, someone must wait by the door to open it before their arrival. Barbarka, the Lithuanian au pair, threw wide the welcoming glass door. Six foot three in height with flaxen hair and a bubbling smile, Barbarka exuded welcome.

"You're looking very well today, Barbarka," said Mara.

"That is . . . . . because it's the way I am."

"Always a smile. Always happy."

The hall was painted in varying shades of primrose and white, while an enormous flower arrangement on a stand, pointed the way to elegant twin staircases with a gallery above, equipped with brass handrails.

"Mara! You've brought her!" and Annie, holding out both hands, kissed Flurry on both cheeks. "And it was you. I thought it was, standing with Bert and the Three Musketeers." She was dressed in cream chiffon trousers and a floating yet severe shirt to enwrap her large body. 'How like a rose she is!' Flurry thought. 'One of those Bourbon roses you see on the covers of expensive magazines. Pale cream, full-blown, yet still perfumed.' There was a quality about her which made everyone she touched feel good about themselves, and there was a wisp of sadness which was impossible to quantify as though she knew and understood the tragedies of life. The polarity of emotions called forth by the outdoor menacing scene and the warmth of the welcome was overpowering.

They went into the small sitting-room with its tall, mahogany, library bookshelves, surmounted by very good sporting pictures. A large, round Empire table stood by the log fire.

"London doesn't go in for tea like we do in the country. This is trout pâté caught by Bert. Or pheasant terrine if you'd rather, shot by the Major."

"Who only helps with the shoot to get a free gun for himself!" interrupted Robert, as he came through the door, holding a glass of whiskey. He gave Flurry a curt nod and she saw that his pupils were pinpoint sharp, when for no apparent reason, she remembered the Major's warning stories.

"Terrine made by Dolly." Annie raised an eyebrow admonishing him.

"Dolly . . . . sorry . . . . . I was . . . . .?" Flurry was confused.

"Your farmer's wife. With the Three Musketeers." Standing together Annie appeared to dwarf Robert, not by size — he was a big man — but as though they had changed identities and she were the husband and he a pliant wife who has made a good marriage and is fairly content. Annie turned to Flurry, "Help yourself to toast." Then sharply, "Robert! Are you eating? Or is it a liquid tea, you're having."

Flurry detected a slight Irish intonation in Annie.

Annie's face had the beauty of a family portrait. Even in middle-age the set of her eyes, the firmness of her mouth, the shape of her nose, were no different compared with other beauties. But it was the flashing radiance, a depth of understanding in her eyes that gave this illusion, and you saw not Annie, but a reflection of yourself in her face. During the pause Flurry asked, "Have you always lived here?"

"Born here and Mara at Bowden's Grove, we're proper Wiltshire."

"And Irish. I often think my wife's more Irish than English."

Mara sat down wearily, thankfully sipping a cup of hot tea. "I can remember visiting your mother when I was small. What a difference Annie's made. The house was terribly dark and old-fashioned, with red damask hangings. You had to thread your way through the drawing-room, there were so many occasional tables and what-nots and hassocks."

"That was because Mummy was very strait-laced and wouldn't have anything changed. She didn't marry until she was forty and kept everything as it was in her girlhood. And Mummy was boss."

"There was O'Callaghan in her, what do you expect. I said my wife was Irish."

"Only half, Robert. On Mummy's side."

"Robert's right," conceded Mara. "Tamzine O'Callaghan always reminds me of Annie's mother."

"Clavincade again. Glad I've only been there once!" snorted Robert.

Flurry thought 'Why do I keep hearing Clavincade, the name's always cropping up.' She felt there was a hidden signal. Looking from one to the other, the cousins seemed locked in their private associations, while Robert kept switching his gaze in an attempt to follow a drift of thought he was not party to, and did not understand. She was sorry for him. When he could bear the conversation no longer he burst out, "Always said Annie should get away from this place."

"What has that to do with it, Robert?" Annie got up to take a cigar from a walnut box on a demi-lune table. The cigar was Dutch. Torpedo-shaped.

"Too many memories. We should modernise. Get on the move."

"We've had this out before."

"You've never said." Mara looked alarmed.

"I've tried to persuade her every year," and he got up to light her cigar, saying, "We should go away. Travel."

"It's an idea," from Mara. "But not for long, I hope."

"Not at all. We're not going," blowing smoke, she dismissed him.

"Would do you good the doctor said — you're not looking well, Annie."

"Are you surprised?" The cousins exchanged looks again and Flurry mused, undercurrents, always a jig-saw puzzle, with some of the pieces pushed under a hearth-rug. Mara and Annie how alike they are! But different, like Janus with two faces on one head. The God of new beginnings. The lintel. The doorway. 'I'm getting obsessed with these people but in exploring their world I'm peering into my own.'

"We can go on a cruise."

"At this time of year?" She drew on her cigar contemplating her husband, to make Flurry think that besides the Bourbon rose beauty she was some tough cookie, and through the aromatic haze of cigar smoke remembered her competence in taking that five-bar gate. "What cruise?" said Flurry surprising herself.

"India. Neither of us has journeyed to the South and East of India. Off the trade routes and the tourists," Robert said, looking at Flurry gratefully.

"How heavenly," sighed Mara. "To get away for some sun. Leave bad debts and endless cooking behind. Not to have to think of anything. Just sleep on deck in the sun. Annie, you should think about it, might make a difference."

"Annie and I met on a cruise," Robert said, addressing Flurry for the first time, so that it surprised her. The cousins were silent. "Both her parents had died after quite long illnesses, and I believe I was some comfort to her. You had been in this house too long, Annie. You're here too long now. We live fifty years behind the times, and it's time to modernise. I've said it over and over again. Like those ridiculous medals."

"We're going to Winncombe Racecourse for the ceremony," Annie agreed. "Two of my farm-workers are being presented with medals for forty years' service to Broxford Court Estate."

"Antediluvian! Staying in one job, on one farm and working for one family for forty years. It's medieval. They should get into the twenty-first century. This is Heartbreak Hotel, where nothing ever gets done. We live our yesterdays. But times are changing. Look at London. You Flurry, as a smart London model, will have seen . . . . ."

Flurry was furious. "Executive!" she snapped.

"Executive," he bowed, "will have seen how the London Docks have been re-built. Put to modern use."

She gasped at his knowledge about her past. Then he went on. "The County Set was killed off when they bombed London." The two cousins looked down at their laps. Saying nothing. Betraying nothing of their thoughts. Then Mara suggested by way of compromise. "Sean says we ought to go to the Fairyhouse Races. That would cheer us all up."

"Sean!" exploded Robert, and then controlling himself. "How much longer is that chap staying? I thought he was only here for a while."

"He's staying."

"For how long? What's it got to do with you Annie?"

She was silent, and Robert looked from one to the other of the women, his hooded eyes were sharp, intensely curious, as though he were alerted to some unexpected signal of alarming proportions.

"I am sure Flurry is not the slightest bit interested in cruising." Annie got up and held out a plump hand. "Come and see my little birds."

She led her into the most spectacular conservatory she had ever seen. Bougainvillaea, and tree geranium scrambled up behind banana palms, lemon, orange and grapefruit. Ferns clustered on a damp brick floor to obscure hot water pipes which conserved flowers and plants of every description from breadfruit shrubs to Begonia rex.

A spacious cage for birds occupied the entire centre of the building beneath a glass roof, lit tonight with angled spotlights. On natural perches, some comprising living bushes, fluttered and darted, chirruped and sang the myriad feathered flashes of tiny birds in colours of yellow, red and blue. Painted tiles attached to the cage depicted the form and name of birds. There were yellow-breasted barbets and the superb blue-backed manakin with a scarlet head, and its metallic call.

"They come from rain forests in the New World, mostly," Annie explained, her eyes alight with enthusiasm. "And we have to cut up

56

fresh fruit for them. In the winter they have figs, raisins, sultanas or currants. This is my Pekin robin, my loved one" and the tiny orange and grey six-inch bird clung to the wire to take a handy spider that Annie supplied for him. "In old houses, stables and barns there are plenty of these about!"

"You have to go insect catching?"

"With Barbarka, of course. She's Lithuanian, although originally her family came from Finland. She adores my little birds and we go out berry hunting to keep my children healthy. Our labour of love."

"What a tremendous beak! And the colours."

"The fruit-sucker. Come and sit down. We can watch. See the red-eared bulbul with his impudent charm? They give you both pardon and peace."

"Have you always been interested in birds and plants and things?"

"Ever since I was a girl. Then I read biology at TCD."

""TCD?" Flurry looked puzzled.

"Trinity College, Dublin. It's a famous university. Specialises in natural sciences." Flurry felt her enthusiasm reaching out with warmth and charm. She sat happily. At peace.

Further from the roof spotlight a violet tanager dazzled like a firefly, when Annie asked, "How are Sean and Bridie getting along?"

Shattered from her reverie, Flurry coloured, "Very well."

"In stables?"

Recovering her composure, "Sean's very much the boss."

"More experience, that's why he came." Flurry had the impression that Annie's eyes were stripping her and that she had the knack of reading a person's thoughts. She hesitated. "I didn't know."

"Why should you! Sean has come to explore the possibility of extending his grandmother's racing stud to England," and she patted Flurry's knee consolingly.

Flurry guessed there must be some blood-tie between Sean and the Bowdens but felt too flustered to ask. "You mean at Bowden's Grove, Annie? Sean is very close."

"Close to you?"

Flurry felt this was a double-take and Annie's charm was getting under her guard. "No. No," she flushed again, "I mean - he doesn't explain or say anything!" and she thought 'Why is Annie probing like this. Cross-questioning me.'

"Close for an Irishman, you mean," Annie smiled to devastating effect so that Flurry said lamely, "I don't know any Irish people."

"You should. Go to County Cork for a holiday. At Easter it's green and fey. Opens your eyes."

"Bowden's Grove is an eye-opener!" But the girl didn't say 'I've

57

never met any woman so magnetic, with no stiffness or formality.'

"You're enjoying it with the Bowdens?"

"Not really — I don't know. Better than it was."

"Better?"

"I know people better. I think I do, but it's difficult to gauge their thoughts. There seems to be an undercurrent. When I first came I thought they were deliberately pecking at me. Laughing at me almost. But now I'm not sure, because I work hard . . . . . please don't laugh . . . . . but I feel as though I'm eighteen, and starting all over again. The past ten years are so far away, that they are dreamlike. As though they never existed."

"And now?"

"Sometimes I long to wake up. To find myself in London again, with work at TorrTechTron and Harry," she corrected herself. "With people I know. But sometimes I think I did not know my London friends either."

"And Harry is?"

"My boss . . . . . or was."

"Which takes us back to Sean."

Flurry got up and walked away, too disconcerted to accept Annie's gaze. She wondered whether she was being assessed for something, or even for her ability to be discreet.

"I was going to ask your advice, you being — as you say, so near and yet so far. May I?"

Flurry stood still, surprised at her own intuition. "My advice?"

"I am thinking of giving Lower Farm to Bridie." Flurry was so taken aback that she could make no comment.

"Give her something of her own. For the future."

"She would be grateful, I'm sure."

"Only grateful?"

"I simply don't know. It would take her away from Bowden's Grove."

"Make life easier. For the future."

"But if the stud's at Bowden's Grove?" Flurry felt that Annie and Harry must have something in common, because she could not divine their thoughts. Were they just devious? Or was there something else? Something she did not know. Some missing or broken piece in the puzzle which prevented her from understanding what either Harry, and now Annie, were trying to say. "It needs thinking about. I just can't give an opinion without considering all the facts."

"Sensible. Think about it and come and see me again." She held out her hand and Flurry was once more mesmerised by Annie's gaze, which was both kind and penetrating. "May I? I'd like that."

Once back in the hall, Annie said, "Flurry, go and have a word with

Barbarka, she's here to improve her English before university. And she wants to come and pick berries for my little birds from your garden."

To Mara, Annie confided, "I like her. Sensible."

"Buttoned up, father and I think."

"Maybe . . . . . older than I imagined from the description.'

"Twenty-eight."

"Looks more. She will melt. And we all know that Sean can be difficult." After a pause, "Who is this Harry?"

"He may have been her boss, but we don't know for certain."

"And her friends?"

"Doesn't seem to have any. Only that she had a tremendous bust-up with a boy-friend, whom we think she was living with. Now she has no flat. Nowhere to go. Although there is more to her than meets the eye. At first I nearly died when she turned up in a Gucci dress and high heels. For the country, darling!"

"What does Bridie think?"

"Just goes vr-oom. Vr-oom."

CHAPTER 5

Big Charlie was a very tall horse and Flurry could only just see over his withers.

"If you can't vault, get up from the mounting block." Bridie was in one of her brusque moods. "Mummy said to take you on the ridge this morning."

Flurry did not feel that she wanted to go, although the frigid house was depressing when you have a cold. Fresh air smelt better.

Bridie opened the wicket gate into Six Acre Covert. As on that day when Flurry first met Robert some weeks ago their hooves were barely heard when the horses walked on fallen larch needles. Fallow deer leaped over felled trunks, scared to watch their passing. They skirted the plough, planted with winter barley, and followed the edge of the U-shaped field enclosed by trees. Across the headland lay Lawson's Cover, but instead of entering the laurel path Bridie turned sharp left and Flurry felt disoriented. The forest parted to form a wide trackway, where the grass was short, lush and rabbit-nibbled. Cantering quietly Flurry gained confidence on the well-behaved Big Charlie. After two miles the ground sloped down slightly and then made a steep ascent towards a rocky ridge. Bridie pushed her Surtees on, and Flurry held Big Charlie's neckstrap having never galloped so fast before, however all was well, when breathless they gained the granite ridge. Throughout the journey Bridie had remained silent, absorbed in her own thoughts, until turning a corner a sharp crag appeared directly ahead. Pointing with her whip she rasped "The Finger of God".

Grass gave way to smooth rock, damp and slippery, and they walked slowly and carefully around the pinnacle, and on to the four great cushions of rock comprising the 'knuckles'. Here, heather and fine, hairlike grass grew from cracks and fissures in the rock and made going safer for horses.

As though diving down to the valley below, a depth of some four hundred feet, was an inclined plane of smashed scree and broken boulders. The floor of the distant plain was a patchwork of brick-red plough, blue-green vegetable fields together with ochre set-aside. In the near distance, the cream elegance of Broxford Court with its Palladian portico and stable blocks resembled a toy house, so small it appeared set on a verdant carpet of lawn and paddocks. The tree-lined drive crossed the Byebrooke over a stone bridge, while smoke curling from chimney-stacks, appeared so wraithlike, that the vapours merged with the December-grey sky. She wondered if Annie was watching her little, flashing, tweeting birds, flitting in a myriad colours, and why she had been so welcoming. So charming. As though she wished to quiet her. Put her off her guard, although what her reason might be was obscure.

Annie and Mara were as English as Marmite-toast, being insular, fortress-like individualists, with strong feelings for entitlement. Flurry tapped Bridie on a shoulder "Bowden's Grove is much higher than the Court. I didn't realise."

"Four hundred and seventy feet." Bridie turned to resume their circular tour. The pathway, although maintaining its height, dipped slightly to the forest which grew up to within two hundred yards of the rock ridge. The air was cold and Flurry was finding it difficult to breathe. Her chest felt tight and cramped with a stabbing pain. Presently Flurry recognised Lawson's Covert on their right, with its weird Blind House, lonely and heavily padlocked, and she knew they had completed yet another of these esoteric, uncanny circles. Stranger still, instead of returning home, Bridie made a complete U-turn left-handed, and led the way down a forty-foot wide trackway which traversed the quarry in an oblique stripe from top to bottom. Flurry remembered seeing this incongruous stripe the night before. Now its presence was revealed. It comprised the main carriageway to harvest granite blocks from the entire face of the quarry, and made a means of transport to the plain below.

"The locals call it the Z-Path."

The going was good. The causeway was constructed of blocks of granite cramped together by engineers to make a smooth surface. This was coated with soft grass and horses walked quietly and confidently down the slope. When they were halfway down, Flurry looked up to see the inclined plane, reaching up to the *Finger*, with its sixty percent slope and loose sliding surface, making a right-angled axis with the road on which they rode.

Gaining the bottom they turned right once more to complete a Z-shaped manoeuvre and cross two fields which ran alongside the lower boundary of the quarry. Between them and Broxford Court lay a stockproof fence which enclosed the parkland.

"I want to put Surtees over these two hedges. You walk on quietly through the hunting-gate."

"Oh! charming. What if Charlie takes off after you!" But Bridie could not hear her complaint.

Flurry seemed to sense Sean's instructions. "You ride with your mind. The horse looks to you to take care of him. It's a big con trick to be riding them and even if you're in a blue funk, don't let the horse know or he'll get worrying." Picking up the reins she walked on confidently, quieting Charlie, and not allowing him to watch Surtees, or have his head. They approached the small handy gate. "Now what do I do?" and back came Sean's instructions. "Place his head by the latch of the gate and turn his quarters alongside. But hold him on the off-side or he'll be walking off and dropping you in the mud." The catch was easy to open and Charlie walked through obediently, just as Surtees hedge-hopped beside him.

"Don't look at Surtees, Charlie," Flurry ordered. "Nothing to do with you!" And the big horse turned to present himself correctly to make the gate easy to shut.

"Thank you. You're just a big softie, Charlie Boy!" and she patted the kind gelding. With mission accomplished they followed Surtees towards the Byebrooke, while his rider looked with surprised approval at Flurry's management of her horse, being only a novice. Bridie, however, had too low opinion of her herself, being both deaf and plain, to be able to give any praise or credit to other people.

Ahead of them, Surtees splashed through the shallows, however, as Flurry approached the river some few yards further down, disaster struck! Charlie hopped off the bank into a deep pool, to frighten the trout standing at station in the watercress! Thoroughly enjoying himself, the gelding splashed across merrily enough, soaking his rider so that Flurry was completely drenched in icy water. She felt petrified with shock, which accentuated her difficulty in breathing. When they trotted up the steep hill towards the hairpin, she was forced to pull Charlie up and keep him walking.

Dragging behind, they finally made the main road, and crawled up through the lodge gates and into the drive, with Flurry slouched over Charlie's neck. Mara was there to greet them, and she, seriously worried at the girl's appearance ordered her to bed immediately, with two hot water bottles and a warm whiskey grog. Flurry choked over the strong drink, and fell into a restless sleep.

Late that night, the telephone ran in Richard's house in north London ordering the chauffeur to return immediately to Henry Pritchard's home in Hampstead. Richard was perplexed.

"Now what's up?" he worried.

Lady Lydia awaited his arrival with impatience, and contrary to her normal routine, asked him to drive her in Harry's limousine rather than driving herself in her own BMW. Lydia was a fast and somewhat erratic driver, who was inclined to take risks, as she believed she possessed a charmed life. That night she appeared withdrawn and harassed saying little to Richard, while he watched her expressionless face in the mirror. Skilfully he negotiated roads still restless with London traffic, as they journeyed towards the West End.

"Put your foot down, Richard" was Lady Lydia's only comment.

"Why don't you drive yourself, rather than making me lose my licence!" muttered the chauffeur.

Passing through Camden Town they approached St John's Wood and the barracks of the King's Troop, Royal Horse Artillery, which held memories for both occupants of the limousine. Lydia's father had commanded the King's Troop, while Richard joined the regiment as a Trooper in the sixties. He and Lydia often talked of the old days, and because of his service with the RHA, Lydia had recommended him to Harry, when the position of chauffeur became vacant. To break the silence, he said "Will you be attending Newmarket Races, m'lady?"

"No!" came the reply, and Richard felt aggrieved.

Baker Street, grubby with black rubbish bags stretched its length beneath orange lights. Forty-ton lorries chivvied night-workers' cars. Nobody seemed interested and Richard negotiated the one-way system, driving towards Harley Street, to stop outside Harry's clinic.

He helped Lydia out of the car. She was wearing her usual pepper-and-salt tweed suit and brown felt hat, although the imperious monocle hung limp on its ribbon.

"You realise his operation for cancer was not a success?" Richard nodded. "They have withdrawn treatment."

He handed Lydia her walking stick, since the car accident that smashed her hip made her unsteady on her feet. That crash happened on a day when Lydia lost one of her charmed lives and Richard led her across the tarmac. He could see that beyond the great glass doors of the clinic, Edward and James, Harry's two sons, were standing with a cousin, and talking to Colin and Elizabeth Goldring.

Lydia squeezed Richard's arm. "You were Harry's friend, so you'd better go in too. You must come and say goodbye!"

The chauffeur removed his cap.

Early the following morning the doctor crossed the front hall at Bowden's Grove thinking that the red and black clay tiles looked cleaner than they had for the past ten years. And surely the sofa covers had been washed and repaired, where they sat before the great inglenook fireplace. Walking upstairs, the country doctor took care not to slip on polished treads as he mounted the oak staircase with its medieval kingpost.

Warmly huddled on a feather-bed, Flurry's eyes looked too large for her pale face, and the doctor was shocked to see how thin the girl had become.

"We're all overworked here," said Mara. "We simply haven't the staff."

Luckily Flurry was only suffering from a severe chill together with a touch of bronchitis, and Mara sent Bridie to town to fetch the antibiotics needed. Dear Grandfather dragged a basket of split logs together with kindling up the stairs to make a fire in her room. It gave out a cheerful blaze, lighting the flowers on her wallpaper, and making the plum-coloured bed-curtains appear warm and comforting, Bridie as though to compensate for past coldness, lugged up the TV set to keep Flurry company, although household finances did not run to the *Radio Times*. Mara brought up a light fish lunch with a sorbet to follow, to soothe sore throats and Flurry was touched to think they had gone to Broxford especially to buy it.

Mara sat on Flurry's bed listening to her reminiscences: "Mother's flat was warm and cosy like this even though it was in a tower block. It was just the concrete stairs and galleries that were frightening. And that awful path under the flyover."

As Mara didn't interrupt she felt she could talk to her. Flurry was putting her feet down into Wiltshire soil and taking small steps towards understanding her own fractured past. "It wasn't all bad — I'm sorry now I didn't appreciate Mother more. Wish she were alive now! On Saturday afternoons we'd walk down to the Limehouse Cut — that's where the canal flows into the Thames. There used to be heaps of birds from the salt-marshes, now it's all contaminated and only seagulls swoop for bread. We could look across to the Isle of Dogs where later they built Canary Wharf and I worked there with TTT." She thought for a while "Strange how there are all sorts of different worlds are lying parallel to each other."

Mara pulled the eiderdown up to Flurry's chin as though she were a little girl. "Sleep tight, darling" and kissing her turned out the light.

As her health improved Flurry began to feel bored. Two days later she asked "Mara, would you like me to tackle some of your paperwork? The business correspondence and book-keeping. I'd love that. Give me something to do."

When Grandfather arrived with the second log-basket of the day, she was supported by a great heap of pillows and was sorting Mara's jumbled papers which were contained in three shoeboxes.

"Mara says 'You're brilliant'. She's thrilled you're taking over her chaotic paperwork. Have no head for figures myself. Different now for modern chaps, I expect. My elder brother Julian had a head for figures, he was a merchant banker y'know and most of Annie's fortune came from her father. Her mother brought the house and land."

"It used to be my forte dealing with bits of paper," Flurry observed. "Things like critical paths and cashflow."

The old man brushed the hearth blowing ash dust off the shelf. He rebalanced the absinthe spoon on the glass which Flurry had placed there on the evening of her arrival. Enjoying the flames, sparkling in the wide metal chimney-piece with its border of flowers and garlands, she contemplated the glass which had once meant so much to her. In the mind's eye the absinthe glowed green. Day-dreaming she went on "Is it possible d'you think Grandfather, to completely change oneself?"

"Once met a very clever fellow. One of those boffin-chaps who helped to design the first computer. He said you can never square a circle."

"How so?"

"Never transform a circle into a square that covers the same area. With scissors you can cut up your circle, but the round pieces refuse to co-operate. However you try there is always a piece left over. He calculated that it might be done, clever chap that computer wallah, if the circle were cut into small enough pieces. But then there would be so many of them they would cover about a tenth of the galaxy. It does not seem sensible to attempt to change ourselves, there will always be a part of ourselves left behind."

In the warmth of a cosy bed Flurry thought of little fragments of matter blowing about the galaxy and wondered if the fragments of her fractured life would really re-form themselves. She knew that in these few, short weeks of living with a country family she had changed. No longer was work a be-all and end-all. She was able to relax. And shopping, travel abroad, night-clubs, restaurants and parties had disappeared unwanted and unmourned. She had simply forgotten them. Outside, the cold gave way to torrential rain which rattled the ancient window-panes. She had never realised before how much she missed her mother. Her thinness. Bony legs and compressed mouth. But love is expressed in many differing ways and Mother had this faithfulness, reliability, she was rock-solid, like London-town in the Blitz and could be depended upon. Nor had Flurry understood how alike she and her mother were. And childhood had not been *all* that bad!

Now Mara? She had earned her respect and the incident of the sorbet had touched her deeply.

Meanwhile Sean kept well away from Flurry's room merely making polite enquiries or sending best wishes through Mara, which she found disappointing. Two days later Flurry decided to get dressed and spend the afternoon in the Smoker.

The blue velvet chairs took on a luxurious tone in the soft firelight, while oriental rugs brought back during the war by Grandfather, told stories of sand, Bedouins and the black tents of Arabia in flickering flames. Grandfather had told her that the Smoker was furnished so that his grandfather could sit here and smoke cigars, because his wife objected to tobacco smoke in the rest of the house. Lucky old great-great-grandfather! Sitting down she slipped her feet into someone's warm carpet slippers, because in this house they are relaxed about them and us. Or mine and yours. You helped yourself to what was available.

Flurry spread out her new account books. Admittedly they were meagre, paper-covered exercise books bought by Mara, and hardly speed icons for an age of information technology, but a huge improvement on scraps of paper. She spent two hours preparing a balance sheet, together with a forecast for the following year's trading. Then, feeling that she could do little more she wandered about the room, idly gazing at the numerous family photographs standing in their silver frames.

There were parents and grandparents, uncles, aunts and cousins, weddings, christenings, hunting pictures and racehorses with their proud owners. On a table with a chenille cloth and glass top, stood pictures of Mara and her husband Alec, and then the happy parents with baby Bridie. Many of the others she could identify, surely that must be Annie with her mother and father. At the back of the alcove there was one black-and-white photograph that made her eyes flick back, and back again, in astonishment. It was Sean! A young Sean, with his dark hair falling over his eyes and wearing the habitual grin. He wore racing silks, and carried whip and cap in one hand. In the background was a racecourse showing horses, jockeys, owners and spectators crowding around, to congratulate him winning the race. Flurry was confounded. On one side of Sean stood Lady Lydia. On the other, Harry was shaking Sean's hand!

What race? Where? Whose horse? Being black-and-white was no help, and Flurry was vague as to Lady Lydia's racing colours. Harry was secretive about this. Is that what he meant by experience changing shape and perspective? This made her think of wormwood in absinthe once more.

Presently both horseboxes returned to the yard and the old house came alive. However, it was disconcerting to see Sean coming through the door of the Smoker with two cups of tea. She jumped with pleasure.

"And isn't that the prettiest face in the whole country, we have here. And her sitting in the dark with no tea!" 'How many times has he said that' Flurry wondered. 'Blast him!' She felt let down and tried to look severe. "Sean. Come and look at these figures. Mara's up to her eyes in debt. What about these bills?" He was leaning against the chimney-piece reading the evening paper.

"It's no good asking Mara is it? She hasn't the money."

Sean looked over the top of the racing page. "Stay them off!"

"We can't ..... some of them are a year old. We're paying interest."

He did not appear perturbed.

"This business could pay, I'm sure of it. It's perfectly viable. Come and look at my projections."

Shoving the newspaper in his pocket, and giving the impression of the acme of boredom, Sean sat down on the threadbare blue velvet sofa.

Together they calculated past profit-and-loss accounts, debts, lost reductions, debts and income tax, together with Flurry's forecast for the next twelve months. She was amazed to find how quick Sean was with figures. How searching were his questions, and how precise his knowledge of market values, turnover and percentage profit. Just before dinner-time they finished the accounts.

"You'll be looking to the books then. And me the horses. Then we'll get along fine." He wandered off, and Flurry felt she wanted to hit him.

The next morning brought several surprises. Mara was overjoyed. "Flurry you're a wonder. You really are. You convinced Sean! I've been hoping for ages he'd put some capital into the business, but no such luck. Now he's agreed and we can get those bills sorted out. What a relief!"

Flurry couldn't believe her ears. "He's paid them? I shouldn't have thought he'd have the money!"

"Are you joking?" Bridie said, looking up from *Hounds* magazine.

Flurry had another surprise at lunch-time when Mara said she and Bridie were out that evening to play bridge. "Bridge is the great consolation of winter nights, too dark for gardening!"

Grandfather was dining with Henry Payne that evening, and to her astonishment Sean asked her to have a drink with him at the local. Bridie dashed upstairs!

Flurry worried that her obvious jealousy was becoming a menace and where it might all lead. Love turns so fast to hate, and Bridie had never grown up, or out of being a selfish child. At least Annie's present of Lower Farm should boost her ego where she would have sufficient land for the horses, to give her some degree of independence. What she needed was a man. A boy-friend. Surely someone would take her on, because she was not too bad looking. It's just she never puts herself out for anybody. Not even her mother and is always pecking at dear Grandfather. If she did get a man, could she keep him, except for the wrong reasons? She'd go crazy with happiness at first, and then drive him mad. 'Besides she's so scruffy, with no taste in clothes.'

Longing for fresh air Flurry went out into the stableyard. Here was confusion. A rat ran from the corn bin with Nimrod the stables terrier in hot pursuit. Then another rat running at right angles to it and going like stink had Bertie on its tail. The two rats were heading for each other when Sean tore out of a loosebox waving a broomhandle. All were on collision course. Sean tripped over Nimrod, Bertie leapt over Sean's back as he lay, and Flurry nearly fell into the water-trough with laughter.

Sean got up slowly, scowling and covered in manure. Flurry giggled until she cried, wondering if he might withdraw his invitation for the evening.

They started off at eight pm. The old White Horse Inn stood by the village pond, where ducks resembling toy china ornaments, were sleeping in the reeds. While Sean parked, Flurry read the 'blurb' on the wall of the porch.

"North Wiltshire can boast of a greater plethora of beautiful and interesting houses than any county in England. The old White Horse was built in medieval times as part of a monastic network of holy houses, and pilgrim rests, to accommodate travellers on the Pilgrim's Way to mystic Glastonbury Abbey. The village pond was once a carp reservoir to provide Friday dinners for Augustinian monks.

King Henry VIII had different ideas. He was hell-bent to modernise, and his new breed of entrepreneurs built black-and-white houses on monastic foundations, while Oliver Cromwell knocked down the inn with gunpowder, to teach Wiltshire a lesson.

However help was at hand. Wool to weave broadcloth from Downs sheep rebuilt the inn until the heavy unwearoutable cloth lost favour with the French. Corn-mills and rope-makers rescued the hostelry, and constructed the present Georgian façade. The old White Horse celebrates seven hundred years of good cheer."

Bert and the Three Musketeers were sitting beneath oak beams at a round table. "Only two weeks to Christmas. What a blessing a deep freeze is," said Dolly. She had exchanged a woolly hat for a tight perm, and a satin blouse covered her ample bosom beneath a Scotch Woolshop cardigan. "Don't know what I'd do without one with all my brood to feed. Not to speak of the Charleville Blazers on New Year's Eve."

"Charleville Blazers?"

"From Ireland. They come every year. Always have. A dozen or twenty of them are here for the New Year's Eve meet, and Hunt Dinner afterwards."

Sean went to the bar for a round of drinks. Bert sat on the other side of Flurry, while Patters decided to lie on her feet.

"Mrs Annie started the tradition. She was joint Master of the Blazers, don't y'know," explained the Major.

"That was years back," put in the haulier ..... "as a young woman. Twenty years!" He sighed stroking greying hair.

"Twenty, if it's a day."

"An' could she ride. Heartbreaking falls though. They say she punctured a lung ..... stake went right through it. Just missed her heart. Always suffered ever since. Has short days."

"Still jumps though. Jumps where no-one else could."

"That's courage."

"Like the Black Widow. She broke her back didn't she?"

"Ssh-ssh. He's coming back. Sean's sensitive if you mention them."

"Don't I know," sighed Flurry. "He's feeling precious because he fell over a rat!"

They all laughed. "What's his Grandmother's name?" Flurry asked the Major softly. He seemed the best informed.

"Tamzine O Callaghan. Tamzine O Callaghan of Clavincade, I should say, they're all O Callaghans but she's the dowager," he whispered as Sean returned. Flurry got up to help, saying quietly "Sorry we laughed, Sean. And sorry about the bruises." Then she blew her nose to stop the giggles. Patters put his lovely scarred head on her knee.

His relaxed ears pleaded for a sausage.

"Patters'll eat they sausages, like moneybox with a one way slit."

She stroked him, "You are the loveliest dog."

"An' you can pet 'im. Takes a lot'er petting does Patters."

"Or throw sticks" laughed Dolly.

The food disappeared at a steady rate and the bartender brought some warm chicken legs to stoke them up. "They do you well here," observed the Major. "Meeting at the Court tomorrow, should be a good run."

"Huntsman likes to stir up they foxes before New Year's Eve. Clear 'em out."

"Had a good run las' Saturday, after it 'ad poured cats and dogs."

"Shouldn't of 'ad."

"Water lying everywhere up to your ankles."

"Shouldn't 'av bin no scent. Scent won't lie on water."

"Hounds screamed all day," put in the haulier. "I saw 'em put up a brace from the brambles by the old barn. Magnificent hunt. That's scent for you."

"Nothin' so strange as scent."

"Don't know as I agree with all this fox 'unting," butted in a red-faced man. He was wearing a round waterproof hat liberally speckled with nymphs for rainbow trout.

"Get on with you, Giddon. What about your fishing. Now that's more cruel than hunting. Hooking him by the mouth, and playing him for twenty minutes or more. Foxes is killed clean."

"Fish don't feel"

" 'Cos they feel. Got nerves haven't they?"

"Met a man once," put in the Major, "he was a zoologist and studied brains in fish. He said fish have more sensitive hearing than any other animal. Like whales, can hear over hundreds of miles, the faint sounds through the ocean."

"What's that got to do with it?'

"If they've got sensory nerves, then they got feel. Stands to reason."

"Whales ain't fish."

"Same principle. Applies to all water creatures. Nerves well-developed. Of course they can feel. Can't understand you chaps."

"Take shooting," agreed the haulier. "Now that is cruel. Alright if they're shot clean. But how many good shots are there? Especially in they commercial syndicates, townies and businessmen from the cities. Many birds are winged. I know they've plenty of gundogs to retrieve, but there's always runners. Creep away and die of gangrene. But with foxes, when they're caught they're killed quick. Too quick for nerves to tell them they're hurt. Far too quick. Nerves respond slowly. That's Mother Nature."

"We need hunting, it's *tradition*, or we lose our souls!" admonished the Major.

"It's the comfort and pleasure of friends," put in Dolly. "That's what our country sports mean. We're a pretty down-to-earth lot and used to mud and manure. Don't think so much of shopping, and my old man won't go for a holiday beyond a weekend's hunting on Exmoor in August. Have to make our own fun."

Flurry's foot was going to sleep and she wriggled it away from underneath the dog. Forty pound Patters stretched out, wagging his tail, to say he quite understood, and agreed to her request. Then the outer door opened and Robert Davies came in. No-one spoke to him, nor did he say good evening. He demanded a double whiskey but the barman paused for a moment before serving him, because Robert was somewhat intoxicated. He paid using a fifty pound note, which the barman changed with a sigh. Robert was well-known for paying even trivial sums with notes of high denomination as it gave him a sense of privilege. Turning away from the bar he swayed towards Sean's table, passing it to go towards a further seat. Unfortunately Patters lay in Robert's path.

"Move your bloody dog can't you!"

Patters stood up, and his eyes appeared to shine red. The kind smile on his dog's face turned to a vicious snarl. Patter's teeth were three-quarter inches of killing chistel sharpness.

"Get out of it!"

"Don't you kick my dog, Davies!" said Bert and the little man pulled his cap down as he stood up to Robert.

"Mr Davies to you!"

"Mister as to those what've earned it."

"And why don't you get yourself a proper job, instead of scrounging about with a bit of fishing and half-a-dozen cows?" Robert moved closer to Bert, "..... fawning on your so-called friends." he sneered, looking at Sean. The dog snarled softly and menacingly. "Barman. Call the landlord and tell him to throw this dog out. He's vicious."

"Dog ain't vicious, he standing 'long o'I. Patter's as quiet as a lamb. Ax' any of they ladies."

The landlord came in puffing his cheeks out with uncertainty. He did not like to annoy Robert because the White Horse was a free house, and he was tenant to Annie, the inn being part of the Broxford Court estate.

"Gentlemen please."

"I want this dog out of my pub."

"It's taking it upon yourself now" Sean said standing up by Bert. The haulier stood up as well, he was taller than Sean, and much fitter than Robert.

"What's it to do with you?"

"Gentlemen please!" If it were a case of losing his licence or losing the tenancy, he believed Annie would see him right. Even against her husband. "You'd best be going home."

"Give me another Scotch. A double."

"Please Mr Davies. You've had enough." The rest of the bar sat silent. Ears pricking. Like cats, with staring eyes, their heads flicked from side to side watching.

"D'you hear. I need a drink in my own pub!"

"Come now," Sean said putting his hand on Robert's shoulder. "I'll take you home."

Flurry saw Robert look at Sean aghast. His face. His skin. His hair. With understanding dawning came an awakening, as though previously he had been unable to penetrate below the surface of Sean's being to see what lay beyond. She saw his gaze travel from Sean to Bert, the haulier, the Major and rest on Dolly, seated, understanding that in their intimacy they had the key to reveal the unimagined. The bar stilled, held its breath, in a corporate knowledge of the profundity of Robert's sudden realization and the crisis it would precipitate. Only Flurry was outside them. Puzzled. For a moment, Flurry and Robert's eyes met in common sympathy and lack of comprehension. The audience looked smug, with compressed lips, heads nodding together, and she was reminded of the word 'speak' and it's indefinable meaning.

Robert forced his shoulder away from Sean's embrace "Don't touch me, Irish *bastard!*" His confusion was so great that the glass he was holding fell from his hand, smashing on the stone floor. Chairs were pushed back with a scraping noise. Patters whimpered.

"You've been trouble ever since you came." Robert was weeping with rage, tears falling down his tie. "You've destroyed me, and everything I've ever wanted."

Fortunately, the door opened emitting a blast of cold air. Heads turned as P C Watts entered on his routine duty call from Chippenham. "Good evening all!" He was a local chap and bred in the village, so he sensed the tension. The PC was six feet seven in height making seven feet with his helmet on. Being a Royal Navy boxing champion before joining the police force, Watts was known as the quickest way of clearing an unruly bar.

"Evening constable," came a chorus.

"The constable here can be taking on the lot of us," Sean said to the haulier. Everyone laughed.

"Time, gentlemen, please," called the landlord with relief.

As they walked out into the frost, the Major said, "Met a chap once about the time of the Algerian troubles, who reckoned he knew Robert Davies, when he was in the Royal Engineers. There was some scandal about an arms deal but it was hushed up. However, Davies was asked to resign his commission, they put pressure on him, and he came out of the army."

Meantime at Broxford Court, Barbarka sensed there was something wrong. She sat up in bed pushing the feather duvet aside. Her window on the second floor looked over a parapet above and to one side of the portico. Outside even in frosty darkness the faint outline of the *Finger* was discernible in front of its mulberry-blue background.

A cold wind rattling the branches of lime trees which bordered the drive, reminded Barbarka of home. Home in Lithuania, with its Baltic winds, spruce forests and lakes. The Court was quiet. No unusual sound spoke of disunity but Barbarka felt a perceptible disturbance in the magnetic shield of the house. Childhood and adolescence living under the Russian Bear made her acutely sensitive to a warning, so she got up and put on a warm wool gown.

The long passageway outside her door was dimly lit by panel lights mounted on the skirtings. Annie had installed these soft night-time lights all over the house, and listening carefully Barbarka made her way to the grand staircase. Two handsome stairways parted and converged from a gallery, and made a horseshoe curve to the hall fifty feet below. Gripping the polished brass handrail Barbarka walked downstairs making no sound on the thick Turkey carpet.

The door to Robert's study stood open. The light, strong and harsh, remained on although the room was empty. Barbarka thought the furnishing incongruous and out of keeping with the Court. It looked as though Robert had purchased the furniture at a hypermarket, simply buying two desks, four plastic covered armchairs, a carpet, desktop computer, Anglepoise light, and other fittings, with no concern for taste or colour.

She continued into the front hall and the large flower arrangement on its pedestal, which she helped Annie to gather and arrange, glowed in the soft light. Barbarka was both au pair and Annie's companion.

The drawing-room was in darkness, but when she entered the sitting-room she was aware of a disturbed twittering. The little birds were awake and restless, and as the spotlights were still on in the conservatory, Barbarka went to investigate.

The birds were flying like fireflies in iridescent cascades. Bougainvillaea and climbing geranium on the walls bowed their petals, asleep, while motionless on a bench Annie sat. Inert. Looking at nothing.

Barbarka sat down beside her and Annie's head dropped on to the tall Viking girl's shoulder, her flaxen hair comforting her face, while Barbarka put her arm round her stout waist.

"Come to bed, Mrs Annie, please, my dear. Come to bed." With Barbarka's help she got up and obediently walked upstairs. The au pair checked the outer doors, switched off the lights, and shut the conservatory doors. As a precaution she dropped the key into her pocket.

In a bedroom decorated in grey and white with rose-coloured curtains, she assisted Annie to undress and slipped a cream satin nightdress over her head. For a middle-aged woman, Annie's soft skin was surprisingly youthful, and the satin accentuated this. Before settling her into the half-tester bed, Barbarka persuaded her to drink a little of the pétillant mineral water, which had been placed on the bedside table. Then instead of returning to her own room the girl tip-toed towards the adjoining dressing-room. Curling her six foot three onto a narrow bateau bed, Barbarka slept. Quietly, deeply, but like her people from the Baltic, with an ear and an eye forever watchful.

That night at the old White Horse Inn it was the landlord's wife with her auburn afro and plastic bosom who tempted Robert up the red-carpeted stairs to a guestroom he had visited before, although he forgot her as soon as he left the inn. He was a man who wanted everything, and gave nothing in return. Comfort for cash. But that night he was outside comfort, knowing he had not appreciated the significance of a hundred small looks, expressions, inflexions, insinuations, whispers, co-incidences, and now he cursed himself for his stupidity.

His life was at a critical stage. He must act. Waste no time. Yet gone were the days of the thick policeman, and plodding copper-boots. With computers talking to international police forces and micro-analysis in forensic science, he must work with extreme care. To facilitate a plan he had come to the conclusion was inevitable, he must go abroad and visit processing networks from a past era. The future was die-cast from the moment Sean placed a hand on his shoulder.

CHAPTER 6

The morning newspaper arrived before eight o'clock, and Flurry liked to see the headlines before Grandfather came down for breakfast. They often completed the Quick Crossword together, he knew answers to the erudite clues, while she could spell! It was one of their small pleasures of a working day.

On the Obituaries page a paragraph caught her eye and she read with surprise and shock:

'HENRY PRITCHARD. Aged 54. Company director. 'The founder of TorrTechTron, he was a pioneer in the field of synergizing technologies and optoelectrics.

A memorial service in thanksgiving for his life was held last Saturday at the Parish Church, Hampstead.'

Harry! It can't be. That's days ago. And heart-sickened she dashed to telephone Elizabeth Goldring, then went to lie on her bed. She was never to hear his voice again, and imagined she saw his face turned towards her, blood on his forehead, and eyes of sorrow looking at her for the last time. Eyes. Voice. His touch. Sorrow for things past never to return, and she felt guilty as though the blood on his forehead had hastened his death in some way. Had she stayed with him she might have extended his life, although with hindsight she had been aware of the inevitable. He was failing, and had been for some time, also being older than her by twenty-five years, one day the end must come. There was a dry taste of shock in her mouth, and for the moment, she could not fully take on board the complexity of feeling his death had aroused. Mourning would expiate emotion and aching grief in due course.

She went to look for Mara in her bedroom, and passing a landing window she looked out towards Home Paddock. A pair of foxes were picking their dainty way along the distant hedge, red-orange against shining green holly, box and lonicera, while bare branches of beech and ash spoke of winter. The larger dog fox was politely following a small light-coloured vixen. By January, the mating season would be with them, with new life and the thrill of coming spring, baby rabbits and close-season for hunting. Flurry now understood that without their quarrel and Harry's death she might never have experienced these precious weeks at Bowden's Grove, and it gave her the incomparable joy of seeing foxes pass daintily by. Finding Mara "I must go to London. Today. Now. Harry has died and I have to see him. Elizabeth, I mean. He's dead ..... " she stammered. Confidences are such flimsy things. Mara was consoling and pitied the girl's grief, she held out her arms and the two women kissed. Normally not an emotional woman, who considered it ill-bred to cry or make a fuss, Flurry was touched by her unusual show of concern, and accepted with gratitude an offer to drive her to the station. In spite of Flurry's haste in leaving London she had packed a trouser suit, navy with a chalk pinstripe, and because of cold weather, Mara insisted on her borrowing Bridie's best camelhair coat. Her daughter became quite co-operative towards Flurry, being inquisitive as to the surprise turn of events.

The train, which was a slow one, travelled towards Swindon on its way to Paddington. Gazing at passing fields and hills numbed with grief and unobservant eyes, she could not have known that Annie, as well as herself, was visiting London that day, Annie was driving her Mercedes up the M4, although Barbarka had not wanted her to travel alone. Annie was insistent, and as Flurry's train crawled over the bridge which spans the motorway before Swindon the Mercedes passed under the train. Neither woman knew that the progress of their lives was now plaited. Entwined. Passing through Acton on its way to Ealing Broadway the train overtook the Mercedes, as the car travelled across Ealing Common, before it stopped to park by the grass opposite a promenade of mid-Victorian houses. Locking the car she walked across to these four-storey, red-brick properties built when Ealing was known as the *Queen of the Suburbs*. At the turn of the century, the houses were lived in by Indian Army or Indian Civil Service officers and their families, home on retirement from Empire duty.

Annie approached No 4 Eastlands Terrace. The stone steps were steep, and below her in the commodious basement was a masseur parlour, garishly decorated in tinsel and gold. On the walls of the vestibule, set between front door and a steel-mesh glass inner door, were photographs of models, while discreet advertisements described 'escorts for all occasions'. The telephone numbers of call-girls and partners were placed beside a list of residents living in the assortment of flats on the upper floors of the building.

Annie looked for the name 'Julie Baker'. Then she rang the bell.

When the train reached Paddington Station, Flurry opened the door and the London world flew in, with its noise, dirt and abrasive style, so that she felt at odds with the objects and influences of city life. She had arranged to meet Elizabeth for lunch, but first she must make her peace with Harry.

Changing to the Underground Flurry knew she had to change at King's Cross and take the Northern Line for Finchley Central, where she had only her map and Elizabeth's scant instructions to guide her. With surprise, she realised that she, a Londoner, did not know the northern part of the city at all. It was a no-go area. Like an invisible frontier Camden Town, Kentish Town and Tufnell Park were out-of-bounds. In mother's day there was no money for tickets, but it was Harry, who without actually saying so, decreed there must be no poaching on his territory. No prying into his family life. No looking at his house. His garden.

Sorrow gave way to rage. Switzerland and Paris they visited for conferences. The USA or Brazil, no! That would mean going with Lady Lydia to buy horses. Harry had stopped her riding and she resented it. A difficult man, money was his icon, it was the only thing on offer. He gave and he took away. On the Underground, stops at Archway and Highgate were alien country and she felt so uncomfortable and disturbed in these suburbs, that migraine jazz-lights in a splintering arc distorted her vision.

"You deserted me. Threw me out. Why didn't you *say*. Explain. You should have said you were sick, rather than have me read about it. I believed you. Trusted you. And you let me down" she raged. Her feelings of being passed over, left out and rejected increased her anger, an anger that later turned back to sorrow.

"I loved you. I thought I did. Did I?" she puzzled. "Or is love so ephemeral a thing that it dies on parting? And only an empty shell of passing memory remains."

Then came East Finchley, and Flurry dimly remembered that Elizabeth had said: 'Get out at Finchley Central'. She scrambled out of the train just as it started to move off, so that the conductor shouted at her. She had a long walk to St Marylebone Cemetery and to find the number that was Harry's grave. So confused was she with rage and sorrow that she had to ask the way twice, and took several wrong turnings, before arriving at black spikey railings and a large Gothic lodge. She sat on the wall near two cedar trees, thankful that her vision was clearing, and trying to bear an insufferable headache. An old woman offered to sell her a bunch of flowers. "For the grave, dearie," she said reverently. "For the grave."

There were pink and white chrysanthemums, and nestling between them early Dutch daffodils and narcissi. The sight of spring flowers made her cry both for herself and Harry.

Any local library would have told Flurry that St Marylebone Cemetery has catered since 1857 for the affluent middle-classes of Highgate and Hampstead. Not knowing this Flurry was unprepared for large monuments flanking broad yew treed avenues. A gardener, standing by a monument incorporating a bronze sculpture, directed her to a more modern part of the burial ground. She trudged past a massive grey and pink sarcophagus, with four bronze angels, one at each corner.

The dun sky seemed solid as in a closed magnetic loop, ionosphere to earth, reflecting back the gravel-crunch of her feet. No birds twittered.

She trekked past evocative anchors, gates into heaven, clasped hands, lilies and a phoenix. A great snake with its tail in its mouth made her flesh creep. Nobody said that it symbolized eternity.

At the cross roads she saw the same gardener again who realized she had walked in a circle. He took pity on her distress and led her to a notice board in a glass case. Here in regimented rows each grave was allotted a number. The new part of the cemetery looked clinically bare with earth scraped clean. The artificial grass surrounding Harry's grave was now removed, and floral tributes, long since faded had been carted away. Only a few scraps of muddy 'In Memoriam' cards, their names obliterated, remained to quantify him.

Flurry knelt down to lay her flowers on his mounded earth. "He cannot be dead. Harry isn't here!"

An obsequious doorman swept open the plate-glass doors of an exclusive St James's Street restaurant for Mrs Elizabeth Goldring. She was a valued lunchtime customer. Gold letters said *Le Tournesol*, while gold petals of sunflowers seemed to flutter across the glass panels.

Sitting at a favourite corner table she pulled off washleather gloves, recollecting the many times that Fleur and herself had occupied these chairs. With her softly tailored alpaca suit and ridiculously fashionable small hat, Elizabeth was always an object of attention, and today knowing that Fleur would be late she ordered drinks from a hovering waiter.

Sipping the drink, she withdrew a long manila envelope from her lizardskin handbag. Colin was an executor for Harry's Will and her husband had asked her to help Fleur understand Harry's wishes.

"Now that she's surfaced," Colin had said "It would be best if you explained the Will to her."

But Elizabeth was uneasy. "Even in death," she said to herself "He makes her dance to his music."

Unfolding the parchment pages she re-read the relevant paragraphs for the umpteenth time. Fleur was to inherit a generous bequest of money. So far so good. Then came the honeyed trap! Colin had annotated the legal jargon of the Will, and she compared his notes with the original document to see they were a correct rendering.

As Elizabeth understood it, should Fleur agree a Contract with the Directors of TorrTechTron for an agreed number of years, to take up an Executive appointment, then she was to receive a substantial number of shares in the Company. The interest only on the shares would be paid to her over and above her salary. However, the actual share capital would be received by her only on retirement, together with the normal pension rights she is entitled to from the Company.

"She's twenty-eight now," Elizabeth mused " ..... and she'll be tied to TorrTechTron for the next twenty or twenty-five years." Finishing her drink the waiter brought her a fresh one without her asking. "Perhaps

Harry knew Fleur better than we do! He ought to! If the girl is institutionalized ..... well perhaps it's a good thing. But if not?"

Let us say she stays with TTT for twenty years odd. She should be happy. Well paid. Good salary and work she knows, or can mature into, while on retirement, she could be quite a rich woman.

But why did Fleur run away in the first place? Did she need space? Time to think about marriage perhaps, or children? Elizabeth smiled because how many times had she seen successful, well-paid career women clinging to the arm of a weed husband! A weedy man. The only man who did not run away. The only man she could get and would actually marry her! But at least he was her weed! He looks after her and runs the children to school by car. He gives her a holiday ..... using her money of course. Elizabeth shrugged, is that what Fleur wants? Harry might be right after all, as he knew her better than any of us.

Taking a pen from her bag to put thoughts to paper, she found herself doodling, and sub-consciously she drew a pitcher-shape with a lip. The lip curled back, tempting her to sketch in hairs. How expressive are our thoughts, made manifest.

Elizabeth recalled that a cousin of hers grew these carnivorous plants. The Green Pitcher, sarracenea oreophilla, was the most beautiful of all. A nectar roll attracts its prey, which is maybe, an unsuspecting fly. Then 'plop' into sticky sweetness! Down she goes to be slowly, exquisitely melted by enzymes, eaten and absorbed by the Pitcher. The ultimate honeyed-trap. She was determined not to influence Fleur in any way whatsoever. However fond she had been of Harry, she was not going to complete his unfinished business.

Looking up, Elizabeth saw Flurry push through the heavy glass and gold leaf doors. No waiter rushed to help her, and Elizabeth was astonished to see how changed was her appearance. The frumpy, shapeless camelhair coat accentuated the girl's straggly red hair, no longer highlighted, and tied back in a loose braid. As Elizabeth took both her hands, she was aware of the rough skin and stained nails, that no nailbrush could whiten.

"It's been so long."

"Ages."

"Seven weeks."

"An eternity. I hadn't realized."

"Sorry it's such a shock, but we didn't know what to do. We put announcements in the paper nearly every day hoping you'd surface."

"Why didn't he *say*. Say he was ill?"

"You know Harry. Devious."

"But to me! He must have hated me."

"Not hated."

"Miscalculated perhaps, but not hated. No. No. He was truly sorry when you went away. He asked 'what news' every day. I think he wanted to spare you grief. Besides he was a proud man and proud of his appearance. He looked ..... well ..... terrible ..... at the end!" They sat in silence, then Elizabeth ordered lunch for both of them as Fleur was in no state to think about food.

"Maybe I shouldn't have told you."

"You were right to say."

"Harrowing."

"I hadn't thought it would be like that."

"Men like Harry are not compassionate. Nor do they have emotions, or feelings for others. It was your tears that infuriated him. If there is illness, even their own, they do not wish to know. They hide. And if it is pushed upon them - they get angry."

After a long pause Fleur asked again: "Did he mention me?"

"Every day. Asked if there was news from the post. Later - we put in announcements."

"Grandfather and I do the crossword puzzle, but there's no time for anything else."

"Grandfather?"

"Mara, she's my employer, and he's Mara's father. Everyone calls him Grandfather. We do the crossword between early stables and breakfast, and there isn't time to read more than the headlines."

"You have stables?" Elizabeth said, thinking of her coarsened hands.

"I'm called Flurry now, it's an Irish name. They're not Irish really, but seem Irish, the whole family do. There's Bridie, she's deaf and then there's Sean ..... he may be family, I'm not sure. Bridie's very jealous because she's deaf and plain."

"Jealous of you because of Sean?" Elizabeth laughed "You go in for devious lovers!"

"He's not my lover."

"Could be?"

"Maybe. But no. I don't know. I don't know anything anymore. Where I am or who I am. Until yesterday I began to feel as though I were finding my feet and was back to normal, but after seeing Harry's grave nothing seems certain."

"Have you any money?"

"I've spent a lot of mine and stable girls don't get much."

Elizabeth withdrew a chequebook from her handbag. "Let me, please. You must have guessed that Harry was generous and left you a legacy, and as Colin is an executor, let me give you something on account, executors can do that." While writing she asked "Why did you run away?"

"I hit him!"

"I heard about that. Good for you." Folding the cheque again she asked "Why run away from your flat and TTT?"

"I don't know, really I don't." This not knowing anything is getting tiresome, Elizabeth said to herself.

"It was instinctive, and I felt there was no going back, I had to think things through and unthink ten years of TTT. I packed nothing in particular because I was going on holiday to Weston-super-Mare."

Elizabeth did not question the extraordinary choice of Weston-super-Mare as a seaside resort in November. She opened the girl's pouchette in a motherly fashion to place the cheque inside, being unsure if Fleur would remember anything about it. Now she wondered if it were the right moment to explain the Will to ..... what does she call herself? "Why Flurry, darling?"

"Bridie didn't like the name Fleur."

Any more questions sounded like a cross-examination, so she just included the copy of Harry's Will with Colin's notes and zipped-up the handbag. Lunch arrived but Fleur did not eat.

"Try some souffle, darling."

"I thought he loved me. But to say nothing and push me away."

"You know he did." She took a deep breath. "Perhaps it'll help knowing he left you shares in TorrTechTron."

Fleur gasped. "I don't want them. I said I wouldn't take anything."

"There are conditions" and Elizabeth thought of 'The Honeyed-Trap', then went on. "He wants you to return to TTT."

"When?"

"In time. When you've thought it over. Considered it through."

"I never dreamed of the possibility." Fleur toyed with her fork. "I can't think about it until after Christmas, as there's too much to do. It's trying to snow and with all the horses in, I can't leave Mara in the lurch, what with the Irish hunt, the Charleville Blazers, coming on New Year's Eve."

"Of course not, if you're committed. They're kind to you? This family?"

"Very. I hated them at first, not being able to see through country eyes and thought they were mocking me, because I don't think as they do. Country people, the real born-and-bred ones, are very parochial. Tribal. It's difficult for anyone else to get in. To get close to them. They say you have to be there twenty-five years before you stop being a 'foreigner'!" The word 'speak' drifted into her mind, its true significance being as far away as ever.

Elizabeth considered that in her bemused state Flurry would be happier over Christmas with the Bowdens and plenty of work to keep her occupied, however, she must get some movement to help Colin. "The solicitors are anxious to see you as soon as possible, to set probate in motion."

"Next week?"

Elizabeth was taken aback "If you can manage that."

"I'd like to buy Christmas presents in London."

"Next week then."

"Grandfather thinks that life is like a magnetic tape. Everything is recorded and you play the same tune over and over again. Hear the same music."

Watching her intense face Elizabeth thought of the pitcher-plant and its form popped up unannounced.

"What time is your train?"

"Five fifteen from Paddington." Getting into the taxi Flurry said "Thank you for everything. In some strange way I feel I'm going home for Christmas to Bowden's Grove."

Annie walked away from Number 4 Eastlands Terrace and returned to her car parked by the church. She was utterly shocked by what she had heard, but not covertly surprised. Sitting in the driver's seat, she looked across the mile-wide open space. Trees were bare of leaves, and outlined suburban grass in stiff ranks, being London-stained an oil-grime ochre. Along bleak pavements, which criss-crossed the Common like a giant crossword puzzle, paper, can-pulls, chip bags and condoms blew restlessly, heedless of time or direction.

Perhaps Barbarka was right and she should have brought her as co-driver. Suddenly the banging of a drum, taken up by the shurrup of a mouth-organ and the snort of an ancient wind-instrument smashed through her reverie with a rendering of *When the Saints come Marching in*. A group of musicians collecting for Christmas charity drew up on the pavement beside her. A man in a donkey-jacket, trainers and top-hat played an ancient sousaphone, while a clown with a pink, green and blue wig banged a tambourine. The mouth-organ was being played by a man in a wheelchair, displaying a placard on his chest which read *Sunlight Soap*. At the same time, a very fat girl in an orange tu-tu and football boots blew her whistle. The clown tapped the car window, sucking a plastic orange and pointing at his collecting box.

"And who is the clown today?" Annie asked him. "You or me?" Very solemnly the clown scratched his head, shook it, sucked the orange and grinned.

"Were I as sane as you!" smiled Annie squeezing a note into his tin. With a deep reverential bow the clown and troupe moved off.

"How true. How right that is," mourned Annie bitterly. "Were we all as sane!"

In her time of distress, Annie like everyone else, retreated to a private daydream of reminiscence. To when she had first met Robert, and fallen for the charm, polish and sexual attraction of this retired Army officer. They became lovers on a luxury cruise, with blue-black nights sailing a velvet sea. And by day, a tropical island enticed their desires, with sandy beaches fringed by gardens and coconut palms. And now? Only her beloved little birds, with their darting, flashing, exotic plumage within a paradise of palms, oranges, lemons and plumbago remained.

Robert told her that he had a business partnership in London with an estate agency. Agency yes! Although the estate part proved to be human flesh, the business being prostitution. It was brought up to date by working luxury cruises with an especial quarry of rich, single, or widowed ladies. By this time Robert and she were married, and she had turned a blind eye to subterfuge, lies and debts because she loved the wimp. But she had never trusted him, nor shared her most treasured secret with him. She thought he didn't know, because no-one, not anybody would tell him.

Turning on the ignition, she drove along the M4 in December gloom, coming off at Junction 18. Approaching home a feeling of loneliness overcame Annie. She was not a woman to let it 'all hang out', nor was she 'modern' in that she would pour out her sorrows to anyone who would listen. Talking about problems does not automatically make them better. Discretion is an art. Tears must be shed alone and secrets shared only with very trusted friends. She knew that Mara would be at a Hunt Supporters meeting with Bridie and dear Sean would be by himself. Driving to Bowden's Grove, she pushed open the back door, calling his name quietly.

Annie always enjoyed the decorations in the back hall, which was painted a warm terracotta and hung around with bunches of hydrangea, rose, lavender and herbs. The cousins' artistic arrangements of flowers and leaves was one of the many bonds between them, and as she walked along the stone passage Annie envied Mara's slovenly, slapdash, yet hospitable housekeeping. Tonight the Court would feel like empty trash. Here on passage walls Barbours, waistcoats, hacking jackets, rubber trousers and hats hung on pegs. But what was this? Annie could not believe her eyes. There were *names!* NAMES printed above the hooks. That must be Flurry's doing. Never in the two hundred year history of Bowden's Grove had anyone's clothes been allotted names. You simply grabbed the cleanest and driest available,and 'hard cheese' to the last man out. It made Annie laugh to contemplate the matter. Sean rattled downstairs.

"My dear, I had to come!"

He held her in his arms and she placing her head on his shoulder clung to him for some time. Then he led her down the steep steps to the Smoker, sitting her in a blue velvet armchair.

"I must discuss ....."

"No. You'll be saying nothing ....." He kicked the keeper, a great walnut hulk at the back of the fireplace into life, piling up coppice-oak sticks like a wigwam, to make the thick bed of ashes glow. When he left the room Annie watched flames turn from blue, to pink and scarlet, and in the mirage she saw the great stone hall of an Irish castle, which were memories of her own youth thirty years ago. She thought she saw a small, chubby boy of three years old astride a wooden rocking-horse, dappled, pitted and patched with age. The smile, the concentration, his unruly hair, was unmistakable. While infant Sean blew 'Gone away' on a little tin hunting horn, the retired old hound Blackwater stood listening, with eyes fixed adoringly on young Master. Annie smelt once more the damp flags of a floor devoid of furniture, a smokey peat fire, onions, stew, boots, apples, paraffin, cabbages and dogs, which always haunt these great family houses of a generation ago. That was before EEC money filled the pot-holes in the Fermoy to Mallow road, and tarted up Main Street in Dear Old Charleville.

Annie sighed knowing that nobody goes through life unscathed and she must bear her grief with fortitude.

Sean returned carrying a tray and Annie opened her eyes to see an omelette next to a tumbler of brandy and hot water, while a bunch of early snowdrops completed the supper tray. She knew Sean could cook, because she had taught him herself and it was homely, because in character the two were alike. Both pushed off an evil day for as long as possible, and neither hurried to make up their mind, but considered how to get over, underneath or round-the-sides of a problem. Annie ate her supper and Sean warmed the seat of his pants by hot coppice-oak. He filled Annie's glass "Have you heard the one about the little man in the pub?"

"Tell me."

"He was lonely. All his friends had left him."

"And?"

"What'll you have to drink? says Murphy. 'A large brandy' replies the little man. 'Is it a wonder then, you being lonely.'" They collapse with laughter.

Annie responded: " 'The drink' said the priest to Andy. 'It's your worst enemy.' 'But father' replies Andy, 'Aren't you forever telling us to love our enemies?' Laughter relaxed the air between them, until she said "..... I thought I'd seen everything. Now I've seen it all! I wasn't surprised, because can you imagine Robert letting himself get caught by one of his call girls." She paused to swallow a sickening sensation. "It was the audacity ..... the sheer wickedness. The Baker girl seems quite a decent little soul, just down on her luck, and with the money dangling before her, it must have seemed to her an easy option to have his child." Continuing more quietly "You may not believe this, but two nights ago Robert asked me to agree to adopt this child. He said it would draw us together and mend our marriage. I said 'no!' He begged me ..... said he loved me, and couldn't bear us to part. He promised the girl was a passing fancy. A mistake and that he was sorry, sorry for everything awry. Drunk or no, and on his knees he begged my forgiveness, praying me to adopt his child.

"Barbarka put me to bed. I could not sleep as dear Barbarka snores. Really terribly. She was asleep in the dressing-room and she snores. Again, you'll never believe this, but lying there alone, I relented. I actually forgave Robert. Perhaps, I thought, it was just a stupid affair and he's learnt his lesson. Thinking of the child, it's his, and not the little one's fault, yes, we would forget about divorce. Start afresh and I would agree to adoption.

"In the morning, I knew that I must see Miss Baker. You know the rest. She was paid to have the child so that Robert could force my hand. His control over my money would be assured."

"And now?" Sean was no longer lounging on the chimney-piece.

"He goes. And I want you to take over the management of the estate as from the first of January. Bridie will have her farm, to get her out of your hair, and you will manage land, farms, cottages, everything. Later on we can plan the projected stud."

They heard Bert's car stopping at the house and Flurry's footsteps as she walked into the kitchen. Their conversation being too intimate to share with others, Annie said goodbye.

"I'll see you home safe. In the Landrover."

"No further than the gates, please!"

He followed the Mercedes through the hairpin and downhill to the wrought-iron gates of the Court. Skeleton trees marked the drive and as Annie's car approached, warm orange lights in the hall were switched on. The watcher in the Landrover saw Barbarka waiting to open the glass inner doors, and skip down the wide stone steps, to pass the columns supporting the portico. The au pair towered above Annie, whom she greeted with a kiss.

'Annie needs a bodyguard' thought Sean. 'And the ever loyal Barbarka can take on anyone.' But he was perturbed and pulled the Land Rover on to the grass, before lighting a cigarette. He smoked the occasional one when he was in a quandary keeping a packet in the glove compartment. Sean was not so self-possessed as he appeared, and being generous, feeling for others cut deep.

To the left lay the quarry, like a black hole, where no lightrays were reflected from it's rough hewn cavity. Its shadow encompassed the Byebrooke cascading and eddying downhill over rocks and boulders. Unseen basket-willow shoots, rattled against rotting bulrushes, while against a paler, pewter sky the *Finger* stood sentinel.

The heavy rains of November had given way to windy cold, leaving the ground parched. Frost, and then snow threatened, weather that every horseman and all huntsmen dread. Ruts, frozen ice-sharp, cut horses' legs and tear a hound's feet to pieces, while ice-bound drinking-troughs add to the general misery.

Considering the present state of affairs, there was one thing that made Sean very glad, and that was Annie's intended gift of Lower Farm to Bridie. "To get her out of your hair" Annie said. He knew that the girl loved him, adored him, and hung on his every word. She often tried to touch his hand, his hair, or finger a cushion, or the arm of a chair where he had sat, as though to steal its warmth. He did not love Bridie and living with her under the same roof was embarrassing. Not only did he not love her, but Sean did not like Bridie, and in his book liking a person is more important than loving them. That was where Annie and Robert had become unstuck. With passion spent, there was no trust, no rapport, no friendly face to cheer and respect.

He recalled Robert's tearful words spewed out of him at the old White Horse pub, as though the smashed glass had unleashed a torrent of woe. "You've been trouble ever since you came, and you've destroyed me and everything I've ever wanted." This was the crux of the matter. It *was* Sean's fault, he should never have accepted Annie's invitation to be near her in England. Robert must have realized that his living so near was a threat, because he was no fool. Maybe he guessed? Sean did not know how much he knew, would ever know.

For now, he believed that he must return home to Ireland and let the divorce, or the reconciliation, whichever way a decision was made, take place in its own time, Annie must make up her mind by herself, and he decided he would not take over the estate management until everything was settled, once and for all.

Tomorrow he would telephone Gran Tamzine and organize their best lad, Diarmid, to travel with the Blazers on New Year's Eve. Then leaving Mara's stables in the man's capable hands, Sean would return with the hunt. That way, nobody would be let down.

He turned on the car lights, and the yellow beam masked the *Finger of God* admonishing with pity, the secrets and plotting at Broxford Court.

CHAPTER 7

As Grandfather dug a garden fork into the hard, unyielding ground of his vegetable patch, he thought that the focus of events was sliding away from Bowden's Grove. His beloved Annie was being wayward and secretive again, which boded ill for the future, and placed the family on the cusp. On the turning-point of change.

Everything that Annie did was secretive. You never knew the full facts, and were only asked to give an opinion years afterwards. It was Mara he was sorry for, as she always seemed to be dragged along against her will, and towed in the wake of Annie's actions.

Rain had made Grandfather's leeks grow long and succulent, but during present frost he had to dig deep to prevent the white, juicy stems breaking off. Much as he disliked Robert, and his restlessness irritated him, he had to admit that up until now the chap had managed Annie rather well, which was no mean achievement. Annie had always been too rich, pretty and spoilt by everyone for her own good. Damn the man, for rocking the boat! Why couldn't he be faithful, like the rest of us! Then with an extra strong heave, a clump of leeks finally gave themselves up, and Grandfather nearly fell over backwards into a row of Brussels sprouts.

When you came to think of it, Robert was only a pawn. A stop-gap in Annie's life. A sexual convenience. A filler-in, until Sean and Annie were ready, when he could be placed on a top shelf and forgotten about. Knowing Annie, who never let her right hand know what her left was doing, she would have told Robert nothing, and he must have married her without being aware. What did he guess? Surmise? Robert was no idiot, and while the Colonel, knowing men, disliked the fellow, and distrusted him, he conceded that Robert had a point.

Grandfather went to inspect the red cabbage, as he was fond of Mara's red cabbage bake, and cut two hearty ones. From Mara's point of view he was uncertain about the Sean-Annie partnership. If that were implemented, it would mean the stud being centred on the Court, rather than here at Bowden's Grove. He knew it had always been Mara's dream to found a racing stud for the thoroughbred racing industry, and sell on young stock. With Sean gone to take over the estate, and without Annie's money, Mara's hopes were smashed. She was left with the shitty end of it. No stud. Just the grind of liveries.

And now? Sean said he was leaving and returning to Ireland, with this Diarmid coming to take his place. He and Mara could only guess why. And who was going to pay the man, the eternal guesswork of Bowden's Grove? Bridie was the only one to come out of this well, with Annie's Christmas gift of Lower Farm. Banging the soil away from the truculent leeks with unaccustomed temper, he laid them out in his beech trug, before carrying them towards the house. Even with one blind eye, and only the long distance sight of the old, Grandfather could see that the white double-gates leading from the orchard to the road had been left open. "Drat! It's that temporary postman again. Taking a short cut!"

The trug was constructed of thick strips of beechwood, bonded by a steel rim to hold the slats together. Placing it in the crook of his right arm he walked through the lavender hedge separating vegetables from orchard, and trudged along the line of orchard trees. He saw that a limb from the aged cherry tree had split, while one of the branches was suspended precariously, perched about its balance-point. It seemed to him an intrusion. An encroachment. In the end maybe everything depended on fate.

The solid wood gates were heavy, and too difficult for his eighty year old arms to close, so he stepped out into the middle of the road to see if someone might be around to give him a hand. He listened. Yes, he could hear the sound of an engine coming up the hill. A high-powered car, driven at a reckless speed for a small country lane, raced round the hairpin and up the straight. Grandfather waved his free arm frantically to attract the attention of the driver sitting hunched at the wheel, but in its furious pace forward the big car swerved without decelerating. The lane was narrow, and the offside wing of the car hit the old man, tossing him into the soft, high bank bordering the road. He fell on his left side. With his good right eye, and before he lost consciousness, he was positive that he recognised the driver as Robert Davies.

The car did not stop, and raced on. Speeding, speeding towards the scheduled destination.

As she arranged with Elizabeth, Flurry's second visit to London took place on a Wednesday, the day before Christmas Eve, and travelling by taxi from the solicitor's office at Canary Wharf to her flat, she felt hurt, disillusioned and friendless. Sitting opposite the solicitor with Elizabeth' a yard or so to the right, at first Flurry felt elated, excited, concerning the size of the legacy she was to inherit. Harry had been generous, although Elizabeth just sat throughout the proceedings, stony-faced. Afterwards the prospect of such a large parcel of shares in TorrTechTron amazed her, even though Elizabeth's expressionless face was unchanged. She did not congratulate the girl. The solicitor cleared his throat.

"There is just one objection, Miss Fleur, which you should be made aware of. I have been approached by the lawyers representing the Pritchard family referring to the terms of your Contract, should you decide to take up employment with TorrTechTron again. They have agreed not to dispute the terms providing the phrase: 'satisfactory service on a yearly assessment', is inserted in the Contract."

Flurry was bemused. "I don't understand." She looked at Elizabeth for help, but received no recognition. "Why should my services not be satisfactory?"

"These are the conditions, otherwise we may leave ourselves open to litigation."

Flushing she countered: "My work has always been more than satisfactory. Ask Colin . . . . ." Her voice tailed away into nothing.

"That, my dear Miss Jones, is open to interpretation."

Perhaps most hurtful of all was Elizabeth not asking her to lunch and a happy exchange of news, nor did she give her a Christmas present as in previous years, Elizabeth just walked away as though she did not want to influence her at all and to Flurry's chagrin drove off in a TTT chauffeur-driven car.

Walking away from the solicitor's office to stand in Westferry Circus she looked up at Harry's former office on the tenth floor of the vast, square tower of Canary Wharf. Someone had shut his window. It was the eighth in a row of seventeen and was always open on Harry's orders. She walked along Heron Quays remembering the powerful lock gates, guarded by steel posts and chains with the top of the ladder dipping into deep, deep, grey-blue water of the rectangular dock, the rungs painted Day-glo yellow, lying alongside a gigantic gas-pipe. She looked across the river to the Greenwich Peninsula recalling the day that as VIPs and guests of English Partnerships a complimentary Thames riverboat had ferried them across to view the early construction of the Millennium Dome and the extraordinary development of the entire peninsula for houses, hotels, offices, Europe's largest cinema, supermarkets, a fifty-acre sanctuary for wildlife, water conservation and recycling. She wondered what she missed about TTT, deciding it was being in the forefront of things. Hearing the news. Flurry then took a taxi to St. Katharine's Dock.

As she crossed the steel-plates which sprung up-and-down on the walkway the dock seemed disjointed. How could she have lived here so long. Once, flats and shops surrounding the restored dock had seemed the apex of good living, but after country air, the noise and sulphurous smell of the city was deadening. In a queer way everything looked smaller and dirtier, however, the inky water lapping St Katharine's dock was the same and yachts bobbed up and down as usual on that salty, tidal, serpentine river although it did not feel familiar. It was no longer home.

She stopped by her favourite restaurant then passed on to collect her keys. The rooms looked amazingly clean and tidy. There was no homely scratched paint, no peeling plaster as at the Grove, while the walls were so white, so pale that they resembled an underdeveloped negative. She wandered through the rooms. Here was limbo, and she felt as though she were blown hither and thither by an intermittent wind. Even the Jacuzzi-type water spluttered in her face. It was her flat and not her flat being only rented, and its decor reflected contemporary living and modern design. Nothing else. Nothing reflected her character. Her personality. Bowden's Grove was the embodiment of a family who had lived there for generations, together with Grandfather's rugs from Persia, Mara's floral decorations and faithful dogs, while even Bridie had an oily motorbike. Living with the family she knew that the gap between childhood and being an adult was being stitched together. Only then could her life begin.

On the table stood a cardboard box filled with post, uncollected for eight weeks. There was the usual junk mail of catalogues, although no bills, as someone must have paid them, and only one letter. Recognising the writing with joy she tore it open, "Mrs Marks! Darling Mrs Marks! She must be ninety by now. I'll go and see her next time I'm here." Mother was always grateful to Mrs. Marks for addressing her as Mrs Jones, with an accent on the Mrs, because in those days being an unmarried mother meant disgrace. Mother's family had been cabinet-makers, and French polishers, while the Marks were East End tailors supplying West End trade. From them Flurry had learnt the cut of a suit and how to dress.

She saw again the paper streamers put up by Mother for Christmas, and the picture saying 'Bless this House'. A pile of mandarin oranges stood by Brazil nuts, while Woolworth's crackers were arranged criss-cross to greet Christmas chicken and sausages. She felt grateful for her babyhood.

Tonight? what should she do? Go out? Stay in? Only early bedtime seemed practicable. Sitting on her white bed, gazing absently at white painted furniture, she wondered how she would respond should Harry be still alive and come through the door, bearing presents, and was surprised to feel nothing. No welcome. No pleasure in seeing his face or hearing his voice. She had moved on. She pondered what she missed about Harry and TTT deciding it was *responsibility* and being in the forefront of things. Hearing the news. She recalled the Conference on Display Systems last June, when Harry left the organisation completely to her for the first time. He must have been failing even then.

A faint winter sun played in swathes of scarlet and yellow on white walls and to Flurry's hypersensitive mind, panels of brightness seemed to appear on each plane surface as a sort of mirage. These were the prototype display panels which have occupied the minds of engineers such as Harry and physicists from academia for decades. On one wall shone a plasma display panel, five feet in diagonal, depicting flowers of breathtaking colour and crispness. On another wall, pictures from space gave a blue earth of incomparable detail and sharpness; while on an adjacent wall, projected from a perfect screen showed sharply focused images of wildlife. The prototype plasma screens, that TTT and other worldwide corporations had engineered were so thin, they could be hung on a sitting-room wall.

The vision faded as the sun set. Although Flurry was not technically qualified in electronics, it had been up to her to target the right people in multi-national companies for the Conference, who might be useful to TTT, and create a show that was interesting, varied and colourful. She was also responsible for arranging the presentation of every paper to be read at the Conference, on her own initiative. Had it been a test? With hindsight TTT was being reorganised prior to Harry's death. This was the paradox. However much she loved the country and was learning from it, she would never have the experience, expertise or capital to start a rural business on her own. Never could she be more than an ill-paid stablehand. One day she must return to London, but never to this soulless flat. She needed somewhere more homely overlooking her beloved river.

She was restless. It was useless to go to bed which made her think of Harry again and why their affair now seemed of so little consequence. Why didn't she miss him? Only now could she question the meaning of their relationship when for ten years he had been her world, work, home, sexual partner and only friend.

Home. This white flat was not home. He came for the evening, took her out to dinner and after bed it was accepted when he said: "I must go back now and get my beauty sleep!" Harry never came on Sundays. There were no Sunday dinners like there had been after church, with Mother's skirt-beef-and-dumplings or end-of-neck with carrots, while Sunday evenings she spent by herself, and her present loneliness made her long for the AGA and Mara's steak-and-kidney pie. Flurry remembered how Mara loved to see Sean's and her own face as the golden-crusted, steak-smelling pie came from the oven, and she realised that Mara was becoming a mother-figure for her. She had to go out and went downstairs, walking towards the river which lay at the opposite end to the entrance over the springy steel bridge, making her think of Mother again and Saturday afternoon walks together down to Limehouse Cut to feed the seagulls, before high tea with herrings-in-oatmeal and mustard. The Thames called. She went to hear what he wanted and met some water-birds on the way who chattered to her. She stood where in nineteen-hundred St. Katharine's Steamboat Wharf was a landing-stage for steamers from the continent, but the tide was on the turn so that conversation with the river was cross-referenced.

Somewhere on the damp air someone was playing a concerto or

fugue, perhaps from a barge or music centre, the music strongly evocative of North Sea and winter river. Rich and powerful the theme seemed quite 'ordinary' in its components of rhythm and melody, with the bass carrying musically related themes. In the distance, a horn was heard used thrillingly with its stirring notes the guiding spirit to a grand idea. This new force gave concreteness to pure 'musical form', while a recurring musical theme in the bass and full orchestra reinforced dramatic point to the notes of the horn, which now drawing nearer, represented an emotion, a destiny.

The music drifted into night and the Thames refused to explain to her what he meant so she went to bed fully dressed and slept.

As Flurry slept quietly, the British Airways plane landed on its scheduled flight from Heathrow to an European provincial capital. The foreign airport was modern enough to allow passengers to walk direct from the aircraft along the endless tiled corridors towards the main foyer. Robert Davies shoved his way past babies-in-buggies piled high with Christmas pressies, students wearing spectacles, and the occasional party of Japanese tourists, who came to view the ski-runs in order to take the obligatory photographs. Robert was here to implement his preconceived plan set in motion on the night of the old White Horse Inn, and he was travelling abroad to cover his tracks. He must take no chances, having too much respect for the expertise of the British police.

Time was pressing. Planned like a military operation, the integration of timetables was paramount. The incident with Colonel Bowden that morning was annoying and Robert hoped the old idiot was too gaga to recognise him. Travelling with a tight schedule was axiomatic to Robert. His parents played as a duo in vaudeville, so while still a young boy he toured a circuit of repertory companies in theatres and clubs and knew every cheap theatrical boarding-house in England.

He passed customs control and immigration without comment on a Cayman Islands passport. Sometimes officials were dubious, however, his expensive leather despatch-case, vicuna overcoat and Hèrmes tie, gave an impression of affluence. Robert often confused form with reality, past with present, so that a character-change held no difficulties for him.

Gaining the foyer, he walked quickly beneath the series of metal canopies and continued through a maze of walkways towards the underground Flughafen. Lifts between floors operated silently, futuristic modern platforms for trains being below the runways. All was steel and concrete, so that the subterranean station with its metallic blue escalators, lift doors, air shafts and service areas resembled a space station from Star Wars. Robert waited impatiently for a train to take him to the city. The first class carriage was luxurious and softly lit. Robert had the ability to detach his conscious mind from the mission on hand if work had to be accomplished, then it must be done. A gearbox in his mind, declutched. He felt nothing.

On arrival in the city he knew he had only two hours before his flight home. Panting slightly as he hurried along concrete tunnels and up staircases, he took the short cut he had known since student days, where a luggage ramp emptied itself into the station yard. Here thousands of university students' bicycles lay propped up row on row. The Engineering Department of the University stood rectangular, immense and impersonal beyond the river. Robert did not cross the river: he only glanced up at the impressive buildings. As a young man with no financial assistance, money had to be acquired if he were to study to be an engineer. Experience told him that working the clubs as a pretty teenage prostitute was the quickest way to earn money. A lot of cash quickly. So, he painted his face, gritted his teeth, and grimaced. The gears of his mind became disengaged and he hardened to necessity.

Studying abroad gave him a new identity, with the past consigned to a mental oubliette. That evening he did not visit old pastures, he ran left-handed towards a series of stone railway arches, over which trains travelled on their way to lakes and mountains capped with perpetual snow.

Beneath the arches one of the doorways led to workshops. Workshops few persons have known existed. Because in sensitive political times they could be of use, the authorities liked to ignore their existence. He pressed a bell to release a locked door and Robert entered the underpass, then mounted a well-worn flight of steps leading to the office.

In London, Christmas presents had to be bought! Flurry bathed, then packed a large suitcase and prepared to leave her flat for the last time. "Whatever the future holds," she promised, "I'll never live here again." West End Christmas shops are a revelation to everyone. Having been in the country for what felt like an eternity, their bright lights and sophistication refreshed Flurry, especially now she had money. Clothes had no allure as when should she wear them? Fashion could wait for her return to town, and Flurry knew that one day she must return. London was both her milieu and her past, with the present only a 'vacation'. She was starting to understand that her commitment to her previous career, together with an adolescent love for Harry as a father figure were no more than a prolonged teenage fantasy. She must square the dilemma of growing into a mature self, as until now she had been a commodity, fashioned, produced, packaged and marketed.

Buying her presents for Mara and Bridie was easy and she chose them a sweater each, while Grandfather would love a book with large print, and many coloured pictures. Sean was difficult, until she saw a toy teddy bear in a shop window. Teddy was covered in cream fur fabric, and sported a check bow-tie. Best of all he was wearing reins. Red reins with bells on. Bells for Sean's cousin little Marie, and she knew it would appeal to his sense of the ridiculous. To be on the safe side, she bought him a bottle of Paddy's as well.

Striking guards decreed that Flurry took the coach from Victoria rather than travel by train. It was quicker for Bert to collect her in Broxford instead of the return journey on crowded roads when trains to Chippenham might be late. Stowing her heavy case in the luggage hold, she chose a seat directly behind the driver, and the route through Kensington and over the Chiswick flyover felt exciting, strongly evocative, yet familiar, as though she had driven this way for years. How quickly the present subdues the past. Condensed water-vapour oozed in rubbery drops down the window-pane, but they no longer resembled tears, while a cassette played 'Jingle Bells' as music to lull passengers to doze.

Long distance coaches travelling west call at Heathrow, to link Bristol, Bath and south Wales with the continent. There was still daylight although vast banks of lights had been switched on to illuminate shady corners. The airport was crystal clear, with frost in the air chasing away mist and traffic pollution. Above, banked aircraft awaited traffic controllers' permission to land in a two minute sequence.

Flurry had excellent eyesight and was a quick, observant person who rarely made a visual mistake. The coach swung with the stream of traffic past a roundabout and alongside the railway which looks as though it is suspended in mid-air. Approaching Terminal One, it stopped at the exterior platform which was sheltered by a hooded, plastic roof. Wire mesh trolleys stood loaded with suitcases, and behind the platform, a wide crossing banded with broad yellow bars led to entrances for arrivals. The yellow and black crossing strobed, as a familiar figure hurried across the carriageway, ignoring taxis,

Flurry stood up and waved, thinking that Robert was hurrying to catch her coach. He looked up. There was one flash of recognition, then the hooded eyes closed to slits.

It *was* Robert. She recognised the crisp grey curling hair and the fawn British Warm overcoat. He walked so near the coach window, that she could see the British Field Sports badge he always wore but Robert passed on rapidly towards the car park. She was puzzled and found herself strangely disturbed.

Bert met Flurry wearing his best suit ready for the traditional Bowden's Grove party, which always took place on Christmas Eve. However, as his toilet was completed with cap and upsidedown pipe, this rather spoilt the picture. The pipe reminded Flurry that she had not bought him a present and as Broxford shops were still open she went into the general stores. After buying four ounces of Gold Block tobacco, she chose a collar for Patters.

"Some tinsel, Flurry. We be wantin' tinsel for 'osses come Boxing Day!"

"Silver okay, Bert?"

He was unusually silent, and told none of his bucolic stories as they drove up tortuous roads, hemmed in by stone walls. Surmounting the rise of one small combe, frosty, glistening tarmac rose to crest another petrified wave, beneath a far backdrop of pine, beech and larch. Cracked, split and broken boughs tormented tree outlines. The close of day was windless, cold and solitary.

When they arrived, the drive was already crowded with parked cars, while the front door stood hospitably open to receive guests. Half of Wiltshire seemed to be arriving. A tall tree decorated with ethereal white lights, sparkled against ashlar stone, while people laughed, kissed and called 'Happy Christmas'.

To Flurry's surprise Bert pulled into the verge, to stop by the wicket gate which leads through marching black-brown larch towards Six Acre Copse. Patters on the back seat sniffed the air, like there was something up.

"It's the Colonel."

"Grandfather. What . . . . ."

Bert sighed. The certainty of life appeared to be knocked out of him. "Don't know as he'll live."

"Whatever . . . . ."

"So they say."

Flurry could see Sean and Bridie welcoming guests, through the columns of the front door.

"Mara and Mrs Annie be with 'im now. In 'orspital."

"An accident?"

Bert started the engine. "Looks as though 'is number's up." Then with a touch of his sense of the ridiculous, "There wer old Bob Adams, ninety an' deaf as a post 'ee were. Lived up to Exford, always walked in the middle of the road 'ee did, that were in the 'thirties mind. 'Is son the shoemaker said: 'Like to see the car what'erd run over father. Like to see the car'." Bert paused for effect. "And 'ee did . . . . . car 'it 'im outside the white gates in the lane."

"Grandfather, you mean?" Flurry was perplexed by the change of location.

"Reckon as you'd like to know, afore going in. Police bin measuring in case of it's manslaughter."

Flurry dragged her suitcase through the back door and fled up the kitchen stairs, to give herself time before meeting people. As usual there was no light and she had to feel her way up by holding on to the torn carpet. A cat fled. The smell of onions was over-powering, and the stairs were old, twisted and warped. Tiny strips of light from the hall glowed between the risers, and through these cracks came the sound of music. Someone had put on a cassette and the party seemed to be warming up.

In the sanctuary of her room, she changed into a plain, black jersey dress, tying an orange scarf about her throat. She then decided to wear her best black Gucci shoes with their very high spiky heels. She was unaccustomed to the extra height, and she was looking down at the holly decorations on top of the long-case clock below her, when she walked down the highly polished oak staircase leading to the main hall. Suddenly Flurry was distracted by the voice of the huntsman to the County and District Foxhounds: "Seems that Bowden has 'Gone to Ground' poor old bugger."

And another voice, "Not the happy hunting ground in the sky!"

Flurry slipped and tobogganed down the last five steps missing the kingpost by inches, at the bottom she found herself in the arms of Robert Davies.

"My dear girl. You should take more water with it!"

The pain and shock made tears very near, while Robert was at his most jovial and truculent. "We'll have to fine you five pounds if you cry."

She looked puzzled and the huntsman laughed. "The hunt should fine you a pound if you fall at a fence. And it's two pounds if you lose your pony. But five pounds if you cry!"

"Quite right" from a subscriber.

Shaking herself free, "I wasn't jumping, thank you," and she forced herself to walk normally across the red and black tiles she had scrubbed so violently and stand by the log fire burning in the great open chimney hearth. Sean left his post at the front door and came across looking very concerned. "It's the ankle that's hurt?" and giving her his arm led her to Dolly in the drawing-room.

Flurry had rarely visited the drawing-room, except to frighten the spiders and shake dead flies and fallen plaster off grubby white dustcovers. In candlelight, and with one low-powered crystal chandelier, the room had pink, green and gold classical charm. No matter that the rose-coloured silk on Regency chairs was threadbare,

Mara's winter flower arrangements accentuated the grace of the room. Annie had sent Barbarka to help that morning, and hothouse carnations, baby roses and dahlias hid the cracked top of the French Empire table. Annie, with her love of botany, looked after the greenhouse herself and only Bridie, talking to a neighbour, jarred on the elegance of the room, because her pale blue dress gave her sallow face a frozen appearance, while the hairdresser's efforts to give her heavy hair a lift had fallen flat. Beetle brows appeared to lower and thicken the forehead arch. Bridie did not speak to Flurry, nor did she take the slightest notice of her, or introduce her to friends. Flurry thought how insular the English could be, and unlike more cosmopolitan parties. Here intruders are ignored and it is up to them to introduce themselves.

The pain in her foot made her take refuge in the kitchen where she could sit down without anyone noticing. The Major dashed in and out helping to fill glasses, because with neither Mara nor Grandfather present they were short-handed. The retired soldier was in his element, chatting to everyone, and joining the laughter. In spite of concern over Grandfather not all the guests were aware of the seriousness of the accident.

To Flurry's surprise, Robert came to the kitchen to look for her. Never doing anything without an ulterior motive, he paced restlessly round the room.

"We shall have to buy you some glasses. Or maybe some contact lenses, so as not to spoil your pretty face."

"I've perfect sight, thank you. You must be the one needing glasses."

He stood still, looking puzzled.

"At Heathrow."

"Heathrow?"

"This afternoon. Terminal One. You passed by, right near the coach."

His puzzlement changed to laughter. "My dear Flurry, you do need glasses. Miles away. I was miles away. Returning from Cornwall, in point of fact." He was watching her face intently. "Went to stay with an old school-friend."

"You were wearing a Hèrmes tie. Like now."

"You never give up, do you. Even so I'm flattered," she looked away. ". . . . . that you should notice. A clever, beautiful girl like you. And rich too. Can't think why you came back."

She got up to move away from him, feeling aware of his sensuality. His iron-grey hair lay in curls so flat and crisp that they resembled leaf-bracts, and his slightly swarthy skin was perpetually sun-tanned.

"We ought to know one another better. We're one of a kind." He followed to stand behind her near the AGA. "Do we call you Miss Fleur now that you're up-market. With my wife and Mara at the hospital with

Bowden." The innuendo was not lost on Flurry. "We are one of a kind. The things we own. Also our thoughts about other people, and what they think of us. We're one kind."

She turned to face him, unable to bear the sensation in her back. When he smiled he was appealing. Evocative. Seduction is the most magical of all arts. And he was the most magical of practitioners. She could think of no reply.

"From London?"

"Yes."

"You always lived in Limehouse."

"How d'you know?"

"Your accent. The arrangement of words. The faintest, elusive trace is there, and nobody can disguise a native accent. I *know*. I study accents. The expressiveness of tonal balance. Tear down bomb damaged houses and rebuild them with concrete tower blocks, the intonation remains. Every street from Limehouse to Tower Hamlets has its distinctive flavour. Now I've rattled you! Blown your cover! Limehouse was the home of craftsmen. Furniture makers. Tailors. Silversmiths. We understand."

She could not guess his motives, or what he was driving at. Only that she was fascinated by him and thoughts of the numbness of her white flat, when sleeping clothed and alone, overcame here. Against her wishes she hoped he would kiss her. "You draw away," he patted her face. "So naive. So experienced yet so naive. So worldly-wise, yet such a baby. Let me help you. Be warned about these people at Bowden's Grove. Run, before you get involved. You have money and opportunity. Go. Back to London." He took her face in both his hands, and she closed her eyes drowning in expectation of his embrace, while the libido of suppressed emotion flooded her aching thighs. But he walked away, leaving her furious. Subdued.

To hide her embarrassment she hurried to her room early, leaving the house to look after itself. She guessed that Robert meant to prostitute her in front of both Annie and Mara because she had seen him at Heathrow, and she wondered if she might have a word with Mara tomorrow. On further consideration she felt too proud to 'sneak' like a common informer, when Annie and Robert were not her business and decided to say nothing. Mother didn't like a 'tell-tale tit'!

Pink roses on the wallpaper turned exotic petals towards the table-light as Flurry switched it on. Bed curtains billowed in the draught to shelter and comfort, while the massive cupboard gathered up her clothes in a vapour of cedar and camphor. Rest eased the pain in her foot. Outside night closed down with a long wild shriek of the stables barn owl. He sat on the clock-tower with an occasional hiss, or yap, then snoring to lull mice, scavenging for fallen corn, into false security. Flurry slept.

At 3 am she was awakened when the emergency floodlights in the stableyard were energised, and immediately extinguished. Getting up and looking through her window, she could see the interior light shining in the tackroom. Burglars stealing saddlery are a constant threat that all stable owners dread. Wide awake, Flurry struggled into trousers and sweater, and limped along the passage. She dared not risk the back stairs with its torn carpet choosing the main staircase instead. It was lit by a single lamp, together with a low glow from the log fire banked up with peat. Holly was strewn on the hall tiles, and a few glasses were hiding on ledges. Flurry stepped around the kingpost, dreading that the spectre of Robert might hold her again.

She listened by the back door wondering if she should press the burglar alarm, then putting one eye to the massive keyhole, she saw Sean. It was pointless to return to bed now and borrowing Grandfather's walking stick, she hobbled down the side-passage and into the yard.

The stable and tackroom were well-built, spacious and equipped with old-fashioned, convenient gadgets beloved by the Edwardians, and of inestimable worth when electricity poles succumb to ice-sheets. Sean had lit a cast-iron cockle stove to preserve watertanks from frost.

"Diamid'll have something to live up to!" laughed Flurry.

"He will. He will. Surely he will be fine! And a happy Christmas to you."

She crept in by the warmth, shivering in zero temperature.

"With that limp, and you shaking, we'll be having you in bed with Grandfather."

"Are you really leaving so soon?" She spoke revealing her deepest feelings, their intensity surprising her. "I thought you were a fixture here."

"And you're needing a friend." He spread a dry blanket over the pile of New Zealand rugs folded on a chest. "A friend to keep you warm," Sean held up a woollen travelling rug, with SRC in gold letters on a blue ground, indicating she should sit down. She fingered the embroidered letters. "Who is SRC?"

"Sean Rory O Callaghan, my hunter's best rug," while covering her up. "And you'll be returning to London surely?"

"Yes."

"Go to sleep now."

She lay in the warm well-being of the temporary bed watching him squat on his heels by the cockle stove, the metalwork giving out a grand heat, and his angular face with its high Celtic cheekbones, a dark silhouette in the firelight.

"Will you write to me, when you're in London?" he said suddenly. She sat up. "If you write to me."

"I will. Lie down and sleep now." Small logs on the stove flared. Later from Flurry, "Robert told me your Gran was the finest horsewoman in all Ireland."

"She was. She was."

"Tell me where you live."

"In a castle on a crag, that Oliver Cromwell knocked the towers into a ruin. We kept in the house while we still had a roof over our heads. There are white doves, they roost under the slates."

She watched him wondering if he'd say more, not liking to ask. She understood that you couldn't push Sean.

"Maybe at Eastertime you'll be coming over to see us."

Taken aback, "Your Gran?"

"She'll be glad to welcome you."

Digesting the turn of events, "I'd love to," and remembering with a shock Annie's words in the exotic conservatory with flashing birds, 'Go to County Cork, it's green and fey. Opens your eyes!' Annie had foretold Sean's invitation! And later, "I've never been to Ireland."

"You fly to Cork city, and I'll drive you."

"To Clavincade isn't it?" He would be drawn no more. She remembered Robert saying when they met in Six Acre, 'Tamzine O Callaghan, little dot of a woman as old as Endor, she can't weigh more than five stone. Dresses in black and wears an ancient feathered hat. I believe she makes flies out of that hat to catch trout or salmon in the Blackwater' and Flurry falling asleep and dreaming. 'She drives down to the bank and fishes. Not much else she can do, except fish and sell horses. Wills her horse over. Throw your heart over and the horse will follow. Then she broke her back.'

While Flurry slept secure in knowing that Sean was no one night stand, he went to the Land Rover to light a cigarette taking one from the glove compartment, as he felt uncertain if he could see his way ahead. Attracted to Flurry by her beauty, charm and smart appearance, he soon recognised her essential goodness, and the very insecurity of her wide-open eyes was appealing. However, he hardly knew her, although believing instinctively that past experiences controlled her spontaneity. At Clavincade, walking together by the delectable river Blackwater, with its leaping trout and hidden paths, they could find each other, embraced in the fleeting sun and scurrying cloud of Easter.

Frost came in hard and sharp with the dawn. "Six o'clock now," he said, shaking her awake. "You must be getting up now, if we're to cook that grand turkey for Christmas dinner."

During the weekend after Christmas, news from the hospital sounded hopeful, although Grandfather, bruised and shaken, was still confused and wandering in his mind. He struggled to tell Mara something but was unable to find coherent words.

On that Sunday morning before visiting hospital, Mara and Bridie attended their local church, and Sean went to Mass in a private chapel belonging to Daisybrooke Farm. Then Bridie rode off on her chug-chug motorbike for the daily visit to Lower Farm, her present from Annie.

Meantime a courier, dressed in black and red leathers with safety helmet and visor, was speeding through three frontiers, before reaching the Dover ferry.

Taking the M25 and M4 motorways on his high-powered motorbike, he speeded amongst Sunday traffic towards the Swindon service station. Then using only a few words of verbal communication to establish identity, he passed a package to Robert Davies, the driver of the BMW who was awaiting his arrival.

Car and motorbike parted, each to his own destination.

New Year's Eve at 4 am was dark, windless and cold when Flurry left the comfort of her bedroom and went down to stables. For several days Diarmid had been teaching her the art of mane plaiting used on hunting mornings to show off the neck and crest of a hunter. Diarmid, with his usual speed and dexterity, was grooming and preparing long manes in readiness when Flurry still sleepy, started plaiting them into eight or twelve equal portions including the forelock.

"I'm mad. Quite mad," she said to Big Charlie, stretching up with cold, aching arms. "Plaiting manes for less than four pounds an hour in the middle of the night. It's all his fault! Why do I listen to him!" But she worked on joining a needle and thread into each plait at the two-thirds stage, then looping the ends of the thread round the completed plait and pulling tight to make a row of neat 'rosettes' down the neck. Diarmid stood by grinning. "It's a thousand fingers we have here this morning," he teased. Flurry threw the water-brush at him.

By ten-o'clock each person seemed to be going in his or her unique direction. Walking across in morning darkness her thoughts turned to the tackroom, come alive in the glow of the cockle-stove lighting Sean's pale face. Flurry was no young teenager dreaming of romance, ten years of Harry's tuition had ensured that. She was too down-to-earth, too world-weary, wary, cautious and prudent to become excited over daydreams of love called forth by Sean's suggestion that they write. But even with iron control over emotions she knew her life-epicentre had shifted, with a swarm of energies emanating from some new point-source, its direction unresolved. She changed into fresh clothes before rugging up and leading Jenny, the elderly pony for Nervous Mum into the small horsebox together with two hunters for clients. Mara gave Flurry explicit instructions on how to look after the owners of liveries.

When Flurry drove cautiously towards the hairpin, every horse in the district was converging on Broxford Court for the traditional joint meet with the Charleville Blazers. Because of extra weight up, she had to take special care, and was perturbed to read an official warning 'MUD ON ROAD' at the entrance to the tree-tunnel. A large fall of earth from the nearside bank had been hastily scraped back, leaving a precarious coating of greasy mud.

Thankful to gain the bottom of the hill with her load in one piece, she waved to Diarmid, who was riding Big Charlie and leading two hunters. He rode looking like a question mark, after years of hard riding, using a jockey's cradle stirrups with feet jammed home and toes pointing downwards.

A group of banner-waving animal liberation rights protesters dressed in yellow tunics were standing outside the wrought-iron gates to the park. On the opposite side of the road were parked two police cars filled with five officers, who were quietly and impartially observing them, determined to keep the Queen's peace. The expression on their faces was impenetrable, and Flurry recognised the tall figure of PC Watts as he sat behind his sergeant.

A steady stream of cars, Land Rovers, vans, horseboxes, hunters, hacks, children-on-leading-reins and fathers running or riding bicycles, passed through the handsome gates, the men gamely holding on to their offspring's bridles.

Flurry parked next to the big horsebox, while Sean unloaded five horses. Bridie still refused to speak to her, and Flurry noted that Mara was riding and leading a second horse, so that her daughter could hunt with Sean. Mara in rat-catcher habit, looked ten years younger, and even handsome on her mare, Polly. Two experienced lady riders met Flurry and helped her to put up Nervous Mum. With much laughter, travelling rugs, boots and tail bandages were deftly removed from their own two mounts, with girths and every keeper carefully checked. The Major strolled across: "Most efficient! Highly competent, my dear. And how smart you look this morning." Flurry was wearing new green, stretch velvet jodhpurs, a wool jacket in Lovat and a flat-crowned velour hat fashionably turned up in front, also in green.

"I've treated myself in the Christmas sales, Major."

"And what a happy face for the New Year!"

Everywhere was joy and excitement, because a local meet is the countryman's day out and the focus of the social round in an otherwise hard-working life. Hospitality is happily given and received. Land, belonging to farmers both great and small, is generously opened up for the Hunt, while supporters wait by gates to open and close them to horses and hounds with a cheerful 'good morning'. This is the companionship of the Hunt. Flurry hated the idea of the day being spoilt by Bridie's unfair rancour.

"Let's be friends, please! It's New Year."

"Why are you all dressed up like that. You're too dressed up!"

Flurry perplexed. "Come on, Bridie!"

"And why have you persuaded Sean to take you to the hunt dinner and dance tonight?" she screamed.

"He asked me."

"Stop it, Bridie," from her mother. Diarmid stood by with his three horses, grinning. He was known to be cheeky, if he thought he could get away with it.

"Have you no pride!" from Sean. "And would I be dating my *cousin* now." This was for Diarmid's consumption, warning him to be careful.

She shouted at Flurry, "Why did you come?" Mara looked out of her depth, and people turned their heads to watch the display. Grabbing Bridie by the lapels of her jacket, Sean hauled her out of sight behind the box, and a resounding slap restored shocked calm. He then untied Surtees, giving the wretched girl a leg up. "Ride with your mother. And go." When Sean looked pompous, Flurry remembered the rat! This time she was determined not to giggle, but walked with the Major down the drive to the front of the house. The meet was being held in a mown field below the ha-ha, which divided it from formal gardens of trees and shrubs. Golden Irish yew trees, as old as the century, were clipped into spheres or pyramids to give the garden a static look, as though frozen in time, like a Seurat painting. Barbarka and two staff were serving drinks from a long table, and sausage rolls and ginger cake was being passed to mounted field and supporters. Sporting terriers, retrievers or spaniels, the working dogs of the countryside, restrained by leads or rope-ends, eyed the pack with respect. Annie wearing her perfectly cut grey riding habit rode Fairytales side-saddle, and mingled with the crowd. She knew every name, where everyone lived, the ages of their children, and their illnesses, she knew corn prices, difficulties for farmers due to lack of fuel and feed, the market for sheep and pigs, Annie understood the heart and mind of the local country, identifying herself, and dedicating herself to it. Robert, resplendent in top hat and red coat, was talking importantly to subscribers.

The Major collected Flurry a drink, and she spoke to Barbarka. "Whoo-ps. Nice . . . ."

"Cherry brandy." Barbarka skipped around with a tray. "I'm dancing tonight with a beau! Mrs Annie bought us two tickets."

"Hope he's a tall beau!"

"Tall. Taller than me. So much higher. Like this high, a policeman." Flurry hoped no local bars needed clearing by PC Watts for 'roughs' that evening. She skipped back. "Mrs Annie's having a short day, so I must make quick time."

A large contingent of guests from the Blazers were brought up by the field Master, with many hat raisings, 'good mornings' and 'great-to-see-you-agains' exchanged. To Flurry's surprise, the Irish Hunt were not wearing traditional black coats, but Barbours with green collars and green velvet hunting caps. Our Master called the field over in order to bid guests welcome, also to thank Annie for the meet and to explain the plan for the day.

Then it was 'Hounds please', when the horn was blown the pack galloped forward with every eye fixed adoringly on the Master who was hunting hounds himself. The C&D kennel has traditionally used many Beaufort sires and the blood is ideally suited to this country. With roads, traffic and wire to contend with, the pack must be biddable and staunchly accurate, although not over-disciplined.

The kennel-huntsman, as first whipper-in, led the nineteen-and-a-half couple hounds towards a gate leading to the series of fields below the quarry. The day was grey cloud, also sun-streaked, with nearby ploughland appearing carmine-pink, behind which verdant green meadow led to the bronze of hedgerows. High above the indigo-hued quarry, the *Finger of God* loomed black and malevolent.

The Master urged his hounds on in front of him to the first draw, while Flurry watched until they were out of sight.

"Best if you walk through the covert over there. I'll find the others, and we'll meet you on the road," advised the Major. Beneath the accusing *Finger* Flurry saw the light change, becoming dark, and making windows of the Court appear empty, sightless. Frightened, she imagined gaping, blackened holes where doors once stood. Turning away hurriedly, she made her way over a well-kept stile and scrambled down a grassy track through a spinney of Lombardy poplar. The bank was steep and at the bottom breeding-cages for young poults had been up-ended ready for next season. Standing by the small road, the land rose up on the far side of the valley. She waited alone. All was quiet, waiting.

She wandered slowly down the road, hands in pockets, on this cold day with minute snowflakes in the air. The horn sounding in the mid-distance was used tootingly, to tell the field that the huntsman was still in covert, although drawing this way. A little later and appearing from nowhere, she saw the sterns of the pack feathering on the brow of the hill not a hundred yards above her. Then the huntsman and hunt staff, their red coats cut off from their mounts, rode along as though dismembered by the rising ground.

Silently like an ethereal spirit Charlie, pale orange in pelt with white tipped ears and a white tag, raced along the hedgerow by Flurry's side. He was a beautiful fox, strong and dashing, and would be a wonderful sire for next year's cubs. Unnerved by her vision she gasped "Now what do I do?" The outline of a lone horseman on a black horse stood on the hill above her. Spectre? Or tribal centaur? Sean's voice, quiet, steady seemed to instruct her. "Take the time and keep quiet." Flurry had learnt enough to know that it isn't sporting to holloa too quickly and raise hounds' heads, thus allowing a fast pack to course a fox, hunting by sight, and bust him. Charlie must be allowed his chance to provide a good run, being hunted fairly by scent, and be given best, which by looking at the strength of the pilot, seemed likely. She knew sufficient to understand that no hunting means no foxes, because they would be gassed, dug or trapped to extinction, and she had learned that a huntsman with hounds hunts selectively, so that old or weak foxes, who are more likely to kill chickens and lambs, are accounted for, leaving the best stock. Too many foxes bring the terror of mange. She was content.

She scrambled on to the hedge. "Yoi!" The high-pitched cry from over the hill echoed round the valley. Within seconds, an excited pack came to the holloa and poured down the slope, the leading hounds giving individual tongue, as yet uncertain of the line. Hounds quickened and swung right-handed along the hedge, then opening with a great burst of joy they pushed their fox down the valley towards open fields.

Meantime the huntsman and whippers-in had to make a U-turn and gallop to a gate at the far end of the field, to turn back and come cantering down the grass verge of the road. Raising his hat, the Master called out "Well done, Flurry!" She had never been so excited. A flood of madness. Expiation. This was what it was all about. "Two minutes, Master. You're two minutes behind."

The field trotted fast down the road behind the field Master, with the local hunt and Irish guests widely distributed, and eagerly exchanging news and gossip. Robert was riding with Bridie, and Flurry was surprised how attentive he was towards her. Mara brought up the rear, walking with her second horse towards the rendez-vous. Then the cars came on at a respectful distance, led by a former joint Master who knew the hunting hazards of engine fume. Dolly opened the door of Bert's truck and pulled Flurry up beside her. The Major sat with Patters on a sack of wood at the back, keeping his foot on a drum of oil in case it rolled.

"They'm going to Daisybrooke Farm" and Bert followed the cavalcade around the hill and along lanes Flurry never knew existed. They held up on seeing second horses, including Mara and Diarmid, standing in a lay-by. Presently the huntsman galloped up, passing between Bert's car and Diarmid, he called out: "Gallop on, and tell the field Master to bring them on!"

"What you got that bloody 'orn for, sir?" was the cheeky reply. Mara rebuked him, but winked at Flurry repressing a storm of laughter. Passing through a village with the cars, she realised they were on a road leading to the Court, but from the opposite direction. They all jumped out and walked along the lane.

Daisybrooke Farm was early Georgian. The house was of brick, chequered in red and dark blue, with a roof of grey slate. It was four bays by three bays, and the windows were all round arched. Pollarded acers, outlining the head-high brick garden wall, appeared as though they were hand-on-shoulders. To the side of the house, and partially concealed by trees and shrubs, stood a small wooden chapel, stained green, with painted windows and a minute bell-tower. Flurry remembered that Sean had said it was rented by a very old lady. Sadly, dear Janie had a dementia and was losing her memory.

The mounted field was standing in a long line, and holding up with their backs to Daisybrooke. In between coffee-housing, they watched the huntsman put in the pack and draw a hanging covert, growing on the side of the steep hill which towered above the road. Taking her bearings, Flurry realised that Bowden's Grove must be further up right-handed and high above them. The huntsman's voice, cheering on the pack, could be heard plainly.

Annie was standing with Sean at the head of the field, some fifty yards away, and she had never looked more beautiful. As foot-followers passed, Sean had a habit of whipping off his hunting hat and curling it in the crook of his arm, while he bent down to talk. He listened or spoke with such intensity that he made his correspondent believe that he or she was the most important person in the whole world.

Time and space were forgotten, Flurry leant against Daisybrooke wall and watched them. She had never felt so happy. An elusive net seemed to bind Sean to Annie, with links of charm and invincibility. Encased in their tightly defined module, Flurry did not feel herself excluded, but as though the web was drawn out and extended towards her. The quietus of the place, together with the enticing sounds of horse, hound, horn, trees, leaves, birds, sheep and friendly voices, melded into a music beyond comprehension. She closed her eyes. Listening. Smiling. And hardly daring to breathe.

The sound of the horn blowing out made the field pick up their reins and walk, then trot down the road, and to push horses through the water-splash above the stone bridge. The Byebrooke glittered in its rocky bed. Overhanging branches of alder and the gold swathes of weeping willow cut the light into strips, which confused the eyes. Flurry ran along behind the horses, thankful that she was much fitter than in London days.

At the T-junction the field passed through a gate, and cantered up the hill over the grass, and while Flurry was hurrying towards the hairpin, Bert caught up with the truck, to save a long walk. They waited in a field listening to a distant horn and intermittent hound music, now near, now going away from them.

In her state of elation Flurry felt she must be alone, and made a solitary way in the direction of Lawson's, with Six Acre distant to her left.

A light wind fluttered emergent grasses and in their companionable solitude she dared confess to the breeze that she was hopelessly in love with Sean. The experience at Daisybrooke was a transition from one parallel world to another, and the new direction her life might take opened up fresh unimagined possibilities for the future. She found herself running along calling amoroso to young grass and crying with joy as though clyst gates on some tidal river had burst open, with the consummation of a longing not consciously perceived but lying submerged, dormant. She knew that at the start of an affair you never know where it will lead, one may end up at the South Pole or going round and round in circles.

As though to break her reverie there was a sudden cacophony of holloas and horn calls from a posse of animal rights activists. They raced past her, intense and sullen, hell-bent on confusing the pack with misleading calls.

Hound music signalled that the pack was coming towards them. Jubilant protesters holloaed, shouted and blew a tumult of horn calls. However, hounds were steady to their huntsman and held the line, and their pilot appeared to be heading through the fence and towards the forest. She hoped to see the fox, and remembering the day when she had ridden this way on Big Charlie led by Bridie, Flurry ran on confidently, and opened the hunting-gate leading to Lawson's Covert. A skinhead with black stubble pushed past, with two frightened-looking girls following him. Flurry felt sorry for them. Another protester with a ginger beard vaulted the fence a little further on, throwing a coke tin on the grass. Infuriated, Flurry picked it up determined to clear litter. The man turned. Then dropped his jeans in front of her, turned back, and farted in her face. Luckily a party of young farmers were tracking them and drove across the field in a Land Rover. "You alright, Flurry?"

"How does everyone know my name?"

A great peal of hound music which grew louder and louder told Flurry that hounds were near. Then she saw the pack pour like an avalanche over the wooden fence and cross the drove and towards the forest, with the treble of the Fell hounds contrasting with the deep bass, bell-like quality of the long-coated, domed-heads of the Welsh cross. Suddenly the note changed as hounds knew their fox was sinking, and success was near. She stood transfixed as the pack disappeared into the trees, when like a shadow she saw the fox flit right-handed across a path.

Hunt staff galloped round the U-shaped field losing time as they skirted the barley, now nearly five inches high, before taking the post-and-rails. The first whipper-in was despatched along the grassy drove which dropped down before making its steep ascent towards the Finger.

"Tally over, Flurry?" enquired a subscriber on point, and Flurry nodded, knowing she had earned Brownie-points, yet again, that day. Everything was right with the world.

The field Master led them over the rails with varying degrees of success, some horses being sticky, causing a couple of fallers. Robert was there with Mara now riding her Polly. Bridie jumped in mid-field. At the check, horses stood quietly while hounds hunted the covert. From her vantage point, Flurry could see Annie and Sean talking together, then after speaking to the field Master, she cantered quietly up the hill, waving 'good night'. Flurry remembered Barbarka saying that Mrs Annie was having a short day. Therefore, she would be making her way home past the *Finger* and along the ridge, before walking down the Z-Path, and home. Flurry watched as her finger grew smaller and smaller in farewell.

Being on a high, she decided to wander on slowly in the direction of Hangman's Copse and then towards the road to look for Bert. Far beyond in Lawson's Meadow the mare and foal had been shut into their field-shelter for safety. All was silent, with hounds being taken on to the next draw, leaving the terriers in the forest. Even the protesters were having a break from horn-blowing and yelling. Only a sparrow-hawk, like a harbinger of evil, hovered, pin-pointing his quarry, before the last lethal pounce on an unexpected victim.

The soft hoof-fall of a cantering horse treading larch needles was heard leaving the forest and entering Hangman's. The sound disappeared. And Flurry thought she might have imagined it. Walking past thick laurels in her green outfit she was invisible to any observer, but looking towards the Blind House with its evil reputation, she was sure she saw a horse, tethered. She waited, intrigued. Surely that was Tiger Bay, Robert's big chestnut. Two white stockings hind, and two white socks fore. The white hairs on the horse's legs shone out in the gloom. But no, it couldn't be. A big man, and one of the Charleville Blazers, being distinguished by a Barbour with a green collar and green velvet cap, was mounting the 'ringer' beside the Blind House.

"Oh well! There's always one chance in a million!"

She could not see the man's face, buried in his collar, although there was something about his appearance that bothered her. Returning home, by driving the small box with her three horses, Flurry spent the next two hours cleaning tack before going in to tea. Sean was nowhere to be seen, and Diarmid was whistling and keeping out of the way while he worked with his accustomed speed and efficiency.

As she made her way towards the house, slight snow was falling. Mara and Bridie were drinking tea at the kitchen refectory table. Both were too engrossed in Bridie's miseries concerning the state of her hair after hunting, to do more than give Flurry a perfunctory nod, so that Flurry, now thoroughly deflated, wondered why she bothered to stay and help. Even so, she was determined to keep the peace.

"I've often wondered whether putting your hair up, would look nice," she said brightly. They looked at her.

"Up?"

"Her hair isn't long enough."

"An Apollo's Knot, say. You don't need it long. Lovely for the party." They did not look convinced and Flurry thought 'It's now or never', so aloud "I'd love to try. May I?" Flurry's spirits were beginning to recover their euphoria of the day, and looking at Mara she wondered if hard work, sadness and trouble had made her employer lose her sense of humour. With no Grandfather present to supply a light touch, Mara was too serious. The fun in life had died. That glorious sense of the ridiculous, lost. Seeing her mounted on Polly that morning had shown how attractive Mara still was. Bridie being a dead weight how right Annie had proved to be to give her Lower Farm, keeping her out of everyone's hair. With a resigned "You can try if you like," and a bad grace, Bridie led the way upstairs. They sat at her dressing-table, supporting drawers so crammed with crumpled clothes that they gave up the unqual struggle and stayed half-open and half-shut. She passed Flurry a hairbrush, stretching her neck up, as though having little faith in the other's competence as a hairdresser.

Flurry combed the hair away from her forehead, to discover that Bridie had an attractive widow's peak. Then drawing the entire head of hair up to the crown, she twisted it into a hard, tight Apollo Knot. The effect was sensational. Her heavy brows appeared better defined, to be balanced by a good, strong jawline.

"How like your mother you are!" and a faint flush of pleasure suffused Bridie's face. Flurry dashed off to produce a length of orange ribbon to tie round the knot.

"Highlights the crown. No wonder Regency ladies adored the fashion."

Looking in the triple mirror Bridie surveyed her head, turning it this way and that, "You're sure. Quite sure I don't look silly?" she sighed, so that Flurry felt sorry about her lack of confidence and only said "It's up to you." And later, "What are you wearing?"

Bridie nodded in the direction of the bed on which lay a frilly creation in hard electric blue. "You don't like it. I can see you don't like it!" with annoyed desperation, "I do, Bridie. I do. Yes, I do," then taking the plunge, "I would love to see you in black. Have you something in black?"

Bridie looked amazed. "Mummy has," and with considerable doubt she brought in a plain, long, black evening gown. Mara stood in the doorway, watching.

"How fashions come back. Wait long enough and everything cycles back, diagonal neck and shoulder, slim and tight, and there must be forty buttons down the back. Kneel down and I'll do them up for you."

"The USA," Mara reminisced leaning her face on the door post and closing her eyes. "I haven't worn that gown since Alec and I went to Ottowa. He was stationed there, seconded for a two year posting on army duty, and they were fabulous years, the best of my life. They had sunshine and sailing in the summer, then winter sports . . . . ." her voice tailed away.

"What do you think Mara? Your daughter will be the belle of the ball." But she had disappeared back to her own room, making Flurry wonder if a crisis were approaching. A crisis in Mara's life, and how much longer could she look after Grandfather, now that Sean was leaving for Clavincade.

Flurry was quite relieved when the front door was closed and they were off. Snow still blew in from the west with a bitter wind. The two would enjoy the dinner at the Imperial Hotel, as Mara had arranged a large table of close friends. Bridie had no partner, however, table numbers being made up of assorted widowers, both temporary and permanent, the eternal bachelors, who are the mainstay of any social function, meant that she would have the polite dance or so. Flurry was unaware of Sean's plans for them that evening. Would they sit with Mara's party or Annie's? Or maybe a special one had been arranged. The Blazers would, as tradition demanded, be evenly split amongst the tables. Sean had not returned, as yet, although it was time for Flurry to wash her hair and get ready.

The freezing draughts in the west wing made wind-braces sob, and she decided to light her bedroom fire when bright blue flames licking split beech logs revived the euphoria of Daisybrooke Farm and the joy of her newfound feelings for Sean. She knelt on the sheepskin hearth rug and on impulse lifted down her absinthe glass to gaze through its conical shape and see the fire splintered into angles, triangles, flash-strikes and jagged edges.

'Sean will write! He will remember me at Eastertime in Ireland. New Year's Day will be hateful without him, although Mara's here and the animals. I must look to the future whatever it may bring.' Bowden's Grove had given her a home and family, love, also horses, dogs, friends and a garden, but the future might resemble an absinthe transformation the change from green to cloudy yellow, as bitter as wormwood. Living in the country troubled her because without Sean would they 'speak' to her? Besides there were so many undercurrents both here and at Broxford Court, things she could not possibly grasp. She wondered if this were a phase, an end to her life's beginnings, but that she had not learnt sufficient to see her way, as yet.

Flurry knew now she was proud of her mother, proud to be a

Londoner, with a family pedigree of craftsmen; cabinet-makers, tailors, silversmiths, goldbeaters, ship-builders and that she could hold her head high as a businesswoman. Should she return to London, however, neither work, success, fashion, design, technology nor regeneration were a panacea for all ills. She must make *time* for friends. Give herself space for love. Time for Sean, to think about him. Find their permanent feelings for each other. On the gentle air of her room she thought someone was playing *Dancing in the Dark*. Far away. Maybe from stables as you never knew with Diarmid. The melody floating in and out of an excited brain reminded her she must get ready for the dance.

Sitting at her mirror and making dozens of corkscrew curls, she knew she looked her best. Better than she could have believed possible, and the past weeks with so many happenings had been a revelation. The brightness of her eyes held a promise of both pleasure and pain for the night.

A small image of concern began as a creeping shadow across her face. Sean had not come back yet. Doubtless she would soon hear his Land Rover, as dinner was at eight-thirty, with dancing and disco at eleven. Finishing dressing in an apple-green satin gown, she put on the black velvet cloak in which she had fled from London more than nine weeks ago. The cloak was prophetic. Being so cold, she nestled into a woollen shawl.

Still no Sean. It was getting late. Puzzled, she entered the kitchen to ask Diarmid if all the horses had returned. He was sitting asleep with his head on the table, a half empty bottle of whiskey by his side, and a partially eaten bacon sandwich, still clutched in his hand. 'Poor Diarmid! Nobody thinks of him. He shall have an extra special dinner tomorrow.'

"Diarmid, wake up. Are all the horses back? And Sean's Hecuba?"

"By Saint Joseph and Saint Patrick, and what would I be doing taking a wee drop, with the horses not all fed and warm in their boxes."

"I'm sure you've done all the work marvellously. But has every horse returned. Every single one. Is Hecuba in stables?"

"And why should they not be? And me failing my duties to the poor creatures."

"You've done nothing wrong, Diarmid. I just want to know if Sean's back yet?" He sat there looking totally vague, gazing first at the whiskey and then at his sandwich. His eyes shifted, suspecting a trap.

"Maybe I'll see him. And maybe not." Flurry gave up the unequal contest, and walked into the Smoker. She looked idly at the photographs in their silver frames, and especially at the picture of Sean standing with Harry and Lady Lydia. The Smoker was very cold, the fire being out and Flurry did not want to make her gown dirty by picking up baulks of wood. She could not believe that Sean had just stood her up, nor was there reason to think that there had been an accident. The hall clock struck nine. 'There goes dinner. Why did I bother to dress? Sean you might have 'phoned.' Was there any point in waiting? She was not going to give up yet, and curled herself up in the battered blue chair, trying to get warmth from her cloak and shawl. Another hour passed. No word. No telephone. No sound.

When the long case clock struck eleven, she went upstairs, because she knew that Mara and Bridie would return early and she did not want to face them. 'Sean, I'm terribly, terribly upset. Perhaps it's as well you're going tomorrow.' She slipped into bed gasping with sudden cold and grief. She felt stunned with a brain confused, atrophied, and struggled with thoughts of affection so long and terribly desired suddenly torn from her. Flurry realised she hardly knew Sean at all and questioned her ingrained trust in him, wondering at her sudden belief that her longings might be fulfilled through him. On a more practical note surely Mara and Bridie would have returned and brought news if anything untoward had happened. Sean was probably talking to the Irish contingent, or maybe he was having too good a party on his last night, and had forgotten. Daydreams end.

After midnight she got up in the dark, to see if there were any lights in the yard. Nothing. Only hard crisp flakes of snow rattled the windowpanes, and sharp, wild, weird cracks were heard as bare larch trunks lurched against each other in the wind. She imagined she saw a flash of light, and the siren of an ambulance as it passed the white double gates. But decided she was hearing things. Then very faintly the sirens of two police cars as they passed each other. In the country, you hear things. Sounds present. Sounds past. Birds mimicking hounds. Cows giving birth, and recreating the souls of all creatures in distress. Taking a grip on her imagination she returned to bed and practised a relaxation exercise to make her sleep.

Maybe it was noise she thought she heard. Maybe the loss of Sean. Whichever way it was, Flurry dreamed she was in the tackroom. A cold tackroom, with everything frozen by frost. In the corner stood the familiar watering-can, used for wetting hay-nets, and keeping down dust. She peeped into the watering-can, seeing it to be half full of solid ice. Wedged into the ice, and barely alive, was a white cat. Rigid. Unable to move. It lay on its back, half upright, its white thighs firmly wedged into the cylindrical can. The cat's dying eyes were glazing. And from its mouth emanated one last tiny mia-ow.

Horrified, Flurry awoke. It was the tiny mia-ow! The resigned cry of death. She leapt out of bed, sickened, and stood on the cold mat. Bed and sleep were impossible now and the entire house seemed to be shaking. Its stones trembling. She threw herself into any clothes and went downstairs to the kitchen.

From sheer habit she opened the muff upon the AGA and placed the coffee percolator on the hob, idly watching as the bubbles rose and fell into its glass dome. On the table the sight of Diarmid's cap sitting on top of the empty whiskey bottle, as though in dedication, made her lift her head and stiffen her back.

"I will go to London as soon as decent," she decided. "On Monday or even Sunday night, and I'll telephone Elizabeth when it's light asking her to book me in at an hotel. I must start again. No regrets." Tears trickled down her face falling on the hotplate with steamy hisses. Bertie came to sit on her feet to comfort her. He was apprehensive. Animals know.

Before she had time to make herself strong coffee, the sound of a Land Rover driving into the yard caught her attention. A minute later came hurried steps and the door opened, bringing in a blast of cold air. Sean stood still with his naturally pale face, ashen. Torn riding clothes were covered with mud. Snow, wet with a curious rock substance had seeped into his Barbour. He was hatless.

"Annie's dead! We've been out searching for her all night!"

CHAPTER 9

The local papers had a field day and Annie was front page news.

"FORMER MFH DIES IN
TRAGIC ACCIDENT"

"Mrs Annie Bowden-Davies, of Broxford Court, was involved in a fatal accident on New Year's Eve. It is believed that her horse missed its footing during their journey home after hunting about 3 p.m., on the afternoon of last Thursday.

The accident happened on a steep incline known as the Z-Path which traverses a disused quarry and leads down to Broxford Court. Mrs Bowden-Davies was thrown and fell one hundred and fifty feet down the rock face. Both she and the horse were found dead at the bottom of the quarry, having received multiple injuries.

When the alarm was raised about 6 p.m., neither she nor her mount having returned home, a party of local farmers and neighbours searched the area. Because of the difficulty of the terrain, and the effects of a heavy snowstorm, Mrs Bowden-Davies was not found until the early hours.

She is survived by her husband, Mr Robert Davies, there being no direct descent. Messages of condolence have been received from all over the British Isles."

The *Broxford Chronicle* gave a front page spread together with several photographs of Annie. Also of the quarry where the body was found, and the supposed direction of the fall.

"DEATH OF MRS ANNIE BOWDEN-DAVIES
LOCAL JP KILLED IN RIDING ACCIDENT

A much loved figure in the community, Mrs Bowden-Davies's family is one of the oldest in Wiltshire. Intensely public spirited she served on many committees, including the Hospital of St. John of Jerusalem, as well as being noted for her work on the County Council, where her forthright views will be sorely missed."

However, the *Bath Evening Messenger* screamed in its leading article:

"How can an experienced horse and rider fall off a forty foot wide road? This newspaper has grave doubts as to the cause of this accident.

Claims that the horse slipped and plunged with its rider to their deaths have been attacked by her cousin, Mrs. Mara Bowden-Hesketh. "It was not snowing when my cousin turned for home. The weather was fine and dry."

And why, we ask, did Mrs Bowden-Davies not slip the safety catch on her saddle and dismount, if she were in trouble?

Why did it take so long to find her? Did it take twelve hours to muster lights from cars and tractors to search the quarry floor and find horse and rider lying locked together? But why spend so long searching the forest? Did someone suspect foul play?

The matter must not be allowed to rest here. We demand a full public investigation."

The house felt like a morgue, with Mara keeping to her room, totally inconsolable, Sean worked like a maniac in stables and then disappeared. Maybe he slept there and except for the disappearance of a loaf of bread he did not seem to eat. Diarmid having returned with the Charleville Blazers three days previously, Bert spent more and more time cleaning tack, so that Flurry felt she was unwelcome in the yard.

Only Bridie detached herself completely from the family. The moment after morning exercise and evening feeding, she was off on her motorbike to Lower Farm. Since Annie had given the house to her fully furnished, she took up permanent residence there, and seemed to signify that she wanted no more to do with anyone.

This left Flurry in charge of the house. The desire to live and work was just as strong in Flurry, even in the presence of death, and especially as they were not able to hold Annie's funeral until after the inquest.

The inquest was held five days later in the old courthouse near the Town Hall in the local market town. The courtroom was packed, the Coroner being a local solicitor. The journalists sat at a table at the back, as the circumstances of Annie's death was of wide interest, and reached the quality national newspapers, which gave a balanced and objective account of the proceedings.

London, Thursday, January 7

A distinguished former MFH fell to her death in curious circumstances on New Year's Eve, an inquest heard. The coroner, Mr. Arthur Brown, sitting at Chipperford, recorded a verdict of death by misadventure, saying that Mrs Annie Bowden-Davies turned for home after hunting at about 3 p.m.

The day was fine and dry, in spite of a later fall of snow. When she failed to return by 5.30 pm, her husband Mr Robert Davies became concerned and sent a party out to look for her by tracing her expected way home along the causeway known as the Z-Path and by the edge of Lawson's Forest.

Finding no trace of horse or rider he alerted the police and a full scale search was initiated. Fearing that she might have been thrown, and the horse bolted, the forest was systematically searched by a cordon of police and helpers. Mrs Bowden-Davies's relative, Mr Sean O Callaghan, recalled: 'It was difficult and frustratingly slow work, hampered by falling snow and in complete darkness, to force a way through the trees and thick undergrowth.'

In the early hours and finding nothing, the search was concentrated on the quarry below the Z-Path. Lit by tractors and 4-wheel drive vehicles, the ring of light closed in on the quarry floor. The snowstorm was intense, and it was not until 4 am that Mrs Bowden-Davies's body was found with her horse, completely buried in snow, both having sustained multiple injuries which caused their deaths.

Referring to both a doctor's and a vet's report, the coroner said there was nothing to suggest either rider or horse had suffered any illness or irregularity that might have contributed to the accident. Nor is robbery or foul play suspected. In spite of unfounded local rumours, the accident remains a mystery.

Mr Brown expressed his gratitude to all those who attended to give evidence. Also the sympathy of the court was extended to Mrs. Bowden-Davies's family for her tragic and unexpected death."

To give herself a break from the mourning atmosphere, Flurry decided to go shopping in Broxford, since there was no food in the larder. It was a wonderful relief to motor down the drive and leave the wrought-iron gates behind. They were still tied up with binder-twine.

She filled up the Traveller with petrol, and bought provisions paying with her own money, as Mara was too agitated to help, and she did not want to beard Sean in the yard during his time of despair. With the last cardboard box loaded on the back seat, she was delighted to see Dolly crossing the road towards her. "Dolly, I am glad!"

"I didn't like to come up. Looked like I was pushing in, but if I can do anything. Anything at all. At anytime. Just say the word and give me a ring. We're all thinking of you. Nobody can quite believe it."

"Such a relief to see people again. Normal people, I mean, and Dolly, I do need a friend to talk to."

"Let's go for a coffee at Kosy Kaf, it's not very good, but homely. We'll see the Major there, as he always goes in the morning. Since his wife died he's lonely, poor lamb, and likes to see his friends. We have to hold each other up."

The Kaf, with its linoleum and paper tablecloths looked smaller but livelier than when she had alighted from the nightmare coach. Today she noticed the owner's heavenly smile of welcome, the tea urn still fizzed steam, the coffee smelt good, and there were sticky buns which appealed to Dolly.

"I've been promised this job in London and said I'd go back yesterday. Now look what's happened! Everyone seems disjointed. Almost as though, if I were to go . . . . . they'd fall apart. Perhaps I'm exaggerating. What gets me is not *knowing*. Grandfather is coming home. When? No-one knows. Mara I can understand, because she's overworked and at the end of her tether. Annie was her prop, and now she's gone. And they're all slaving away over the funeral.

It's up to Bridie, it really is. She gets everything she goes for.

Everyone's as wax in her hands. Still let that go. She has her farm, horses and she's not bad looking. Not really. But she's so selfish, won't do a thing to help. She hasn't the sense to value or understand people. Take Sean. She just likes to have him around, at times I don't think she's sincere even about him. She just uses everyone. Then there are the solicitors. They keep coming and going every day, spending hours and hours in the dining-room with the family. I do think they might say something. Sean seems to be staying on. But is he? It's not knowing."

Dolly's nostrils flared. "Sean?" Flurry nodded. "They do say. But it's not for me to gossip."

"What? I'm not with you?" Flurry looked perplexed.

"I'd better not say."

"Help if you did."

"Another time perhaps." Dolly helped herself to a second sticky bun. "Look, here's the Major. All you can do is live one day at a time."

The tall figure of Barbarka obliterated light from the glass door. The Major held it open and helped her carry in two enormous suitcases.

"I can not stay. I can not."

"You don't mean you've carried those the whole way from the Court?"

Barbarka nodded. "Oh! You did! Why on earth didn't you ring?"

She shook her head, and the Major showed signs of impatience. "We haven't had our coffee yet. What about these ladies?"

"Had ours . . . . ."

"Two coffees please. And Barbarka, *please* sit down. I don't know what's the matter but you make us weary looking at you."

"I am not wanted."

"Rubbish! Take no notice of him," from Dolly. "He's tetchy this morning."

"Why can't you stay!"

"He's sold Mrs. Annie's little birds! Madame not buried in her grave and he's sold them. The dealer came with a van this morning, went into the cage and caught Mrs Annie's birds. All of them. I heard them crying."

"Birds don't cry."

"S-sh."

"They cried. I heard them. The man packed them into cages and put them into the van. Then drove off. 'Why did you sell them, Mr Davies?' He just laughed. I can *not* stay. And look . . . ." She took a handkerchief from her pocket. "And look!" She opened it out. "All of Mrs Annie's little birds, from the cage for the last time." A current of air stirred the tiny pile of blue, red, green, yellow and white baby feathers, so that they floated into the air over the table, fluttering up towards the ceiling.

Standing on the pavement outside the cafe, Flurry asked, "Have you visited Grandfather today, Major?"

"Funny you should say that. Seems to have recovered his onions completely. Very weak of course. But compos mentis, y'know. Can't wait to come home." He blew out his cheeks, considering the matter. "Claims it was Robert who hit him!"

"Robert?"

"Yes. Strange isn't it? Said he was going towards the motorway in a devil of a hurry. Terrific speed. Couldn't take the corner. Only the vegetable trug saved him." He paused then went on. "First Bowden. Then Mrs. Annie. Don't know what to make of it. Strange. Strange, Reckon Barbarka has a point."

Flurry had to have time to think and wandered towards the small stone bridge over the river. 'It *was* Robert,' she thought. 'I *was* right. At Heathrow, I knew Robert passed the coach. If he went to Cornwall, he would have driven the other way and not hit Grandfather. And if the Major says it was Robert who hit him, what will the rest of the district think?'

Steep hills, fold on fold, stood across the river, where sheep clinging to almost vertical pasture, and looking like cottonwool buds, grazed alongside strips of kale planted to encourage pheasant. Over the distant hill, a hunting horn could be heard and presently the small box, driven by Bert, came steadily along the road towards her on its way home. Bert waved.

"My box! The small box! That's my box. Why didn't they ask me?" To Flurry, her whole position at Bowden's Grove was being called into question. Until now, she assumed that it was her decision whether she should go or stay. But had she a place there at all? Was it an illusion that she was needed? Maybe no-one cared anyway. Or they might not want her? The fresh thought was a shock, and also an unpleasant possibility. Understandably, Sean had not come indoors or spoken to her for days. He had a lot on his mind. Besides no-one could do anything until after Annie's funeral and the effect of her death had been so devastating that Flurry found it difficult to grasp, especially with regard to Sean. Before New Year's Eve he had decided to return to Ireland. Then Annie died. Were the two events connected? And what was the position now?

Annie's funeral service and burial was to take place at the small church of St Mary Magdalene as no-one could bear the thought of a sanitised cremation. Flowers were arriving by the cart load, Annie's Will already bequeathing a considerable amount to charity, people believed that the scent of flowers were for the comfort of the living more than the quiet dead. Flurry went to the church to take the names of those who sent flowers, and she looked up at the picturesque tower circa 1300 with its bell-opening and Y-tracery. The impressive porch she knew was given by the Bowden family in memory of King Charles the Martyr, while within, she smiled at carved bench-ends depicting mediaeval scenes, including one of a fox dressed as a Bishop, preaching to a flock of birds. A card said they commemorated a bitter feud of the parish with its worthy Bishop.

The churchyard was sombre with yew and cypress trees. Many of the table-tombs were collapsing, with slipped sides, revealing cramped vaults where families lay buried.

Bert was helping the verger dig the six-foot deep grave, down into clay and rock, while rain drizzled in dreary misery. The last of the snow had turned to slush. The verger had steel-rimmed glasses and a stutter and he and Bert were at school together forty years previously. They spread out the green artificial grass sheet to cover sliding mud with the usual carping banter of close neighbours.

Cordial relations between Bowden's Grove and the Court had been maintained for the sake of appearances during the past week, with the order of service sheets being organised by Robert and Mara and despatched for printing. Funeral arrangements became a joint effort. It kept everyone sane, at least at Bowden's Grove, as well as in answering the hundreds of letters of sympathy received from friends and acquaintances.

On the day of the funeral it poured with rain and the wind tore through the cypresses on the church path, ripping apart vertical branches and making the verger weep at the mess. The tenor bell was ringing as the Brigade Colour of St. John Ambulance was carried into church, followed by representatives of the County Council. The church was packed, the aisles a solid crush, and the oak doors leading to the tower were opened to keep more people out of the rain. Even so, a silent phalanx of locals guarded the path as Annie's coffin was borne into St. Mary's accompanied by the Bowden family. Some distant cousins had flown over from Ireland, together with an ancient relative from the Peak district.

It was only someone of Sean's sensitivity who could have chosen the indefinable nuances of the *Londonderry Air* as a setting to the first hymn, symbolically joining north to southern Ireland and thence to Wiltshire. The congregation was amazed and there were a few heads nodding in knowing comprehension. Previously there had been raised eyebrows when the family seated themselves in front of the pulpit, as Robert sat with Bridie in the front pew. Mara sat behind with Grandfather in a wheelchair, together with Sean and the cousins.

Flurry was jam-packed into a four-seater box-pew with the Three

Musketeers and Barbarka, Bert being one of the bearers. In the congregation, many ladies wore black, the blackest-black, surprising in those secular days. And there were grand hats too, in honour of the funeral. Even Mara had hired one from the local hat shop because a hunt country makes a lot of the etiquette of respect for such occasions.

Robert was his most obsequious self during the prayers, helping Bridie to find the correct page. The rector gave the eulogy and many of the congregation wept genuine tears. Mara was too heavily sedated to feel emotion, while Grandfather portrayed a soldier's stoicism. Only Sean saw a ghost.

The aisles had to be cleared of people before Annie could be carried towards her grave. A cross of pink carnations, her favourite flower, bore the giver's name as Sean Rory O Callaghan, as though in communion between quick and dead. The rector read the sentences from St John, Job and Timothy from the 1662 prayer book. Nothing was cut out by church or family. It was expected.

Standing in the churchyard, even the dogs-in-cars, the subsidiary pack of all country people, did not bark. The cars were parked in an adjoining field and continuous rain beat on metal roofs to give a sound of muffled drums. Everyone came to the graveside. They stood, heads bared, seven-deep in a hollow square, beneath blue-and-white umbrellas, reminiscent of a dozen race-meetings. Unseasonable daffodils still in bud looked on peeping between huge clumps of snowdrops.

Only Robert and Bridie sprinkled earth on Annie's coffin. The others stood apart, Sean resolute and shaking his head, as though this were unfinished business. The Master of Hounds blew a double recheate, the huntsman's farewell, at the side of the grave and Dolly tried to pacify Barbarka. Then she started to scream and the Major held an umbrella over the au-pair to hide her face. The congregation shuffled, embarrassed, to break ranks. Robert, holding Bridie's hand, walked towards the church path.

Barbarka broke loose, dashing up to Robert and shaking her fist. She towered over him so that off-guard he fell back.

"Murderer!" she screamed. "Mrs Annie, you killed her. Murder! . . . . murder!"

Flurry looked from one person to another and then to the corporate face of the countryside swinging into action. Is this when they 'speak' to each other? She could feel, like prickly heat under her skin, a corporate identity, with people seemingly welded together to think and act as one as though they knew what was going to happen before it finally did.

"Tea is the normal finale to the funeral," whispered Dolly. "You mayn't go without tea. It's thought unkind not to go, being like a wake to comfort the family who feel thoroughly let down, and at a loose end."

Flurry heard whispers flying from mouth to mouth. She caught only fragments of conversation but it seemed that Barbarka's explosion was no more than an expression of corporate understanding. A consensus of opinion. They looked smug, nodding their heads, and she was reminded of that evening at the old White Horse Inn when a sudden dawning of understanding came to Robert. And a glass smashed. But the immediate difficulty seemed to be 'tea'. A thorny problem. Dolly looked worried.

"Is it Broxford Court or Bowden's Grove?" she confided softly. "We don't seem sure!"

Dogs on leads jumped from cars and lifted their legs, before a good bark-up. Then a Range Rover driven by a stout lady in uniform drove slowly round the field and Dolly trotted across. They conferred. On driving off again other cars followed in a hearty rush not to be left behind. Uncertain, the cavalcade made towards the bridge, then still following, turned left-handed taking the Range Rover's lead, past the hairpin, past the gates where Grandfather was nearly killed, and did not stop until they reached those metal gates which were tied back with binder twine. Then they made a careful way up the drive to Bowden's Grove.

It was eleven o'clock before the family went to bed, and gloom settled into the old house once more. Flurry was not ready for sleep, and sat up in bed with her note pad, to write to Elizabeth with the latest news. First she described the funeral and Barbarka's outburst.

"I am still shocked, and just don't know what to think. Murders don't happen to ordinary people like us, and I'm sure Barbarka was just overwrought. During the past week it never dawned on me that it was other than a tragic accident. Obviously everybody else seems to know a great deal more about it than I do.

And then, Elizabeth, there was the tea! Sometimes I'm just thankful that we're more modern in London. How country fashions, country-ages-old-customs cling, are they or us real?

They all came back here to Bowden's Grove. Heaven only knows how many, the drive was packed with cars, and Bert had to open the gates into the paddock. I was devastated, it had never dawned on me that people would return for tea! We had simply done nothing about it. And then the country swung into action.

Dolly must have guessed, when we met at Kosy Kaf that day, that there would be a problem, because I exploded to her about Bridie and everybody being flat on their backs. How do country women manage to make dozens of cakes, biscuits, sandwiches and filled rolls, and even know where the cups and plates are kept at Bowden's Grove? She just said she got up early, and made the things before her brood wanted their breakfast, and were sent off to school with packed lunches. Dolly did add as an afterthought that the ladies of St John Ambulance helped with cakes.

I disgraced myself utterly, because I fell asleep in the big leather chair in the dining-room, in spite of all the noise and everyone talking at once. It was like a lullaby! When I came to, the kitchen was immaculate. Even the glass cloths had been washed and were hanging up to dry by the AGA, with the dogs and house-cats all fed. Dear Dolly and Co.

And that wasn't the end of it! We were just going up to bed when Grandfather (he's back now. He returned with us after the funeral), Grandfather said 'Where's Mara?' We looked everywhere, all over the house and finally found she had fallen down those dreadful back stairs, she'd tripped and knocked herself out — but OK now.

So Elizabeth you see how things are." Flurry sucked the end of her pen like she did at school when puzzled and did not know what to write. She chose her words carefully. "I think I must return to London. I have to earn a living. I love being here but there's no real opening as far as I can see, although must stay and help for a day or two. Will phone tomorrow with news.

Love,
Flurry."

Feeling much more relaxed and rested she got up later than usual. She walked downstairs to put the letter to Elizabeth in the rack for the post. The postman always arrived bringing morning letters and if he were early took a cup of tea in the kitchen before collecting any house mail. She was surprised to hear the sound of a car, rather than a van, retreating down the drive.

Meantime Sean at the front door was saying thank you to the doctor for calling to see Mara so promptly and also for his advice, before continuing on morning rounds. Although Sean knew he must say goodbye to sorrow and mourning, as Annie would hate any sign of weakness, there were many problems. His must be an over-riding quest, a consuming passion to solve the mystery of her death. As regards Mara, the doctor was adamant that she should go away on holiday, otherwise he predicted a complete mental breakdown. Grandfather and Bridie he could deal with. But then there was Flurry and he was delighted to see her on the steps, a letter in one hand.

Smiling, Sean stretched out his hands, to kiss her on both cheeks. He was unaware of how like Annie he was, as though he had taken on her mantle within the guise of her mannerisms and he could see pleasure written all over Flurry's face. He must be careful. Careful not to hurt her, being unsure of his feelings within turmoil. He knew he respected her for loyalty, courage and controlled emotions. "I didn't forget you! I would have phoned but no-one had a car phone. Then we found Annie."

They stood for a minute. "Thank you for all you're doing here. It's most appreciated." A weak sun came out to brighten the arch of rusty larch trees, now yawning and awakening to spring, while the grass edge to the drive was white with thousands of snowdrops. Somewhere a lark sang, way, way up, in pale cloud.

Bridie drove to the house on her motorbike from Lower Farm.

He called out "Come in! At once. We've got to decide now!"

"You're not boss," she muttered.

"You shouldn't shout at Bridie," from Flurry.

"You be wanting a thick ear!" Flurry laughed at him.

They went into the kitchen, to find on the well-scrubbed refectory table a clean cloth covering a jar of home-made marmalade, fresh-baked bread, some eggs and a message in Dolly's school-child hand. "Bacon and clotted cream in the fridge. Love D."

"How kind. How very, very kind."

Grandfather was sitting by the AGA wearing his dressing-gown. "I can't find my trousers. Where've they put my trousers? I can't find anything."

"Grandfather, what are you doing out of bed?"

"I couldn't find my trousers. Not hanging in their usual place, always hang them in one place. Always have."

"Ever since you were out of Africa."

"Any more 'cat' Bridie?" from Flurry.

"I thought you were going back to town."

"I am."

"How can I cook breakfast if I haven't my trousers."

"And isn't it myself that's cooking the breakfast?" When working Sean slipped back into the vernacular.

"These pyjamas fall down."

"These eggs'll burn. I'll help you in a few minutes." Sean was an efficient cook.

"What do you want Sean? Decide what?" Bridie interrupted.

"Your mother. She must go on holiday."

"Who says?"

"The doctor. Don't prevaricate."

"Where? Where do you suggest?" from Flurry. "Grandfather have you any ideas?"

"Strawberry fields."

"Ye Gods!" snapped Bridie.

"Strawberry fields and Cheddar cheese."

"He's bonkers!"

"Listen."

"Fairbrother . . . . . Dick . . . . . no, that was his brother Charles. That's it. Charlie Fairbrother, a Major when we went out to Haifa. Took the horses all across France by train. It was wartime, y'know, and then ship to Haifa."

"Yes, Grandfather." Flurry knelt down beside him. "You said Cheddar, darling."

"Yes. Yes, I forgot. I'm just a stupid old man."

"Mara. What has Mara to do with Cheddar?"

"That's the girl!" Sean looked approvingly at her eager face, and glorious colouring.

"Muriel. Dick Fairbrother . . . . . no, it was Charlie. Charlie Fairbrother's daughter Muriel. They used to stay together in Cheddar at their farm and pick strawberries. Haven't seen Mu for years. She inherited it from Charles y'know."

"She still lives there then?" Flurry asked quietly.

"Married. What's her name? Bridie, what's Auntie Mu's name, child."

"McGregor. And she isn't my aunt, she's godmother."

"Knew it was. Fetch the address book, girl."

"If Mummy goes away, who's going to look after Grandfather?"

"You are!" Sean was feeling mad.

"I have the farm. *She is!*"

"By Jesus. Fetch the address book will you!"

The address book found, Sean spoke to Muriel using his usual Celtic charm, and she was delighted to have Mara to stay. The family then settled down to breakfast.

"And who's going to drive her down?"

"I will if it helps. That is so long as the Traveller stays together."

There was little difficulty in persuading Mara to go and stay at Cheddar, she was thrilled at the prospect of holidays with Mu. Flurry and Bridie packed, and putting Bertie the Jack Russell on the back seat, they waved goodbye to Bowden's Grove.

"Brilliant. Brilliant, you really are. I can't believe it! What would we do without you!" The little car puffed and panted along the M4 motorway with Flurry keeping to the inside lane near the hard shoulder in case of trouble. They negotiated the transition from M4 to M5 successfully towards Junction 21, and looking at the road signs Flurry realised that this was the exit for Weston-super-Mare, and was intrigued to remember how childhood holidays had brought her to Broxford.

Mara piloted them through Sidcot and Axbridge and on to the Somerset levels, infusing Flurry with her own excitement by telling stories of schoolgirl memories. The restaurant where they enjoyed cream teas, the streams where they hunted crayfish, were joyfully pointed out, until Flurry had the heartfelt realisation that she could enjoy Mara's teenage reminiscences without grief. At Bowden's Grove she had come to terms with the turmoil of her lonely youth, and learnt to respect Mother, and to have pride in her EastEnder family.

Muriel McGregor's farm lay in a south-facing combe sheltered by the Mendip Hills. Cheddar red soil of strawberry fields looked as though they were combed into the hillsides, although the miles of polythene tunnels were not yet in place for early fruit.

Flurry refused lunch as she was still concerned about the roadworthiness of the Traveller, and with Bertie bouncing up and down on the back seat, she made her way to Axbridge. She had to look at the narrow streets, where she and mother had wandered during their coach trip from Weston. And surely they had bought ice cream near King John's hunting lodge. Across the road a used car saleroom caught her attention. "Why do I put up with this ghastly Traveller?" she said. "I'll buy myself a little car."

Sports cars brought back memories of Harry, but there was a nice, small, grey Peugeot 205 which attracted her, with the price well within her means. Production of her driving licence, and after a telephone call to the bank manager, Flurry found herself test-driving the Peugeot along sandy roads once covered by salt-marsh. Seagulls followed her, the smell of salt was everywhere, and the Bristol Channel drew her in quiet excitement to the A370 towards Weston-super-Mare. Strangely nothing was familiar. Although Westlands aeroplane factory was the same, she was amazed at the extent of the industrial estates, also, the road took her to the western end of the seaside resort, rather than to the centre of town.

Then she saw the tower of Uphill church on its low eminence. How small it looked, how shrunk it appeared. Only sea-blasted fir trees, bent and distorted by wind, appeared in tune with the brave, tiny, mediaeval church, calling fisherfolk to prayer and sympathy.

Flurry drove the car onto Uphill beach. Bertie whimpered to chase along the brown sand, excitedly sniffing the heavenly sea-salt smells mingled with shells, fish and the play of other dogs, horses, gulls and cormorants which is so fascinating to both town and country dogs. To the west she could see Burnham Bay behind Brean Down, where she and Mother had walked day after happy day. Uphill village was cheaper than Weston town, and the lodgings more economical.

The January day was pale grey, with mist obliterating South Wales, before merging into a Payne's grey sea. The tide was far out, its muddy low tide-line being edged with a black band. She took the dog to see a sea-worn, driftwood tree, beaten into a sea-serpent and sat on its nose, its tail furling gracefully behind her, while Bertie paddled and looked for sand-worms.

"Why do I sit here, relaxed. Happy?" she said to the distant pier, its white super-structure standing on black iron legs.

Scraps of conversation lingered on the mist. 'I didn't forget you.' 'Thank you for being here. Appreciated.' 'That's the girl!' 'I can't find my trousers.' 'Who's going to look after Grandfather?' 'Brilliant you really are.' Bertie swung round on his lead, frantic to meet a lady Westie Terrier.

'How can I leave now. Or should I go? TorrTechTron will get fed up and find another executive, it's a wonderful chance. Do any of us women know?' she ruminated, thinking of Sean. 'What do we really want? We have freedom to choose what we want to do, but we choose not to choose in so many cases, because are we any better off. Have we destroyed our true function?' She wondered if her love for Sean was only an illusion.

A faded photograph of a soldier in uniform floated like a hologram across the sand. Flurry had found it in Mother's handkerchief drawer but never dared to ask who the man was. Mother must have loved and lost. Perhaps that was her fate too, and the idea of 'last times' took hold of her. Last family breakfasts. No more dogs with pleading eyes. Last rides, even the loss of tack to clean. No wonder the sacrament of 'The Last Things' held such mortal dread. 'I must stay on just once more, Mother. Only a little while. A little longer,' she pleaded, 'or I'll regret it for the rest of my life.'

Flurry's car was delivered a few days later to the admiring looks of everyone in the stable yard.

"Mus' o' won Lottery!"

"Nice to have rich friends."

Bert rubbed the numberplate with his finger. "YC number."

"YC?"

"Exmoor. Where I was born to. All YCs."

"I bought her in Axbridge."

"Still Zomerset."

"Oh! I see. Yes, of course. The registration number. I'll look in the logbook. It'll say where the last owner lived."

"Up to Exford. That's Exmoor."

"So I'm Exmoor now, am I. Same as you."

"Exford always do have YC."

CHAPTER 10

For nearly a week Robert had been unable to sleep, and spent hour after hour sitting in the artificial leather armchair in his study. With its everyday office furniture, the room was the only one in which he felt comfortable. He even kept the light shining from his anglepoise lamp to keep the shadows away, and the directed light played on his wall-shelves, containing a series of plastic wood boxes, with files, books, a plate decorated to resemble a carousel, a sailing vessel, compact discs and a model of the Tower of Pisa.

After Annie's death, the chirruping and twittering of her birds had played on his nerves like screechowls, and now that Barbarka had taken umbrage and left, the Court was completely empty of life. Even the flower arrangements, so dear to his wife, had withered and been thrown away by the daily cleaners.

His hand rested on documents spread out on his desk. He could not believe what he read and for days he had re-read those parchment sheets over and over again. It was not credible. For months past he had realized that life with Annie had soured, and guessed that divorce was possible. However, immediately before Annie's death, he believed the danger had passed at any rate for the time after their long passionate conversation in that blasted conservatory. Damn those birds again!

God knows he had borne it as long as he could. If only she had been reasonable. Imprisonment at Broxford Court, bound in chains by the estate, the estate workers, country friends and country ways was a life sentence. He had never been one of them, and it was as if he were hanged on a tree and left there to rot.

It was that broken glass on the stone floor of the White Horse, when he saw Sean for what he was. What he really was. That evening, the realization had come to him like the conversion of Saul on the road to Damascus.

Then he had flipped.

There had always been periods when he was not really sure what was real and what was imaginary, however, these documents written in crabbed legal phrases were real enough. Annie had disinherited him, given him a mere pittance under her Will, and tied him to Broxford Court, which he hated. All because of Sean. Blind! Blind! He'd always prided himself on his perception and his quick interpretation of unfolding events, but they had tricked him. Been too quick for him. It was impossible to comprehend the enormity of the insult.

Wearily working over these thoughts for the hundredth time, he could only see one slender chance of making the best of his impossible predicament.

His own London solicitors had already briefed counsel to challenge

Annie's Will. It was to be expected that Colonel Bowden and his daughter, Mara, would be given handsome legacies, also that Annie had left a great deal to charity, together with the gift of their cottages to her estate tenants. This was in Annie's nature. Everyone knew of her generosity and her gifts to the county. But the residue! The ultimate beneficiaries! Surely she must have been unduly influenced? Something ruthless had to be done. In the meantime, his wife's early demise meant that death duties would be massive, and his best hope was to wait and see, to give himself time to watch and manipulate. Time was of the essence, he greedily conceded.

The solicitors were also employing land agents to explore the legality of Robert being able to let the Court, together with its land, to a rich and valued client who wished for a country retreat. It was a beautiful house and elegantly furnished, and had been equipped by Annie to the highest standard. This would give him a further income and enable him to live abroad. Perhaps ways-and-means could be arranged for a trade-off between opposing interests.

And yet. And yet. There was a way. Perhaps a slender chance, but an undoubted possibility. For the moment all he could do was wait, and exploit favourable circumstances at the appropriate time.

Leaving the anglepoise light to burn all night, he walked into the hall. Above, the outline of the skirting lights illuminated twin staircases, with their brass rails and filigree ironwork balustrades. Large prestigious pictures of scenes from country life decorated the fifty-foot high walls, while the pedestals for flowers stood empty and unadorned. The glow of soft lights spoke of safety to welcome guests of the house, but to Robert the lights were a restriction.

To a maverick such as he, these lights delineated a strictly controlled path, and recalled to him the wooden bars of his childhood cot. One nightlight fractured his nursery gloom. Beyond lay forbidden curiosity.

Deep in reverie, the insistent ringing of the telephone brought Robert back to the present. 'F*****' it was the third time today that his private line had rung and he knew exactly who it would be. Julie Baker! It was those f***** journalists' fault splashing Annie's death across the tabloids. He'd known it was inevitable but he wasn't going to answer, as he feared people he had used. Something had to be done, as he realized he was on a downward curve, and he must abort one plan before conceiving another. The woman Julie had served her purpose even though her child had not persuaded Annie to forget divorce proceedings. Now she was dead he was in a worse position than before. Surely Julie must realize it was pointless to try and blackmail him. She had been paid off, and that was that. He walked upstairs to his spartan bedroom to lie down but not to sleep.

It was Bridie, riding her bike from Lower Farm to the Grove before breakfast, who saw the white van first. It was standing by the paddock gate, and two men unloading fence posts and wire were stacking them for use.

"What are you doing, chaps? We haven't asked for a fence."

"Mr Davies's order. He said to fence off your paddock, leaving a three metre pathway from gate to your yard."

"*Who* said?"

"Mr Davies, Broxford Court."

"Rubbish. It's nothing to do with him. There's a mistake. I'll see Mr O Callaghan."

Sean phoned Robert's land agents. They confirmed that, because their client was anxious to let the Court together with its land, they must end the present arrangement whereby Bowden's Grove had made use of a hundred acres of the Court's land comprising Home Paddock and Lawson's Meadow. The agent pointed out that there was no formal agreement between Annie and Colonel Bowden. No tenancy was in place. And no rent had ever been paid. It was a grace-and-favour grass-let, which could be concluded at any time.

Sadly Grandfather had to concede that the agents were correct. Originally there had been a gentleman's agreement between himself and his brother Julian, after Bowden's Grove land was sold, that they could use the land for stock. Annie had merely honoured her father's arrangements.

Grandfather knew that his friend Henry Payne, the solicitor, was a worried man when he called to see him. They went together into the dining room.

Henry tapped the tips of his fingers together. "I warned Annie, that I was uneasy and could see terrible problems arising. Litigation is out of the question both from the view of expense, time, and the ambiguity of any outcome. Robert has the tenancy of Broxford Court, including land and other property. As Annie's husband we are unable to eject him — as at present."

"But isn't there a clause prohibiting him sub-letting?" asked Colonel Bowden.

"I fear not." The solicitor shook his head. "The Trust Fund was set up in haste, and was ill-thought out. I could see difficulties at the time but Annie was insistent. Light a fire and no-one knows what'll go up in flames." The two sat in silence. "However we have time. The Will has to be proved and death duties paid by whatever means we can. Either the Court or the land may have to be sacrificed ..... so there is room for compromise. We don't know what's in Robert's mind."

"Strange chap! Bad business" agreed the Colonel. "He hates the

Court, always has done. But it's Bridie, she's the one I'm worried sick over. What about her? Annie gave her Lower Farm with the promise that rates, insurance and services would be paid. Now where's she to find the money with nothing coming in? *I* haven't any."

"Everything's in the melting-pot. And although I hate the expression horse-trading ..... in the circumstances ..... we'll see ....."

Talking over lunch the family worried that with only a few acres remaining to them at Bowden's Grove, together with the orchard for old Jenny, what were they to do with the horses? There was insufficient grass or exercise paddocks. In the long run, due to future changed circumstances, it would be possible to buy land in the near vicinity and construct extra stabling. In the short term it was disaster.

They were reduced to riding out on exercise all the morning. Sean led two, with Flurry riding Big Charlie, and leading two, being sandwiched between Sean and Bert with his two behind her. Even Barbarka, who was staying with Dolly, was pressed into service. Exuding merriment and many high-pitched giggles, Barbarka brought up the rear, riding one and leading one. Bridie was rarely seen. She was rapidly becoming more and more useless in stables, so that Sean warned her that he could not pay her wages. During the afternoons, on non-hunting days, they were in the ludicrous position of boxing the remaining hunter liveries to a friendly farmer who had suitable meadows at the end of the village. Bert drove his pick-up behind the big box to carry extra head-collars, NZ rugs and emergency oil-drums, *because the truck was known to leak oil.* Patters sat on top of Bert's dinner and the hay-nets. It was easier for him to drive straight to the meadows, while Sean parked at the entrance of a narrow lane. Then he and Flurry unloaded and led the hunters a hundred yards to the field. Flurry began to understand how Mara felt when she described the house as *chaos,* before Flurry arrived to lend a hand. The Colonel was getting stronger every day, and with his indomitable spirit, he insisted on doing most of the cooking. His beloved garden became sadly neglected, and Flurry vowed she would never leave until she had weeded it thoroughly for dear Grandfather.

Meanwhile Robert was making a special study of the times that Bridie rode backwards and forwards to her farm, as she was the key to his future. After Annie's death and her unexpected Will leaving him a virtual 'pauper' he had to work to change things to his advantage. He and Bridie must get to know one another better. Often she journeyed two or three times a day, and Robert guessed that the girl had become restless and how well he understood her predicament! This made her unable to stay in one place for long, and he never saw her go out hunting, maybe it had lost its charm! As yet, he was not to know that she had begun to hate horses!

130

From his vantage point in the second-floor front bedroom once occupied by Barbarka, Robert using binoculars, could watch the small bridge which crossed the Byebrooke. He always had a strange premonition of other worlds, and the au pair's room haunted him, especially as a string of dried out berries, nuts and seeds, prepared for Annie's little birds, hung like an invocation near the window. Robert turned his back on it, unable to touch the string, or throw it away.

Each morning, each evening and sometimes at lunchtime, Robert could see Bridie pass and re-pass the bridge on her phut-phut motorcycle. He was fascinated by the girl. Having predicted her movements correctly he decided to take his walk at these selected times. At first he merely raised his cap and smiled. Next day he waved 'good morning' so that by the following evening they stopped for a chat. Very soon afterwards he bought her a pile of *Country Life* magazines, which he knew she couldn't afford for herself. And it was not long before he heard with secret amusement Bridie's troubles with Surtees.

"It's Sean, of course, he says Surtees is my horse and I must look after him. I already have my mare and foal, and Mummy's Polly, which means I haven't enough land at Lower Farm. But Sean is adamant, and he's Lord God Almighty in Mummy and Grandfather's eyes."

"But my dear, how simple!" with a click-click of reassurance. "Bring him to me. Since I sold my hunters, except for Tiger Bay, the groom has precious little to do except lounge about."

One evening Flurry went into the kitchen to find Sean fast asleep in his chair. His tea, completely untouched, still lay on the table. 'How tired he looks' she thought, and sat down quietly in the Windsor chair with its sack cushion. She rested by the plates, dishes and saucepans threaded on massive wooden plate-racks and left to dry over the AGA by Grandfather, while Tweedles the cat with one eye, jumped on her lap, as he had done when she first met Robert. Flurry remembered crying with cold and loneliness, as though bereft.

Now her problems were different. She had taken this family on board as her own, and her energies were directed in helping Bowden's Grove get over its troubles. Who bothered that the kitchen was beginning to look distinctly grubby and back to its slovenly usual self! Deep down she realized that the immediate problems of the horses, Mara and Bridie were mere pinpricks soon to be resolved. There were other hidden meanings that she could only guess at.

Why had Robert closed his land to the horses? She understood that he wanted to let the Court, and tenants might require the seclusion and privacy of covert and meadows. The rich and successful hid from photo lens and prying eyes. But agreement might be months away. Robert's jealous vendetta against Sean pulled in his words across the previous months.

" ..... that Sean, don't trust him. They never ought to have taken him on. I did warn them!" Tiger Bay had walked with a slow even pace to match her speed across Six Acre Copse. "I've told Mara time and time again to get rid of him. She never listens." The big chestnut then jumped over fallen trunks, near the Blind House, with Robert leaning forward on the mane to avoid overhanging branches. Another vision stole across her mind, of the 'ringer' standing by the Blind House, but she could not remember what was remarkable about it. And Annie's voice with Mara breaking in: "Sean says we ought to go to the Fairyhouse races to cheer ourselves up!"

"Sean!" From Robert. "How much longer is that chap staying?"

And Annie's voice "He's staying."

"For how long? What's it got to do with you, Annie?"

What of Daisybrooke Farm, and Dolly's insinuations. The "oh ayes" from Bert, and Sean promising to take her to see the house?

She was unable to ask Sean directly because their relationship was too fragile. However, for the immediate future something had to be done about obtaining extra help. She knew that he rose at five each day and rarely went to bed before midnight. He refused to employ local labour, saying that they did not have the experience to follow his his exacting standards, and if clients paid high livery charges they expected the best. And would get it. On hunting mornings every horse must be turned out impeccably.

Looking at him sleeping and oblivious to the evening she felt an intense longing for him and a tenderness towards his utter fatigue. Perhaps it was his hands curled around a dark blue, empty teamug saying in white letters 'Cadbury's Easter Egg' which was poignant. His tousled hair was framing fine pale skin, and she bent towards him longing to kiss it, to hold his head close. Mother him. Protect him. Draw him into her. His long lashes flicked, dreaming like a child allowing her for a brief flash to perceive the unexpected turmoil of his soul, as yet undeciphered.

She made some fresh tea, shared out Sean's frigid egg and chips with Tweedles and Bertie, and fried him a fresh egg on bread. He did not stir.

"Wake up. Come on and eat. The animals cannot manage a second tea!"

She sat him up at the table, putting knife and fork into his hands. All Sean said was "Yes'm."

"We've got to have Diarmid back."

"Diarmid?"

"To come and help."

"We can manage."

" ..... with the work. Drink your tea."

"I haven't a spoon." She did not tell him to get it himself as she might have done some weeks past, but got up obediently from her chair and fetched a teaspoon from the drawer. She stood there looking into the mirror above the clock from where she could see his tousled head. "You must ask your Gran."

"He's needed at Clavincade."

"Not as much as here. No harm at any rate to ask her."

"You don't know my Gran."

"I can guess. Don't tell me you're afraid of her!" She dumped the spoon in his tea.

"What if I am?"

"Seems to me." Reaching across the table, she took his plate, scraped it, and washed up. "Does she know about Annie?"

"She knows."

"And our troubles with Robert? The land. No Bridie even, and Mara away. You're working your guts out, what for? For us, distant cousins."

"I can't presume."

The atmosphere thickened, as though air had changed. "She must understand the position."

"She does. And isn't it herself that's founding the stud?"

"Who?"

"Gran Tamzine."

"Where?" Flurry was perplexed.

"Daisybrooke."

Flurry could not believe her ears. Here they were in chaos, with everything changed. No land, the Court to be let. But nothing had changed, and things were going along as if nothing had happened, as if she had stepped into Annie's shoes. A little woman dressed in black, taking over from the voluptuous Annie, making her live again. A take-over. That name Clavincade, but at Daisybrooke.

"It isn't the first time."

"What's that supposed to mean?"

"Any cake?" She did not press him, noting the warning signals. "When you've rung your Gran."

"Tomorrow."

"No. This evening."

"Too late."

"Don't prevaricate. Up you get." She grabbed him under the armpits. "Into the hall, or no cake." He put his arm around her giving her an unexpected kiss. She pulled away from him unwilling to show that she loved him.

"Cake, when you've phoned your Gran."

133

"A promise?"

They went into the hall and the dark landing above showed that Bridie had not come home. He made a cage of kindling amongst the ashes on the hearth to create a cheerful blaze.

"I'll do that. You telephone."

He seemed undecided.

"Tell her it's urgent. Surely she can get extra staff. Not like here."

Flurry fed the fire with dry branch-loppings from the forest, which smelt vaguely of autumn mushrooms and heard him dialling a number.

"Oh! Who's that? And how are you. It doesn't matter. Tell herself it's urgent." The phone went silent. He waited, whistling softly like a lullaby.

The unexpected kiss hovered on her skin. Longed for, making her heart leap. But she was determined to be mundane about it, to treat it as of no importance, as a mere amused salutation. The sort of incident they could both take in their stride when he felt he was being presumed upon. She forced back intoxication. Rejoicing. The atmosphere crackled and he was listening again. Explaining.

"Wondered if you could ..... whether ..... how much? You see it like that? Well it's nice to know! So you've heard? Let him be. Not much? You are thinking that of us!" Sean rubbed his ear, holding the phone away in dumb show. "I'll be trying to remember. In future."

Brown shadows withered in the corners of the hall as firelight brightened. In an attempt to bring herself back to reality Flurry ran her hands over the patches she had sewn to repair the worn chintz, from a length of bird-and-flower material she had found in someone's workbasket. Sofa springs felt hard and concentrating on the present she forced herself to say to the sofa "I will make a couple of cushions, there's plenty of stuff."

Sean held the phone at arm's length letting Flurry hear the determined cackle of a voice resembling a parrot. He rubbed his ear. Put his finger in it, wiped it around as though to clear his head.

"Yes'm ..... understood ..... try harder," grinning at Flurry. "And you be looking after yourself!" He put down the phone.

"What did she say?"

"Putting Diarmid on the plane from Dublin next week."

"Whoo-pee!" They jigged round and round the sofa. Flurry was determined not to let him get away with it. "You promised to take me to Daisybrooke."

"Did I now?"

She pushed him, and he collapsed on the sofa as though in obedient despair, then he pulled her towards him.

She struggled. "Not until you promise."

"Next Tuesday then."

The cotton chintz was rough to the skin, the birds and flowers of the pattern looming large and out of proportion. Springs jangled. His were no inconsequential kisses. And yet restrained, with passion controlled, and no beast let loose. Always a private person who held his secrets well yet gave them up one by one at the apposite time when trust was revealed.

As when lightning strikes to illuminate the material world, a stream of electrons is carried from cloud to earth. So it was between them. But each lightning bolt gives off elves or sprites, and such pulses propagate in all directions, away from the discharge of energy.

For Sean, he was so often beset by his own uncertainties. And as for Flurry, experienced and yet naive, hers were incoherent feelings. Unexpected. Half suspected. Not thought out. She was only beginning to permit herself the luxury of describing even to herself, her feelings for him, and she could not begin to guess what his feelings were for herself.

She knew what it could be like. Guessed what it should be. She knew all her life that love would be like that, and this was a vision of love. When she was younger she would lie in her white bed, in her pale flat, looking out at the wide grey river and see the morning sun like a slit, a crack in the sky. And dreamed that one day it would be like this. She knew the suffocated disappointments. Had experienced the sense of loss. The let-downs. The never-was. The abuse she would never admit to herself, that she was abused. That Harry had abused her, and taken her youth. She knew now that the ice in her heart had melted, as Annie prophesied. Learnt, grown up a little, changed. And without guilt, stress giving way to peace. In his restraint lay her confidence.

A day or so later a card from Mara arrived. The postman leant against the kitchen table drinking his tea and hoping to hear the news to carry on to the next farmhouse. The picture postcard depicted the pale limestone of Burrington Combe, which rises up vertically each side of the narrow, twisting road, wild and spectacular. Not as famous as Cheddar Gorge, where to walk every yard costs money, it is a charming place to explore. On the left of the photograph stands the great rock where the Reverend Augustus Toplady was inspired to write the hymn Rock of Ages, Cleft for me.

Rock Farm
Cheddar

Darlings!

I know how the parson felt about this place! Reminds me of home and the Finger. Having a brilliant time. Can't believe it. Went out hunting twice with the Mendip. Lunch and two parties. Francie Fairbrother remembers Haifa,

Father, and sends love and kisses.
Longing to return home. Can Flurry fetch me? Bring
Bertie.
Love to all
Mara.
Everyone started to talk at once. When? Is she well enough. Flurry
has her Peugeot. Will you get her, please. And what about us giving
ourselves a treat?

Consulting the racing calendar they decided they would go to the
Winncombe Races for the next National Hunt fixture. Diarmid would be
here and it gave enough time to organize themselves, and tell Mara that
Flurry would collect her. Sean wanted it to be a surprise, but
Grandfather said "No!" He insisted they tell Mara, otherwise she would
be disappointed should she wear the wrong suit and hat.

Opportunity comes to those who plan, wait and watch. That
afternoon it poured with rain when Bridie rode her motorbike towards
the hairpin, having failed to turn on her headlights, as she was inclined
to live in a dream-world and not to think. Her goggles were opaque
with water droplets, so she was unable to see a fresh fall of liquid mud
streaming across the roadway. The narrow wheels of her bike skidded.
Bridie panicked and tried to right herself, but only accelerated the skid,
to make her crash over the far bank. Fortunately, her fall down the
precipitous drop was broken,when the forks of the bike jammed
themselves between a stand of young hazel coppice.

A few minutes later headlights searched the scene, and Robert
appearing as though he were greatly distressed helped the crying girl
into his car. The motorbike looked beyond repair, but Bridie appeared
unhurt except for a few bruises.

He insisted on taking her to the local hospital, making much of the
poor condition of the road, and her bravery at travelling by herself.
Assisting her through reception he saw her settled comfortably on a
waiting room chair, with magazines to read and a welcome cup of tea.
Then went out into the town.

He knew he must be careful not to overwhelm her, as she was unused
to those little attentions beloved by women. He must initiate her slowly
as attracting her was crucial to his plan. Through Annie's Will Bridie
would inherit money, which he felt was his by rights and he was
determined to get it for his own use. Ethics, the rights and wrongs of a
case meant nothing to Robert. Holding on to his position, money and
power were paramount. Flowers? A bunch of Parma violets would be
adequate as a first small gift, although he spent longer choosing his
purchases in the wineshop, after which he drove Bridie home to the
farm, kissed her demurely and promised to call at teatime tomorrow.

The telephone was ringing at Broxford Court, this time he answered it as at last plans could be laid down. He must arrange the exact time and place of a meeting with Julie. Timing was of the essence, and he knew she was greedy enough to obey his instructions exactly.

At tea next day he visited Bridie taking his briefcase with him. Now the floodgates were open she talked on and on. "Unfair! Why is it always me? They always pick on me! Anyone goes short? Who is it? D'you know who 'tis?" Robert nodded tactfully and she gave him a mug of tea. He winced behind her back, as the brew was strong enough for a spoon to stand up by itself and years of Annie's company had made him fastidious.

"It was alright when Daddy died. There wasn't enough money for me to stay at school, and the army wouldn't pay. Just Mummy and me running the yard with a couple of teenagers from the village. I was happy, and it was bliss after boarding school. Happier than when Daddy was alive, as Mummy looked to me."

The fire through the bars of the iron duck's nest grate glowed with heat, blue and white Dutch tiles below the pinewood mantelshelf looked homely, and Robert knew he must listen and wait.

" ..... happier than when Daddy kept taking her off with him to Germany, Ireland, the USA, or whatever. They never thought of me. It wasn't my fault that I went down with measles, a lot of us did, the san looked like it was a war, with Daddy in the army they didn't think much about it. Just thought I was dreamy and not concentrating."

Determined not to look bored, Robert saw that Annie had had the paint stripped from pine doors, cottage cupboards and china shelves to give pleasant soft finish to the small room with its white walls and dark beams. New curtains were cotton chintz to match the small two-seater sofa.

" 'Bridie must learn to concentrate,' they said. The school was run on bracing lines and it was very bad up there on the Moors, most of us were army. Parents posted abroad. It was alright if you were good at work or games, but I just wanted to be at home."

He understood her predicament, although despising her as a woman. A small new kitten lay on a cushion in a wooden chair and it was curled round a childish toy dog.

"One holidays I got an awful wigging for a bad school report, and then they found I couldn't hear. I hadn't said. Not told anybody I'd gone deaf. Mummy was very upset and I had to go to specialists and things."

Robert got up and went to the dresser, on it a vase of pussy-willow and very early jasmine stood by a musical jug that played *Scarborough Fair* when you wound it up. He opened a bottle of apricot brandy, bought yesterdeay, and gave her a generous portion. She would suit his purpose nicely, but he must go very gently as she was suspicious and jealous.

"Then you know what happens? HE comes, Mr Lordy-Boy. The village teenagers weren't good enough, and we had to pull our socks up. 'The horses aren't finished' he'd say ..... " she gulped down the sweet drink, hardly noticing, but held out the glass for more. She picked up her new kitten and sat on the wooden chair rearranging the fluffy dog alongside her grubby corduroy skirt. The stale smell appalled him.

"Kitty. Kitty."

"What's his name?"

"Rags. I had a doll."

"Doll?"

"Rag doll," she smiled, amusing herself at the childish joke, to make him wonder if she were really stupid. "Drink your drink."

"I'd like to kill her!" she exploded

"The doll."

"No, silly. Flurry."

"Of no consequence. She's of no consequence. She cannot possibly make any difference to us. She'll be off as she has no part to play. Not like you. You must think of your future."

"That's years away, if I ever inherit, and then it's only half. Mr Payne warned me against spending anything and said I must put it to the back of my mind, and anyway it depended on death duties and the state of the market. I wasn't listening."

"You must listen. It's important. You should think of marriage and children of your own."

"Kitty. Kitty. So soft."

"Would you like a child? Children of your own?"

"Don't know." He did not press her. "I hate horses. They steal all your day. I wish. I wish ....."

"Wish what?"

"I wish I could just stay at home and breed cats. Exotic cats."

Judging that she had sufficient to drink, he knelt down on the handmade rug by her side. Gently removing the kitten, Robert placed his head in her lap, feeling with his hand beneath her skirt." "We're all desolate," she stroked his hair tingling with unknown pleasure at his caress. "We are both wronged!" His hair had enticing, shining, grey curls, faintly scented as a practised, inventive seducer.

The next morning Robert spoke to Bridie in a faintly hectoring tone, knowing that mood changes enhanced his value as a confidant. "You must write to the Council. Write to them immediately. The local suveryor."

"Wouldn't know what to say."

He opened his briefcase and placed notepaper, an envelope and pen on the kitchen table, but leaving a scent-spray and his 'little toys' undisturbed. Kitty jumped down.

"Perhaps later," looking sulky.

"Now. And you shall have a treat. Good girls get treats." Robert knew to the finest nuance how to please, and then, to withdraw his good offices to create unease.

"Special treats. Sit down and write," he dictated:

"Dear Sir,

While riding my motorbike home to Lower Farm the day before yesterday, I skidded on the roadway beneath the tunnel of trees which leads to the hairpin. Only good fortune prevented me from crashing over the edge of the steep bank to the Byebrooke below. The state of the roadway is quite unacceptable, being covered with mud from the collapsed bank. Lights or road signs must be put in place ....."

In evening firelight, he sprayed her arm, and the tops of her legs with the lightest of French perfume.

When Sean went to the airport to collect Diarmid, he stopped for diesel at an out-of-town used car mart and was distressed to see Annie's Mercedes exhibited for sale. He was unable to leave it in a saleroom for anyone to buy, which was why when the family were motoring to the races, Sean drove Grandfather in a Mercedes.

CHAPTER 11

On the morning that Flurry went to collect Mara she felt far more confident in her little car than when driving the worldweary Traveller. Bertie liked it too, there being less fume from between the floorboards. Terrier and girl had taken a deep liking to one another, "I will always have a dog. A dog like you" she said kissing his nose.

Mara was thrilled when she saw her best hat on the back seat. "Brilliant. You're brilliant. I don't believe it!" Even so, she was disappointed that Bridie had refused to come, in spite of Grandfather's offer to pay for her ticket.

"Difficult. She's always been difficult. I hardly know her."

Cheddar to Winncombe was about forty miles as the crow flies, and they had to cut across country to reach the racecourse in time for lunch. Entering the Members Only car park, Grandfather stepped out of Sean's Merc wearing his good thirty-year-old Savile Row suit.

"How priceless! My dear father!"

However, it was a glimpse of the well-known figure of Richard, in his chauffeur's uniform, who made Flurry gasp with surprise. He was standing by Lady Lydia's limousine which was parked by the rails overlooking the course.

"You're looking well, Miss Fleur, but thinner, if you don't mind my saying so. We must build you up, as I hear you are coming back to us."

"Dear Richard. How do you know?"

"They say."

"And you listen."

"Only if it's my business to hear, Miss. You know that." Mara's nose was twitching, intrigued.

The wind blows strong and chill at Winncombe and Flurry was glad she was wearing her fauxfur coat brought from London, also her expensive kid boots. It was like old times, and she half-hoped to see Lady Lydia and gauge how her return to TorrTechTron might be received. Lady Lydia being a non-executive director of the company.

An official opened a plastics tubular section of the fence to admit them, and Flurry was surprised to find that the family was well-known by everybody at the racecourse. The secretary hurried forward to shake hands, and Sean seemed the centre of attention.

As they passed the pre-parade ring. Flurry read the pictorial plan on the back of her racecard to identify paddock, stands, bars and bookmakers. Behind the raised viewing platform overlooking the paddock, gaily striped tents held trade stands offering signed prints, sporting cartoons or copies of Victorian hunting maps. A green trailer exhibited animal portraits executed from photographs. Next to it Flurry found she could buy anything for the horse from grooming kits to stable rugs, saddles, bridles and halters to sheepskin saddle covers, while a huge cardboard box held wildly reduced knitted pullovers.

Flurry paused at the Countryside Alliance stall, with its popular ties, cards, books, pens and dog leads and bought a memento key-ring for Richard, because she felt she owed it to him for his kindness, before following Mara towards lunch.

The upstairs member's dining-room, as part of a special suite, was located behind the owners' and trainers' bar, which led to private boxes with glass fronts. From a wide terrace both the steeplechase and hurdle racetracks could be viewed, as they were laid out in a clockwise circle between an eighteenth-century barn and the grandstand, Tattersalls and car parks. Flurry crossed the vestibule with its cloakroom desk and attendant and approached a steep stairway leading to the first floor. Behind her, the outside door flew open with an extravagant gesture to admit a party of persons.

"Thank you kindly, Gaylord, but Fleur can help me up these damned stairs!" And Flurry turned to see Lady Lydia limping towards her. "Dratted steep. Would think they could put in a lift for racegoers. We pay enough." Lydia was as thin and wiry as a stick-inset, with her right hand she held the stair rail, gripping Flurry's arm with a skinny left which was laden with diamond and ruby rings.

"Won't ask you how you are. Richard said you're alright but too thin." A remark that coming from Lydia seemed to be out of context. "How are the Bowden's treating you? Was talking to them. And my young Sean. Rode one of my horses at seventeen. And won. Outrode the professionals. Now he's afraid of his weight."

"I saw a photograph."

When they reached the landing, Mara and Grandfather were standing waiting for them.

"Don't have much to say for yourself do you? Though Harry said you chatted enough, too much sometimes." Flurry blushed with embarrassment and pushed her face into the collar of her coat.

To Grandfather. "Behaving herself is she? Taught her to ride yet?" Was Lady Lydia being provocative? But as Grandfather was smiling and nodding, Flurry decided it was just her abrupt way of preventing any needless explanations and was grateful to her.

Sean opened the dining-room double doors. "And how was your holiday?" Lydia asked the middle-aged receptionist with a smile, brown-haired perm and a South African accent, then to her secretary, an earnest young man in glasses whom Flurry remembered, "Jonathan, we'll need an extra four at table. And the usual."

The dining-room was large, with cream walls and cream curtains making it fade to eternity, when given boundaries only by lines of troughs filled with brilliant cyclamen and baby-green fern. Blue chairs held damask tablecloths in contrast, while cones of napkins hid bread-rolls on sideplates and glasses were many and varied. A booth for the Tote, located in one corner, had a red stripe, while a resplendent bar was doing a brisk trade for the hopeful and unfortunate alike.

"Fleur, or Flurry, whatever we call ye now, you don't know everyone. John and Patsy Camelot." Sir John Camelot shook hands, she waved. "Have a horse in training. And this is Gaylord Pring, who answers to Bruin if you treat him kindly, Jonathan you remember, as he's been milling around for ever."

Champagne was served at a round table set like an island in the centre of the room, staff moved with alacrity as they knew Lady Lydia hated to be kept waiting for a drink. Also she tipped well. "Sean, I want you next to me. Patsy can sit next to Father Bowden, as you both know the Middle East. Gaylord talk to Flurry, as you're working together, and Mara, I'm sure you can put up with John, but he don't know much when it comes to horseflesh." Johnathan squeezed in near his employer ready for any cuffs she might feel inclined to give him.

"How fortunate we meet under such interesting circumstances." Gaylord pulled out Flurry's chair. He was taller than at first glance, slim, suave, courteous and with a somewhat scholarly, studious air, and Flurry was unsure how to place him, wondering if he were associated with the company.

"I'm very out of touch with TTT news."

"Forgive me, let me introduce myself." He sat next to her, giving the impression of presenting his very fullest attention. "Gaylord Pring. I have taken over from Colin Goldring as Chief Executive, when he became Chairman after Henry Pritchard."

Flurry thought that he looked more like an Oxford don than the Chief Executive of an electronics company. Time would tell. Strange that Elizabeth had said nothing about him, which made her wonder if there had been a strong leadership challenge for control of TorrtechTron after Harry's death. And whether Colin had been 'kicked upstairs', leaving Gaylord Pring, being Lady Lydia's protege, as the victor. She must tread carefully. Sitting at this round table of corporate entertainment, Flurry felt she had been ejected into manipulative business environment with no Harry to guide her, or give instructions on how to act. Maybe it would be wise to watch and take her cue from Lady Lydia, who seemed friendly enough.

But what was Lydia's attitude towards herself? A widow and an ex-mistress, albeit sufficiently recompensed by Harry's Will. Maybe she herself was just a pawn, with a simple part to play in the networking.

Gaylord was an attentive listener, while she explained her work with horses. He seemed genuinely interested, while she chose each word carefully, keeping a watchful eye on Sean and Lydia who appeared consummate friends. Champagne was drunk, salmon mousse with dill sauce consumed. Each pair at the round table seemed absorbed in each other's company.

A waitress with brown shoulder-length curls brought fillet steak. Lydia patted her hand and congratulated her on the successes of her nephew, an amateur jockey. Still at college, he already had many winners to his credit, and that afternoon was riding two horses for a well-known trainer. She seemed to know everyone, and Flurry felt she ought to learn more facts about racing before returning to the company. During Poire Béllè Helene Mara was selling the advantages of a hunter-livery to Sir John, while Grandfather reminisced on the part played by the Yeomanry Cavalry in Egypt with Patsy Camelot, and was delighted that they had mutual friends through her father a tank Colonel.

"What's this about Robert letting Broxford Court, Mara?" Lydia asked.

"Letting?" As yet no-one had told her.

"In *Country Life*," with Gaylord joining in. "Could be exciting, Lydia."

"Gaylord here thinks so."

"I don't believe it! Not a word." Maria struggled to gain composure. "Whatever do you want with the Court?"

"Entertainment."

"Oh!"

"Gaylord's a great believer in treating 'em right!"

"Where's Robert going then, if you take the Court?"

"On his travels. You know Robert, restless."

"Why? Do you?" Mara snapped. "I thought it was only Annie."

"Robert knows more than you think. He's no fool. Resourceful. Wily." Lady Lydia grinned at Mara's discomforture. "Don't look so put out!" she added.

They agreed to take coffee after the first race, and Flurry was glad to be out of the tense atmosphere, and in the fresh air. She hoped that Sean would accompany her to the paddock, but it was Gaylord who became her escort. Standing by the paddock she attacked her racecard once more, learning how to understand the hieroglyphics of name, sire, dam, age, weight carried, last ran, owner, trainer's name and jockey. Then there was form to consider and rating. She must find out where starting prices were exhibited.

"You must each me all about racing!" He smiled gravely. There was something reserved, unassuming, about Gaylord which appealed to the girl. "This is my first time, I know no more than you. Presumably only owners and trainers go into the paddock."

"Perhaps we shall be asked, who knows."

"Asked?"

"Lady Lydia has a horse running in the fourth race. That's why we're here."

"I didn't know." To fill in the pause, while she sized up the horses led round by their stable hands. "Have you known Lydia long?"

"Three weeks. Only three weeks. Since I was appointed by the Board." She did not ask him if he were an engineer, and divining her thoughts "I have a merchant banking background. And you, if you don't mind my saying so, you seem to have a quick perception of everything you undertake!"

Each horse was tacked up and wearing a rug with its owner's or sponsor's initials, also its number in the race. Flurry returned to her racecard trying to learn the colours that jockeys were carrying.

"Which horse would you back?" he asked.

"One can only go by other people's opinions. Form and rating. What the experts say, until you get that eye for an animal. That indefinable something that comes with experience. Sometimes I think that now I've learnt a little about horses . . . . . I know nothing at all."

"Lady Lydia has a great eye for a horse."

"And Sean."

"They've known each other for ever." Flurry thought there was little that escaped him. "Sad about his father being drowned!" Gaylord told her.

"I didn't realise. Lydia must know Tamzine O Callaghan."

"They were at school together. She is much older than her late husband Henry Pritchard. Old enough, or nearly, to be your grandmother!"

Gaylord was quick to divine secrets and it made her blush, or was it his interpretation of Lydia's attitude? There was nothing objectionable about him and nothing you could take offence at. She wondered how old he was with his pepper-and-salt hair, and felt drawn towards him, he being unusually sensitive for a businessman. She gently bit the corner of her racecard, wondering, while Gaylord watched, without assuming.

"And what may I call you? Miss Jones sounds so formal. Do you like Fleur or Flurry?"

"I'm still not entirely sure what my interests are. Where I fit in."

"Clarity of purpose can be superficial. What really interests us may be stored away out of reach."

Horses were led to the centre grass lawn, Newmarket blankets folded to quarters and girths tightened for jockeys to mount, then complete two circuits of the paddock before removing rugs and commencing a long walk to the course. Gaylord and Flurry moved towards the private boxes in order to watch the start. Taking an opportunity to speak seriously he said "At TTT I believe it is in our interests to diversify. The global challenge of increased production beings increased leisure, which we have scarcely begun to study seriously. Many alternatives in growth opportunities exist in markets around the world, and TorrTechTron must expand, think of a world-wide spread of business."

Flurry had to concentrate to follow his drift, which was concise but difficult to follow. He continued, "I believe our spearhead could be in the world of sport, making it a flagship to illuminate our name. Using computer simulations we can examine and design new equipment using materials originating from the space programme, which will bring unheard of advantages to sportsmen and women."

They talked for some time, hardly observing the racing from their position on the outside terrace.

"If my ideas appeal to you, perhaps you might consider an outline as to how we might capitalise on sport, and generate valuable publicity for TTT."

Flurry was only half-consciously aware that they were being watched by Lady Lydia from the glass-covered private boxes reserved for owners and trainers, and located on the first floor of the stand above them.

"May we say after Easter then, when your new office will be ready for you?"

At Lower Farm, Bridie waited impatiently for Robert to arrive. She was wearing her new blue suit, bought yesterday in Bath. The coat was a little tight, and she wondered whether the skirt was too short and revealing. She had not dared buy a hat, as her bank account was overdrawn. Waiting at the door she felt like a naughty schoolgirl by going out with Robert in secret, rather than attending the family day-out. "Good girls get treats," Robert had said, and this made her scared of being found out especially concerning his seductive sexual attentions. During those last five minutes before his car arrived, Bridie pressed her face for comfort into kitty's warm fur, as her mother, once loved, was becoming an adversary.

Robert drove her to the most prestigious hotel in the district and about thirty miles from home. He did not worry that they might be seen lunching together, as the hotel had international pretensions and was too expensive for local tastes. It was not that people couldn't afford the lunch-bill, but because opinion felt it was waste of money.

A mile long avenue of beech trees led from gold embossed black iron gates across moss-grassed acres of park and lawn, to the three-gabled Jacobean house. Added wings and pillared portico were frescoed in earth pigments of yellow ochre sandstone, reducing to pale lemon, while shadows were copper green and blue, and the iron oxide in a restored water-tower reflected red light. A new annex of grandiose proportions spoke of modern prosperity. Bridie was childishly intrigued by the rose-pink strip of carpet beneath a striped awning, adorned with great vases of roses, lilies and chrysanthemums for a wedding-party, which led to the front door. She felt flattered and vaguely excited to walk along it towards the entrance to the hotel.

She sat on a Chippendale-style sofa in the pitch-pine and oak-ply library, restored in a country house design and waited for Robert, listening all the while to the faint laughter as wedding guests, in formal morning suits, arrived for luncheon. Unable to contain her curiosity any longer, she stood by the curtains to watch the bride's arrival during this fashionable, up-market wedding. Older than she expected, the lady wore a gorgeous hat decorated with butterflies, toned to match her gown of floating chiffon, while a pearl choker with a diamond clasp circled her neck. Envy consumed Bridie that a woman so much older than herself should have such glamour, and be so feted as, on murderously high heels, she tripped amongst the flowers. Then Robert took her arm leading her away. Several drinks later they went in for lunch.

Having consumed nearly a bottle of sweet Australian wine, as Robert did not buy expensive wine for someone who could not appreciate it, Bridie began to feel faintly nauseated. The painted ceiling of the dining-room moved forward and back in a spectrum of colour, and they withdrew to take coffee in a pavilion positioned on the far side of the drawing-room.

Across the lawns a Rolls Royce, decorated with white ribbon favours, drew up to the accompaniment of chinese firecrackers.

"She looks old for a bride."

"She is."

"You know her."

"Don't we all. In all the papers. The tabloids at least."

"I didn't see."

"Her fifth."

"Fifth what?"

"Marriage. Fifth husband."

"I wouldn't stand for that. Not ever. If I were once left, or deceived, or I thought there was someone else around, I would never forgive him. Never. Fancy anyone doing a terrible thing like that to you. Adultery. I don't care what he did, or whose fault it was, who was in the right, or who was in the wrong. I am not a person who ever forgives. Or forgets a wrong. I'd do anything to get even, as I don't believe in letting bygones-be-bygones."

Robert understanding the extent of her bitterness was clenching his coffee cup so tightly, that his fingers turned white. Then the pressure exerted broke off the handle of the cup, to make Bridie start with tension.

Mara and Grandfather sat in unexpected winter sun on a wooden bench near the paddock, when she saw Flurry wander quietly towards the saddling boxes. Horses were receiving final touches before the next race, and surcingles, essential in case of a slipping saddle or even a broken girth, when galloping at thirty miles an hour, were being buckled over racing saddles. Lady Lydia's black mare Heliotrope, with her blue, red and green rug, was being waited on at the far end of the line. Grandfather had fallen asleep.

Something about her appearance suggested that Flurry was feeling at a loose end, because Mara knew her well enough to infer that she never wandered aimlessly about, and without purpose. Knowing that she had had a long interview with Gaylord Pring, who was obviously a protege of Lady Lydia, she wondered what was on offer, and hoped that Flurry knew what she was getting herself into. Mara had great respect for Lydia Pritchard. However, she was well aware of the other's habit of using people, and then discarding them. Mara waved, and Flurry walked over to sit down. Grandfather slept.

"I'm feeling dreadfully in two minds. Gaylord does not need me until after Easter."

"Wondered. thought you might be."

"Might be?"

"At a loose end."

"Unexpected, as I'd been wondering if they'll still want me. So I've done well."

"When do they want you?"

"After Easter. I did say."

"But did they say? Their terms, I mean."

"Extraordinary really. I've read lots about science in sport. Oh! Rackets for tennis balls at a hundred and forty miles an hour, and clever sails for racing yachts."

"Always a great reader."

"Didn't think you'd notice. Now I don't know what he means, whether it's to work on ways-and-means between science and sport, or using sport to boost a 'can-do' attitude within TTT."

"Double-think!"

"Surprised you'd mention that. He's so nice! Charming really. Unassuming. But frighteningly intense, and sounds like a dissertation on a specialised subject."

"Complicated. Out of my depth."

"You're kind."

"Not always. I'm not always kind. But you are so worth it. I do admire you. I really do. Don't take offence darling, but you've matured since you've been with us. You've always played fair, and you're still what you always were but opened out, blossomed. Like you've been set free, but retaining your roots, your sincerity. Well I'm telling you now, that you can. You can do anything. At the same time I'm a little frightened for you, as I know how one can be manipulated. But I'm forgetting, come along quickly and let's put our bets on, they'll be going to the start in a minute."

So occupied were they by their own conversation that Mara felt Flurry was unaware of Lady Lydia and Gaylord standing with the trainer in the paddock. She was giving her instructions to the jockey.

"Heliotrope, the black mare," from Mara.

"Will she win?"

"You'll see what I mean. Wake up Father, come and put on our bets. Thirty-three to one. The mare's done well on the flat, and the going's good to firm. Should be an advantage."

"What's the odds," from Grandfather.

"Thirty-three to one, I told you, unless it's shortened. Not many in the know. Where's the Camelots? Surprised they're not with Lydia, unless they're having second thoughts about joining her. Don't blame them."

Flurry was towed along in Mara's wake, towards the lines of bookmakers standing by the course under striped umbrellas.

"What are they giving? I haven't my glasses, only a six horse steeplechase, I'm surprised no takers. Oh! I see, there's Green Man, local horse, local trainer, done well coming up through the point-to-points and won at Didmarton last year, so all the money's there."

"'Av it one with Avalon! Thank you Madam."

"Go on Flurry. You'll see."

She looked at her racecard reading:

2. HELIOTROPE (Ire)
     Owner Lady Lydia Pritchard
     Breeder Clavincade Stud

"I might have known," she said. "Ten pounds?"

"Twenty, if you can, Sean'll put his shirt on. Quick before they shorten. Told you so, people are watching, you're okay though. Come on lets watch from the stands rather than go back to the private boxes, we can enjoy ourselves without having to think about every word we say."

"I was going to ask you. Can I stay?"

"With us? But of course, aren't you one of us, one of the family." Her face told Mara that Flurry felt happy, enchanted, as though life was all worth it.

"Climb up to the seats, windy but see better. Give Father a hand, it's steep.'

Sitting high up above the course they watched the starting-price come up on the electronic board.

"We've only just made it. There's our *friends* putting on the main bets."

"Do we get our bets?"

"Should do. Odds written on."

The commentator coughed into the public address system.

"Ladies and Gentlemen. We now have the fourth race, the Winncombe Steeplechase Cup for five year olds and upwards of two miles and about four furlongs. There are five runners, as number six is a non-runner. The first on the course is number four Green Man with purple and crimson hoops, white cap."

Mara was in her element. Her hazel eyes, behind half-moon, fine gold-rimmed glasses were bright, while her brown curls beneath a feathered hat had been freshly coiffured. This was what a holiday away from care had done for her.

"My daughter's excited," Grandfather confided. "Used to ride point-to-point. Wonderful rider. Raced in Singapore, don't y'know. And Kentucky."

"Today she's like a mother-hen," Flurry whispered, ". . . . . enjoying the pleasure of others." As though in recognition of her thoughts, Mara turned, "Stay as long as you like. Now we've got Diarmid, and we're back to normal, we must take it easy and have some fun . . . . . point-to-points. I'll introduce you to some people."

"Number Two. Heliotrope. Blue and green diamonds, red star and cap."

"Classy horse," Mara observed.

"What's it like being a jockey? In a steeplechase."

"Better than sex!" then adding, "you mustn't get nervous or you become tense. Take it as it comes."

Horses galloped to the start and they could see them trotting in a circle awaiting starter's orders.

"And they're off! Racing on the far side of the track they come to two plain fences, and are safely over with Burnt Umber taking the lead."

Mara focused her binoculars on the water-jump.

"With a sloppy jump from Thyme Tells over the water,

and they're turning across the top of the track towards the long straight run in front of the stands. It's Burnt Umber, Green Man, Naylor's Grose, then Heliotrope last. And we have a faller in Thyme Tells, an indifferent jumper. The jockey is up, and both on their feet."

"Loose horses play a big part," from Mara. "Heliotrope doesn't give me heart failure every time she jumps."

"Safety over the next two jumps which will be the last on the next round. All tightly bunched. Burnt Umber still in the lead with Green Man, then Naylor's Gorse with Heliotrope bringing up the rear. As they race in front of the stands, Heliotrope is preparing to make a move and keeping well up on the outside, as they go away from us."

"The way she travels shows a touch of class," from Mara.

"Now Green Man is taking over from Burnt Amber as they complete the circuit. Then Naylor's Gorse."

A great ah-h-h from the crowd as the loose horse cuts across the plain fence nearly unseating Burnt Umber's jockey.

"They must see a fence or they can't jump it. But they're well clear," Mara cut in.

"They've settled down again into a nice easy rhythm on the far side. Coming to the first of the far plain fences, still going very fast. This is a cracking pace. Green Man, then Heliotrope moving into second, with Naylor's Gorse and Burnt Umber. Coming up to the water, safely over, and they're sorting themselves out. Heliotrope gets a reminder from her jockey, and she's putting in her challenge."

Mara explained, "Races are won or lost on the run-in. Horses must stay well, and be made to keep their concentration. Listen to their jockey to lengthen or shorten before a fence."

"The final two fences. And it's Green Man then Heliotrope."

The stands erupted with excitement. "Come on my son," was the cry. That haunting cry. "Green Man. Come on. Up the Man."

"Local horse. Local Derby," and Mara smiled quietly. "Watch," she said.

"The last fence neck and neck. Stride for stride. Heliotrope jumps it a shade better, and is taking the lead. Green Man being driven on."

The noise in the stands was unbearable. "Come on, my son."

"Heliotrope shows her class and is three lengths in front of Green Man. She grabs the ground. Digs into it. It's Heliotrope. Past the post a five lengths winner!"

"Green Man threw it away on the last fence," agreed Mara. "Then Heliotrope beat him off." They held each other with joy as they scrambled down the steep terrace steps.

"Not enjoyed myself so much since Newmarket Races." The old man's face was flushed with pleasure. Flurry was glad Bridie wasn't there to spoil Grandfather's day!

Leaving the stands, they passed through gates guarded by officials and entered Tattersalls, joining the crowd by the bookmakers, who were having a good day. Mara spied Sean. "Bet his winnings have made a good hole in the bill for Annie's Merc! Marvellously lucky is Sean."

Grandfather muttered "Spends all day reading the racing papers!" Sean came across while Flurry collected her winnings, stuffing the notes into her handbag. He grabbed her, swinging her round and round, so that the crowd had to part in wolf-whistling amusement.

Mara watched, looking over the tops of her half-moon glasses and wondered how far their affair had progressed in her absence. 'I am not sure,' she thought. 'Not at all sure if she's the right one for Sean,' and began to worry in case these dear young people got hurt. Richard, too, was standing near the barrier ready to collect his own small winnings. The chauffeur exchanged a glance with Mara, whom he knew slightly. His eyes said 'Well here's a turn-up for the books. Him and 'er. Wonder what Mr Prithard would've said!'

"Dear Richard!' from Flurry. "I've never been so excited! You must have had something on. And please, please remember this day." Flurry took the key-ring out of her purse and gave it to him. Richard thanked her, then when their backs were turned took off his cap and scratched his head.

As a group the Bowden contingent decided to celebrate in the Tattersall's bar rather than return to Owners', Trainers' and Members'. Sean bought drinks, and they found a chair for Mara at a crowded table.

"'Ere Missey, you sit down too!" There are still manners at a race-meeting. "An' get a chair for the Colonel." The smell of beer, stout and whiskey fume was overpowering, while the floor was littered with discarded betting slips and muddy marks. Everyone was jam-packed together commiserating with each other on the defeat of Green Man, so that Sean brought drinks all round to cheer them up and was loudly thanked. An old man with a scarf sat thoughtful. Two farmers discussed the price of pigs. At the far end of the bar, the tote was doing good business, the girls wearing scarlet blazers.

"I can't drink much, I'm driving." And Flurry pushed her half-finished whiskey towards Mara, who put her arm halfway round her waist to make Flurry dream in a fog of cigarette, cigar and pipe smoke. "My life only seems to have begun since I've been at Bowden's Grove."

One dark night with no moon, an open-backed truck manoeuvred slowly and carefully up the Z-Path. No headlights, not even sidelights were switched on, but by watching the dark shadow on the right hand side, the driver could steer a straight course. Reaching the top, the vehicle bumped its way along leaf-strewn paths to the Blind House. Still showing no light, the lock was unfastened and only then was a torch used to roll out a five-gallon drum of lubricating oil. Relocking the door, the driver lifted the heavy drum with some difficulty, and staggered forward with it in the direction of Lawson's Meadow. Should a night-watchman or poacher have been abroad, he would not have recognised the man, being dressed in an oily Barbour, stocking cap pulled well down, and rubber gloves.

With the night so dark and the ground littered with roots and broken branches, the driver found it hard going. But he staggered on, clutching the drum to his chest and walking across the meadow. The road with the hairpin lay on the far side behind a hedge.

After about half an hour the man finally reached the gate located above the field. By it's side lay a pile of round straw-bales from a previous year covered with rotten webbing. The man scraped away some of the decaying straw and stowed the oil drum away in the pile of bales. He then retreated towards the Z-Path with as much alacrity as he could manage.

CHAPTER 12

Mara decided she must see Bridie immediately after breakfast, as she had not arrived at Bowden's Grove that morning, nor had she telephoned to welcome her mother home. Unfortunately, Mara found that two tyres on the Traveller were flat, so she had to borrow Flurry's Peugeot.

The day was cold, damp and misty, and she was glad of the car's newer and reliable brakes, as she made her way towards the hairpin.

"KEEP LEFT" said the red and white board at the head of a row of red lamps, now dim in daylight, and Mara hoped that she would be directed to KEEP RIGHT on the way up. She did not fancy the embankment side.

She turned towards Lower Farm to find the curtains drawn over windows, and wondered if her daughter were ill. Then she saw the new motorbike by the hedge which worried her, because she knew Bridie had no money. 'I must ask Henry Payne' she thought. 'Not yet surely, she can't have been pestering him!' And an unpleasant thought 'And not a money-lender with their unpledged loans! The child's immature enough to be taken in by an unscrupulous anybody.'

She knocked. "Anyone at home?" A thick crescent of laurel, lonicera and box sheltered the cottage from wind racing across the meadow, blowing furry clouds over the sky like demented sheep.

"Bridie darling. You there?" A curtain twitched, and Mara wondered what Bridie had to hide. "It's me. Mummy." Presently the door was opened unwillingly, to show Bridie still wearing a shabby dressing-gown.

"You alright, darling?" and fibbing "I was just passing! No ill-effects, I hope from the accident. Grandfather said you were OK. Let me draw your curtains."

"It's alright. Leave them. They're alright. Leave them alone, I said." Any hint of disapproval called out a tantrum. She held her head in one hand. Mara, who could be both kind and generous, was not a woman to pander to modern pampering, nor was she fashionably sentimental, but came to the point. "Darling, we must talk. You simply haven't been pulling your weight. Away for days at a time, and not riding out. I can't have it, I simply can't." Getting no reply. "You're sure you're alright? A headache?" She had the unpleasant impression that the girl had been drinking, which was why Grandfather kept the key to the drinks cabinet in his pocket, a slight that humiliated Bridie. Mara went on "I know you love living here, but you are spending too much time at the farm."

"So what!"

"I can't pay you. I simply can't. And Lower Farm isn't yours until everything's sorted out!"

"It was alright before he came."

Ignoring this "We need more help after Uncle Robert shut Home Paddock and Lawson's"

"He isn't my uncle."

"You called Annie, Auntie, when you were small."

"She was your cousin. Robert's no relation. No relation at all. You know that, so don't say Uncle Robert ever again."

"Why bother about it, as if it mattered." Mara sighed, exasperated.

"Does to me."

She asked softly "Why not?"

"Nothing."

"We're getting nowhere. Let me make you a cup of tea."

Mara went into the small well-equipped kitchen. Once a narrow outshut, Annie did everything well. Small or large nothing was too much trouble, and she had a flair for getting things right. But had it been wise to give Bridie Lower Farm when she was so immature? With hindsight perhaps it was a mistake, and one of Annie's few mistakes. Always a plain difficult child, you could never get near Bridie. "No," she'd scream. "Don't want to," as though baby speech had given expression to pent-up rage. Mara hated to admit it, but she'd always been thankful when term began and Bridie went back to school.

The kettle was boiling, and Mara peeled off a red and silver foil milk bottle top, and opened the door to the ashcan to throw it away, then stood stupefied, amazed. She counted, one, two, three whiskey bottles, and brandy, apricot, cherry. Two gin. "I don't believe it!"

The sound of foot-stamping as Bridie dashed upstairs rattled the cups in the glass cupboard. Mara switched off the boiling kettle "Bridie!" Then followed her daughter up the uncarpeted spiral staircase, with its copies of primitive paintings of eighteenth century sheep and cattle.

"Bridie! You can't do this." No reply. Silence behind a locked door, and Mara alarmed, perplexed, went into a second bedroom to sit down on the single bed. On a corner dressing-table were two Staffordshire dogs and a flowered comb-tray. Through the casement window at the back of the house she could see her own mare, Polly, grazing, and looking slightly stout. 'I must exercise her more,' she thought, to give her aching head and mind a rest. Bridie's mare and foal moved across beside the hedge. But there was no Surtees. He was not to be seen. Mara opened the casement to get a better view, and the fresh air revived flagging spirits. Being a little short-sighted she screwed up her eyes and then she saw him. It was Surtees, grazing three fields over on Robert's land.

Remembering Bridie's words "He's no relation. You know that. No relation at all," understanding began to dawn. There was the new motorbike and the whiskey, gin and brandy. "Oh no! Not him," she spoke aloud in anguish. But she knew she was right. "I must not be too precipitous. I must stop. Stop and think. Not say anything now. This is too big for me to handle by myself, and I must discuss it with Father. You can see Robert's point as marrying Bridie would save his bacon, and let him get his hands on her money."

Bridie hid by her bedroom curtains, looking down on Mara as she left the house, closed the front door and went down the path. Seeing the crown of her brown felt hat above a loose Loden coat, as if in plan, her mother appeared stouter and more upright than before her restful holiday.

In her silent world, no birds sang. No music enchanted or soothed her. What can she hear? Only the beat of drums, ear-drums, beating a tattoo of discontent, angry that she was born before the days of MMR vaccine which protected children from measles. Being deaf, being odd, Bridie became the butt of others who bullied the odd-girl-out.

Mara opened the driver's door of the Peugeot, to make Bridie throw open the casement in a fit of rage. "You've got her car! You never loved me. Never. It's your fault I'm deaf. Why couldn't you die instead of Daddy. I hate you. I hate both of you. And I'm never coming back. Ever. I don't need your f***** money. Bugger off. I want nothing from any of you."

Her stream of abuse could be heard by Bert in his cottage further down the lane, as he banked up his early potatoes with a mulch of garden compost. He leant on his spade, remembering the car lights that went as far as the cottage. Stopped. And then left in the early hours of the morning.

Meantime Mara drove home troubled as to how to help a daughter who was so vulnerable. Bridie had been a no-no child. Always had been. She would stamp her little foot and scream "No. Won't, shan't." Perhaps a young psychiatrist, more in tune with this sentimental society might advise. Mara had enjoyed boarding-school and made lifelong friends, so that she and Alec thought they were doing their best for the child. She sighed and wondered if she should talk to Henry about an allowance for Bridie.

"Annie, it is your fault," she said to the steering-wheel. "You did make mistakes, and brought it on all of us. You should never have left Robert in such a tight corner!" However, she was glad that at the hairpin corner the large red-and -white board said KEEP RIGHT. Entering her own drive she remembered the three hundred pounds she had won at Winncombe and meant to give to Bridie. "Oh well! It can go to charity. I'll let Sean have it to pay towards repairs for the chapel roof at Daisybrooke."

Without stopping to dress, Bridie grabbed a hunting-whip and dashed

155

out into the meadow, even though she knew her rage was stimulating her to make a weak animal suffer. "Polly! Polly! Come on, good girl." Bridie's eyes were fiendish and the horse was suspicious, walking across to her very slowly. She grabbed the headcollar, pushing the mare into a corner, then hit her quarters a ferocious blow.

"I hate you." Polly swung round alarmed. Bridie held on. "Take your f***** money," she screamed raining blows on the hind quarters. The horse reared up and would have kicked with an off-fore, if Bridie had not leapt backwards tripping over her long dressing-gown and fallen into the mud. Polly seeing an opportunity to escape, jumped the five-bar gate, turned right-handed and galloped up the lane to Bowden's Grove where she met Flurry in the stable yard. Appalled at the whip marks she called Diarmid. "God! They'll be furious! Don't tell them. Don't say anything to Sean or Mara. Please!"

Diarmid grinned. 'Wasn't she Sean's woman? Maybe a future Missus.' He ran his hands down the neck and shoulders of the terrified mare, quieting her. "Come on ol'girl. Let's hide you away. It's a magic potion I've here, made by the leprechauns." He figured it could be worth a bottle of Paddy's.

"Diarmid, you're a star."

For four days, and working with Bert they kept Polly in the lane behind the hedge, or when Flurry signalled, sneaked her into the field across the road which was owned by Bert's friend. Then a smart brush down and a New Zealand rug hid the damage from view. It was Bert who explained about the lack of grass at Lower Farm due to the late spring. Mara was content to believe him.

Returning home after the euphoria of Winncombe Races there was a feeling of anticlimax made worse by worry over Bridie, whose conduct was chewed over in great detail. Grandfather was especially concerned as he had always been sorry for the child. She was his only grand-daughter and all their hopes were pinned on her. It was he, who when her deafness became known, arranged for her to go for a year to Germany and attended a German clinic specialising in treatment for the deaf. Their help was outstanding, which was why Bridie could understand so much.

Sean was becoming more and more introspective and withdrawn, as though Annie's death had drawn energy from him and to Flurry's chagrin he took little notice of her. She was puzzled. He had been so warm, affectionate, on the night he had telephoned Gran Tamzine. Restrained, yes. He had neither committed himself, nor compromised her in any way. But knowing something of men, his restraint was unpredictable, and she wondered if he regretted kissing her. Bertie came to sit on her feet again, it was as though both Sean and the terrier were waiting, extrapolating their consciousness into the future, and the exaggerated antipathy between Robert and Sean appeared as though they were linked in unholy bondage.

For the livery yard, grass was the great problem, and Sean's expertise had reached interested ears. He successfully negotiated livery for some young yearling racehorses, and also the breaking and schooling, as well as keep and bringing back into work, a string of polo ponies, to be prepared for summer chukkas. Things were looking up, with Flurry doing the books, the business was viable as her figures had predicted and they were making money. It was time to take the longer view and lease suitable pasture. Land belonging to Bert's farmer friend opposite was ideal, but in poor condition which meant raking, rolling, weedkillers, then fertilising and re-seeding, before calling in the haulier and friends to erect stockproof fencing.

As she had promised, and longing to be in the fresh air away from the house, Flurry helped Grandfather in the garden which was becoming too much for him. She dug, raked and weeded, then helped him to start begonias, dahlia and chrysanthemums in potting-house trays. She loved the old man, at times, however, his endless reminiscences of the Middle East and El Alamain, retold a dozen times, like a tape which starts and has no end, began to cloy. Besides she found herself listening. Always listening. Interpreting sounds from the stableyard and longing for Sean to come and ask her to ride out with him alone. But he didn't come. To ease the tension in strained nerves she decided to see how the fencing-party was getting along and volunteered to take coffee and fruitcake to the fields opposite.

"We're marching with the boundaries for you" called the haulier with his usual charm.

"Marching? I don't understand."

" 'Marching with the boundaries' an old Wiltshire expression, Miss Flurry." The haulier, being a lady's man, prized himself on being respectful. "A 'march' is a tract of land on the border of a country."

"A debatable tract," put in Violet.

"This land ain't 'batable. 'Tis leased."

"You can always get a rise out of Bert," mocked the haulier.

"Anyroads. 'Tis 'oss pasture. No need thiccy." He looked around at the rough grasses. "Better'n spray grass with whiskey. Then'll be half-cut!" They all laughed.

"Daft buggers!" chorused Violet, digging out an extra tough ragwort root.

"Did you hear the one about Bert and his calves, Miss Flurry?" went on the haulier, as he drove in a wooden fencing post. "Took a couple of his calves to market and they ran away. He unloaded them by the passage leading to the cattle-pens, when they decided they didn't want to be veal and took a butchers by jumping straight over the fence. Down the road they went and into a meadow by the river, with Bert, drovers with electric probes, a constable on duty, and the lot of 'em, chasing after."

"They'm daft!"

"Calves swam the river and were off. One gave himself up. But the other, he went into some sorta Green Sanctuary. Now you've got to pay to see him! In a Theme Park!"

"Buggers'll make you pay to see a bleeding cow soon."

"Twern't like that. Biggest liar in Wiltshire that 'aulier," and Bert nailed a wooden cross-member, taking such a blow with his four-pound hammer, that he nearly knocked his friend's head off.

"Let's be having that fruitcake then. Take no notice of them silly buggers," snorted Violet. " 'Cor! Gets me knickers wet sitting on damp grass." Flurry was glad Violet wore knickers, being a further proof that She was not a He. But the picture of Violet, in her man's cord trousers, waistcoat and cap, wearing pink knickers, foxed the imagination. The haulier winked.

Henry Payne sat in his office contemplating Mara and Colonel Bowden's telephone call regarding Bridie and Robert. Already he had trouble enough with Davies. Not only had he shut his land to the Bowdens, putting them to endless expense, and threatened to dispute Annie's Will, but now for the third time he had refused to allow valuers for probate to enter Broxford Court. Robert always had some stupid excuse.

To value Annie's furniture, jewellery, pictures and effects would take a long time. Why was he prevaricating? Payne was suspicious that certain items might have been removed, but to apply for a Court order would create gossip, just as if there were not enough already and the solicitor hated unpleasantness. It was bad for business. He would send a sharp letter, and hope that Robert would comply with his demands.

As so often in an English mid-winter, sunny weather turned nasty again. Clouds closed in with black ice, to make driving treacherous. People stayed at home unless their journeys were urgent.

It was a cold night with freezing fog as a car with it's YC number-plates drove along the M4 towards Chippenham, and afterwards the B roads towards Broxford which had sudden sumps of fog in the hollows. The windscreen wipers hardly cleared frozen mist from the windscreen, making visibility difficult in evening darkness. Several times the driver considered turning back. But no. The arrangements for such an important meeting might never present themselves again.

The car halted near the Bowden's Grove turning, and a pen and ink sketch map sent by post to the driver was carefully consulted. Continuing the journey, the car was driven with extreme care along the lane towards the hairpin. The road appeared to be closed. Or was it? A string of lights, barely visible in the darkness, was spread along in a confusing ribbon. What did the roadsign say? KEEP RIGHT.

Turning the wheel sharply towards the unaccustomed right side of the road the car skidded. The driver, afraid to steer into the skid, and risk hitting the row of danger lights, applied the brakes, causing the car's rear end to skew round. Brakes did not hold. In the lethal mixture of wet, ice and lubricating oil it gyrated in a figure of eight totally out of control. Back wheels spun. And the car twisted and somersaulted twice as it took it's terminal course down the steep embankment towards the Byebrooke river below.

A thin, terrified wail, as from some small animal, came from the rear seat, as it's occupant was tossed around the car like a mothball in a butterfly net. This in concert with the driver springing from floor to ceiling on the seatbelt as the car gyrated. A tree bent one door. A stump drove the near wing through the bonnet. Decelerating abruptly, the car finally came to rest on the naked rocks of the river. The driver was too shocked, too concussed, to be aware of a can of petrol being thrown over the hot engine, causing a sheet of flame to engulf car and occupant. The wailing ceased.

It was Bert who saw the inferno first, when he took Patters out to his kennel for the night. Plumes of scarlet, orange and lemon flame like a Vesuvius, illuminated bare trees and hedges across the fields, while intense black smoke was visible against the purple depths of a winter sky. He guessed what had happened, and ran with the dog across the fields. Bert was more agile than his elderly frame would suggest.

The air stank. Reeked. It spluttered with water, burning paint and rubber tyres amidst exploding glass. Steam fizzed from the Byebrooke which was already dousing the flames.

Bert and Patters squeezed through a blackthorn hedge, the petals from its white flowers descending on them like snow. The dog barked as though sensing an intruder, then together they made the treacherous descent towards the river which dipped down on the opposite side of the steep embankment which supported the road. High above them shadows played on the hairpin where a flickering movement back and forth along the line of red lamps, whose warning was extinguished by the glare of the blaze, added an urgent requiem. The dog whimpered uncertain, as though he sensed a presence. Bert looked up. Someone was there. "Patters heel!"

The inferno died as they watched until only a ruby glow of smouldering fabric and molten plastics, saturated with lethal gas was all that remained of the blaze. Bert paused. Anyone passing had gone. The car body was an integral whole, with shut doors. "Nobody 'b'aint alive. No-one ain't." He approached the vehicle and in a spurt of flame, he read the number plate, aghast! 'YC!! "Flurry," ' and he started up the steep twisting ivy-covered trail alongside the slope which led to the road, falling twice over grabbing fingers of dead vine. He made his boots rattle along the tarmac, never stopping until over a mile later, Bert and his dog walked alarmed and afraid up the Bowden's Grove drive. Then with relief they saw the Peugeot car, with its special number-plate, standing quietly in the stableyard. It was some ten minutes before Bert recovered enough to knock on the kitchen door and ask to telephone the police.

"Gave I a turn, it did. Gave I a turn."

The evening of the fire Robert had coaxed Bridie up to bed early, as the drink he had prepared for her made the girl sleepy. She was in no mood to resist, as she enjoyed his attentions, the way he undressed her and slipped the plain cotton nightdress over her head. Then plumping up the pillows he put her down to sleep, like a tired child.

The sound of the front door opening, then shutting again woke Bridie, when she too, saw the blaze. Light from the fire flickered along the walls, as her bedroom was in the front of the house and facing the hills.

"Robert? Robert? Are you there?" she called in alarm. She stumbled across the room, unbalanced by the suddenness of her awakening, to totter down the stairs, meeting him in the gloom of the tiny hall.

"Where have you been?"

"Go back to bed."

"But where?"

"Went to check."

"Why did you go out?"

Exasperated at her insistence over a trifle "Go back to bed!"

"I want to know why you went out." She infuriated him, so that struggling to hold his temper, he repeated. "Seeing the flames. Went to check."

"They're in front. Up the fields and hairpin no doubt." Then stroking his coat "You're wet."

He pushed her upstairs, wondering how long he could stand this woman. She, turning on the landing "You're wet. Why are you wet? 'T'isn't raining. You can see from here," and she went to the window to find that the flames had died down and only an acrid smoke troubled the night.

Somewhere a dog was barking.

"We'll call Bert."

A flicker of interest, of meaning, crossed his taut face hidden in the darkness of the room. "Bert?"

"Phone him. He'll know."

"Know what?"

"He always knows. I'll phone him."

"No. Not now. Tomorrow."

"What good's that. Maybe there's a car crash. I'm going down to call Bert." She switched on the light, to see his face was ashen. "You can't stop me."

Out of focus, he flipped, with dreamwork beating reality. He snapped out the light and threw her on the bed with a sharp slap. Bridie burst into tears. Self-preservation gained over violence, and he cried:

"Darling! I'm so sorry. I was afraid ..... afraid you'd get cold." She wept with noisy tears. Then kneeling down by the bed, he pulled up her nightdress exposing a naked back. Gently, seductively, caressingly, he licked her skin, with long, soft, dry strokes.

How he hated her, despised her. Her petulance, and slovenly habits. His beautiful Annie, with her flowers and perfume, how had it come to this? If only Annie had been reasonable and not kept him like a dog on a lead. Robert was no countryman, his restless, soulless spirit ached for movement. Travel. Anywhere. To submit to the country you must be born to it. It's a different world. A world behind reality and few find its secrets without the accident of birth.

He licked on like a dog, down her backbone, her hips, fawning to fortune. To keep expediency alive.

A picture of a cruiseship floated into his mind, sailing across blue seas, with tropical palms waving over gold sands and the long boats that Polynesians paddle. The fishermen were handling and hauling up a great dead fish with legs and seaweed floating from its head like hair. The eyes were open, staring.

He continued licking, caressing until she quietened, responded to him, and finally yielded with furtive delight. Robert had no belief in right or wrong, only a sense of self-preservation. Sirens sounded across the darkness as police, fire-engines and an ambulance attended the accident.

The following morning an anonymous telephone message from a callbox in Gloucester to police headquarters, suggested that Bert Rawle of Lowers Cottage was responsible for the accident, as he was in the habit of carrying drums of lubricating oil, loose, unroped and in an unsafe condition in the back of his pick-up truck. The sergeant in charge of the case recorded in his notebook that an opened drum of oil had been found near the warning lights at the scene of the accident, but had been removed by the fire brigade on the night in question. The man referred to by telephone should be interviewed immediately, so he sent an officer to see Bert.

The *Bath Evening Messenger* gave the accident a front page spread.

"INFAMOUS HAIRPIN CLAIMS
TWO VICTIMS
COUNTY WORKS DEPT
CENSURED

A woman and her newborn baby met their deaths in an horrific accident on the road between Broxford and South Parkington, last Monday night at about 9pm.

The accident happened on a hairpin bend, notorious for its mud slides, causing the car to turn over and crash down a steep embankment. Bursting into flames, neither police nor fire brigade could save the occupants.

The driver of the car was a woman between 25 and 30 years of age, and is believed to come from London. The body of a newborn child was found with its presumed mother and it is understood the police are continuing with their enquiries.

Letters of complaint regarding the condition of the road have been previously received by the Surveyor to the Council. An urgent enquiry must be held, and the erecting of permanent barriers given priority."

Some time after the report, Sean gave Bert a 'lend' of his wagon which he used for collecting feed, to take six more calves to market. They drove together and stood waiting on one of the wide, raised viewing steps near the auctioneers rostrum. Prices were depressed! Farmers leant on sticks around the high metal bars surrounding the ring. Fat cattle were weighed, came in, were auctioned, were sold or taken home in despair. Ruin haunted the community, and there were few jokes.

"Won't have no farm soon. All be Theme Parks!"

Indigenous families would stay, welded together, wedded to the land. Many of the bored young would leave, enticed by pop culture, advertisements, peer pressure and drugs.

Driving home, Bert told Sean that a police officer had called to see him, asking about the oil. "Didn't drop no oil."

"I'm sure you didn't".

"What would I be dropping oil for? Expensive is oil. Only carries one. Know'd if 'ee were broke."

"You told him."

" 'Sides why was top not screwed on. I axed. Weren't burst nor nothing." They were silent for some time. "I seed 'im. Waving betwixt the lights. Patters seed 'im too. Whimpered. Bloke up there. Muckin' 'bout."

Sean digested the information. Some time later, the Somerset man went on " bin thinking. About Annie ..... could've bin. 'Tis possible.

162

Thought 'bout that s'mornin'. Could've bin like that."

Sean trusted Bert and confided in him with confidence. He also knew that he was far from stupid, and had sensible native wit.

It was still dark when Sean made early morning tea, and carried a tray to Mara. He sat on the bed, waking her quietly.

"What is it? What's happened?"

"Nothing. Did you have a good sleep, now."

She sipped the hot tea, waiting.

"Months ago. Think back to before Christmas and about the time Flurry came, when Annie first mentioned divorce. Isn't it true she mentioned Robert's woman, and we haven't heard of her again until this day?"

"Heard of her. Annie mentioned this Julie, what's her name? Baker wasn't it? But I've never thought about her since. 'S'pose she was paid off."

"And if she wasn't? The woman and her newborn."

"Sean, no. It couldn't be."

"The number now. The number of the car. What did Annie say?"

"He's bought her a car. I said 'How killing.' From Somerset. Oh no! I remember I said 'How killing.' I did. 'Somerset, that's miles away.' "

"And Bert was explaining?"

The penny dropped "YC"

"All Exmoor's YC. That's in Somerset, you must know someone in authority, someone who can help."

Chief Superintendent Saul Parker CID (retired) had been a great friend of Major Alec Hesketh. The two men often played golf together, so he was delighted to see Sean after Mara telephoned an introduction.

"Clever. Very clever. Ingenious. Of course it's possible, there's no doubt it would work. But there's nothing for the police to go on. No action they can take, as it's only surmise. A theory. There would be no burn marks even, to give us a clue, or cause for DNA testing.

I will certainly do anything I can to help, as I have many friends in the force. You certainly may have a point with regard to this latest incident. London, you say. In confidence, I understand the car was stolen from a London Property Company, and I will see what I can do regarding their address.

Shocking business. One wonders why the poor woman drove that way, if she hadn't intended to go to the Court. If she were visiting the village, she would have taken the direct route. Pleased to do anything I can!"

With the address in his wallet, Sean drove to Bath in order to visit the Public Reference Library. Situated on the first floor of the Podium, a cream confection, comprising a modern complex of buildings, it stood on the bank of the Bath Avon river and Sean paused at an exterior stall selling cut flowers. Their scent had momentarily deflected his concentration from the task in hand and made him think of Flurry. It was not that he had forgotten her, but the complexity of the present task so occupied his subjective mind, that his own personal satisfactions were overpowered and drained from him. This nearness to death had augmented his priorities and his own personal tragedy made him review life from a different angle, to feel despair at the confusion of his emotions. It worried him to think that she was in love with him and that he was disappointing her, knowing that Flurry was not in a position to appreciate the full implication of Annie's death. How could she? She hadn't the facts. But the time was not right, as he had to study the task in hand. Review the part he must play.

He walked up the stairs, and asked for directories from the reference library. While waiting he wandered across to where palms in pots, Muzak and little tables beneath trailing plastic ivy tempted visitors to morning coffee. He ordered a cup thinking: 'Perhaps I should have asked her to come.' Then he walked to the bar and bought a packet of cigarettes and having finished his coffee he made his way towards the library, leaving the packet of twenty cigarettes minus one in the shop.

The reference books were on a table detailing the private companies and their directors extant in Great Britain that year. Turning the pages 'I could have taken her to lunch at the Bay Tree. Annie and I used to go there when we wanted a bit of peace and some time to ourselves.' The smell of fresh flowers mocked his concentration.

Even so, it was not long before he matched the Capricorn Property Company of Number 4, Ealing Broadway, London (the address of which had been given him by retired Chief Superintendent Saul Parker), with the appropriate entry of companies. As legally required, the names of the four directors were given, one of which was R. Davies.

He was almost sure he had three murders to fight for. But how to prove it? They had nothing to go on. And what was Bridie's life worth? He knew he had little time, because once Robert had let the Court and acquired money he would be off abroad, taking Bridie with him. And then? When they were married and sailing on some liner to South America where life is cheap, what then? This was what Annie had feared, and why she never wished to go away, or leave home.

Tomorrow he must drive to London and search for facts. Attempt to prove that the incinerated woman with her newborn was Julie Baker. However, he stopped at the flower stall and bought two bunches of iris.

CHAPTER 13

Flurry rarely went into the morning-room as it was cold and little used by the family. Lemon painted walls and soft lime-green alcoves with shelves still retained their Victorian flavour, and a wrought-iron fireplace with scrolls, garlands of flowers and cherubs looked mournful, with its pile of soot cluttering the grate. The furniture was an odd assortment of bookcases, a heavy oak desk, together with a ladies' bureau complete with a painted picture on the inside. A plaster cast of the Emperor Hadrian had a cracked nose, while someone's spinning-wheel and embroidery frame spoke of days when there were still housemaids to look after the home.

She sat on the window-seat and waited, as this was the only room with a window commanding the length of the drive. Presently doors slammed and with 'Goodbyes' from Mara, Grandfather and Bert, the Mercedes started on its journey in dignified efficiency. 'He might have taken me!' Flurry was depressed when she saw the car disappear from view and the thought made her sadder than ever. She walked down to the Smoker, built up the fire and returned to a pile of books, accounts and letters awaiting her attention on a table by the window. Once her work at TTT was an aim in itself, to be completed with efficiency and ambition, but without love. Now every order for hay, straw or feed was charged with innuendo. She was becoming more sensitive, more vulnerable to the feelings and actions of others now that those 'gap' years had been filled. "I'm so uncertain," she said to the blue velvet armchair, "I'd like to stay as I love it here, but I have my living to earn and the thought of Sean moving to Daisybrooke is a shock! Mara can't employ me here without him as the keep is too meagre. Gaylord said 'After Easter' so it looks as if I must go." She refused to admit that her world was revolving around Sean because his charm and easy manner veiled a very private person, and she had no idea what his feelings were for her. At Bowden's Grove she was happier than she had ever been in, her life.

Flurry was not so artificially self-assured as she was once. To belong, or not to belong. There was this on-edgeness. She thought she might not be there much longer in this centre of unlikely storms, and the realisation was a kind of grief.

She was finding it difficult to work on the question of Diarmid's tax position between the British and Irish Taxation Departments, as it did not seem to be of immediate relevance to a question of suspected murder. She had never liked Robert and was slightly afraid of him, in spite of physical attraction. But murder. That was far-fetched. He could not possibly have picked up Julie's car and thrown it over the embankment, or a horse and rider. It always came back to Annie. She thought that she might be in a Looking Glass world, where there is no reality and only surmise.

Outside in the stable yard, she could see Diarmid strapping a horse, to make its coat shine like polished steel, while padded stable rugs and wool Newmarkets had been washed and were drying on a heavy duty washing-line. Nothing was slipshod. No corners cut.

It was a relief to go out into the yard when the *Animal Feeds Ltd* lorry arrived. She counted in the number of sacks containing two short tons of horse nuts and wished she could buy more for extra discount. But too much might become mouldy. Diarmid had hardly been sober since Winncombe Races, while Bert had a smug expression on his face. Even Patters had a new bowl.

They went into the tackroom for a brew-up with Diarmid, whose coffee always tasted of hoof-oil. He slept in the rooms above the stables and was most hospitable when anyone called. "Bell's or Paddy's?" he would say. Drunk or sober, the horses never went short for anything.

They discussed the two horses going to Ardingly with Sean to compete in dressage trials. Winning classes would be a good advertisement for bringing on young stock. Diarmid was to go with Mara to groom for Sean, while Grandfather expected to stay with cousins. Flurry had not been asked and she realised this was only an oversight, but thought she might use the two days they were away to see the solicitors in the City.

Meanwhile, like a replay of the day when Annie had made her fateful journey to London before Christmas, Sean drove the Mercedes up the M4 and through Acton towards Ealing Common. London was an unknown quantity to him. The USA and France he knew, Berlin, Warsaw and even the Caucasus, when they travelled to buy the best horses, but London, other than Heathrow or Gatwick airports, was an enigma. He did not know how to gauge its quality. The unknown is always a challenge, because when you do not know the essence of a group of people, it is easy to overplay your hand and succeed at nothing.

He remembered he must park on the grass by a church as Annie said, leave the car, and cross towards the open common with its outline of trees, to a crescent of red brick flats situated across the main road. He rang the bell which had no name-plate as presumably the flat had not been re-let. He waited, noting that the 'Rent-A-Stud' cards on the address-board suited Robert's enterprises. In the distance, the strains of *When the Saints come Marching In* breathed across the noise of traffic like discordant mewing, then a thin woman in trousers, striped shirt, trainers and an apron opened the door.

"Julie Baker, m'dear?"

"She isn't here. Left." The woman did not take the fag from her mouth, and began to shut the door.

"How long ago, dearie?"

"Don't know."

"A week. Several weeks. Days?"

"None of my business."

"And to be sure, it's me coming all the way from County Cork to see Julie, and she's not here!" He gave the woman his most enchanting smile, sweeping back the tousled hair from his forehead. She hestitated long enough for Sean to take his wallet from his pocket. It was a good pigskin wallet, and the woman eyed it with curiosity.

"Would Julie be taking her car with her?"

"Packed everything up and scarpered."

'Round one to us', he thought. 'Capricorn Property Company said it was their car.' "And the baby?"

"Don't know nothing 'bout that." Angrily she tried to shut the door, but Sean had his foot in it. "And isn't it me coming all this way to give presents for the baby." She hesitated too long. "Let's be having her address then, dearie."

"Don't know about that," she was still wary.

"But you know then." Extracting a ten pound note between finger and thumb, "And you'll be letting Julie have a present for the baby, when you are asking me in for a cup of tea." She eyed him, distrust competing with avarice, then unwillingly she opened the door wide enough for him to enter. He made a quick bee-line for the stairs.

"'Ere. Down the office."

"Fourth floor. Her flat's on the fourth floor. Her name-plate is saying so."

"Flat's empty."

"To be sure the flat's empty, and haven't I nowhere to stay in London?" He scampered up to the first floor. The flats were constructed from several tall, narrow town houses, each house retaining its original staircase and individual flavour. Passages on the upper floors connected the buildings together to make one integral whole. The front upstairs drawing-room in each case, was divided into two smaller rooms and it was easy to envisage prosperous Victorian families taking tea, playing cards and gossiping as they looked over the Common.

Peering over the banisters, which zigzagged down the stairwell, "And what may we be calling you, Mrs . . . . ." Sean called down.

"Sharon."

On the second floor a woman with suicide blonde hair was collecting her milk and the *Sun* newspaper, she yawned. "Why here's a pretty boy. Won't you come in, darling?" Sean mounted to the third floor nearly knocking over a bleary old man, wearing a bowler hat.

"If you must, go up again and third door on the left," Sharon panted.

The two room flat with added kitchenette and bathroom was surprisingly pleasant, with long windows looking over the open space as far as Uxbridge. The carpet, three-piece suite, dining-table, chairs and bookcase were ordinary and entirely non-committal. They gave no hint as to the taste or habits of the recent occupant. The bedroom too, with its double-bed, dressing-table and wardrobe had nothing to say about Julie Baker. Sean opened the drawers and each cupboard-door in turn. Nothing. Everything was completely empty. Even the bathroom had no soap, hairspray or talc. Only the kitchen gave him a clue. He held his breath. He must not appear too eager. "And now Sharon," he said, lolling against the sink. "Will you be giving me Julie's address."

"Don't know her address. Honest. She scarpered."

"But you'll be seeing her. Give her this for the baby. Was it boy or girl?" He handed her the tenner.

"Girl". The woman pocketed the money without thanks.

He turned sharply. "Maybe just what I'm needing. An old pair of tights. My car door is coming loose and tights are just the job to tie it up." Sharon shrugged.

"The only thing she didn't take. Left me to do the clearing up." Sean retreated from Number 4 quickly, in case Sharon changed her mind.

As he approached his car, a troupe of musicians patted, caressed and were kissing the Merc in dumb show, shaking their collecting box with exaggerated vigour. One knelt down imploringly.

"Let's be having a tune then," and the band struck up *Get Me to the Church on Time* with Sean conducting. Giving them a donation he asked "I'm looking for something to eat — is there somewhere you can suggest?"

The fat girl, grotesque in orange tu-tu shrugged. The clown looked mournful. "Nothing five-star. Just pie and chips."

"Chips! Chips!" they mouthed. The sousaphone player, sporting a top hat, took Sean's arm bundling him along. They walked down a side alley by the church, to turn into the church hall behind it. A mouth-watering smell of home-made shepherd's pie, sausages, hot treacle tart and creamy rice assailed nostrils of the hungry troupe.

The hall was neo-Gothic in style which was so beloved by the Victorians. Posters pinned to cream walls between the corbels of varnished pairs of arched braces supporting a hammerbeam roof, were enlivened by posters of London scenes. A bar, serving steaming savoury dishes was attended by ladies-who-help. Generous portions filled hot plates and Sean started to pay.

"Very kind. Most generous. But no, we're not destitute. The band is a week-end gag for charity, to build a community centre," said the top hat taking off his threadbare donkey-jacket. "In point of fact, I'm a dental surgeon, Frances in the tu-tu is a patents lawyer, and our clown with his plastic orange, advises us, because he's a social worker." The clown hooked his pink, blue and green wig on the back of the wheelchair, while the cripple got up from the seat, "I'm just going for a pee," he said running off.

"That's Ken. He plays ice-hockey."

Sitting together at one of the trestle-tables the dental surgeon said "I thought I recognised the car. Some months ago."

"You did."

"With a lady."

"She died . . . . . I have her car."

"I'm sorry to hear that. Not very old." Then went on "You're from Ireland?"

"County Cork."

"I was at TCD for five happy years. Had quite a few days out hunting with the Kildare."

"Never with the Charleville Blazers, then?"

"Only once. they had a lady Master, I remember. Beautiful she was. Rode side-saddle."

"Annie. The Merc was her car. That was Annie."

"Double sorrow."

"It's because of Annie that I'm here." There was hardly any trace of his Irish accent, and his companion didn't interrupt his thoughts.

"Did you know a Julie Baker?" The dental surgeon raised one eyebrow. "Nothing like that. Nothing at all. I never met the woman. But Annie was interested." He considered how much he should say, then decided, "Charity. To do with charity." The other seemed satisfied. "May I ask you. Did you know of her?"

"She's the sort of girl we're trying to reach."

"Girl?"

"She was when she first came here. A typical teenager. Nice little soul, but not very bright, and easily taken for a ride. They run away from home and come to London with city lights, then drift into prostitution. Our projected community club would give them friends. Somewhere to go and helps to keep them off the streets, then hopefully into training and work."

"There was an accident near where we live. A woman and newborn were killed in a car crash." The dental surgeon was listening carefully. "We have reason to think it was Julie. Perhaps I shouldn't ask, but if, if there were an official request, would you know who her dentist was?" He searched the man's face. "Her dental records?"

Taking a card from his case, "This is the name and address of our dental practice. I know we can help."

Sean left the church after many goodbyes and promises to return. He drove towards Ealing Common Underground, near there was a Post Office. Buying a large envelope, he stuffed the tights inside, addressing the parcel to Chief Superintendent Saul Parker. He was satisfied with his work, having both material for a DNA test and dental records. Even so, showing that the dead woman was Julie was no proof that she had been murdered, only that the accident was exacerbated by a drum of lubricating oil dropped on the road by a person suspected. It was strange, that the car steered right, rather than left, as demonstrated by the skid marks. Also, why did the Capricorn Property Company say the car was stolen? And what part did Robert, as director, play in the deception? As for motive Robert would have wanted Julie and the child out of the way, because everyone knew of Bridie's insane jealousies.

Regarding Annie, there was no evidence that she was murdered. Only gossip, and a plausible method as envisaged by Bert. However, Robert's motive was strong, being his love of money, and his restless, greedy character.

"Time. Time. If only Robert would make a mistake. And soon," he said to the car. But he knew he must not allow himself to become demoralised, otherwise good luck flies out of the window.

At the time Sean went into lunch with his new friends, the telephone rang in Robert's study.

"I am thinking you would be liking to know," said his co-director of Capricorn, ". . . . . that today a fella was asking many, many questions."

"What sort of fella?" Robert accentuated Mr Singh's clipped English.

"An Irish fella."

"Asking who. What questions?"

"Sharon is telling me he was saying he comes from Cork."

"Asking what?"

"Asking her many, many times about Julie's address, and where she is living now."

"She doesn't know." How much Mr Singh guessed, Robert could only surmise.

"That is what I keep telling her, when he came in to be looking at Julie's flat."

"She let him in?" Robert was furious.

"A cock-with-the-bull story. He is telling her he is looking to rent the flat. Another thing is very, very strange. He is driving an expensive Mercedes car."

Robert was silent for a while. "Sharon took everything that Julie left behind and dumped it, like we arranged."

"Everything, dear God. Except perhaps for some dirty old laundry."

"Dirty old laundry?"

"Just dirty old laundry. Sharon is telling me the fella wanted some dirty ol' tights for his car."

Robert was aghast. "He took them! She let him take them!"

Mr Singh seemed to think it prudent to say no more until Robert had quietened down, when after a long pause he asked "Anything else I should know?"

"Only goodness gracious me! Sharon is saying that the fella was talking to the crazy, crazy band of drop-outs, as though he was knowing them."

Contemplating Singh's information Robert was severely shaken, and mystified as to how Sean had stumbled on the truth of Julie's identity. He thought it might be wise if he made a visit to the Blind House, so he tacked up Tiger Bay throwing a saddle-bag over the horse's neck.

At Bowden's Grove Flurry did not return to the house, but asked Diarmid if he would catch and tack up Jenny the pony. She felt like a quiet ride. Road work was dull and they had been having too much of it lately, so she decided to risk riding the byeway which led through Robert's land.

Opening the little hunting-gate that is the entrance to Six Acre Copse, she experienced the unease that gripped her on the day she met Robert for the first time. There were more deer about than previously, as they were breeding fast, and one of those strange, timid muntjac flittered by. Jenny was quite unconcerned and walked quietly on. They passed along the edge of the field near the U-shaped belt of trees, noting that the corn was ten inches high and approached the hunting-gate which led to Lawson's Copse, Flurry turned left-handed, as she had on the day of the New Year's Eve hunt. No hounds poured like an avalanche over the fence, no huntsman and hunt staff took the post-and-rails. The woodland no longer echoed to the excitement of the horn. The air was silent, without the clamour of hound music, and a fitful breeze shook the crowns of forest trees, to threaten rain. Flurry felt scared. She pined for the companionship of the hunt, their happy, friendly faces. Their dedication. There is more to hunting than running after foxes.

Jenny trotted down the wide grass drove, hoping for a canter up the rising ground which led to the *Finger*. Flurry recalled the spot where Annie had said 'Good Night', when she turned that last fateful time towards the Court. Jenny cantered. Forest boughs chattered. Flurry wished she had kept to well-known roads and pushed the pony on, thankful when they reached the granite ridge. Turning right-handed, the sharp crag of the *Finger* was directly ahead, and she decided to circumvent the smooth rock to take the lower path which led below the four great cushions comprising the 'knuckles'. The sky darkened. Flurry clung to the outline of the forest edge, afraid to continue along the ridge or approach the Z-Path. To her right, a forest track appeared to take a shorter route towards Lawson's Copse, and Jenny seemed confident of the quicker way back to her stable.

The track they followed was wide, but rutted where tractor wheels had pulled out extracted timber, so that the going became heavy and sodden. The occasional open clearing was darkened by black cloud, while the journey seemed endless, and only the pony's confidence quietened Flurry's fears.

Suddenly the path narrowed through a thicket of tall laurel. Great sarsens impeded the pathway, and at that moment the black cloud condensed to precipitate biting hailstones. Pony and rider crouched under a particularly dense patch of laurel, when Flurry, peeping through the leaves, saw to her relief that they had approached the Blind House by a back route.

As on New Year's Eve Flurry found herself sheltering in the same green laurel, and like some old newsreel, the pictures showed a horse with two white stockings hind and two white socks fore tied up to the circular wall. This time the horse was Tiger Bay because Robert, attired in tweed coat and cap, was carrying a saddlebag from the interior and padlocking the door behind him. Suddenly the hailstorm stopped.

Flurry sat quietly thinking of the 'ringer' with the rider in Barbour and green velvet cap of the Charleville Blazers. The forgotten image which had tantalised her for weeks suddenly came to her as she contrasted the appearance of Robert with the stranger rider! And its implication gave substance to ephemeral fear. Robert mounted his horse. Unfortunately, Jenny whinnied at Tiger Bay who answered her back with a cheery greeting and made Robert turn round. Flurry emerged from her hiding place, flustered and afraid. Robert raised his cap slowly, staring at her with his hooded eyes.

"I'm sorry . . . . . I rode off the Byeway track . . . . . it was raining!"

Robert collected himself instantaneously. "Feel free, my dear! Feel free! Ride where you like! A gal like you must please herself, though I'm surprised to see you out alone." He stretched out one hand and grasped Jenny's right rein. The animal tossed her head uncertain of his hold.

"I'll lead you to the road. And where are your friends today?"

"They're out!"

"Leaving you alone. Why didn't you give me a ring and I'd have kept you company. Let us ride to my house, and I'll give you lunch. You must be famished, it's getting late."

"I must be back."

"Still working for them are you?" he laughed. "When are you returning to London? I hear from Gaylord Pring that you're to be a high-up executive in TTT. Well done, my dear. Did they tell you they've decided to rent the Court as a conference centre? That'll wake up the neighbourhood a bit, shake some of these sulky estate workers to the seat of their pants. Get a bit of business management into the place. And about time too! This hierarchical system is all very well and it needs a revolution to change it!" He rattled on as they rode across Lawson's Meadow towards the road.

The meadow lay high above the lane and trees forming the upper portion of the beech-tunnel were part of the field's hedge. Robert led the way to the gate, dropping Jenny's rein in order to open the latch with his whip. The pony fell behind Tiger Bay, so that Flurry was standing next to the pile of last year's rotten bales. Idly, she prodded the soggy straw with the long cane which Diarmid had lent her.

"Looks like a badger's hole. Are they digging yet?" And to her surprise the pale straw-coloured cane was streaked with a smear of oil. Robert watched her like a cat. Then he shrugged. "Maybe. Damn nuisance, badgers." They passed through a gate and down the steep bank into the lane, when Flurry put Jenny into a trot and with a thankful 'goodbye' continued on her way towards home. Robert stood puzzled. First there was Sean visiting Ealing and now the girl hanging around the Blind House. Whatever had put them on to that? And looking for what? Co-incidence? He thought not, they might guess but they could never know and never prove anything. Robert was sure of himself, and confident. He did not like Flurry, because he saw something of himself in her. They were both street-wise, and living on the outside looking in. He suspected that she had been her late employer's mistress, as Robert was acutely perceptive towards misalliances of others, but being dead to the spirit he could not appreciate her essential goodness.

As he contemplated pony and rider trotting away from him at best speed, their combined form becoming smaller and smaller, he considered how her seat as a horsewoman had improved and how much she had learnt in a few months. Awakening from reverie, he decided he must not break contact with her, the information he might glean was too important. "I'll ring you. We must ride out together . . . . . in a few days . . . . . I'll give you a buzz," he shouted after her.

He turned for home by way of the road, rather than taking the Z-Path. There was much to be done, with little time to lose, and first he must organise transport with London.

Sean arrived home about five o'clock. In fading winter light, he glanced through the uncurtained window of the Smoker. Grandfather was sitting in one of the blue velvet chairs in front of silver-framed family photographs, while Flurry knelt by the wide, open log fire, in her hands a toasting fork. Grandfather was spreading butter and Marmite with increasingly shaky fingers. As Sean watched she laughed inclining her head with its long ponytail towards his knee. How well they understood each other. In old age, Grandfather's detachment from the everyday world gave him a bird's-eye view of proceedings, without having to become involved. For Flurry, he knew she did not take sides being both within the family, but not a member of it. Sean thought that she loved them all and he opened out his arms towards her in symbolic embrace.

The time had come. It was not fair to keep Flurry waiting longer. He must discuss with her the ramifications of Annie's Will and how it came about that he and Bridie shared, due to the intricacies of the Bowden and O Callaghan histories.

While they were enjoying tea Flurry described her encounter with Robert and the unexpected signs of oil.

Later that night Bert placed a rope lead with a slipknot round Patters' neck and without locking his cottage door walked quietly out into the darkness. He had no need of a torch, because the old man's eyes were as penetrating in the night as day time. Clever people might say that owing to his life outdoors, increased oxygen levels gave him a sharper sight and awareness.

He walked from his cottage past Lower Farm towards the forest and sneered with disgust when he noted Robert's car in the drive. Davies no longer bothered to hide visits to his cousin-by-marriage. A moment later the farmhouse door slammed in annoyance, and with hurried footsteps Robert approached his car, turned on the engine and backed it hastily and noisily into the lane. Bert and Patters leapt through a handy hole in the hedge so as not to be observed.

"Now where's 'e'm off to," said he to the dog, as they watched the cone of the BMW's lights search out the lane and turn right towards the gates of the Court. He wondered if he should alert Sean but thought better of it, as Robert appeared to be returning home.

Bert continued his clandestine way across fields which led to the hanging covert. The path was steep, slippery and February cold, while on a bank above him a fox speed by hunting for a nocturnal dinner, which might include an early lamb or free-ranging chicken. Patters whimpered. Bert gave him a disciplinary jerk to the halter, silence being imperative, as poacher and dog were, like Charlie Fox, looking for an illegitimate feast. Unlike the fox, Bert's was a nod-and-wink affair, because traditional landowners, and certainly the late Annie Bowden-Davies, turned a blind eye to the taking of a few pheasants, trout or salmon. The poacher is the gamekeeper's extra eye and ears, his secret

174

night-watch movements are quick to detect escaped cattle, sheep in distress, badger setts near jumps, and most importantly city gangs with 4-wheel drive and rifles, poaching venison for restaurants, or salmon netted from streams. To Bert, it was a point of honour that he never sold his gleanings, he either ate them himself or gave them to friends, which included Bowdens! Annie and Mara often had a good laugh when they enjoyed a delicious pheasant casserole, after a brace of birds had been left in a carrier bag on the handle of the back door. Origin unknown.

The old man sat on a sarsen stone and from his satchel he removed a skein of fine twine, upon which was threaded seeds of Indian corn. Patters waited, understanding the patient drill, although they were not needed till first light, Bert liked to prepare. Strangely, sounds of heavy diesel engines came from across the valley to their observant ears. It seemed as though one or more large lorries had halted near the fork where the road divided leading to either the village or Broxford Court, the drivers being unsure of their way. It was unusual. Narrow local roads were rarely frequented by heavy traffic unless fulfilling some special task, especially not in the early hours of a February night.

From his elevated position Bert watched and to his amazement saw by their lights two large covered lorries drive slowly up Robert's avenue, the headlights of one vehicle illuminating the outline of the monster in front. There was no time to telephone Sean and he must watch alone, so making a hound-jog of five miles an hour he ran towards the Court.

In spite of the darkness, Bert took every precaution not to be seen and eschewed the main tree-lined avenue, as it meant crossing the open lawns in front of the house. He preferred to travel by the outside fence of the paddocks and approach the stableblock at the back entrance.

Ancient brick gateposts were topped by age-worn stone hawks, the family crest, their wings half-open as though in perpetual vigilance. Man and dog took advantage of tall box hedges which protected gardens from coach-house and stableyard, and then moved warily towards the house.

Grey shadows passed back and across the ashlar facings of the stone arch to the yard bordered by coach-house, groom's lodgings and the back door to kitchens, pantry and stillroom of the Court. Bert heard men's voices and the scraping of boxes as they were unloaded from wheeled trucks to lorry ramps, to be stacked at the interiors. Holding Patters on a very tight lead Bert drew nearer, taking advantage of the shadow thrown by the door of the open feedstore. Two covered vans of the type used by house removal companies were parked by the door, their side-lights switched on, while two teams of three men each worked to load under the instructions of Robert and a stevedore foreman.

All was black and grey except where dull yellow light hit steel edgings to the trucks. The men conferred, then acted in dumb show. Bert surmised that large pictures were being removed, together with cabinets and assorted chests of objets d'art.

Knowing that he could do little more than watch, Bert decided to withdraw and crept silently back the way he had come. When they were out of earshot he gave Patters a special piece of cheese, his favourite tit-bit.

Henry Payne tapped the tips of his fingers together in his habitual manner when he felt uneasy, because Sean, sitting on the opposite side of the solicitor's desk, was recounting Bert's story.

"Pictures, perhaps silver and antiques, he thinks!" he sighed. "I'm not surprised! Robert has been evading our valuers for weeks and the only inventory we have is twenty years old. Robert can concoct any story he likes." He opened his desk drawer and drew out a letter. "And now we have received this from Robert's London solicitors.

"Dear Sirs,

Our client Robert Davies Esq is deeply concerned at the constant Threats and Harrying made by your firm with regard to the Valuation of the contents of Broxford Court.

Under the terms of his late wife's Will, Mr Davies is enabled to continue to live at the matrimonial house and this includes all furniture, works of art and appurtenances. Since no death duties are payable on estates passing from wife to husband, a valuation is irrelevant. Our client has instructed us to make a claim that all the said contents of the Court are his by right etc etc . . . ."

"Would a solicitor write a letter like that?"

"Depends which firm you go to . . . . . when buying time."

"Scurrilous."

Henry Payne continued mournfully, "You and I both know that this is nonsense, and quite out of order. Their claim will not stand up in Court. He is playing for time."

CHAPTER 14

Grandfather was initiating Flurry into the art of pruning roses. He liked to shorten their stems in October so that the wind would not shake their roots, then prune to two buds in early spring. Roses to Flurry had grown in public parks, or were cut for florists' shops, so his skill fascinated her and she was quick to learn the rudiments of the art. She was equally aware of Sean schooling a pair of young horses ready for the spring dressage trials at Ardingly in the outdoor manège on the far side of the hedge.

She admired Sean's graceful air of relaxed and easy competency, allied to an independent seat in all the movements the horse was able to make. His exacting balance was due to concentration, and use of his body as a counterweight to the horse. He was patient with each animal, persevering and utterly persistent in his schooling, and inviting the horse to do well for both itself and rider. After about forty minutes with each mount, he put each one in turn over a few small fences, using a variety of approaches and distances to keep the young animals fresh and enthusiastic and to improve their confidence and gait.

At coffee time, Sean came from the stables into the garden and helped to sweep up rose prunings and carry them away for burning. He pulled Flurry to him speaking quietly. "Will you come with me to Daisybrooke?"

Flurry was surprised, because each time he had promised to take her, something untoward had disrupted their plan, until she thought there must be something strange, sinister and unexpected about the place.

They drove in the Land Rover past Lower Farm which looked deserted and empty and neither allowed themselves to speak of the affair developing between Robert and Bridie. Further along, Bert was preparing his garden for early broad beans, while Patters gave a cheery bark. But they did not stop and drove on until the chequered dark blue and rose-coloured brick of Daisybrooke came into view, then they passed by the pollarded trees with their hands-on-shoulders to a far gate in the high garden wall. Sean opened the wicket leading to a small wooden chapel, where Flurry knew he attended Mass on Sundays, and took her hand. Flurry, wearing blue jeans and a brown check tweed jacket, with a well-tied cravat looked up at him with childlike confidence. The long, thick red plait down her back gave her the look of some elfin sprite. Her eyes were luminous.

Taking a key from his pocket he opened the steel security lock and picked up some letters and bills delivered to the doormat, making Flurry wonder if he were in charge of the chapel. Although built entirely of wood with a Queen-strut roof, it was more spacious than its green-painted exterior would suggest. Several large religious pictures, suggesting a wealthy patron, hung on buff-painted walls, and light from pink-tinted window glass lit the small altar with its fair linen cloths, crucifix, two candlesticks and missal, placed upon a cushion. Before it on a step, an arrangement of fresh flowers made her think of Barbarka. She sat quietly on one of the thirty or so rush-seated chairs, while Sean stood in prayer at the altar-step.

He remained there for a long time detached from the present and Flurry thought he had forgotten her, so with trepidation and in painful recollection, she remembered another time, place and country. This was in Switzerland, eleven months ago, when she and Harry had attended a scientific conference at Lucerne. For some reason, best known to himself, they visited the gorgeous baroque Abbey of Einsiedeln.

Entering the Lady Chapel of the Abbey, she had felt overwhelmed by the magnificent abundance of colour and shapes in the pulpit and cupola area. Clouds, painted in gold and white, revealed frescos of heavenly groupings, while the entire splendour was concentrated on the statue of the Black Madonna, who was adorned and clothed in the gold embroidered style of dress of the mediaeval Spanish Court. Harry, it appeared, was making his pilgrimage to the divinely consecrated chapel itself. How little she knew about the man whose bed she had shared for nearly ten years, she, being unaware even, that he was Catholic. The girl waited puzzled and not knowing how to act. Should she kneel with him? But his cold, isolated demeanour made her reluctant to approach him. She felt shut-out, disregarded, uneasy.

After a long time Harry rose from his knees. He did not look at his companion but merely walked away, to admire ostentatiously the golden pulpit with its red curtain high up beneath an exploding sunburst. She watched his tall, proud figure walk slowly down the aisle, and then she knew, knew for certain, that she had no part in his life and would never be accepted into the inner circle of his family. She was on the outside looking in.

Had he brought her to this solemn place to tell her just that? To inform her without committing himself. Without creating a scene? Then she had understood for the first time, that Harry had taken ten years from her life and she was old before her time. For them there was nothing. Only oblivion.

Flurry rested her head against the wooden back of the chair in front of her in this small English chapel a million miles from the ornate splendour of Einsiedelm. She was too stricken for tears, until she felt a warm arm round her waist.

"Come and light our candles now."

He led her to the back of the chapel. Here below a strutted extension, pale-coloured paint gave way to the green of the exterior, and in the gloom stood a row of candles, those lamps of faith, in their wire holders. A paper envelope had written on it the words 'Red 50p. Yellow 25p.' Flurry felt in her pocket and to her chagrin could only muster ten pence.

The votive light glowed from three candles.

"For the family. For Annie and for us."

Flurry nestled against him and could feel his heart beating. She stretched out her hands to collect the warmth from the candles, until presently he said: *"Annie was my mother!"*

Startled, she looked up, searching his face. Slowly recollections, memories, half-insinuations flooded her mind. Pictures of Sean and Annie jumping a gate, the two always riding together. 'Sean's Gran taught Annie to ride,' from Bert. 'They do say,' Dolly had said. 'But it's not for me to gossip.'

The day of the Charleville Blazers, when they stood alongside the wall of Daisybrooke in New Year's sunshine before bitter snow, how alike they were, the timbre of their voices, every gesture, the intensity of the eyes. And the heat of the candles melded to the moment when time and space were forgotten.

Flurry thought, 'I think I must have known, but never allowed myself to speculate.' As he said no more, Flurry volunteered "Gaylord said your father was drowned."

"That was years later. The affair started when Annie went to Trinity College, Dublin, where she read biology, as she loved plants and animals, I think she told you. The O Callaghans and Bowdens are distant cousins, so it was natural that Granny Tamzine asked her to stay at Clavincade and she spent the long summer vacations riding our horses and fishing for trout and salmon with Gran on the Blackwater. I believe she felt more at home with us than living with her parents. They were very old and very backward-looking. Annie wasn't like that, and she and Rory liked to build hides for the shoot, and sail from Youghal in the wild and treacherous swell of the Atlantic. The challenge excited her."

"Rory? Your father?"

"He was Tamzine's only son and he and Annie fell for each other, theirs was the great love of their lives. Unfortunately, they could never marry as in those days divorce was impossible, he being Catholic, and Rory was married to an estranged wife. They had lived apart for many years. Annie left Trinity and the following year I was born."

Later he continued, "Annie gave birth in the great four-poster bed with red velvet curtains where all Clavincade heirs come into the world. There was never any attempt to hide the affair from neighbours, and people who worked for us, as we are very relaxed about that sort of thing and I was officially adopted by my father as Sean Rory O

Callaghan." There was no trace of the Irish vernacular in Sean's speech, as though he wished to emphasise his English roots. "As Annie told you when you visited her, her parents were very strait-laced, as well as being elderly."

"I remember."

"She liked you."

Flurry was perplexed . "I wasn't . . . . ."

"On approval? Now whatever put that into your head!"

"Some intonation."

"Annie was very perceptive."

"And you?"

He changed the subject, unwilling to speculate on the future. "She couldn't bring me back to the Court. It was too English. Too stultifying, no love-child would ever have been happy. My father was Master of the Charleville Blazers and he asked Annie to be his joint Master."

"That was why."

"Annie lived at home with us, so she could look after me, and she helped father hunt hounds. Gran Tazmine taught her all she needed to know, and more, much more, as she adored Annie. Gran was the best horsewoman in all Ireland, there's nothing she doesn't know about horses. Or hounds for that matter.

"About the time I went away to prep school, Annie's parents fell ill, first Grandpa and then Grandma followed, so Annie went home for over three years of harrowing illness. It drained her. Then, just when she and father could plan for the future he was drowned in a great storm off Youghal, when several ships were wrecked and even the car ferry capsized with all souls lost. Rory was an experienced yachtsman, but never used an auxiliary engine." There seemed to be little more to explain, and Flurry understood how easy it had been for the charming, seductive Robert to capture Annie on a romantic cruise.

"We'll go outside," he added. "It's stifling in here," and Sean locked the door, leading her towards the garden.

Flurry wondered what the effect had been on Robert, knowing that Sean was his stepson! The implications were too — she hardly liked to think the word — ludicrous, to be contemplated! She now understood the antagonism between the two men, but did Robert know the truth before Annie died? The answer to that altered the complexion of everything.

Primroses in mown grass were peeping amongst early daffodils, while pink bergenia had burst into full flower in a raised wall-bed, in front of a large grouping of shrubs, their contrasting green and white leaves gossamer against eucalyptus, which had survived winter winds. Iris was showing broad fronds, at the feet of jasmine pinned to six-foot enclosing walls, and early buds of rose, blue geranium, peony and poppy were alert and thinking of spring.

They walked to the back of the house and Flurry was entranced to see how beautiful the domicile was, parts being sixteenth century in origin. Facing three acres of broad lawn and formal garden, was a large window of eight lights with two transoms, and Sean waved to a small white-haired old lady sitting in a Jacobean wing-chair. Her companion, standing beside her, attempted to draw the patient's attention to Sean and Flurry.

"Dear Janey, she has Alzheimer's. I think she's forgotten who I am again."

'And what', Flurry thought, 'might the fact of Sean being Annie's son bring to the heady mixture of Wiltshire gossip?' However, she only said "Who does the chapel belong to?"

"To all of us. It's a gift." Then shedding the Wiltshire part of his character usually so reticent. "But Daisybrooke belongs to me. Janey only leases it. It was Annie's gift and I was to live here when we formed the stud."

Flurry considered 'And now the project's dead? But is it?' And continued to keep silent, while the image of Tamzine O Callaghan, dressed in black, came into her mind. Gran Tamzine who adored Annie, seemed to be a perpetual presence. She kept turning up, as though part of her lived in Broxford Court, and that she was with them, and always had been. She remembered that day in Lawson's when Robert said: "His Grandmother's a witch!" Flurry realised that she had had all the pieces of this strange puzzle available to her from the very beginning, except that she had never known how to arrange them. Like a jigsaw with no picture. Looking at Daisybrooke's beautiful architecture, with its mellow fullness, it seemed exactly right for Sean and she envied him, until he said, "I should never have come!" and, with extreme bitterness in his voice, "I blame myself for Annie's death, I caused her killing, it was because of me she died. Nothing, but nothing will come between me and bringing Robert to book."

"You didn't know. How could you. You can't torment yourself for something you didn't do, even though with hindsight you might have acted differently."

He was not convinced and jumped off the wall. "Now you understand why Bridie and I share the residue of the estate. Bridie because the Bowdens made the money in the first place as merchant bankers. And me. Me . . . . . if I hadn't come Robert would never have known and would not have felt threatened."

"Did Robert know you were Annie's son?"

He waited a few seconds. "No. She didn't trust him. He must have guessed."

Flurry remembered the night in the old White Horse. The smug looks from Bert and the Three Musketeers. They knew. The Charleville Blazers had 'spoken' to them. They knew. And Robert had guessed. Flurry now understood the appalling consequences when people do not 'listen' and have nobody to 'put them right'.

"You can't prove it," Flurry stormed. "You can't prove anything. It might have been an accident." Sean walked away laughing. A noisy, animal laugh, that made Flurry shudder. There were so many facets, many layers to the character of this enigmatic man.

Above them four miles to the west, the *Finger* peered towards the garden over tall, brick chimney-stacks. Encased in its pale blue background, the rock crag appeared less menacing then usual, as though in promise of a solution and towards future calm, while Sean's intensity of purpose persuaded her of his genuine intentions towards herself.

The police car with a detective sergeant in plain clothes and his companion the tall, severe-looking Chief Inspector Saul Parker, passed through the wrought-iron gates leading to the park at Broxford Court. Being February, chestnut buds in the avenue were shedding their sticky bracts to show fresh green fingers. To a casual eye, the facade, with its giant portico of Corinthian columns surmounted by a pediment, appeared as it always had, but to Parker something was lacking. No welcoming Barbarka was waiting to open the glass door to guests. No lights shone, its sash-windows looking dead. The door-bell echoed as through empty, deserted depths from somewhere in the lower quarters of the Court and it was a full five minutes before Robert appeared in the hall.

Parker's eyebrows raised a fraction on seeing Robert, although his face showed no other comment or sign of recognition. However, he was shocked at Davies's appearance. Instead of the usual smart, rather overstated country clothes, the man was dressed in old corduroy trousers and a sweater that had seen better days. His face was tired and careworn. He was unshaven, and there were dark rings below his eyes, while even the crisp curls were lank, making him look ten years older than a few months previously. Parker doubted that his changed look was due to grief.

The detective sergeant showed Robert his card, but Parker being present as an unofficial observer was not introduced, and Robert led the two men across the hall. The house was cold, and how different it appeared to Parker from the day when Annie had given a reception to the worthies of the county. Representatives of the County Council, police department, St John Ambulance, together with many other organisations had been graciously entertained. The hall was welcoming with flowers, and surely the staircase held many more pictures.

They entered the study. "You live alone, sir?" said the detective sergeant.

"Can't afford staff now. How can I afford to pay staff on the pittance left me?" Robert was inconsolably bitter. "Besides, the place is let. To a city firm."

They sat down on comfortless plastics covered chairs. The fax machine seemed to be the only operative thing in that austere room. Its colours, Parker thought, were depressing. A large pile of papers were laid out on the office-type desk.

"And you'll be living where?" went on the sergeant.

"Does it matter?"

"Doubtless you'll be leaving your address."

Robert did not volunteer any more information. The detective continued, "There are a few routine questions I would like to ask you, sir."

Parker watched Robert intently. It seemed as though part of him was acutely focused on the coming interview, while the other half of his mind was completely split away, disassociated from the present.

"Miss Julie Baker was an employee of yours, I believe."

"Of the Company, yes."

"And you knew her personally."

"Of course. I make a point of knowing all my people who work for me." There was no hesitation on Robert's part in answering the sergeant's restrained, probing questions, and he seemed to be a policeman's perfect witness, being composed, accurate and confident.

"Is it correct, sir, that Miss Baker's car was reported as stolen?"

"Technically yes. She had left our employment, taking the car with her."

Parker didn't like Robert, although he kept any sign of antipathy from his face as, long ago, he had imposed a rigid control over his emotions.

"When did you become aware sir, that the woman who died on the road to Broxford Court might be one of your employees?"

"On the road which *could* lead to my home," corrected Robert. "The car might have been going to several different places!" He blew out his cheeks. "But to answer your question . . . . . . by slow degrees. A matter of deduction, I suppose. The newspaper report was obviously a factor. When a horrific accident happens near your home, it's natural to take an interest. And the paper cited London to be where she lived. Later I had a call from Mr Singh, saying that the company car lent to Julie had crashed and the *Wiltshire* police were investigating. It was the word Wiltshire which first made me think."

The sergeant made a mental note to ascertain whether any mention of the Wiltshire police had been divulged and if the fact could be verified.

"Then, of course, there was the question of the telephone call!" Did Parker imagine it or was there a suspicion of triumph in his voice. Of trumping their ace!

"Telephone call, sir?"

"Implicating Rawle of Lower Cottage. He lives nearly opposite my cousin-by-marriage Miss Bridie Hesketh. She said he was screaming blue-murder up and down the lane. Apparently, one of your chaps had called because an anonymous phone call had told them he was in the habit of carrying unsecured oil drums in the back of his pick-up truck and had contributed to the accident, a charge he strongly denied. Bridie said he was utterly furious, stumping up and down, and it was some time before she could get any sense out of him."

"Did he say the source of the telephone call?" asked the sergeant.

"Not as far as I'm aware of. He didn't say. But remember, I have it second-hand from my cousin. There may have been omissions or embroidery on the way, so you might verify my account with her." After a moment's pause he went on "Later I heard from Mr Singh that a distant cousin of my wife's, a Mr Sean O Callaghan, was interested, but I expect you know that."

Parker wondered whether Robert was being disingenuous and leading them where he wished the questions to go.

"Which brings me to a rather delicate question, if I may say so, sir. Did you ever have any personal relations with Julie Baker, other than as an employee?"

Robert paused, longer this time, to make a dramatic effect. "May I enquire. Is it possible for the police to be discreet, if there is no question of the public interest being at stake?"

The sergeant inclined his head, and Robert got up to pace the room, thrusting his hands into trouser pockets as though in embarrassment. He pouted a lower lip. "You know how it is when we get older, towards that middle time of life. And my wife had not been well . . . . . I knew I could depend on Julie to be discreet, and my visit to the flats would call for no comment. The affair did not last long and meant absolutely nothing to me, as I was a happily married man." He sat down again as if drained, but looked up with such innocence as though thankful to have confessed.

The sergeant continued relentlessly. "And Baker left your employ when?"

"When in Mr Singh's opinion she was not fit enough for work."

"She was pregnant, I understand."

"So Mr Singh tells me."

"And you have no occasion . . . . . ?"

"None," he chipped in too quickly, "I can assure you of that." He laughed nervously ". . . . . of that I will assure you."

"One last question. If Baker were travelling to the Court, and we must take this into consideration, can you tell us why that was?"

"I have no idea. Singh thinks she might have come to ask for my help. For money. By law, we had to keep her employment open for her, but she could have been in financial difficulty and had no-one else to turn to."

As they entered the hall and walked towards the front door, the sergeant said suddenly, "Were you aware that your late wife visited Miss Baker?"

Robert's eyes twinkled beneath the heavy, shaded lids. "So she told me. Very charitable was my darling Annie."

".It was no secret?"

"Why should it be?" And with the last parting shot they left the Court.

"And that, if Sean O Callaghan is correct," said the former Chief Superintendent Saul Parker to the sergeant as they drove away ". . . . . is the performance of a lifetime." And he wondered if Robert had any formal stage training.

The detective sergeant was inclined to agree with him.

Bridie took the bus for her local market town. Beyond a handsome market place and near the imposing town hall with its centre an ample bow and rusticated ground floor, lay an historic, mediaeval alley, where Bridie knew she could find a milliners, with hats-for-hire. She looked through the extensive shop windows. Spring was in the air. There were mouth-watering hats to suit every taste, type and occasion. Wedding hats, for Ascot, for lunch, opera or evening parties were arranged in a plethora of colours. Bridie had one idea in mind. She wanted a hat for a bride-to-be.

The Edwardian shop-bell tinkled, and Bridie walked down two stone steps. The owner came forward as Mara sometimes hired one of their hats for a formal occasion. Everyone seemed to be doing it these days, being so much cheaper, and it was no surprise that Bridie asked for a hat for a very special day, although other than that she would be wearing a blue suit, the girl seemed vague. Bridie hoped that Madame Fez would not think it best to have a word with Mummy, even though she looked surprised that Bridie needed the hat immediately. Today. White hats did not seem to suit her slightly swarthy face with its eyebrows like minute clothes-brushes. She did not like cream or pink, besides so many of that year's hats were for the chic, the ultra-smart woman, which made choosing difficult. It was a great year for clothes. She could not carry off the high crowns like bowler-hats with their exotic feathers, or the swept-up brims, and not flowers accentuating a hat's excessive width. Madame tried to tempt her with a small, close-fitting cloche, which had style but little trim.

Then Bridie saw it! An amazing creation in burnt straw! It was an enormous hat, very beautiful, but the sort that only an extremely thin model, of at least six feet in height, could carry off. Madame had bought it for the shop, as a kind of sales motif.

She pointed, and asked to try it on.

"Really? . . . . . is it really you? What occasion is the hat for exactly?"

But she did not answer, and took the creation off the stand, placing it on her head. She looked in the mirror. The straw crown was decorated with silken flowers, exotic velvet fruits and sprays of corn, constructed from tiny, shining shells and sequins. Bridie closed her eyes. It was perfect. And she imagined the tropical paradise that Robert had, in great secret, described to her. A fantastic sea-jewel where they would be married.

"I will take it!" Now Bridie had no money and the hat had cost a thousand pounds, making its hire charge high. She was chagrined that Robert was less free with his money than he had promised. Madame appeared dubious, as Bridie looked a bit sad in the over-decorated, over-powering hat. However, she didn't want to offend good customers and took Bridie's cheque, the girl knowing by her face that she would ask Mara to pay if there was any doubt. Discretion with ladies' secrets in a small town is vital.

Bridie went to the bus stop rejoicing, knowing she would be far away when the cheque bounced. The hat was packaged in a large, striped hatbox, for all the world to see, but she dare not shout out "I'm a bride-to-be. I'm to be married, so shucks-to-you, you mothers with pretty daughters!"

Flurry walked up the polished, fumed-oak staircase to her bedroom. At evening stables, they had been busy preparing the two boxes for tomorrow's event. Sean, Mara and Grandfather were to travel together, and start off early, while Diarmid followed driving the horsebox. His battered, plastics suitcase was already packed with all his worldly goods, comprising best breeches, well-cut boots, tweed jacket and cap inherited from Rory many years ago, because no-one looked smarter than Diarmid, or his horses, at a horse show. Even his hand-made shirt from the best shirtmakers in Dublin was one of Sean's, who gave it to him in a fit of generosity,

Flurry sat on her bed in the dark with only a crack of light showing under an uneven bottom to the door. Since his revelation at Daisybrooke, her relationship with Sean seemed more complicated than before, as the situation created more problems than it solved. Unlike him, she believed there was little to be done to unravel the mystery of his mother's death and it was better to leave crime to the patient and careful work of the police, rather than play at amateur detective.

Her chief concern was that in the intensity of his fury at Annie's death, Sean would, like *The Flying Dutchman*, sail the world looking for Robert to bring him to justice. Should, as Sean suspected, Robert leave Britain, then he would follow him and never let go, this was to assuage his imagined guilt at being the cause of his adored mother's murder. And self-reproach is the most bitter of all follies. It destroys a man. But was it murder? Obviously Sean and Bert had access to information of which she had no idea. But to be realistic, pushing a heavy, fit horse together with its rider over a cliff seemed far-fetched, unless they used a tractor and chain! Even the police had no suspicions, because they had nothing concrete to investigate, except a strong motive and vague rumour.

Flurry knew that as long as the mystery was unresolved, the future for Sean and herself was hopeless. They had no future together and Annie would always be between them, egging Sean on. How alike these two were. They possessed the same intensity of purpose, and she had to admit it, the same selfish determination to have it their way. She got up quickly and turned on the light.

Standing in the middle of the room Flurry felt lonely and at a loose end, as she now began to feel guilty herself! How much of this had she brought on them both by her not leaving Sean alone? He must have guessed she loved him and his feelings for her were compassionate, sincere and warm, but was any commitment by him to her an added burden? She could not know him in the few months of their acquaintance. Had she given him time to know her?

She decided she must live one day after another, and as she was not seeing the London solicitors until the day after tomorrow, also knowing the date for the MOT test on her car was drawing near, she decided to have it serviced and spend the waiting time in Bath. That would take care of the next day. She further thought that she might ring Gaylord in the morning and seek an interview with him.

Gaylord Pring had impressed her far more than she realised and the emotional strain of the past few weeks made her half-wish for a comparatively straight-forward business life. Cash flow, sales charts, forward planning, market research and computing demand models were at least rational, they did not tear heart from body.

Yes, she would telephone Gaylord. He had said "After Easter," and she looked forward to working with TTT once more. Besides she must find herself a furnished flat, somewhere near her beloved river Thames so that she could watch the lapping tide and hear wild seabirds to still her soul. She must go forward however painful that was. Not reminisce. Not cling to Bowden's Grove. Not look to the past, although as she lay down, her heart was in mourning.

CHAPTER 15

There is an old saying that because of the loss of a horseshoe nail, a whole kingdom was lost. An estate may not be a kingdom, but although Robert undoubtedly knew the ancient proverb, he could not have been aware that it applied to him, on the morning he decided to do urgent business in Bath.

The day before, the Broxford farm manager had put thirty young store cattle into a meadow behind Robert's stableyard. The following morning early, being both young and inquisitive, they had broken a wooden fencing post and pulled out nails holding their barbed-wire fence. Smashing through the fence-hedge, three steers escaped into the lane. Robert's only groom-cum-handyman stopped washing his employer's cars, to give chase to lost cattle. This meant that hurrying to journey to Bath, Robert found his BMW covered in detergent suds, and was forced to take the Land Rover instead.

Driving along the A4 Robert was about twenty minutes behind Flurry's Peugeot, which she was taking to the garage for service, and Robert entering the outskirts of the city saw Flurry get into a hire car on the garage forecourt by the petrol pumps.

Her near presence made him consider a possible fresh course of reasoning, as the visit from the police had scared him more than he dared admit. It made him wonder what, if any, fresh evidence they had to hand and it was imperative that he kept one jump ahead of the sergeant, and in particular the tall man whom he suspected as being a high-powered officer.

Flurry intrigued him. She was intelligent, fiercely loyal to the Bowdens and especially Sean, but with an openness which could be outwitted. He began to regard her as a 'window' through which he could see any moves the opposition might make. He must ensure he had adequate time.

Mid-morning traffic was heavy and he was aware that Flurry's taxi was three cars behind him. Keeping to the inside lane, he manoeuvred to let the other vehicle pass him, in order to follow it as far as Milsom Street. Here, he saw Flurry get out, wave to the driver and cross the road to enter a large department store.

Luckily, Robert found a clearway and quickly turning left, then left again, he was able to park in a small enclosed yard known to local people. Giving the attendant a tip to park the Land Rover, Robert hurried down a narrow passage and crossing Milsom Street followed his quarry into the shop.

It was not long before he spied her in the hat department, and waiting for an opportunity when no assistant was hovering. "Charming. Charming, my dear. You should always wear pretty hats. For London, I presume.'

The cinnamon-coloured silk hat with its self-silk rose brought out the tone of her red hair, and shading her face accentuated green flecks in her eyes.

"Yes," and not wishing to appear rude, "I'm going to town tomorrow."

"They're away *again*, are they?"

"Why not?"

"Leaving you."

"I could have gone, had I wanted to."

"London must be more fun for a gal like you. And seeing Gaylord Pring."

Flurry was flabbergasted, having only telephoned his secretary that morning. 'How is it,' she thought, 'that Robert seems to predict my every move' but only said "I'm not as it happens," and correcting herself "Well not until the day after."

"Lucky Gaylord."

"Not at all. I'm simply lunching with a future boss."

"So you've decided."

"Decided what?"

"To take his offer."

"How do you know? What's it to do with you?"

"Nothin' m'dear. Absolutely nothing . . . . . just passing the time of day to be sociable. There's not much of it nowadays."

"Not much what?" She felt she was being rude.

"Polite social contact."

Flurry found herself saying "You started it."

"Started what?"

"I'm sorry. I didn't mean anything. Nothing at all." Now she was apologising.

"We can be friends. What are they to us?" The assistant came with Flurry's account, placing the hat in a plastic bag. "Won't you wear your hat?"

"No."

"For lunch," and he took her arm. "Please. Please be kind, and have lunch with me. The hat looks lovely, but perhaps you'll wear it another time."

Standing close, although not noticeably so, and slightly behind her, he took her arm and piloted her towards the rear door of the shop. Flurry did not want to go, but Robert had taken control. She tried to think of an excuse, but couldn't find one. Robert was unlike any person she had ever met, and nothing you could say to him, would he take amiss. You could not touch him. Insult him. Offend him. He simply turned the jibe, the point of thrust, to his own advantage, nor could she imagine him losing his temper, he was too dangerous for that.

They turned through two narrow streets to enter the elegance of Queen's Square. Ornamental trees shimmered with expectant green, and a party of Chinese tourists were smiling at everything and taking photographs of each other in front of the obelisk erected by Beau Nash. He led her along the south side of the square while he relaxed her with his small talk at which he was an expert, and Flurry felt drawn to him. He was at his best, the perfect luncheon escort. Robert introduced her to a select French restaurant she did not know existed, where the front window was stacked high with corks from a thousand French wines. A bell tinkled as they pressed the brass latch, while sticks of French bread crowded a dresser opposite the fire, burning in its eighteenth century, wrought-iron grate. Naughty Parisian prints crowded walls, and hundreds of picture postcards decorated the cash desk.

Flurry realised she was tried after a taut, restless night, and was thankful to sit on a velvet sofa holding a welcome glass of gin and tonic. Robert ordered lunch and she wondered how he guessed what her favourite dishes might be. He regarded the wine list, and knowing that she must have learnt something about the grape, he chose a wine which was expensive, but not pretentious, seeming about right.

"You like your steak rare, I believe. Pink in the middle and charcoal grilled outside. The meat here is good. French butchered."

The collection of ethnic fans decorating the open beams appeared to cool the air. He patted her hand. "I believe we think alike, and the bucolic lives we lead can be less than inspiring. It's nice to get away." With no introduction he said ". . . . . had a call from the police recently. About Bert."

"Bert? Whatever for?"

"Storing oil. It gave me quite a shock, you finding that oil . . . . . and Sean informing them!"

Flurry was confused as to how she should answer and said nothing, allowing him to rattle on. "I told the police that your Rawle had probably been pinching oil, and storing it under the straw."

"You didn't!"

"Of course I didn't, darling, as I know he's a friend of yours. Your face is a picture, my sweet!" Then with a sudden change of tack "Is Bert with them today. Has he gone away too?"

"No. Someone has to look after the horses."

"And you're off tomorrow and not coming back till the day after."

Flurry tackled her cheese while Robert poured the coffee. She shook her head to brandy.

"While the cat's away, why don't us mice play! Come out for a ride tomorrow."

"Really I must go. Thank you for lunch, it was brilliant, but I have to catch my bus."

"I'll take you home."

Flurry said goodbye with as much grace as she could muster, wishing she had not come. She escaped to the door. Unfortunately it was raining cats and dogs, heavy rain, which poured off over-filled gutters and flooded the pavement. Robert caught her up, taking her arm. The car park attendant had placed the Land Rover close to others, one each side of it and Robert had to open the narrow back door to help Flurry up, guiding her towards a front seat.

When they drove up to Bowden's Grove Bert was watching from the stableyard. He was leaning his chin on the handle of a broom when Robert kissed Flurry goodbye, and she hurried into the house. A moment later she came out again, looking anxiously at Robert's Land Rover as it disappeared down the drive. Then, without a word to Bert she took Mara's Traveller, even though it was sadly down on its wheels, and dashed off towards the Court. Bert watched and waited until she came back. Meanwhile he sorted the large bunch of keys Sean had entrusted to him and spelt out his instructions for their use.

No-one answered the doorbell to the Court, and it had a hollow sound echoing down into the empty mansion. Flurry wandered up and down the shallow stone steps under the portico, then decided to find her way round the house towards the backyard. She passed the lawns with their formal, clipped yew trees, and saw once more the ha-ha, where on New Year's Eve the great hunt had enjoyed Annie's last meet.

Looking under the archway, Flurry saw Robert's Land Rover parked, and she tapped at the kitchen door. No answer. No dogs. No cat. Nobody seemed to work here any more, however, she had to find her handbag left behind in the car, and with sudden trepidation she made her way towards the vehicle. Trying the narrow rear door it opened and she climbed up.

There was no handbag anywhere, although she was sure she had left it by the front seat. She lifted a pile of odd coats and mackintoshes and looked in a cardboard box. No handbag. In desperation she investigated a large saddlebag tucked under one of the backseats. First she lifted out a green velvet hunting cap, thinking that perhaps Robert had put her bag away for safety, and then turned over a Barbour with it's green collar. At first the significance of the find did not dawn on her. Then as recollection flooded back, she sat there quite still, aghast.

The horse standing by the Blind House was no 'ringer': it was Tiger Bay tied up on that fateful New Year's Eve, and the man wearing Charleville Blazer coat and cap was Robert because he was wearing *mahogany-top* boots! And she knew that no-one wore mahogany-tops unless they were wearing a red coat. She closed her eyes to shut out the image of a triple murderer.

"I took your handbag into the house. If you'd waited I'd have brought it up!" Robert was standing there. He indicated the coat and cap she was holding. "I see you've found darling Annie's green hat. I keep it with me as it reminds me . . . . . of happier days!"

She struggled not to faint, he was patting the handbag evocatively, and sat down on the tailgate. "You must have guessed . . . . . I'm desperately lonely." His body blocked escape. "Annie's loss has hurt more than I could have believed possible."

Not daring to move, she understood that Sean was right. Why hadn't she listened to him.

"Annie," he leaned reflectively against the door. "She was a Master y'know." He took the coat and cap from Flurry. "Charleville Blazers. Wore the green hat," and opening the Barbour "See, it's hers. Extra large size."

Flurry said nothing, with her knees drawn up to the chin as though in protection, while he diving into the pocket "Her handkerchief, look," and held it out pressing his nose into the velvet collar. "Her perfume." He waved a hand as though to waft it towards her. "There was face powder too," and sadly "It shook off!"

It was Sean's truth or his, and Flurry wondered if Robert knew that Sean was Annie's son. Again, did he realise that she knew? How could she tell Sean about the mahogany-tops in time, before it was too late? Why was no-one here?

"You look tired, darling. Won't you come into the house?"

Finding her voice. "No, I've got to go."

"Make you a cup of tea."

"No. Let me go." He was laughing at her.

"If you wish. Why shouldn't you go? I'm not keeping you, just being friendly, that's all, as I know you're lonely too, they all being away, only want to help, because I can read you like a book. You listen to Sean too much, and you can't trust him, y'know. Born wrong side of the bed, if you get my meaning!" She ran over to the Traveller. "Ghastly car! Don't forget your handbag m'dear." He handed it to her, then prattled on. "Would have thought Mara'd buy herself a new motor with all the money they're inheriting. But they'll never learn. They think poor, so they always will be. Poor and slovenly." Shutting the door as she turned on the engine. "Don't forget tomorrow, I'll be up about eight-thirty. Get Bert to tack you up, we'll have our ride, then I'll take you to the station . . . . . wish I were coming to London too. But too busy."

He saw Flurry drive out accelerating so fast that she nearly crashed into the stone gateway, then he turned to the Land Rover throwing himself down on the wooden floor with an exhaustion following iron control. It must be hours now. Not days. He knew they had locked on to him, how or why he might never know, and Flurry was the chief danger because she must never be allowed to speak to Sean. Once in Panama City he could travel as to where extradition was impossible, while working his finance through Zurich friends. He dreaded dragging Bridie with him, although she was an expendable store and it would not be for long. What a pleasure it'd be to get shot of her! Laughter returned to him. He had the advantage. Time. Precious hours before Sean came home, and he got up with his face runnelled from the lines of the boards used to repair the floor.

Yet Flurry was the danger, she being the gluon, the energy, that held the pack together, and he feared her, admired her, felt an affinity with her, knowing how well they could have worked together in different circumstances.

Different. Indifferent. The sound of the word to his over-energised synapses recalled that indifference had cost Annie, his darling Annie, her life. She was so perfect, but she never listened to his tears. The tears of the disaffectionados. The lost ones.

And Sean. How he loved him! Was proud of him beyond dreams, as his son, albeit he being only a step-father. Sean was everything he had ever wanted to be. Curling forward as though in pain, the tears came when he remembered the lack of trust, slights, injustices, secrecy and petty snubs he had endured. He, Robert Davies, sophisticated, polished, internationally educated, clever, but he cut no ice. And would never be accepted.

Take Bert. That clown or goon, with a cap bigger than his brains. That waster and shirker. *He* knew that Sean was Annie's son and tears poured down his face at the shame of it, the humiliation of knowing that no-one would 'speak' to him. Oh yes! Sean had plenty of time to waste with Bert.

He recalled a certain market day after the pair had sold half a dozen of Bert's calves. Returning from shopping, Robert had seen the two having lunch in a pub. Bert with his cap on was shovelling in black pudding and mushy peas, even though he was Somerset! Sean was discussing something interesting and Robert knew he daren't join them, be friendly with them, or they would have some excuse to go off home. Sean had plenty of time to waste with Bert!

Even Annie! She had time for Dolly and they'd often have a laugh and gossip together. Also, Robert was beside himself at the thought of that asinine Major being asked to join the shoot as guest. Annie's shoot, where even he, her husband, felt out-of-place, all due to this British hierarchy. This social cohesiveness.

Annie's indifference! If only she had told him about Sean she would have been alive now. Robert was capable of cutting out the actual manner of her death from his mind, like a clothes-moth he could cut holes in his memory. And if only Sean had once, just once, spoken to him as father, step-father would do, he could have loved him and given him anything he wanted, because Sean was everything he would be proud to be. Robert knew he would have been perfectly happy for Sean to take over the estate. Do as he pleased, manage the farm, land, stud, bloody tenants, Sean could have the lot, leaving him with dignity, with a place, money to travel a little. Be free of claustrophobia. She had to die to ensure he, Robert, was not cheated out of inheriting Annie's money. Money was his idol.

Now Flurry? Things might be neutralised. Robert always thought of saving his own skin first, as a main priority, and co-incident with his feelings for the girl, it would expiate part of his own identity. Recovering from over-charged reverie, Robert dashed over to his pristine BMW, to drive at high speed towards the city. This time his business was very urgent indeed.

Two hours later Bridie received a telephone call from him, with explicit instructions as to what she must do, then wondering, and somewhat scared, she went upstairs to pack. She was to marry a man she hardly knew, was twenty years older than herself, and of whom she was even a little frightened. She had learnt that Robert had a character that could never be crossed or argued with.

Until now marriage had been a pleasant daydream, but she had never considered the hard facts of giving herself in marriage. Robert's telephone call had instructed her to prepare for a night flight to Panama City, and also that she was not to tell a soul. She wondered why Robert had leaked their destination if it were a secret, but realised that complications could occur at the airport control.

A hurried night flight! This was Bridie's first alarm to reality. In her pipedream, she had envisaged an ocean liner sailing from Portsmouth, like she had seen in films, with bands playing and flags waving amidst cheers from the dockside, perhaps to the tune of *We Are Sailing*. Bridie had always been a fan of Rod Stewart. But no! She was facing fourteen hours of flight with Robert in a cramped seat. This reminded her of the plane to Frankfurt.

Taking down her school suitcase, the various labels recalled those journeys to Germany and to a clinic for the deaf. It brought back her fear of flying and of being trapped in a narrow airborne coffin, but most of all her terror at leaving the home she felt safe in at Bowden's Grove. Another label spoke of her many journeys to Skegness and to boarding-school. She fingered the picture of the little sailor with his sea-boots and fisherman's hat, and the caption *Skegness is so Bracing!* Strangely, Bridie wished she were only going to school and not halfway round the world with a man she distrusted. Suddenly she realised that she must sleep in a bed vacated by dead Aunt Annie! An old aunt who had fallen over a cliff!

Her stomach in turmoil, she started to pack the few clothes she had. Robert had promised much, but it was always "When my money arrives." And Bridie had begun to think it was likely to be when her money arrived! Unable to bear the tension any longer she sped down the narrow stairs and went to the gate. No-one was about and only the dim light from Bert's cottage could be seen further down the lane. She went back indoors and wrote:

"Dear Mummy," then crossed it out and wrote:

"Darling Mumsie,

Robert wants to marry him and we are flying to Panama City starting tomorrow. Will you come and see us off. Please don't be angry.

Love,

Bridie XXXXX."

Pushing it into a used envelope she wrote, "Mummy. Urgent" on the front and running down the lane tapped on Bert's door. It took some time for him to quieten the girl, whom he had known since babyhood. After taking her home and making her promise to go to bed, he opened the envelope, read the contents, and set to work.

Meanwhile, nobody appeared to be at home when Flurry returned to Bowden's Grove as it was getting dark. Mara had taken the dogs with her because they loved a holiday and staying in an hotel enjoying chef's best bones. It had been habit and pure routine that brought Flurry safely back and she still shook with fear when she turned off the Traveller's engine. All the terrors of square faces, tower blocks and the Greenwich Foot tunnel was melded into Robert's grey curls and hooded eyes as he held up the Barbour and green velvet cap like some hideous garrotte.

He had murdered Annie. How, she dared not speculate. Why else had he disguised himself as a Charleville Blazer subscriber? 'I must tell Sean. Now. Immediately,' and she raced upstairs to the sanctuary of her room, locking her bedroom door for safety, knowing that entrances to the old house had a very fluid quality. There were either no keys, they were lost, or various windows could be opened with a kitchen knife, and a visit from Robert was always a possibility.

She wanted to find Sean. Warn him. Hold him. All thoughts of

TorrTechTron being banished from her mind. As quietude and confidence returned the logistics of driving to Ardingly surfaced, and with it a brightness, a spreading joy surging over her face, head, chest flowing like a honeystream, because at last he knew she had a part to play and she had made up her mind to stay with Sean to see his tragedy through.

She felt elated, perplexed at her intoxication that at last she had made a decision to remain at Bowden's Grove to stand and fight. TTT was a total irrelevance. Is this what the river was trying to say when on the night-breeze she heard a horn, used thrillingly as an emotion, a destiny?

But where was Ardingly? They had said Sussex. "I'll ring Dolly as she'll know someone with dressage horses who'll put me right, then drive down this evening." Unlocking her door to walk along the passage and telephone from Mara's room she listened. There was no mistake! Someone was downstairs. Old houses possess their own creaks, groans and footsteps. This sound was different. The noise was positive and more substantial than ephemeral creaks and scuffles, as if a door were being unlocked and she could hear faint metallic rasps. Not daring to wait any longer, Flurry crept up the second flight of stairs on hands and knees, it being too dark to proceed with safety.

Draught in the windbraces purred softly, and she felt her way along the wall by rubbing hands gently over the raised panelling, this part of the house being less familiar than her own first floor landing. Sean slept up here and she felt the frame of his door, which was shut tight, with her right hand. Listening again, the furtive footsteps downstairs seemed to have retreated, although she could not be positive of anything. Someone might be waiting, but fear gave her courage. Once, Mara had described the boxroom at the far end of the passage, and had shown her how an ancient door, half-concealed behind a forgotten wardrobe led to a supposed priest-hole now blocked about eight feet down from its second-floor opening. Nobody, not even Robert, a burglar, a ghost or poltergeist was likely to know about the priest-hole, and Flurry, entering the boxroom, could see by the star-lit sky through a window the outline of an unwanted cupboard.

She waited, cold and miserable for a long time, not daring to return to her room. The euphoria of her decision to stay was diluted by the uncertainty of her precarious position. She studied her watch in the moonlight calculating that it would be ten frigid, shivering hours before dawn, she then sat down on the curved lid of a black leather cabin-trunk, while the waxing moon shifted millimetre by millimetre in its trajectory across the skylight. She listened and waited refusing to allow herself the distraction of thought.

Then she heard a car coming up the drive, and peeping through the window saw to her surprise that it was the Mercedes with Sean and Mara. Stopping by the front door, he jumped out and hurried into the house. Lights were switched on, Mara brought in the dogs, and Sean was running upstairs, as Flurry emerged from the boxroom to meet him too cold and stiff to walk, and calling faintly "I'm here."

He rushed up to her. "Are you alright? Bert phoned, said you might be in trouble."

"Phoned? I didn't know."

"What's this about Robert?"

"I was so frightened. Someone was creeping about. I could hear them from the lower landing."

"Impossible!" He paused, then realising. "That was Bert. He didn't want to scare you, and came in through the coalhole, went into the gunroom and drew out my shotgun and ammo. Darling, you were well protected." She thought of Bert climbing over the coal with his cap on which made them both laugh and broke the tension.

She clung to him and he carried her into his bedroom throwing back several duvets and eiderdowns. Sean liked a selection of warm, soft bedclothes and goose-feathered pillows. He tucked her in, and cautioning her to lie still, went downstairs for some brandy and hot water. Faintly, she could hear Mara and him consulting.

In bed, they talked with an outpouring of half-concealed confidences. Flurry told him about the Blind House, Tiger Bay, Robert's mahogany-tops, Annie's cap and the green velvet collar, the perfume, her powder and about its being Annie's when she was Master of the Blazers.

"Except she never wore a green velvet cap, nor a Barbour."

"No?"

"It's a recent democratic ideal, to make the hunt more accessible to everyone."

"What did she wear then?"

"Charcoal grey riding-habit, she has always ridden side-saddle, and top-hat with a veil." For the moment, Sean decided not to say anything about Robert and Bridie's flight the next day, as he did not wish to disturb any further recollections she might have. After a few minutes and as though in obedience to his hopes, she said: "That decides me! I am *not*, absolutely, definitely *not*, going to ride out with Robert tomorrow. In fact, now you and Mara are back I shall think twice about going to town. I've become quite cowardly!"

"Riding out?"

"Robert said, to get Bert to tack a horse up, and he'd come at eight-thirty for us to ride out together. Something about his being lonely, and wanting us to depart as friends. I told him I was going to London tomorrow, and he appeared to know that Gaylord had offered me a job.

He seems to know everything I do. At lunch, he said he could read me like a book. It's uncanny."

"At last!"

"What?"

"His first mistake!" Excited, he got up, and walked round the room. "Then it was dangerous . . . . . my being there!"

Going to the window, he drew back the curtains and looked out as if to clear his mind. Neither said anything, seeming to know that this was the turning-point, where the past changes direction towards the future.

"How often do we say to ourselves, 'I wish I had done this, rather than that.' Or 'If only we'd had the opportunity to . . . . .'."

"To do what?" She thought she saw his point of view, and time stood still for both of them, until finally he observed, "You are right. It's too dangerous."

"Shall I never be allowed to do anything?"

"You don't have to."

"I want to know." She wondered if in his private tragedy, love and terror lay underneath, partially controlled, because always he would care more for the living than the dead.

"It's not feasible."

"Why do you always have to be so obtuse. Secretive. You're such a concentrated person. You feel guilty for your mother's death, but would it have happened if your parenthood had been acknowledged by more than a nod-and-a-wink, amongst people you know. Within a certain magic circle? Can't you trust anyone? Or don't you feel you can trust yourselves?"

"Real trust explains itself? You cannot choose for others."

"How can I choose? Or choose not to choose, when you hardly explain anything."

"There's no reason why you should." Then more quietly. "I don't wish to be clandestine."

"If you trusted me you would leave me to make up my own mind."

"And place you in danger?"

"That's a new one. It was me who spoke of danger. But there you go again . . . . . you speak of Robert's first mistake, then refuse to explain."

"If I did you would anticipate. It would come to nothing."

She got out of bed and came to face him by the window. "I wish. I wish you to trust me whatever the outcome. I understand that I have a part to play and if you have ever believed in anyone, allow me to make my own decision, whatever it costs."

He waited, licking his tongue over dry teeth, critical reserve in conflict with a glint of excitement.

Then he smiled, it seemed with relief, and taking both her hands.

"You will go to bed now. Get up about eight o'clock so there's no time left to be thinking." The infection in his voice sounded to Flurry like a harp. "Go downstairs and don't be forgetting that you have never seen me or Mara this night. Only that you'll be off to London tomorrow afternoon. If Robert calls, do exactly as he suggests."

They went to bed but not to sleep, the past behind them it was the present standing still. He kissed her pushing aside a cloud of red hair broken loose from its plait. She closed her eyes, lips swelling with desire. He took off her shirt gently caressing her as he slid off her clothes, and she was acutely aware that he trusted her and was allowing her to share his closely guarded id.

She settled into the erotic swansdown duvet, feather soft, drowning with happiness. This is what I am. I have come home. She longed to bring him closer to her now that she understood his past, his passion to keep justice alive. It was not only love but deep affection blended with uncertainty dispersed, reflected in her vision at Daisybrooke when an invisible net bound Sean to Annie and she was not excluded, but as though the elusive web bound her to them.

She longed for him to begin, his caresses becoming too much for her to bear. "Please, darling, please."

"Flurry, you're so beautiful. I believe we are both in love."

She pulled him into her. Claiming him, knowing that love was like this without abuse, guilt or stress, only exhilaration, acceptance. She was made complete as he impaled her, the last breaks, gaps, fears of faces, tunnels, loneliness and disillusions mended as their flesh fused into one being.

CHAPTER 16

She awoke refreshed, having passed through a transcendent state between dreaming and waking. She was surprised to see morning light filtering through chenille curtains so that it made a fine web on plain painted walls. Sean's room was very large, being the main bedroom on the second floor. Flurry sat up aware that she was wearing her lover's blue pyjamas and she felt something metallic round her left wrist. It was a gold cross and chain and one he always wore under his shirt. This was Sean's most precious possession.

Tension surrounded her in this cocoon of hand, cross and eye, yet she no longer suffered from the debilitating migraine that had plagued her all her life. Brain and sight were clear, attention being focused on the crucial day ahead. At eight o'clock she stepped into the unknown, the little cross worn under her sweater.

Coffee was percolating on the AGA hotplate and in its sweet, pungent aroma Flurry caught a breath of salt breeze. She imagined she was holding Mother's Saturday afternoon hand when they stood together at Limehouse Cut feeding the seagulls. Down river, black clouds were piling in from the North Sea and birds were restless. Wheeling and screaming. Occasionally one would fly in distractedly to grab a mouthful of bread. Storm clouds resembled oil-smoke. Black. Smothering. But Mother stood her ground doggedly defying wind, rain and hail. Flurry knew that when crisis breaks you must seek the eye of a storm. Look into it. Dive into the maelstrom. Its blackness. Ride the cloud to defy river, sea and murder. In the faint distance a hunting-horn was blowing Saint Hewit's Recheate thrillingly, calling her to obtain justice for Annie and Annie's son. This is what the river Thames meant! She must trust the companionship, the 'holdfast' of those who 'speak' together. Are of the same mind. She accepted the package.

There was a light tap on the back door.

"Nothing more charming than a lady who knows how to make good coffee! May I come in?"

"I didn't expect you so early, Robert."

"I like the jeans, Gucci, I suspect, like the shoes!" His memory, his attention to detail was unbounded. He forgot nothing and could comment on every eventuality. He relaxed her, making her forget the danger of the unexpected.

"Bert called at the Court this morning, hawking his trout and hoping to drum up custom with my new tenants."

"I thought this was the closed season for trout."

"Not for rainbows it isn't. They factory breed them, in stews."

"Ugh!"

"Taste alright. Let me make the toast," and taking the loaf from her he brushed her hand with his own. "Bert said, to tell you he won't be along this morning, he's going to market. Up 'sarternoon!"

"I was hoping he'd take me to the station."

"Nothing simpler. We'll ride. Have a snack-lunch at my place, then we'll collect your case, is that it over there?" He threw his tweed cap down on the bench, but kept his heavy hunting whip round his neck, like a groom leading second-horse. They sat at the bare boards of the refectory table, with the cat curled up on yesterday's newspaper. He was eating quickly as though toast-munching were an obstacle race and time was of the essence, but he gave nothing away only observing nonchalantly "Where are they staying?"

"Hotel, I think, although Grandfather's with friends and dining with them." She poured him another cup of coffee, black with no sugar.

"How did it go? The dressage."

Flurry was thankful that the pen of a lie-detector was not there to peak from its normal chatter. "He didn't . . . . . phone!" Then Flurry knew that she too, was able to tune in to his wavelength. To detect his probing questions.

They walked to the stables together. The yard was deserted with the Mercedes and large horsebox absent. All horses were out to grass except for Jenny who was in her box. Tiger Bay stood tethered to the metal bar, where horses had their legs and feet washed down. He collected the mare's saddle and bridle from the tackroom while Flurry brushed mane and tail, trying to hold on to her thoughts, which were being swept away by the tideforce of his persuasion.

She got up on her pony, watching with surprise, but no comment, as he fetched her suitcase placing it in the tackroom. He smiled, as though to reassure, then untying Tiger Bay they set off towards the wicket-gate leading to Five Acre Copse. Little traffic was passing on the main road.

The copse had come alive. Deer were fleeing in all directions as though in alarm, while no muntjac were to be seen and even the rabbits scampered off. The breeze waited, holding its breath. After the high of last night, Flurry felt a depression coming on because she had always feared Five Acre and wondered if this were the last time she would take this path. Last night's rain left ash leaves and pine needles saturated and water poured over the riders making them wet with brushing drops. Jenny shook herself, jogging now to keep up with Tiger Bay.

Verges of the U-shaped field were knee-deep in grass, through which Jenny picked her way, and tight ashtree buds threatened to burst before the oak to portend a wet summer. Cows beyond the strip wood were lying down to keep their personal patches dry. A flight of wood pigeons took fright due to nothing in particular, whirr-rr-ing straight up in alarm. The aether, that harbinger of things to come, felt edgy. Scratchy.

Robert opened the hunting-gate by hand rather than with his whip and they trotted along the track through Lawson's Covert towards the Blind House. Then he turned off through rough grass avoiding broken sarsen stones. Clicking his tongue and with "Follow me, let her hop over," he led the way to jump a string of small, fallen pine trunks. "Good for the horses. Quietens them down to have a few jumps. A little fun."

Jenny was enjoying herself when a fox, alerted by the clatter, sneaked like a straight, red line across their path. Jenny spooked in surprise, and Flurry had to sit tight.

"Just let her find her way over this little triple. You'll be alright."

Flurry closed her eyes and held the neck-strap, having hardly ever jumped before, but did not want to appear 'chicken', and strangely the small jumps relaxed her, made her feel less anxious.

At the edge of the copse, she turned to cross Lawson's Meadow and ride on the road, but Robert put out his hand to take Jenny's right rein.

"We go this way!"

As they turned back from the gate leading to the hairpin. Flurry saw the haulier's lorry pass by and she wanted to call out. But he did not appear to see them.

Meanwhile at Lower Farm, Bridie dragged her school suitcase with its memory-teasing labels down the narrow staircase. The fire had not been lit and there was no oil for central heating so the house felt chill. Heaving the case on to the pine table she opened it to pack the fluffy, toy dog who was sharing the Windsor chair with the cat.

Bridie had put on weight during the latter weeks of inactivity. A big-boned woman, lack of riding together with no energetic stablework, meant that muscle was giving way to fat. The trouble was compounded by her diet of bread and chips with little expensive fruit or meat. Money was a headache to Bridie and she had managed during the past few weeks by selling small pieces of jewellery left to her by her grandmother. The blue suit with its micro skirt felt tight, however, Robert had said she was to be ready early and there was nothing she could do about it. She kept pulling it down with annoyance.

The cat, bereft of its toy companion, rolled and stretched on the cushion, and Bridie picked it up burying her nose in the soft, warm fur. "How I wish you were coming too. I don't want to go. Why can't we just stay here and be happy!"

Then she walked over to the dresser and wrote on the back of a circular

"Dear Mummy,

Just in case I don't see you please look after Kitty.

B."

and attached the message to the front door with sticky tape.

It seemed like a 'last supper' when she emptied a whole tin of catfood into a pie dish and placed it on the floor for her kitten. Holding back tears she put on the enormous hat with its fruit and flowers, opened the front door, dragged her suitcase to it and sat on the upturned side.

The enormity of the step she was taking overwhelmed her, because she now suspected that Robert's brittle charm resembled a toffee-apple, with the scintillating glaze of golden sugar hiding black, rotten fruit at the core.

What could she do? In childish, confused misery she thought of the worthless cheque given to the hat shop, "If I don't go away with Robert, who will pay for the hat? And Mummy will be very, very cross."

She sat waiting for Robert with the ridiculous creation tipped over her heavy eyebrows.

As Robert and Flurry turned back towards the forest Jenny objected to his gripping her bridle, and tossed her head up and down, with Flurry feeling they had been captured. She couldn't try to release his hold and knew it would be useless to remonstrate.

"Which way do we go?"

"Home!"

Then Flurry knew it was to be the Z-Path, and even if she persuaded Robert to relinquish Jenny's rein, running away was impossible as Tiger Bay could gallop her down in a minute.

They were being towed along with every step marked out as though on a grid of possibilities. In the utter loneliness of field and forest there were no friendly footsteps, no greetings, as 'PRIVATE, KEEP OUT' notices and firmly shut gates discouraged local walkers and hikers.

Robert was not chatting to her now and his mood had changed to dour contemplation. In a weak voice, that did not seem to belong to her, Flurry said "I would like to return now. I have things to do."

He took no notice, neither looking at her face nor attempting to answer.

Sean did not know where she was and even Bert was far away. Step by step they passed through the trees to approach the track that led along the edge of the forest. Step by step in walk-march they took the road which widens and changes to dried earth. Ahead was the escarpment, its rocky fingers like teeth at the entrance to the abyss of the quarry. Step by step, Tiger Bay's head nodded up and down to the rhythm of his rider's legs. A work-horse, he knew it were best not to think, not to be companionable with his master, being only a bought, fed and groomed servant.

Pace by pace they proceeded, and Jenny had to do an occasional jog to keep up with the big horse, while Flurry could no nothing but wait as she was ahead of alarm or even fear. Dragged along to the beat of horses' feet, her body felt in tune with the nervousness of a beloved pony. Putting down a hand stiff with apprehension, she patted Jenny's grey neck in an attempt to soothe her fear.

They reached the edge of the quarry. Above, the panoramic expanse of rock piling tier above ranked tier rose up to the enigmatic crag of the *Finger of God* in front of a lemon-grey sky. Ahead was a great pile of black rocks delineating the far extremity to the quarry, while to the right the abandoned workings described a semi-circle arena, the floor of which was two hundred feet below. Plunging down in a diagonal stripe was the stone-bonded, inclined-plane of the Z-Path.

Robert turned his head to face her, his skin ashen-grey, and seemingly he had no eyes, they being deeply embedded in hooded lids like a puff-adder.

"You shouldn't have trusted that Sean. I did warn you. He's never there when he's wanted." He shook his head. "We could have been friends."

The ring of a four-time walk changed, as steel-shod hooves met smooth, stone pavement of the Z-Path. Robert had been riding on her right, when dropping his hold on Jenny he appeared to rein back slightly to leave a void. Flurry dared not look down the quarry face where vortices of air were too rarefied, too thin, to hold her body which in chaos, appeared to float above it. She felt, not saw, Robert drop behind her, then move left with Jenny squealing and kicking in agony, and being nudged, edged . . . . .

"*Yoi!*" The huntsman's call ricocheted from crag to rock, and looking up she saw a black horse and rider standing by the *Finger of God*. A trickle of loose scree, rocks and stones slithered and chased each other as the horseman attempted to descend the forty-five degree drop towards the Z-Path.

"Annie's bastard! Break your back like the Black Witch!" Robert cried.

Hecuba, with every confidence in her rider, which is the love between animal and man, squatted on her quarters, pounding with her front feet while Sean, leaning back, held her head up high, as the trickle of loose scree turned to an avalanche racing ahead of them.

The scene exploded. Behind Flurry galloping hooves changed to a higher note as a second horse raced down the Z-Path.

"Mara. Don't let him escape. Get his whip, we've no case without it!"

Rising the deerhorn handle of her heavy, cropped whip Mara hit Robert on his neck, belabouring him over shoulders and back with the muscular power of a fit, athletic woman, until exhausted, he fell to the ground. Out of the tail of her eye Flurry could see Barbarka taking the hedges on Big Charlie, while with the exaggerated roar of an engine encircled by rock, Bert's pick-up truck, with Patters standing on the front seat, spluttered up the stone paving in third gear. In the mid-distance the haulier's lorry was bumping along the track between Court and quarry.

Sean descended safely to the Z-Path, while a stream of small boulders continued to slip down the slope, then bounce across the pavement, before crashing over the precipice, splintering and fragmenting as they split on the rocks below.

Recovering from Mara's blows Robert awaited his antagonist, crouching low over a tightly held whip, and as Sean attempted to grab it from him, he lunged, jabbing him in the stomach with a vicious thrust. Recoiling with sudden pain, he fell back to give Robert an opportunity to mount Tiger Bay, who with unaccustomed restlessness cavorted round, with Robert's foot in the stirrup.

Above the mélèe of stones, upset horses and fighting figures, Bert drove up and commanded. "Patters . . . . . go . . . . . grip!"

The black-brown dog, his eyes blazing red, leapt down from his perch, and never forgetting an enemy raced up the slope, his three-quarter inch teeth bared. As Robert fought to mount, Patters rushed under Tiger Bay and, grabbing his arm, made Robert relinquish the stirrup iron.

"Call off your bloody dog!"

He made a sudden prod with his whip, but Patters never whimpered, because neither iron bars nor electronic probes, but only death, or his master's voice, will dislodge the grip of a faithful Patterdale. Exhausted at last, Robert dropped the whip and Mara grabbed it from beneath his feet, only then did Bert call his dog to heel.

"I'll have the law on you . . . . . for this ambush," gasped Robert holding his arm. At that moment, a second plain, black car drove quietly up the path. The retired Chief Inspector Saul Parker stayed unobtrusively on the back seat, while grim-faced, the detective sergeant approached Robert. His face showed that such proceedings ought to be left to the police, he was not keen on amateurs playing at histrionics, but still, "Robert Davies, I am arresting you for the attempted murder of Fleur Jones, also the murder of your wife Annie, together with that of Julie Baker and her child. Anything you may say . . . . ." as he read Robert his rights, the Chief Inspector walked up and took the whip from Mara.

"Let me," Robert said in an almost inaudible voice. "Let me . . . . . put my horse away."

"Of you go then. He can't get anywhere. My chaps are coming," and the sergeant appeared to be glad to get rid of him.

"It's a pleasure!" And Barbarka, jumping off Big Charlie grabbed Robert by the left ankle, throwing him up on Tiger Bay so that he cried out, before ambling off and holding his bitten arm below a bowed head, subdued in shame of failure. At the bottom of the Z-Path Robert stopped, turned, and with his undamaged hand, raised his cap in salute to his step-son. Then rode towards the Court.

Flurry was sitting on the ground too overwrought to stand, and Patters, joining in with his great, sloppy kisses, licked her face and neck, then tugging at the front of her tweed coat, and with an extra-special heave, pulled her to her feet and into Mara's arms.

"Can you ever forgive us for putting you into this!"

"Very ingenious," said Parker. "Just as you predicted, and I've never seen this done before. It does work, because the proximity of whip and horse's flesh means there are no burn marks."

"I don't understand," from Flurry.

"My dear young lady, you were in great danger." He looked disapprovingly at Sean. "Although I must congratulate you on timing."

"We were watching every step of the way."

"I nearly died when that fox got up!" Mara exclaimed.

Flurry touched the whip and Parker curled it up holding it to his side. "Now it's an ordinary hunting-whip. Now . . . . ." and he turned it over straightening thong and lash. "You see this silver band? Rotate it, to switch on the power from an electric battery hidden beneath the leather of the handle." He prodded the weapon forward as Robert had done. "The high current would send any horse crazy when pushed up its behind."

"Don't I know!" from Sean rubbing his stomach.

"That's how he killed Annie! And Miss Flurry if he hadn't been stopped."

"It was Bert seeing the cattle handlers at market who guessed," from Sean.

"The runaway calves!" The haulier had ambled up leaving his lorry at the bottom. "Bert here" patting him on the shoulder. "Reckon he gets to the bottom of most things," and there was a countryman's pride in his voice.

Flurry was still puzzled. "How?" Then realisation dawned. "Is that why he was at Heathrow?"

The Chief Inspector raised an eyebrow. "That's what we surmise. He had to be careful as manufacture of an electronic whip in this country would invite blackmail."

The group broke up when the police backed down the path. Sean helped Flurry on to Jenny, there being no need for words. No call for exhibitions of affectionate exuberance. Their feelings for each other ran too deep for that.

The others wandered down the path. Jenny took Hecuba's left side holding on close to the black mare for comfort, while Sean smoothed his horse's cuts and bruises from loose stones on her quarters.

"Seems Diarmid will be needing to mend her with his leprechaum ointment."

He held Flurry's hand and following the others some fifty yards behind they reached the bottom of the Z-Path, to stand and look at the stables of Broxford Court for the last time.

On the misty spring morning, they could see that a light, showing no stronger than a candle-flame, had been switched on in the tackroom.

"Robert!"

Across the still air the sound of a shot rang out!